Someone

Else's

Love

Story

Also by Joshilyn Jackson

gods in Alabama

Between, Georgia

The Girl Who Stopped Swimming

Backseat Saints

A Grown-Up Kind of Pretty

Someone Else's Love Story

Joshilyn Jackson

wm

WILLIAM MORROW
An Imprint of HarperCollins

SOMEONE ELSE'S LOVE STORY. Copyright © 2013 by Joshilyn Jackson. All rights reserved. Printed in the United States of America. No part of this book may be used or reproduced in any manner whatsoever without written permission except in the case of brief quotations embodied in critical articles and reviews. For information address HarperCollins Publishers, 10 East 53rd Street, New York, NY 10022.

HarperCollins books may be purchased for educational, business, or sales promotional use. For information please e-mail the Special Markets Department at SPsales@harpercollins.com.

FIRST EDITION

Designed by Jamie Lynn Kerner

Library of Congress Cataloging-in-Publication Data has been applied for.

ISBN 978-0-06-210565-3

13 14 15 16 17   OV/RRD   10 9 8 7 6 5 4 3 2 1

*For Bobby Jackson, who married the right girl,
and Julie Jackson, a custom job*

"Hope" is the thing with feathers—
That perches in the soul—
And sings the tune without the words—
And never stops—at all—

EMILY DICKINSON

Acknowledgments

Huge (and oddly long-standing) thanks to my sharp-eyed, canny editor, Carolyn Marino—I met her when my very first novel was at auction. What an unmitigated pleasure to work with her at last! I have such deep-set gratitude to everyone at William Morrow for the warm response to my work, especially Liate Stehlik, Lynn Grady, Tavia Kowalchuk, Ben Bruton, Mary Ann Petyak, and Amanda Bergeron. As always, I must thank my wonderful agent, Jacques de Spoelberch.

A few years ago, at the Vermont College of Fine Arts, I heard poet Robin Behn read her glorious and earthy poem "It Is Not Always Possible to Fall in Love in Blackberry Season." Her poem's incantatory female voice evokes a pair of lovers, addressing the woman as *you*.

Rereading it obsessively, I started imagining a man who might speak *to* a woman in this way. The result was Walcott, a young male poet whose history and personality would let him write comfortably in such lush and visceral terms about his female lover's sexuality as well as his own. Robin Behn kindly

allowed me to put a few lines of the poem that spawned Walcott into Walcott's mouth, but the poem is absolutely hers, and
was first published in the inaugural issue of *TAB: The Journal
of Poetry & Poetics* from Chapman University. You can read the
piece in its entirety on my website at joshilynjackson.com/behn.

Walcott should write a poem celebrating the patience and
kindness of genetic counselor and researcher Dawn Jacob Laney,
MS, CGC, CCRC. William would not have been possible without her.

And not just Dawn—this book is full of cops and crime and
chemistry and genetics and forensics and Judaism and nuns and
many other things outside of my direct experience. The following human beings deserve better poems than I could write for
being invaluable fonts of information. Any stupid mistakes are
mine.

Science geek Scott Winn; RN Julie Oestreich; Lieutenant
Jay Baker of the Cherokee County Sheriff's Department; chemist
Deawna Echols; memoirist Jessica Handler; Sister Joan Gannon;
biologist Kerry Kilburn; college football player Bob Jackson; nov-
elist Susan Rebecca White; family therapist Dr. Michael Bris-
sett; D. P. Lyle, MD, author of *Forensics for Dummies* and the Dub
Walker series; technophile Alison Law; and the so-awesome-you-
wish-you-were-on-fire-so-he-could-save-you fireman/paramedic
Daniel Jackson. And he *would* save you, too.

I cannot function as a human, much less as a writer, without
the following four posses:

My reader posse: That's pretty much you, Person Who Bought
This Book. You are letting me keep this job I love. Thank you.
If you're one of those passionate and miraculous bookstore hand-
sellers or big-mouthed, wonderful readers who recommend my
books to other people, then I feel so warmly toward you, we
should probably make out a little. You are directly responsible for
this book, for good or ill. Thank you doesn't cover it.

My writer posse: These people have, for years now, consistently and lovingly slapped me into being better and braver, on the page and off. They are each an essential nutrient, so I list them in alphabetical order: Anna Schachner, Caryn Karmatz Rudy, Karen Abbott, Lydia Netzer, Reid Jensen, and Sara Gruen.

My family posse: Scott, Sam, Maisy Jane, Jane, Alison, Bob, Betty, Bobby, Julie, Daniel, and Erin Virginia.

My Jesus posse: First Baptist Church of Decatur, smallgroup, and my slanted sidewalkers. Shalom, y'all.

PART ONE

Bullets

"Faith" is a fine invention
When Gentlemen can see—
But Microscopes are prudent
In an Emergency.
EMILY DICKINSON

Chapter 1

I fell in love with William Ashe at gunpoint, in a Circle K. It was on a Friday afternoon at the tail end of a Georgia summer so ungodly hot the air felt like it had all been boiled red. We were both staring down the barrel of an ancient, creaky .32 that could kill us just as dead as a really nice gun could.

I thought then that I had landed in my own worst dream, not a love story. Love stories start with a kiss or a meet-cute, not with someone getting shot in a gas station minimart. Well, no, two people, because that lady cop took a bullet first.

But there we were, William gone still as a pond rock, me holding a green glass bottle of Coca-Cola and shaking so hard it was like a seizure. Both of us were caught under the black eye of that pistol. And yet, seventeen seconds later, before I so much as knew his name, I'd fallen dizzy-down in love with him.

I've never had an angel on my right shoulder; I was born with a pointy-tailed devil, who crept back and forth across my neck to get his whispers into both my ears. I didn't get a fairy godmother or even a discount-talking cricket-bug to be my conscience. But someone should have told me. That afternoon in the Circle K, I deserved to know, right off, that I had landed bang in the middle of a love story. Especially since it wasn't—it isn't—it could never be my own.

At eleven o'clock that same morning, walking into gunfire and someone else's love story was the last thing on my mind. I was busy dragging a duffel bag full of most of what I owned down the stairs, trying not to cry or, worse, let my happy show. My mother, never one for mixed feelings, had composed herself into the perfect picture of dejection, backlit and framed in the doorway to the kitchen.

I wanted to go, but if I met her eyes, I'd bawl like a toddler anyhow. This tidy brick bungalow on the mountainside had been my home for seventeen years now, ever since I was four and my parents split up. But if I cried, she'd cry, too, and then my sweet kid would lose his ever-loving crap. We'd all stand wailing and hugging it out in the den, and Natty and I would never get on the road. I tightened my mouth and looked over her head instead. That's when I noticed she'd taken down the Praying Hands Jesus who'd been hanging over the sofa for as long as I'd had concrete memory. She'd replaced him with a Good Shepherd version who stopped me dead in the middle of the stairs.

The new Jesus looked exactly like her.

He was super pretty, slim and elegant. He was backlit, too, standing in front of a meadow instead of a kitchen, cradling a lamb instead of a spatula. My mother had never once gone into direct sunlight without a hat and SPF 50, and this Jesus shared her ivory-bloom complexion. I looked more Jewish than he did. They had the same rich brown hair glowing with honey-gold highlights, the same cornflower blue eyes cast sorrowfully upward to watch me struggle a fifty-pound duffel down the stairs. Neither offered to give me a hand.

Mimmy wasn't anywhere near ready to let me go, and the thought of having to fight my way out of here made me want to flop down onto my butt and die on the staircase.

"Please don't make this awful. This is the best thing," I said, but Mimmy only stood there, radiating lovely sorrow. The pretty my mom has, it's an unfair amount. Simply ungodly, and it worked on everyone, even me sometimes.

"Maybe for you," she acknowledged. "But Natty?"

That scored a hit; I was trading Mimmy's mountain full of trees and deer and sunshine for my dad's three-bedroom condo, sleek and modern, bang in the middle of the city. But all I said was, "Oh, Mims."

We'd been having this fight all week. Dad's condo was ten minutes from the Georgia State campus, and from Mimmy's, I drove about four hours round-trip. I had to register my classes around Atlanta's rush hour and make sure they all met either Tuesday/Thursday or Monday/Wednesday/Friday. This was enough to make a simple coffee date an exercise in logistics, and Mimmy didn't help my social life go easier. She'd been boycotting anything with a Y chromosome for going on seventeen years now. Even her cat was female, and she'd been known to change my shifts at her candy shop if she knew I had a date. I would've moved to the condo long before if my stepmother, Bethany, had ever let my father make the offer.

She hadn't. Not until last week, when the results of Natty's tests came back. Dad had set them up after Natty taught himself to read. The tests said my kid was rocking an IQ north of 140, which put him firmly in the genius category. My three-year-old could probably apply to freakin' Mensa.

Bethany—Bethany herself, not Dad—called to tell me I could have the condo. This was unusual. Bethany was the heavy who told me I was getting uninvited from Passover because her entire family was coming and the dining room table only had so many leaves. A few days later, Dad would do something huge and beautiful and thoughtful for me, as if these events were wholly unconnected. But this time, Bethany had wanted to talk to me badly enough to dial Mimmy's house phone when she missed me on my cell. A risky move. Mimmy and Bethany were matter and antimatter. Contact between them could trigger a blast that would knock the planet clean off its hinges and plummet us all right into the sun.

Luckily, I was the one who picked up. We had the briefest exchange of cool politenesses, and I waited for her to drop whatever awful bomb she'd primed this time. She cleared her throat and delivered what sounded like an overrehearsed monologue:

"So! Given Nathan's unusual intellect, David wants to help you place him at a more academically focused preschool. We understand how limited the choices are out there in the weeds."

I swear I could *hear* the narrow nostrils of Bethany's long, elegant nose flaring in distaste through the phone as she said that last bit. It was a carefully worded piece of code. Last year, I'd almost killed my Jewish father by sending Natty to preschool at Mimmy's Baptist church. Natty and I no longer attended synagogue *or* church, which was better than when I was a kid and had to go to both. Dad offered to pay all tuition if I moved Natty to a "better" school.

"Surely there is more than one close preschool," he'd said.

"Of course," I'd told him. "If you prefer, Natty can go to the one run by the Methodists."

Now Bethany went on, "It means moving to Atlanta. I know that your mother isn't likely to see this as an opportunity. Country people can be shortsighted, especially when it comes to education. But the benefits . . . I think any decent parent could see them." She sniffed a little huff of disparaging air and finally came to the heart of it. "You and Natty could stay at the condo. We'd put your own phone line in, and you could decorate the third-floor bedrooms as you please. I'm not sure your father is prepared to suffer the on-call rooms with the residents, so sometimes you'd have him napping in the master. But otherwise, you could think of it as your own place." There was a pause, and she added, pointedly, "For the year." Then, in case I hadn't gotten it, "Until you graduate, I mean."

This was an amazing number of long-standing, guaranteed

fight starters to pack into a single speech. Even a dig at Lumpkin County! Sure, we were rural, but not the kind of rural in *Deliverance*, and she damn well knew it. If she'd hoped to goad me into turning down the condo I'd been coveting—fat chance. I summoned all my inner sugar and said, hell, oh hell, oh hell-hell yes, and then I got off the phone fast as I could.

Now I dumped my heavy duffel by the front door, next to Natty's *Blue's Clues* suitcase and the stacked laundry baskets full of books and socks and toys. I went to Mimmy and looped my arms around her little waist and put my face in her hair. She smelled like vanilla.

"You're the best Mimmy in all the world. I don't know how I would have gotten through Natty's baby years without you. I couldn't have, not and gone to college. But I'm twenty-one. Natty and I have to stand on our own at some point. This is a nice step."

She shook her head. "You and Natty setting up house ought to be exciting. It's a rite of passage. I ought to sew you curtains and throw a housewarming. But I don't know how to celebrate you moving into that awful man's place."

I let the *awful man* part go and only said, "I am not moving to the *house* house."

Bethany and Dad and my three little stepbrothers lived in a huge stucco and stone McMansion out in Sandy Springs. No way I could ever share a roof with Bethany. I called her my Step-Refrigerator to my mother and much worse things to my best friend, Walcott. She'd earned all her names, though to be fair, I'm pretty sure I'd earned whatever she privately called me.

Mimmy started to speak again, but just then we heard Walcott coming down, his long feet slapping the stairs. He had most of my hanging clothes in a fat fold he held against his chest.

"Why do you have so many dresses?" he asked.

"Because I'm a girl," I said.

My mother eyed my things and said, "A better question is, why do you dress like a forty-year-old French divorcée?"

"I like vintage," I said, going to unburden Walcott. It was a huge stack; I found most of my clothes at rummage sales and thrift shops, digging through mounds of acid-washed mom jeans for the one good circle skirt or perfect two-dollar wrap dress.

He waved me off with one hand, arms still clutched tight around my clothes, heading for the front door.

Mimmy said, pinchy-voiced, "You can't load hanging clothes first. They'll get smushed and have to be re-ironed."

Walcott stopped obediently and draped my clothes over the duffel, giving me a Walcott look, wry and mock-martyred. He'd walked over yesterday from his momses' place to help me pack, as his hundred-millionth proof of best-friendhood. Today he'd help load my car and keep Natty entertained on the drive to the condo. The condo was built in a stack of three small floors. The kitchen and living space were at ground, and Dad's master suite took up the whole middle. Natty and I were taking the two rooms that shared a bath at the very top. Walcott, being Walcott, would carry the heaviest things up all those stairs, while we toted in pillows and Target bags full of shoes. I didn't even have to drive him home, just drop him at his girlfriend's place in Inman Park.

He'd been doing crap like this for me since we were both five, the outsiders at a milk-white elementary school in a so-white-it-was-practically-Wonder-Bread county. I was the only half-a-Jew for miles, and Walcott was the sperm-donated product of a pair of lesbians who left Atlanta to grow organic veggies and run a mountain bed-and-breakfast for like-minded ladies. Walcott's momses engaged in all manner of suspicious behaviors, including Zen meditation and hydroponics. Where we lived, those words were as foreign as Rosh Hashanah or Pesach Seder, strange rites that got me extra days off school and sent me to my dad's place in Atlanta, where I no doubt painted the doors with lamb blood and burned up doves.

Me and Walcott, we'd stood back-to-back with our swords up, together surviving the savage playgrounds; yet here was Mimmy, giving him the glare she saved for any poor, male fool who got caught by all her immaculately groomed pretty and tried to ask her out. She knew darn well that Walcott didn't have a sex-crazed man-genda for helping me move, but every now and then, she remembered he technically belonged to the penis-having half of the human race. She'd flick that suspicious, baleful look at him. She'd done it when he was in kindergarten, even. Back then, he'd showed me his penis on a dare, and it had been an innocent pink speck, clearly incapable of plotting.

"This is the last from upstairs. Let's pack the car after we eat," Walcott said.

"As long as we get on the road by two. I don't want to unload in the dark."

"I'll dish up lunch," my mother said, wilting into acceptance. The wilt was a feint. I caught her sloe-eyed side-peek at me as she rolled away against the doorway on her shoulder and disappeared into the kitchen.

"Hoo! You're so screwed," Walcott said, grinning. To an outsider, my mother would seem to be in a state of mild, ladylike displeasure, but mainly at peace with the world and all its denizens. But Walcott and I had grown up together, in and out of each other's houses all day long our whole lives. He could decode the state of the Once and Future Belle from her lipstick colors and the angle of the tortoiseshell combs in her hair almost as well as I could.

"She's loaded for bear. And I'm bear," I said.

"I can't help you with that. No one can." He flopped into a lanky heap of string on the wingback chair. "But I could say you a poem? I've been working on one for you, for this exact occasion."

"No, thank you," I said primly.

"It's really good," Walcott said. He cleared his throat, putting on a faux beat-poet reading voice, really boomy and pretentious. "Alas! The Jew of Lumpkin County, exiled once more. Like Moses—"

"Poem me no poems, Walcott. I know what you use those things for." Before he got hooked up kinda serious with CeeCee, his signature move was to quote hot lines from John Donne or Shakespeare to mildly drunken girls in the Math Department.

"They work, though," he said. "I used to get a lot of play, for a skinny English major with a big nose."

"Bah! It's a noble nose."

"It's overnoble. It's noble plus plus. Lucky for me, chicks dig iambic pentameter. But this poem? It's not for seduction. It's free verse and quite brilliant. You wander forty days and forty nights in Piedmont Park, following the smoke from a crack pipe by day and a flaming tranny hooker in the night."

"You're a goof," I said, but as always, he'd made me feel better. "Stop it. I have to pacify The Mimmy. Maybe we could crawl to the kitchen with fruit? Throw a virgin into her volcano?"

"Now where are you and I going to find a virgin?" he asked, droll.

I started for the kitchen, then paused under the painting. The new Jesus, with his salon-fresh highlights, had those kind of Uncle Sam eyes that seemed to track after me.

Walcott followed my gaze, craning his head back to look. "Holy crap! Where is Praying Hands Jesus?"

I shrugged. "I know, right?"

"Shandi, that's your mother in a beard."

"Yeah. Super unnerving. I don't expect Jesus to be that . . ."

"Hot," Walcott said, but he was looking toward the kitchen now, where my mom was. I scooped up one of Natty's stuffies from the closest laundry basket and chucked it at him. He caught it, laughing. "Aw, don't throw Yellow Friend!" He tucked this most important blue patchwork rabbit gently back in Natty's things. "I know she's your mom. But come on."

I couldn't blame him. My mother was forty-four, but she looked ten years younger, and she was nowhere near ready to recover from being beautiful. If I'd been born with a lush mouth and crazy-razor cheekbones, instead of round-faced and regulation cute, I'm not sure I'd recover, either.

"Lunch," Mimmy called, and we went through to the kitchen table. Natty was there already, perched in the booster so his nose cleared the surface of the high wooden table. Most of his face was hidden by his *Big Book of Bugs*, but I could tell the move was worrying him. All his Matchbox police and EMS vehicles were lined up in front of his plate, and he had big chunks of three of his bravest costumes on: fireman's yellow slicker, astronaut's white jumpsuit, airplane pilot's hat.

"Goodness, Captain Space Fireman, have you seen my kid?"

Natty said, "I am me."

Walcott said, "Weird. How did a Pilot Space Fireman turn into a Natty Bumppo?"

My tiny literalist lowered the thick volume to give Walcott a grave stare. "These are costumes, Walcott. I was me the whole time."

I took the seat by him and said, "Oh good, because you are my favorite."

Walcott sat down across from me.

"Mimmy made cobbler," Natty told me in his solemn Natty voice.

I nodded, taking it very seriously. "Excellent."

"Mimmy says I must eat peas," Natty said next, same tone, but I could tell he believed this to be an injustice.

"Mimmy is very right," I said.

All our plates were filled and sitting centered on the tatted lace mats. My mother took her place at the head of the table, and we all bowed our heads.

Looking down at my plate while my mother had a cozy premeal chat with Jesus, I realized I'd clocked her mood wrong. She wasn't sad or wrecked. She'd made chicken-fried steak and mashed potatoes and peas and fresh biscuits, then swamped the plate in her velvety-fat gravy.

She only cooked for me like this when she was furious. She thought the meanest thing you could do to a woman was to give her a fudge basket; she lived on green salad and broiled chicken, and Mimmy would have still fit into her wedding dress if she hadn't set it on fire in the middle of the living room when I was Natty's age. Then she packed me up and moved back here, where she'd grown up.

My angry mother prayed a litany of thanks for food and health and family and put in a word for the Bulldogs approaching fall season. She didn't go off-book, didn't exhort the Lord to bring her wayward daughter to a better understanding of His will. In the past, God's will had so often matched up exactly with my mother's that she found it worth mentioning. But she closed after the football with a sweet "Amen," and I upgraded her from merely furious to livid.

Natty amen-ed and then started zooming one of his cop cars back and forth. Walcott dug in, moaning with pleasure at the first bite. He'd eat everything on his plate and then probably finish mine, and I had no idea where it would go. He was six feet tall and built like a Twizzler.

"Eat up, baby," I told Natty.

"I will. I have to consider the peas," he said, and I grinned at his little-old-man vocabulary.

My mother had served herself a big old portion as well, and she whacked off a huge bite of fried meat and swabbed it through the potatoes, then put the whole thing directly into her mouth. My eyes widened. I think the last time my mother ate a starch was three years back, when Dad paid my tuition at GSU in full.

I always knew he would, but Mimmy worried he'd cut me off once court-ordered child support for me ended. I wasn't eligible for most scholarships, even though I'd been an honor student in high school. I'd spent my senior year at home, baking Natty and studying for the GED. When Dad's check came, she'd gone to the ancient box of Girl Scout Thin Mints in the freezer and had two, which was for her a caloric orgy. She'd purchased those cookies at least four years ago, and she hadn't so much as worked her way into the second sleeve.

Now she sat quiet, chewing what had to be the best bite to enter her mouth this decade, but it was like she wasn't even tasting it. She tried to swallow, then stopped. Her face changed and cracked, like she'd been told she was eating the thigh meat of her dearest friend. She spat the wad into a napkin and stood abruptly, chair scraping against the old hardwood floor.

Natty kept right on zooming his cop car across the tabletop, but I saw his eyes cut after her as she hurried from the room.

"Mimmy is fine," I said to him.

"Mimmy is fine," Natty repeated, zooming his car back and forth to a mournful inner rhythm. "It's only because we are going far away for all eternity."

I was already getting up to go talk to my mother, but I paused. "Natty! We aren't going far, and we can visit anytime we like."

Natty said, "Not far, we can visit," with absolutely no conviction.

"It's going to be fun, living in Atlanta. We'll get to hang with Walcott tons once school starts, and you can go to preschool and make nice friends." I met Walcott's eyes across the table, because he knew *all* my reasons for moving. Up where we lived, everyone knew about Natty's geniushood, probably mere seconds after I did. It had reopened all the worm-can speculation about who Natty's dad might be. Natty, who picked up on so much more than your average three-year-old, was starting to ask questions. Up until this year, his baby understanding of biology had allowed me to tell him the simplest truth: He didn't have one.

How do you explain to a preschooler, even one as bright as Natty, that his mother was a virgin until a solid year *after* he was born? A virgin in every sense, because when I finally did have sex, I learned my hymen had survived the C-section. How could I tell my son that his existence was the only miracle I'd ever believed in?

If neighbors or acquaintances were pushy enough to ask, I told them the dad was "None O'YourBeeswax," that randy Irish fellow who had fathered a host of babies all across the country. But I owed Natty more than that. Maybe a good made-up story? Something about star-crossed true love, probably war, a convenient death. I hadn't made it up yet, mostly because I didn't want to lie to him. And yet the truth was so impossible.

Telling the truth also meant that I'd have to explain how sex worked normally, while Natty was still quite happy with "A daddy gives a sperm and a mommy gives an egg, and bingo-bango-bongo, it makes a baby." He wasn't interested in exactly how the sperm and egg would meet. Much less how they might meet inside a girl before she'd ever once gone past second base.

But Natty had an entirely different question for me. "Is Mimmy going to die?"

"No!" I said. "Where did you get that idea?"

"I heard her tell the phone that she would die, just die, just die when we are gone," Natty said. I could hear my mother's inflections coming out of him on the *die, just die, just die* parts.

"Mimmy will outlive us all," I said and added sotto voce to Walcott, "If I don't kill her."

Walcott made a smile for Natty and said, "Yup. Mimmy will outlive every single one of us and look hot at our funerals."

"We'll come back and visit Mimmy lots, and she won't die," I said, shooting Walcott a quelling look. "Let me go get her, and she can tell you herself."

I left Natty with Walcott, who, saint that he was, was asking if Natty would like to hear a dramatic recitation of a poem called "Jabberwocky."

I went back to my mother's amber-rose confection of a bedroom. I'd done it as part of my portfolio to get in GSU's competitive interior design program. It was ultrafeminine without being fluffy, and the faint blush of pink in the eggshell walls suited her coloring. She sat in it like a jewel in its proper setting, but just now, she was in a mood much too heavy for the delicate curtains.

"Not cool, Mims," I said. "Not cool at all. You need to rein it in."

I had more to say, but as she turned to me, her mouth crumpled up and fat tears began falling out of her eyes. She lunged at me and hugged me. "I'm so sorry! I'm so sorry!"

I patted at her, thoroughly disarmed, and said, "Momma . . ." My own name for her, now mostly replaced by Natty's.

"That was completely out of line, in front of Nathan. Completely." She spoke in a vehement whisper, tears splashing down. "I'm an awful thing. Just slimy with pure awful, but, oh, Shandi, I can hardly bear it. He'll forget his Mimmy and be all cozied up and close with that man, that man, that dreadful man! Worse, he'll forget who he is!"

I breathed through the dig at Dad and said, "He won't. I won't let him."

We sank down to sit together on the bed, her hands still clutching my arms. She firmed her chin at me bravely.

"I want you to put something in the condo, Shandi," She waved one hand past me. I glanced over my shoulder and saw her favorite picture, from last summer at Myrtle Beach. It showed Mimmy hand in hand with two-year-old Natty, the ocean swirling up around their ankles. She'd blown it up to a nine-by-fourteen, framed it, and hung it in her room. Now it was perched on her bedside table, leaning against the wall. "I want him to remember me. More than that. I want Nathan to never, never forget for a second *who he is*."

"Okay," I said, though I wasn't sure how Dad would feel about me hanging a big-ass picture of his ex-wife rocking a red bikini. I was positive how Bethany would feel. "I can probably do that."

"No. No 'probably.' Say you will," my mother said.

I sighed, but Natty had never spent more than a weekend away from Mimmy. He might need the picture. I could hang it in Natty's room so Dad wouldn't have to look at it. And Bethany never came south of the rich people's mall in Buckhead. If she did drop by for some unfathomable reason, I could stuff it under the bed.

"Fine. I'll hang it."

Mimmy shook her head, fierce. "I need you to swear. Swear by something you hold absolutely holy that you will hang that at the condo, no matter what." Her fingers dug into my arms.

I thought for a second. I'd grown up between religions, at the center of a culture war, each side snipping away at the other's icons until I was numb to much of it. There were not many things I held as holy.

Finally, I said, "I swear on the grave of my good dog Boscoe, and all the parts of Walcott, and—I won't swear anything on Natty proper, but I could maybe swear this on his eyelashes. Those are the holiest things I know."

My mother smiled, instantly glorious, her big eyes shiny from the tears and her nose unswollen. She even cried pretty.

"Good," she said. "Good."

She stood and dusted her hands off and stretched, then walked past me to the bedside table. I pivoted to watch, but she didn't pick up the beach picture. Instead, she reached past it, to a much larger rectangle, wrapped and ready to go in brown butcher paper. It was behind the table, but it was tall enough to have been visible.

"I already wrapped Him up."

I knew what the package was, of course, by size and shape. The Myrtle Beach pic had been a decoy, with the real picture she wanted hung at Dad's place hiding in plain sight behind it. And she wasn't angry at all; I should have known that when she didn't swallow the bite, but I'd missed it. Damn, she was good, and in her arms she cradled Praying Hands Jesus, the Jesus who had hung over my mother's sofa for as long as I could remember. Man, oh man, had I been played.

My mother dashed her last tears away and added, smiling, "I also pulled down this picture of me and Natty. He asked if he could take it."

With that she picked both up and left the room, practically skipping as she went to add the weight of Jesus and herself to the pile of things that I was taking to my father's house.

*A*fter lunch, Mimmy had to get to work. She owned the Olde Timey Fudge Shoppe in a nearby mountain village that was surrounded by rent-a-cabins and vacation homes. The village had a picturesque downtown with an independent bookstore, some "antique" marts, local wine-tasting rooms, and half a dozen Southern-themed restaurants. She drifted, mournful, to her car, looking prettier in the sherbet-colored sash-dress uniform than all the little high school and college girls who worked for her. I'd been one of them myself, until last week.

After a hundred hugs from Natty and a thousand promises from me to visit soon, she drove off to hand-dip the chocolates she would never sample. Walcott and I finished loading and got on the road.

Less than two hours' worth of kudzu-soaked rural highway separated us from the city condo, even with the detour to bounce by Bethany's Stately Manor to pick up the keys. Still, it wasn't like The Fridge was going to invite us in for kosher crumpets and a heart-to-heart. I figured I'd be unloaded and moved before sunset. When everything you own will go into a VW Beetle, along with your three-year-old and your best friend hanging his bare feet out the side window, how long can moving take?

We drove along singing, then I told tall tales for a bit. Natty loved Paul Bunyan and Babe the Big Blue Ox, and I had learned the art of packing these tales with filthy double entendres for Walcott. When that got old, Walcott recited poetry, until he got to Emily Dickinson and started freaking Natty right the hell out, what with the corpses hearing the flies buzzing and capital *D* Death himself pulling up in a carriage. So we canned it, and Walcott plugged his iPod into my port and blasted his Natty playlist, heavy on the They Might Be Giants, as my car ate the miles. We were listening to "Mammal" when I noticed that the kind of quiet that Natty was being had changed.

"You okay, baby?" I called, glancing in the rearview. His skin looked like milk that was just going off.

"Yes," he said. But he added, "My throat feels tickle-y."

I shot Walcott a panicky glance. We both knew "tickle-y throated" was Natty-speak for "thirty seconds from puking." We were in the last few miles of kudzu and wilderness. In another ten minutes, the exits would change from having a single ancient Shell station into fast-food meccas. A few exits after that, we'd be able to find a Starbucks, and then we'd officially be in the wealthy North Atlanta suburbs.

But for now, there was no safe direction I could aim him. Most of his toys were piled high in a laundry basket under his feet, and the thought of cleaning puke out of the crevices of that many Star Wars action figures and Matchbox cars gave me a wave of sympathy nausea. The passenger seat beside him was full of our hanging clothes. Walcott began searching frantically for a bag, and I rolled down every window and hit the gas. A better mother would have realized this move would be spooky for Natty; he got motion sick if he was worried.

An exit appeared, mercifully, magically close, and I yelled, "Hold on, baby!" as we sailed down the ramp. It ended in a two-lane road with a defunct Hardee's with boarded-up windows on one side and a Circle K on the other. I swung into the Hardee's parking lot and stopped. Walcott wedged his top body between the front seats and unbuckled Natty, while I popped my door open and leapt out so I could shove the driver's side seat forward. Natty leaned out and released his lunch, mercifully, onto the blacktop.

"Oh, good job, Natty," Walcott crowed, patting his back while I dug in my purse for some wet wipes. "Bingo! Bull's-eye!"

When Natty stopped heaving, I passed the wipes to Walcott and said, "Everyone out!"

Walcott lifted Natty out and cleaned his face, carrying him across the quiet road to the Circle K lot. I moved the car across, too. Walcott set Natty down and the three of us marched around in the sunshine. After a couple of minutes, Natty's wobblety walk had turned into storm-trooper marching. He started making the

DUN DUN DUN music of Darth Vader's first entrance, and Walcott and I leaned side by side on the Bug and watched him.

I was thinking we could risk driving on soon when a green Ford Explorer pulled in to get gas. The guy who got out of it caught my attention. Hard not to notice a big, thick-armed guy with a mop of sandy-colored hair, maybe six two, deep-chested as a lion. He was past thirty, his skin very tanned for a guy with that color hair. He was wearing scuffed-up old work boots with weathered blue jeans that were doing all kinds of good things for him. For me, too.

Walcott said, quiet, only to me, "Gawking at the wrinklies again."

I flushed, busted, and looked away. Walcott liked to give me crap because my first real boyfriend after I had Natty had been thirty-five. The guy after that, the one I'd stopped seeing a few months ago, had been thirty-nine.

The guy in the Explorer finished at the pump and went inside. I had to work not to watch him make the walk, and Walcott shook his head, amused. "It's like you have reverse cougar."

"I'm already raising one little boy. I don't need another," I said, arch, just as Natty passed.

Natty said, "I would like a brother, please."

Walcott laughed, and I gave him a fast knuckle punch.

"Maybe later," I told Natty. His skin had lost that curdling sheen, but he still looked peaked. I got my bank card out and said to Walcott, "Can you fill the car up? I'm going to take Mr. Bumppo here in and get him a ginger ale."

Walcott waved the card away. "I got this tank. Grab me a Dr Pepper?"

I tossed him the keys, and Natty and I went on in. The door made a jingling noise as we opened it; someone had wrapped a string of bells around the bar for Christmas, and they were still up.

The hot, older guy from the parking lot was standing dead still with his hands clasped in front of him in the second aisle. He was facing us, towering over the shelves, right at our end. As we came abreast, I saw the aisle was a weird mix of motor oil and diapers and air fresheners all jumbled in together. He was stationed in front of the overpriced detergent, looking at a box of laundry soap like someone had put the secret of the universe there, but they'd written it in hieroglyphics.

Natty paused to scrub his eyes; it was dim inside after marching around in the sunshine. I realized I was staring at the guy, maybe as hard as he was checking out the box, but he didn't even notice. When Natty was with me, I got rendered invisible to college guys, but a kid didn't stop guys his age from looking. Heck, he probably had one or two himself. While I would never be a certified beauty like my mom, I was cute enough in my red and yellow summer dress with its short, swirly skirt that he should've spared a glance.

Especially since it was pretty obvious to me that he was single. Newly. It all added up: the shaggy hair, the interest in detergent boxes. He was trying to learn how to not be married anymore. Divorced guy meets laundry. Walcott said I was getting a little too familiar with the syndrome.

As we passed, I checked his marriage finger for that tattletale ring of paler flesh. Bingo. Add the broad shoulders, the permanent worry lines in his forehead, the wide mouth, serious eyebrows, and there he was: my type, down to the last, yummy detail.

If I'd been alone, I would have sauntered over, done the thing where I tucked my long hair behind my ears, showed him the teeth that Dad had paid several thousand bucks to straighten. If he'd had a good voice, I might have let him take me back to his place and introduced him to the mysteries of fabric softener, maybe let him get to second base on his newly Downy'd sheets. Looking at him, the football player build, I got a flash of what it might feel like to be down under that much man, pinned to fresh-smelling bedding by the great god Thor. It was a sideways thrill of bedazzled feeling, snaking through my belly.

It surprised me, and I found myself smiling. Sex had never

quite worked out for me yet. When I looked at this guy, I knew my body still believed it would. Probably. Eventually. After all, I'd only tried sex with two men. Well, two and a half, I guess, because a year after I had Natty, I'd lost my virginity with Walcott, but I didn't count that at all. He'd been doing me a favor, and we'd never even kissed.

Then Natty tugged my hand, steering me past the hot guy, heading for the candy aisle. Since Walcott wasn't there to prang me, I gave myself a half second to check out the ass as I went by. Passed, flying colors. But then I went on, because Natty was with me, which meant no other man in the world could claim more than a look or two. They mostly didn't exist for me in Natty's presence. Not even Norse godlings. Policy.

Natty paused at the treat aisle and said in solemn tones, "They have Sno Balls."

"Interesting," I said, internally shuddering at the thought of Natty puking nuclear-pink coconut down my back as we drove on. "You know what's even more interesting? They have ginger ale." I said *ginger ale* like Mimmy said *Jesus*, walleyed with excitement, using long, ecstatic vowels.

"That's not interesting," Natty said, but he let himself be towed past the Sno Balls with the same good-natured disappointment I'd used to let him tug me past the blond guy.

The refrigerated cases at the back of the store were full of weird zero-calorie water drinks and Gatorade and Frappucinos, all in a tumble. Diet Coke by the Power Milk, orange juices stacked behind the Sprite. While I hunted ginger ale, Natty tugged his hand away to dig his Blue Angels jet plane out of his pocket. He started zooming it around.

I called, "You got ginger ale?" across the store to the scraggly, henna-haired object behind the counter.

"Do what?" she called back. We were closing in on Atlanta, but her Georgia-mountain accent was so thick I knew that she'd been brought up saying *you'uns* instead of *y'all*.

"Ginger ale?" I turned so she could hear me.

"Just two liters. And they ain't cold," she said.

I shook my head and opened the case to get Natty a Sprite, but I didn't have any faith in it. Mimmy had raised me to believe that ginger ale and a topical application of Mary Kay Night Cream could cure anything but cancer.

I grabbed a couple of Dr Peppers, too, for Walcott and me. Natty had zoomed his way over to a tin tub full of ice, and as I passed him on the way to the register, I saw that it was full of green-glass-bottle Coca-Colas. The sign said ninety-nine cents. It used to be only country people remembered that green-glass-bottle Cokes tasted better than any other kind, but the in-town hipsters had gotten all nostalgic for them. They cost two, even three bucks a pop inside the perimeter.

If I'd gotten the damn Dr Pepper, Natty and I would have walked out clean, but I wanted a Coke in a green glass bottle. I grabbed one and said, "Just a sec, Natty Bumppo."

He stayed by the tub, flying the jet low over the ice as I put one soda back. He was in plain sight, so I left him there and headed for the register to pay.

I passed the blond man, still standing at the end of the aisle. He was breathing shallow, eyes slightly unfocused, like he was looking a thousand years into the future instead of at a box of soap.

The girl behind the counter watched me approaching with her mouth hanging slack. She had big boobs, swinging free in a tight knit top that was cut low enough to show me a Tweety Bird tattoo on the right one. Her bobbed flop of dyed magenta hair ended in frizzles, and as I got close, I saw both her front teeth were broken off into jagged stumps.

"That all?" she asked.

"Yes," I said. It was very hard not to look at the teeth. She started ringing me up.

Then the cheery jingle bells on the door rang out. It was an odd Christmas-y sound on a late summer day, unexpected enough to make me look, even though I knew the bells were there.

I glanced at the door, at the stumpy little guy coming in.

He had a broad, pale face with a wide nose under a baseball cap, pulled low. Then my gaze stuck. My whole body stopped moving and the very air changed, because the guy brought his hand up as the door swung jangling closed behind him, and I was looking down the barrel of a silver revolver, really old and rusty.

All at once, I couldn't see the guy behind the gun as anything more than a vague person shape. I only saw the shine of fluorescent light along the silver barrel, only heard a voice behind it saying in a redneck twang, "Get on the ground! Get on the ground right now, before I put shoot holes in you."

His voice was low and raspy, like he was talking in a growl on purpose, but very loud, and I believed him. He would do it.

"On the ground!"

I couldn't move, though. My joints refused to bend and take me to the floor. I was closest to the gunman, by the register, then the big guy in the detergent aisle, and beyond him, standing tiny and alone in the path of the gun as it swept back and forth, was Natty. Natty gone still with his plane clutched in his hand.

I felt my head shake, back and forth. No.

A gun had come, rusted with anger and ill use, loaded and alive in human hands, into the same room where Natty stood in his honorary pilot's cap, hovering his Blue Angels plane over an ice bucket full of Cokes. Natty looked at the gun, his eyes so round that his fringe of thick, ridiculous lashes made them look like field daisies. The gun looked back.

It was not okay. It was not allowed. That gravelled voice told us all again to get on the ground, but I couldn't get on the ground. I couldn't move or breathe in a room where Natty stood far, so far away from me, too far for me to get there faster than a bullet could, under that gun's shining gaze. His little fingers were white, clutched hard onto his plastic jet.

Then the guy by the detergent moved. Just a couple of steps. A step and a half, really. Barely a move at all for a guy that tall and big, but it changed my life a thousand ways.

It wasn't a threatening move. He moved parallel to the gun,

and his palms were up and pointed forward in surrender. He sank down, folding into the seated shape that Natty called crisscross applesauce, palms flat on the ground, spine straight.

That sliding half step put his big body between the gun's black, unwinking eyehole and everything that mattered to me on this green earth.

And that was it. That was when it happened. I lowered my body to the ground, and all of me was falling, faster than I could physically move, way further than a glance or an attraction, falling so hard into deep, red, desperate love. I lay flat on the Circle K's dirty, cool floor, but the heart of me kept tumbling down. It fell all the way to the molten center of the earth, blazing into total, perfect feeling for the big blond wall of a man who had put himself between my child and bullets, before our eyes had ever met, before I so much as knew his name.

Chapter 2

William Ashe stares at the detergent. All morning at work he ignored the ever-rising restlessness that invaded his body. His jaw would not stop grinding itself closed. His hands would not stop fisting. He's left the lab early, heading for the mountains to exhaust it out of himself rock climbing. But now he's been waylaid by a cleaning product. He holds his body very still, though his spine shudders and twangs inside him. The internal, tooth-jarring vibration of all his nerves feels endless. Meanwhile, the detergent sits in its mundane cardboard box, oblivious, as William fights not to shove the whole shelf over. He wants to rip the box in half, stomp in the powder until it is sullied black and kicked away, ruined and gone.

He breathes in. The detergent only *seems* like the perverse agent of some dark destiny. It isn't. It is soap.

William Ashe doesn't believe in destiny. The word itself is actually shorthand people use when they wish to mysticize random events or externalize the results of their own willful choices.

William's own large, athletic father used to tell him he was destined to play football. All he really meant was that William was a big kid with excellent hand-eye coordination. His mother, in direct and endless opposition, insisted he was destined to unlock the secrets of the universe. Her own father was a physicist, and William had inherited the same aptitude. William grew up torn between these destinies; both his parents seemed so sure. By the time he was a teenager, he had formed two vertical wrinkles—his mother called them "stress horns"—between his eyebrows from the constant furrowing.

Then one day he saw Bridget, and he chose his own destiny. He chose her.

It was his junior year of high school, and she was ripping out the corpses of old phlox plants in the green space all the Morningside kids called Shit Park. Morningside was riddled with little parks and a nature preserve, but this one, the one near William's house, had no playground equipment and very few trees. It was a square of brown grass with some flower beds flanked by sagging wooden benches.

Bridget, a stranger in his neighborhood, a new girl, was on her knees, her ponytail and the right-triangle points of her small breasts bouncing in tandem. It wasn't only the way her hair shone copper in the sunshine as she tore up the flower bed. It wasn't only that her geometry was perfect in a way that felt specific to William, as if the slope of her narrow waist as it widened into hips had been crafted for him exactly. It was more than that. Though to be fair, these things mattered. They mattered a great deal.

Puberty had made him overly aware of the pleasing shape of girls: their high, light voices, their distracting smells. In the girl-free environment of his own home, he had expanded his old chemistry set, spending all his accumulated birthday and Christmas money on it, until the bulk of it was probably illegal. Then he'd found Dartmouth College's Chem. II and III labs online and worked his way through them. His grandfather's university connections gave him access to the labs at Emory when his own became insufficient. Last year, he'd decisively ended the long-standing kitchen-ant infestation without harming the dog. It could not be called an unqualified success; William had vomited for three days straight. His parents now discouraged testing in this vein. Still, he had outgrown the online labs, and most of his experiments were of his own design now. His place at the State Science Fair was a foregone conclusion. But at school? A cheerleader passing his lab desk in a swirl of short skirt could muddle even a simple attempt to grow a bismuth crystal.

Sophomore year, he'd been bumped to start on Varsity, a promotion that had allowed him to sink himself into several girls. He was amazed at how the simple pumping action of it quieted his rowdy body, let him think clearly for hours after. It had been a great convenience to have sex available.

But it wasn't only the curvy-girl shape of Bridget, sweaty and in filthy shorts, that caught him as she knelt in the loamy earth, tossing the leprous old phlox plants into a heap behind her. She hummed to herself as she tore up the flower bed with cheerful authority, altering ground that absolutely was not hers to change. Nearby he saw she had a bucket of tulip bulbs, a flat box full of black-eyed Susans and new chicory blooms, a wrought-iron post with a hook, and a brightly painted birdhouse. She was fixing Shit Park with no permission, ripping up phlox in mad handfuls. She hummed and streaked dirt across her face as she wiped sweat away. She either didn't know or didn't care that anyone was watching.

He recognized her.

She was a shiny picture of how he was in the lab when he followed an experiment he should not be doing down its next step and its next, until the reactions had fulfilled themselves in the chain he had predicted, once again not blowing anyone up. She was . . . He couldn't find the word, but then he found it. The word was *complete*. She was complete. Watching her, his mind and body both surged into an electric, vibrating agreement that was final: *That one. There.*

He felt a huge unclenching in all the cells that drove his working parts. All the destiny he needed was murdering old phlox and wearing Converse high-tops. His eyebrows stopped their constant press toward each other, shifting back into the slot where eyebrows go. It felt good and easing, but a little painful, the way a lunge felt in his legs after a hard run.

He understood what his parents meant by destiny then: that they wanted a specific thing. That they would be relentless until they got it.

This understanding made his own course feel preset, but difficult. This one specific girl was a subset of all girls, and all girls didn't like him. He was weird. All girls told him so. Even the ones he had sex with told him so, and the sex was mostly secret. They weren't his girlfriends. Even Paula told him so, and she was his best friend.

On the plus side, for the last year and change, all girls *had* liked to look at him. The soft pads of fat on his hips and belly had melted away, and his shoulders had spread themselves apart, until he was shaped like a triangle built out of hardened flesh. This made the girls forget that they'd called him Moosetard in middle school. Now they mostly called him William.

He'd broken himself of the comfort of covering his lips in spit bubbles. All girls did not like that. He carried a secret penny in his mouth instead, liking the tang of the copper on his tongue. In middle school, he sometimes cried and punched his hands into walls or the faces or stomachs of his classmates. Football helped stop that. His therapist had delighted his father by suggesting it, saying contact sports were exceptional stress relief, though William couldn't see what he had to be stressed about. His grades were perfect. Still, he had learned to save the internal pulse and heave for football, and now it felt good to feel it building up red inside him, to let it spend itself in the hard smashing of his body into other bodies. He won games, and his face was symmetrical in ways that pleased all girls, so sometimes he got to spend the rest in sex.

Then he saw Bridget, this subset who mattered in a way all girls did not, and wanted her.

He still wants her. He holds his angry body rigid in the Circle K minimart, staring at the kind of detergent she used to buy, hearing her say, *It smells like the color green*, in his head. He uses Arm & Hammer now, which smells like clean nothing. The smell of nothing is another way to never have her voice sound in his mind. There were five very bad months of external silence, and after that, he had to push the voice of Bridget that he still heard internally out of him, away entirely, banished. She has not existed in his thoughts, not for seven months now.

Not until this moment, which makes sense, mathematically. He didn't see it before because he's not good at following the passage of time. When he's in the lab, he'll wind himself so deep into the helixes, unraveling the secret language of the viral RNA, then suddenly realize his body has become ravenous and desperate for a bathroom. But, seven months plus five months equals twelve, and twelve is a year.

A year ago, today.

Last night, Father Lewis came by the house again, for the first time in weeks. William wouldn't let him in.

He looked blandly at Father Lewis and said, "I am not up to having company," even though Paula was there, sitting in plain sight on the sofa, reading case files.

Paula told him to say it because these days, he is unable to tolerate people in the house that aren't her. It is a social convention that should have driven the priest off, but Father Lewis only looked at William with his eyes all moist and said, "Anniversaries are hard, William. They can open up a wound that might feel closed, make it fresh again."

Now William connects this speech to the current date, and sees that Father Lewis was not making a random observation. He was being personal. But Father Lewis has shown up on the porch and said so many things over the last year, most of them not relevant.

"You can always call me, if you want to talk," the priest went on. "I understand your anger with God." But William is no more angry with God than he is angry with unicorns. Neither was present at the accident.

Policemen came to explain it to him, and the words they said were not words he could process. They were not words that he could hear. Eventually, he caught their meaning, and then William told it to himself this way: Bridget's Saturn has no backseat anymore, and the backseat was where Twyla sat, strapped into her car seat. Therefore, now, there is no Twyla. Simple physics. There is no need to move past that bald fact, that way of stating it. When there was a backseat, there was a Twyla. Now, there isn't.

Most of the parts of his life have split themselves neatly into before and now, and it is this dividing line that kept William from opening the door wide enough to allow priests, not any kind of rage at Bridget's deity. Before, his involvement with the church was important to his wife. Now, Father Lewis is not relevant.

He closed the door and sat back down with Paula.

"Need some space, Bubba?" she asked.

"To do what in?" he said, deliberately overliteral.

She chuckled and propped her long copper-brown legs over his. "No space for you."

Paula, his best friend since high school, is one of the few things from before that has come with him into now. In the before, she was both his best man and Bridget's maid of honor. The three of them played pool every Thursday, and Paula always came to Sunday brunch, usually with whatever man was following her about. Bridget learned the guys' names, but William called them all "Buddy," because month by month the guy might have a different job, a different skin color, a different car, but he was always pretty much the same guy.

Now, Paula is what he has in lieu of family. He never minds her.

He also doesn't mind the maid service. She—or maybe they—refreshes the house while William is at work. With such limited company, the house stays clean, and the air inside feels cool and barely used, rich with oxygen. He is not angry with Bridget's imaginary God inside his quiet house.

I am only angry with Bridget, he thinks. He stares at the box of detergent, understanding that an anniversary, the one Father Lewis said could open up old wounds, is here upon him, now. It is hard, as he was warned. He is both in desperate pain and furious. He simply did not know it, because Bridget is not here to tell him.

When he was a child, sometimes a thing would swell up inside him, a huge, unnamed, inflating thing, pressed hard and tight against the walls of his skin, thinning it. He would sob in hard, angry barks. He sounded like a circus seal, the other kids would say, and laugh. Then he would hit things, walls and trees and other children, his own thighs, anything to make the swelling pop or go down. He would end red-faced and sweaty and suspended again. Now he knows it was always and only his old friend, chemistry, acting on his brain, making him have some kind of a feeling. It helps when he can name the feeling. Naming lets him own it, makes it finish faster.

He tells it to himself again, so he can ride it instead of having it ride him. *I am angry with Bridget.*

Not because she was driving. She was only taking their toddler to St. Thomas for Mother's Morning Out. Bridget's wagon was a solid object, existing in space and time, and a semi-truck's brakes failed, so that it slid until it was occupying the same space at the same time. Something had to give. He can't fault Bridget because her car obeyed physics.

He's angry because of what Bridget did next.

And he's angry about the detergent. These days William sleeps alone in a bed that smells like the blankest kind of clean. He's angry that he knows this box, remembers the green scent rising up in his memory from the sheets where they so many times lay tangled and replete, where they woke together every morning, where they once made Twyla. It's wrong for Bridget to be a physical presence in his mind. He can't unsee her body, pale and soft, the hip deep-curved to fit his hand. The constellation Orion caught in the freckles of her left shoulder. The cord of muscle in her runner's calf. He doesn't want to think of that body, personal and perfect to him, twisted into the car's body, both of them broken. They had to use the Jaws of Life to get her out.

As they lifted her free, she saw. She saw the place where the backseat had been.

William does not believe in an afterlife. People reproduce, preserving their genetic traits via their offspring, and then they die. Bridget saw the absence of Twyla as they lifted her, and Bridget believed in Christ, in resurrection, in a literal heaven. She couldn't let Twyla go alone. She'd belonged wholly to God before she was ever William's, and in that moment, she let God win her wholly back.

That's as far as he can get. Remembering washes swarms of chemicals into his red blood. It's all he can do to stop his hands from tearing out his eyes, pulling the walls down. He hauls his thoughts backward, to thirty seconds before. There's no reason to allow this. He has not allowed himself to so much as think her name for months now. He must stop looking at detergent and remembering. He must stop now, in his next breath, because there's nothing that happened after Bridget's heartbeat ceased that William can forgive. Not one damn minute of any piece of life.

He hears Christmas bells then, a cheery tinkle of discordant, grating sound. It helps William look away from the detergent. He sees a young man has come into the minimart. He is twitchy and pale, and he's holding a gun. He waves the gun back and forth, yelling for everyone to get on the floor. It's surprising.

It is purely out of habit that William looks around first, to see what the other people are doing. He does this because of Bridget, whose name cannot be so easily rebanished. She wanted William to be more interested in people, so in college he studied biology and genetics as well as chemistry. He knows that people are herd animals. They like to go wheeling in the same directions, and they feel more comfortable around William when he wheels with them.

The gun makes it important to keep the people comfortable. So William looks, and no one is getting on the ground. Not the clerk, standing slack-mouthed by the register. Not the dark-haired girl in the flowered dress.

He looks the other way and sees a little boy, a few feet behind him and to his right, shining bright in a yellow fireman's slicker and a black cap. This child is about the age Twyla would be now. He is staring at the gun. Eyes wide. Breath short. William, who is both taller and broader than the robber, decides he should take the initiative and comply, so as to look less threatening.

William steps sideways, slowly, hands up, and gets between the frightened child and the man with the gun before he sinks down.

He checks himself over carefully for terror, but there isn't any. It's curious, because fear would be appropriate. This might simply be a dearth of proper chemicals. There cannot be a lot of adrenaline left to dump into his blood. He's spent so much on his ridiculous, ongoing rage against the anniversary, the detergent, his wife.

The robber has pink-rimmed eyes and damp nostrils. His hands jerk the gun around and his finger is on the trigger. Every time he blinks, he squeezes his eyes shut hard, and his mouth works, too. His whole face clenches and unclenches. His gaze darts about, trying to look at all of them at once. He appears to be under the influence of a stimulant, likely illegal, and he is engaged in a stressful activity. He cannot be trusted to make good decisions.

William hears a door opening behind him. It's the door by the soda case with the Employees Only sign hanging on it; an old man comes stumping through it with his eyebrows beetled down. An old lady follows right behind him. They are different from each other, but clearly a set. She has pastel Bermuda shorts and a stiff bubble of lavender hair; he has plaid golf pants and a cap. The man is looking toward the register at the clerk, saying, "Carrie, what is—"

He stops so abruptly that the lady behind him bangs into him. The old man stares from William, sitting on the floor, to the man with the gun. He puts one arm out, herding the lady behind him, and in this simple gesture William understands that they have been married for a long time.

The lady sees the gun then and puts her hands up, the way robbed people do in the movies. Her mouth drops open into a bright, uneven circle. She is wearing orange lipstick that has bled into all the wrinkles around her mouth.

"Get on the floor!" the gunman yells again.

Now the dark-haired girl is sinking down to the ground, the poppy-covered skirt of her dress belling around her, and then the old couple does, too. The herd animals are all doing the same thing. This is a stress reliever for all of them. Even the gunman's next blink is less of a squeeze.

"Not you," he says to the clerk, gesturing with the gun. "Come on out from back there first."

The clerk comes around the counter and lies down beside the dark-haired girl. It's happening quickly. This is an efficient robbery, so far, but William doesn't trust it to remain so. The person with all the power in the room is on drugs.

William considers what to do next. The robber is a small man with a narrow chest, a potbelly, and skinny arms. He has a patch of thin brown beard on his chin that he keeps petting with his free hand. If William could get to him fast enough, he could twist him into separate pieces, easily. It would be a useful spending of the angry chemicals that he's been riding.

But he can feel the presence of the child sheltered behind him. He doesn't want this boy, who, in a different universe might have gone to school with Twyla, might have been her friend, to be shot if William is not fast enough. He stays where he is.

"Open the safe, you old piece a shit," the gunman says, jerking the gun at the old man.

"It's on a timer!" the old man says.

The robber uses his free hand to wipe at his damp nose. "You think I'm stupid? I been watching you, weeks now. You think I don't know about when the safe's timer goes off? I'mma start shooting all these people if you don't get a bag and fill it up for me. And you"—now the guy is talking to William—"you can lay all the way down flat on your stomach on your own, or you can lay down flat because I've put one in your brain pan."

If William complies, he will lose some options. Still, the child is directly behind William. If William stands and the man fires toward him, the bullets will be moving in the direction of the child. William lies flat on his belly.

He makes his arms into a pillow and rests his cheek on it. His face is now pointed directly at the dark-haired girl in the poppy dress. She stares intently at William, communicating urgency, and then her gaze slides past him to the child. So they are a set, too, like the old couple is a set.

He hears a scuffling sound behind him, then feels a small weight pressing into his side. The child has scooted along the floor to him, and now he fists his hands in William's shirt. He is panting into William's armpit.

William scans the room. The old lady is looking at him. The clerk, down on the ground, glances his way, too. Even the old man shifts his gaze to William as he goes behind the counter with the gunman to empty the safe. The herd is following his lead, so he lies still and quiet and waits for it to be over.

Now the gunman has the bag. He says, "That's all?"

The old man says, "We don't keep much cash. Everyone has a bank card these days." He sounds both defensive and apologetic.

The gunman empties the register drawer, too, and directs the old man to lie down with the rest of them. He grabs two cartons of cigarettes, stuffs them into his plastic grocery bag on top of the money, then swings the gun around back and forth, sweeping his gaze across all of them in turn.

"No one move for ten minutes, or I will surely come back

here and shoot you," he says, which is truly the stupidest threat William has ever heard.

The gunman starts to turn away. In thirty seconds he will be gone. It seems the decision to lie quietly down will pay off.

Then William hears the Christmas bells, chiming again.

He thinks three words: *Here we go.*

It's a cop. A female state cop in her uniform, swinging cheerfully through the door with an environmentally sound travel mug for coffee in her hand.

The gunman and the state cop see each other, both reacting with a whole-body shock that reverberates through them and opens their faces up into circles, eyes and mouths widening at the same time. She halts directly in the doorway.

She drops her mug and reaches for the gun at her hip, but the door swings shut and bangs her in the back. She fumbles it. William is faster than she is. He should have moved when he had the chance. Now he is flat on his belly with a little boy clutching his shirt. He can't stand up and run toward gunplay with a child clinging and dangling down his side.

The gunman pulls the trigger, and it seems to William that he smells the sulphur before he hears the bang. This isn't possible, but this is how he experiences it, in spite of science. He barely clocks the blood that appears in a wash on the shoulder of her blue uniform shirt; he is noticing instead her face, how it stretches and thins, as if the entry of a bullet into the closed system of her body is fundamentally changing her already. The late-coming sound feels loud in the small market. It starts a ringing in his ears. The child makes a noise and pushes his face into William. The face feels wet, and the wetness is absorbed by William's shirt, coming through the cloth to touch his skin.

The bullet shoves the state cop backward, against the door, which opens. It spills her onto the ground outside. She is already rolling to the side as the door swings shut behind her in a cheery jangle of bells.

The clerk on the floor says, "Oh no. Oh no, no, no," in a soft, conversational tone.

William's body has more adrenaline after all. It is dumping into his bloodstream, and he can feel his heartbeat pounding through all his limbs and in his spine, even in his eyes. He closes them against the rhythm, knowing now that the gun in the room is real and powerful. It can change and end things in an instant. William, of all people, should have understood this. An unaccountable longing rises up inside him, and what he feels for the cop in that moment is both beautiful and terrible. He has no name for it.

He hears the gunman yelling, "Holy shit! Holy shit!"

When he opens his eyes, he sees the gunman has his back to them all, scrabbling to lock the door, then wheeling back around to face them, all lying still and obedient on the ground.

"This is not the plan," the gunman says helplessly to the old couple, and William sees how young he is now, too. His nose is running; his upper lip shines with sweat and mucus. The clerk is young. The girl in the poppy-covered dress is young. The room is full of children, and one of them has a gun. He brings his gun now to bear on William, then the dark-haired girl, then the old couple. He swings it back and forth like this is still pretend, a television show. It isn't. It is real.

The gunman says it again, this time to the clerk. "This is not the fucking plan."

You are angry, William thinks at the gunman. The thought comes in the voice of a young Bridget, her high school voice. *You are angry because your robbery has been thwarted.* The gunshot, the real gun in the room, has banged her banished voice back into his aching head. He doesn't know how he will ever shove it out again.

"How can I get out of here?" the gunman asks.

The old man opens his mouth and closes it, like a fish gulping its way through an air drowning.

"Got'damn tell me!" the gunman hollers.

It is the clerk who finally answers. "Go out the back. It's not locked from inside, but can't no one come in thattaway."

The *th* sound comes out airy and too soft as her tongue pushes against the empty place where most of her front teeth should be. William feels his tongue make an inadvertent checking gesture, running across his own front teeth, intact.

Out in the lot, there is a shot cop. William wonders if there is anyone to help her, or if she is conscious and using her radio. Maybe she has her own gun out now, pointed at the door, waiting for the gunman to step through.

The gunman must also be wondering all these things, only slower, through the cloud of drugs that have made him so glossy-eyed and frantic.

"She's out there right by my damn car," he says accusingly, to the old man. "I'm screwed! I'm screwed!"

The old man says nothing, and the gunman stamps his feet, making a terrible, inarticulate gargling noise. The little boy still presses his wet face into William's side, and William threads his other arm beneath himself to pat at the boy, awkwardly, as best he can while lying on his stomach.

The gunman should leave. Most likely the cop is too busy bleeding into the gravel to stop him if he is fast. She might be dying.

William does not want her to be dying, and this is the right thing to want. He is having a good and human reaction. No one would want that for her. But the voice of Bridget, loose inside his head, won't let him stop there. She is naming it. She is naming the terrible, beautiful thing.

You are envious. You are envious of that cop because for her, everything will go dark and be quiet and stop.

William's gaze finds the gun. It is a .32 revolver, probably a six-shooter. That means there are five more bullets in it.

And then, for the second time in his life, he finds himself at the center of a huge reverberating truth. He recognizes destiny, this shorthand word that means nothing beyond the strength of his own will, in a way he has not since he saw Bridget, whole and beautiful in pink high-tops, her jaw set, saving Shit Park.

This is what he knows: Five bullets left, and he owns one. At least one is for him.

He recognizes the feeling that rises at this certainty. He can name this blend of chemicals, though it has been a while since it washed along his blood. It is what Bridget always called "the thing with feathers." It is hope.

His moment will come. He only needs to watch for it. He only needs to take it. He stares with new eyes at the loaded gun. He waits.

Chapter 3

*H*e shot that lady cop. In front of Natty. Natty had already wiggle-wormed over to the big blond guy, and now it looked like he was trying to burrow into the guy's side. I found myself hoping to someone's God or other that Natty was reacting to the noise, that he hadn't seen the blood opening up in the shape of a fast-blooming flower on her blue top.

Then the gunman twisted around and turned the deadbolt, fast, trapping Natty and me and everyone in with him and the gun and the stink of copper and sulphur.

He also locked Walcott out, and I fell into a pure, almost holy terror. I don't know what I expected Walcott to do. Burst in and save us with the power of T. S. Eliot? It didn't matter. What mattered was, Natty and I were stuck without Walcott in a room where the air still rang with the residue of gun sound. I felt white inside and out, eaten up by bad light like a roadside animal.

Then the gunman paused, half turned again, and flipped the door sign over so the word CLOSED faced out. Did he truly think someone might step over the bleeding policewoman and try to pop in for a pack of Camels?

He started yelling at us to move, to crawl back away from the plate-glass front; I found myself nodding. Moving was a thing to do, and doing felt better than lying still and helpless. Also, it was a smart thing for him to pick. It was a small relief, that he would think of a smart thing. I'd lost faith in him when he paused to flip that sign.

I followed his instructions, got to my trembling hands and knees and crawled along the floor toward the freezer cases. I tried to stay between Natty and where I thought the gun might be. I could feel the air on my thighs as my skirt tangled in my knees and hiked up in the back. I reached with one hand to yank it down as far as it would go.

I was wishing I'd worn ugly panties, and that made me realize I was a scant six inches from hysterical. I made myself breathe deep and slow. I crawled and tried not to think of the gun's black-hole eye looking at Natty. All the while, the bare backs of my thighs buzzed and clenched like the gunman's gaze was dirty beetles walking on my legs. Surely he wasn't watching me crawl. Surely he had other things on his mind just now. But I wished my dress was longer.

The big blond guy was in front of us, lifting one hand to open the door with the Employees Only sign. I felt a praying feeling, and it was aimed at him. Crazy. He might look like a Norse deity, and he had put himself between my kid and danger, but that didn't mean he was going to whip out a thunder hammer and smite the gun and save us.

It was up to Walcott, locked outside so far away from us and, oh please, calling 911.

Natty shadowed Thor through the doorway. I crawled faster, getting close, so Natty could feel me behind him.

The gunman, still using a fake, growly voice, said, "Don't even try to let that door swing shut between us. Push it all the way open, to the wall."

I said to Natty, softly, "Gonna be okay, baby." I was surprised at how true it sounded, how steady my voice was. Motherhood and a gunshot had insta-morphed me into an excellent liar. Mostly

I got red and blinked too much. Natty paused and peered at me over his shoulder, eyebrows pressed into a worried crinkle. "Keep going!" I smiled at him, very bright-eyed and glorious, like I was encouraging him to jump off the side of some fancy hotel pool near Disneyland. "Gonna be fine!" I sounded so firm and steady that I almost believed me.

Then the gunman ruined it, dropping the yelling rasp and saying to us all, "Aw, hell. I'm Stevie, by the way," in this insanely friendly tone, like he was about to tell us he would be our hostage taker today. Like he might next ask what he could do to make crawling along the filthy linoleum with the gun's black gaze skittering back and forth across my naked legs more pleasant. It struck me as wildly unprofessional.

We crawled single file down a hall that dumped us into a long, thin office. It ran the whole width of the store, and the two outside walls were exposed brick. On the longest brick wall, light spilled through a row of narrow windows in a horizontal line right up by the ceiling.

Stevie had us sit on our bottoms in a row against the long inside wall, like Natty's preschool class waiting to go to recess. Thor had gone in first, so he was all the way at the far end of the room, right by a desk that stood longways to him. Natty sat beside him, squeezed between us. I leaned in and Thor leaned in, too, as if he felt me willing him to help me make a tent over my son, to press in toward each other, to make Natty be the narrowest, most tiny slice of target.

"You're squooshing me," Natty said, both hands moving to hold his cap on.

I said, "Shhhh," half a heartbeat behind.

I eased my bottom an inch away, but stayed leaned. Thor did the same thing, and I was so glad to be seated near him. So glad that Natty was even nearer. Close to him felt like the safest place in the room.

I heard a soft plopping noise on my other side. The clerk was sitting with her knees up in a tent, hunched forward over them, her broken front teeth showing through her open mouth. Her head was tilted down in profile to me, and the plops were tears falling out of her and down onto her jeans, making wet spots. I wasn't crying, I realized, and felt strangely proud. It would scare Natty more if I cried, so I wasn't doing it, and that was all. On the other end was the old couple, first the woman, and then the man tucked into the corner. On the short wall next to him was the only door in.

Stevie—God, what a stupid name for a grown man with a pistol—grabbed one of the twin rolling office chairs and pulled it under the windows, beside a file cabinet. The top of his baseball cap didn't even clear the windows when he was standing, but he sat anyway. His T-shirt was dirty and it said SHAZAM! across the front in peeling letters. The chair was high for him, so only his toes touched the floor. He swiveled it back and forth, not even noticing he was doing it, the same way Natty might.

The afternoon sun coming through the window slits made us all squint. He swayed in the chair, looking at us with the sun in our eyes, and said, "Sorry about that. I need to be under these here windows in case of they send snipers."

I heard a person say, "That's okay!" all cheery, and it was me.

Stevie stared at me then like I was being a bad hostage instead of him sucking at robbing. But I hadn't been able to help it, just like I couldn't help smiling at him, an encouraging, big-ass smile that showed all my teeth.

The voice in the back of my mind said, *Are you trying to make friends with this shithead?* And I was. I had a whole push of words rising up in my throat that I had to work to swallow: *Hey, Stevie! I'm a Pisces who loves sweet pickles and early David Bowie songs, and did you know my son is a certified genius and a miracle? He'll probably cure cancer one day, Stevie. Do you want to shoot the boy who'll stamp out cancer?*

Because Stevie had told us his name and apologized for the

sun glare, like we were people, I wanted to be a whole, real person to Stevie, so he wouldn't hurt my son. I wanted it so bad I was shaking.

I made myself pull a bunch of air in through my nose. The room smelled like Vicks VapoRub and tuna salad sandwiches. Old-people smells. I pushed the air out and kept right on smiling, trying to make a face that told Stevie that I might not know him well, but I already liked him an ungodly amount. He looked away.

I peeked at Thor. He looked a ready kind of still. Was he going to make a move? I wanted him to, but what if it went wrong? What if Stevie got angry and started shooting, and Natty— I couldn't think past that.

I let my gaze slide sideways to the desk beside Thor, seeking something that might help us. It looked like something from a dorm room, cheap and modern. No drawers. On top was an old square monitor that had to weigh a thousand pounds and a bunch of other useless crap in a jumble: keys, envelopes, pens, a ceramic dish full of paper clips. The computer tower was on the floor underneath, and the other side of the desk had some open shelving. The bottom shelf had the printer, and above that was a stack of white paper held down by a big glass globe paperweight. It was shaped like a squashed softball, with a huge, perfect orange Gerber daisy trapped in the glass.

No drawers. That seemed important. I badly wanted the desk to have at least one drawer.

Then I stopped looking because Stevie got out of his chair and walked to the door.

He locked it. He literally turned the flip lock on the doorknob, like he was in here going to the bathroom. Like a flip lock could stop cops or bullets.

I looked to Thor, but he wasn't looking back. He was watching Stevie, too, and he gave a faint, incredulous headshake. He knew, and I knew, too. Stevie was a novice or incompetent or maybe just plain stupid. He was going to eff this whole thing up.

Thinking that was like being gut-punched. I felt my waist jackknife and fold me forward in a twitch because I saw what Stevie effing it all up might look like. It looked like me dead, like Natty traumatized and motherless.

That wasn't even the worst that could happen, but the thing that was worse than my own death could not be allowed. It could not even be considered. I would curl up all the way around my son, and I would eat up every bullet with my body, before I let the worst thing be. Natty would walk out of here. That was non-negotiable.

"Now what?" Stevie said, loud and not calm at all.

He banged his gun-free hand into his forehead, like he was trying to beat his brain into thinking. I wanted to kill him for asking us. For not knowing what to do, and quietly and powerfully doing it until he was away with his bag of cash and smokes and we were all out safe. My heart flailed and pulsed against my ribs in what felt like a million beats a minute. I couldn't stop any of this. Stevie needed to step up and be a damn pro. But he was going to eff it up.

Stevie had a gun, so Stevie, who was otherwise as viable as dog crap, owned us. If I died here, Natty would be an orphan. Would he go looking for his father? But what could he find, when there was no such thing? When Natty happened, he was born wholly mine and perfect. This is what I whispered into the pink coil of his newborn ear: *My body made you up, because the world is so much better with you in it.*

I didn't say that to anyone else, not even my parents. They would have questioned it, tried to make me test it. Me, I knew what I knew.

But why hadn't I already invented that tragic hero-soldier father, fallen in Afghanistan, in case I walked under a bus one day? I'd thought I had time. I'd assumed I had a whole long lifetime to invent Natty a nice, dead father, perfectly loving and permanently absent.

.If Natty went looking, there were other stories he could find. He might dig up that distant, deep blue night, the misty not-quite-memory story that Walcott told my parents. It was a fairy tale in Grimm's tradition, and I'd never told it to anyone. I hadn't even told it to myself, because I knew that night had nothing to do with Natty. Walcott and my parents saw it differently, though.

I didn't know squat about guns, but right then I wanted Stevie's anyway. The gun in my hands and not his would change everything. I would own *him*, and suddenly it was hard to put my eyes on anything else. I had to physically turn my head to stop staring at it. That meant I was looking at the drawerless desk again.

I knew then why I wanted it to have drawers. Because it was close to me, and people hid things in desk drawers. Things like weapons. How did I know, really, for sure, that Stevie had the only gun in the room?

The Circle K near Mimmy's house, I knew, was chock-full of weaponry. It was owned by Mrs. Quincy and it was a craphole, a lot like this one. All the candy was dusty. One or another of Mrs. Quincy's hairy, tattooed sons manned the counter. Her boys, all four of them, could each throw a Coke bottle up high, high into the sky and shoot it into a rain of glass on the way down. Walcott called it Redneck Skeet, and back when we were kids we used to bike up and get dip cones at the DQ, then walk over to the meadows behind that Circle K to watch them do it. They had guns tucked all over that store.

Like as not, there was a gun here, too.

The old people on the end of the row were the owners, I thought. This office was full of old-people smells, and they had come out of the door that led back here. I didn't think these two spent their weekends shooting at Coke bottles; she had on resort wear, and her bag exactly, exactly matched her shoes. He was wearing a thin summer cardigan. But this was Georgia, and not city Georgia, either. Not for quite a few miles yet. These old folks were country people, and they sure as hell looked like Republicans. They had to have at least a pistol hidden here. Maybe a shotgun, too.

Stevie scratched his head, pushing his fingers up under the cap to get at his scalp, muttering to himself. I risked a slight lean toward the clerk and whispered, "Gun?"

She turned her face to me, her eyes black-ringed with cried-away mascara. She shook her head, a rapid back-and-forth so subtle it was barely more than a tremble. But it wasn't a no. It was an animal move, uncomprehending.

I looked all around the room, and then mouthed, "Gun?" again. Her eyebrows knit, still puzzled. Finally, I made a gun out of my fingers, showing it to her in the shelter of my legs. "Where is it?"

Her eyes went wide, and this time the tremble back and forth was a definite no. At the same time, her gaze darted away from me to a two-drawer metal file cabinet by the door. The cowardly little object was lying. The file cabinet had a weapon in it, I was sure.

Stevie had turned toward me. "Are you talking to her? What are you saying to her?"

Stevie took a step in my direction.

As the gun turned our way and Stevie stepped close with such intent, I could feel Thor coiling. The muscles in his big body tensed, readying for fast movement, but he wasn't really Thor. He was just some big blond guy, sitting close to Natty. I couldn't let gunfire happen this close to my son.

I started talking, my voice all high and shaky. "Nothing, just . . . nothing, just . . ."

"Just what? Just what?" Stevie said, and the gun seemed to grow and swell in his hand as he approached. With every step he took, the blond guy wound himself tighter, and that huge and huger gun came closer to my kid.

I said, desperate, "I was checking on her. She seems real scared."

Stevie drew up short, and the gun tilted a little sideways. Off Natty. Now it was pointing at Thor himself, and I felt Thor's tension ease a notch. It made me love him more, that he would rather have its eye on him than Natty.

Stevie blinked. "Well, that's nice then." After a second he added, "She don't need to be scared."

Now that he had stepped in close, I saw how red and quivery the skin around his nostrils looked. His pupils were huge, though the room was bright. Dear God, but Stevie was jacked up on something. He started to back away, his twitchy gaze pinging to the door.

"We're all scared," I said. He paused like this was a new idea to him, and I kept talking, because now I had something human and not crazy to say. "My son here, Natty, he is only three. Natty is so scared. He shouldn't be in here."

Now Stevie looked at Natty, and I could feel Natty shrink into me. "You scared?" Stevie asked.

I felt more than saw Natty's head dip in a nod.

"Well, don't be. I like little kids. I'm a daddy myself. I ain't gonna shoot no little kids, okay?" Then he walked backward, glancing all around the room so it looked like his eyes were rolling. "Oh Christ, what next?"

Stevie, who would be our hostage taker today, was floundering. The gun wobbled in his hand.

"I gotta get out of here," he said. "Should I run? Maybe I should run."

I stared at him, too frozen with hope to answer. The clerk beside me made a honking noise, swallowing her tears, and his gaze went to her.

She said, "Yes. Run. You should run now." Her voice was low and trembly, but she sounded so sure. I could have kissed her.

He made a move for the flip-locked door, and my heart fluttered and flapped, wild with hope. But then Stevie stopped and cocked his head like a dog. It was a full three seconds before I understood.

Sirens. I could hear them in the distance, wailing their way closer every second. We all froze then, listening to the cops coming. Lots of them. An ambulance for the downed Statie, too, I bet. Walcott was doing what he could for us, but why couldn't the cops have been two minutes later?

Stevie moved first, stamping his feet in a blurring frenzy of a rage dance, then hopping up and down like a redneck Rumpelstiltskin. He kicked backward, like a vicious mule, the sole of his boot banging at the wall behind him five or six times. It made flat slaps of ugly sound against the brick. He said a long chain of words, most ones that Natty had never heard before.

I put my head down, made myself smaller, squeezing Natty close into my side. I had to make everything be different. I needed a gun. Stevie had one, and that meant Natty could be hurt, could be worse than hurt. I could not allow it.

I had this crazy trapped-on-the-playground-seesaw feeling then, like I was jacked up in the air with my legs hanging down, clutching Natty close, and Stevie-Our-Robber-Today was a mean kid on the other end, having a temper tantrum. He held us helpless in the air, and he was flailing around, not in control. He could drop us down hard, any second. I hated it. I hated it.

He could kill me, and it was worse than not leaving a nice story behind for my son. I could die here, and I had never told myself the truth.

I'd closed my eyes to it four years ago, when Natty stopped my period. When he made me puke up all my breakfasts and switched my sweet-set mouth to loving onions and hot peppers. I had Walcott's momses take me to a doctor, and I let the doctor tell them what I already knew: I was a virgin. I was pregnant.

I decided that meant Natty was a gift. For more than nine months, he and I were one thing. After they took him out, I saw two tiny, pink-toed versions of my father's feet. I saw my small, round skull and face, the shape of my own jaw. I saw Mimmy's outsize eyes, the long lashes crumpled up from the cramped quarters. I only saw the things that made him mine.

I never let myself connect Natty to that dark, blue velvet night when I woke and found myself outside, sprawled in a beanbag chair, alone. I saw all the crazy stars swinging back and forth, like they were hanging down on strings. I heard Walcott's frantic yells. *Marco! Marco!* and I knew that I'd been lost. I'd been afraid. I'd called Walcott, and here he was at last, come to find me.

I was more than half an hour away from Dad's house, on the Emory campus.

Walcott drove me back to Dad's in my VW, so it wouldn't be missing in the morning. The road looked lined in light. It felt fake, like a movie I was watching from inside itself. I kept graying out, the whole ride home. I have no idea how Walcott got back to the Prius. A taxi? I never asked.

Dad's driveway shimmered and shifted as Walcott helped me up it, but I wouldn't let him in the door. Inside, it was dark and quiet, my three little half brothers tucked into their beds upstairs, Dad and Bethany in their room with the door closed. They'd gone to sleep, thinking I was eating burgers and then heading to the midnight movie with some kids from synagogue. Thinking I'd come home straight after the film and slip quietly to bed, the way I often did on my every-other weekends.

I stumbled down to my room in the basement. I don't remember changing, but I woke up hours later, tucked under my covers in a clean T-shirt. The sun was up. Last night's clothes were in a scatter on the floor. My top, streaked with dried red Georgia clay, had my bra inside it. I unfurled the skirt from its filthy twist. No underwear. No shoes.

I went right to the bathroom to turn the shower on. I let the water work its way to scalding, then got in and stayed until I threw up. I only got out to brush my sour teeth.

I picked up the clothes that were in a scatter on the floor. If I left them, in two weeks I'd find them hanging in my closet. They'd be clean and pressed, courtesy of Martha, Bethany's three-days-a-week housekeeper. I realized that I didn't want to see these clothes again. I couldn't put them in a trash can, though. Not in this house. Bethany would find them. She'd hold up this clay-stained skirt with its dried crust of something white staining the back, asking me why I was throwing out the nice things my dad bought me.

I stuffed them in a gym bag. I shoved the bag deep into my closet, behind a stack of shoe boxes.

Later, when Natty happened, Walcott told my parents about coming to find me, as if Natty and the dark blue night were connected. I didn't see how they could be, because I already loved him so. He floated and bobbed inside me, the two of us alone conspiring to invent his hands, his serious, wide brow, his knobby knees.

Natty was real, and that night wasn't. Even so, Mimmy made me see a pastoral counselor three counties over. He's the only one I ever tried to tell, saying only that my son *felt* like a miracle. Some man of God he turned out to be; he actually made a pooh-pooh noise, blowing out air in two fat, dismissive pops. So I sat on his flowered sofa and agreed with whatever words his mouth made until our time was up. At the end, he told me I'd have trust issues with men and gave me a book called *Godly Wifehood*. Dad sent me to a shrink, and it was much the same. Dr. Fleiss told me I'd have control issues with sex and gave me a scrip for the pill.

I refused to go back to either one of them, ever, but I threw the book away and filled the prescription. Score one for Judaism.

Now, with Natty tucked so close I didn't know whose scared heartbeat I felt pounding through me, his or mine, I was filled with crazy regret. That night, this child—they *were* connected. I looked at my lovely boy, and for the first time, I admitted I had no idea where he'd gotten that wide mouth, his stompy walk, his boxy little shoulders. I'd always thought of these things as purely his, afraid that if I didn't, then I couldn't love him. Oh but how foolish! How small-minded! I loved him now, so hard, inside this Circle K, that I would die to keep him safe. I loved every single piece, no matter where it came from. That had always been true, but I had been too cowardly to know it.

Now I understood exactly how a baby started knitting himself together inside me, how he got born a full year and seventeen days before Walcott finally popped my cherry, and nothing about the way I loved him changed.

I couldn't die here, though. I had no story in place to protect my son from the truth I'd just acknowledged. Unthinkable, that Natty could grow up without me there to tell him that I loved his every cell, always, no matter what.

I had to get at that file cabinet. I had to get that gun. I would shoot Stevie a hundred times and end this, and then I would take Natty outside into the sunshine where Walcott was waiting to drive us to Atlanta. I could almost see an alternate version of me, some superhero girl, bold and unmerciful, fixing everything. But I kept on sitting on my ass, holding Natty, and not being her. Guns might be powerful, might be fearless, but I wasn't.

The sirens stopped. Whoever had been coming, they were here. Stevie stood by the wall, his tantrum spent, panting. His eyes looked wild and there was spit on his bottom lip, making it look glossy and girlish in spite of his soul-patch beard.

We all sat, me pickling myself sour in my own helplessness, waiting to see what the police would do. Waiting to see what Stevie would do. He chose pacing, close up under the windows, twitchy and jerky.

"Shut up and let me think," Stevie yelled, though none of us had spoken. He sounded angry and scared.

Then the phone rang.

It was a cordless phone in a wall charger hanging above the desk. It made Stevie jump and swing the gun toward it. I jumped, too, and Natty jumped, and the clerk made a gasping noise. It rang again.

"Should I get that?" Stevie asked. He jammed his empty hand up under his cap and scratched savagely at his head.

None of us answered. He asked again, this time looking directly at the clerk. She was the one who had answered his last question, but she sat weeping, fat tears plopping endlessly onto her jeans.

It rang five times, and then I guess it went to voice mail.

Stevie gave up on her and glared from one of us to another, spook-eyed, like a panicked horse. An endless thirty seconds passed.

The phone rang again.

"Shit!" Stevie said, between the next two rings.

Thor spoke then, and his voice was low and so calm I felt it like a soothing herbal wrap. "You should answer it." He sounded very sure.

Stevie started toward the phone, then stopped, uncertain. He waffled, and it rang for the fifth time. It stopped again.

"Next time," Thor said, calm. "They'll call again."

Stevie looked at him, then nodded.

We waited, but the phone didn't ring again.

We all sat there, breathing hard, staring at one another, not sure how to proceed. A solid minute passed.

"Dammit all to hell!" Stevie yelled. He kicked backward at the wall again. "This is bullshit." He looked at us, from one to another, like he was looking for backup. "Bullshit, right?"

"They'll call," Thor said.

Another minute, maybe two. It felt like ten.

"Naw," Stevie said. "I have to do something. I have to show them that I am some serious business. You know?" Now he was talking to himself, not Thor, like he was gearing himself up. I wanted to tell him that shooting the cop would have clued them in. The cops knew he was some serious business. We all knew. But I didn't want to call his attention to us, so instead I looked at Thor. We all were looking at him, even Stevie.

"Someone has to do something," Stevie said. His voice was shaking. His hands were shaking.

Thor nodded. "Soon. But not yet. They will call." He sounded like he was soothing a collicky baby. But Stevie was munching at his own mouth and blinking too much, gearing himself up. He was going to do something awful, unless someone else did something first.

I think Thor knew it, too. Because Thor did something.

He started moving. Very slowly. So slowly. He twisted at the waist toward the desk, one long arm moving across his body, reaching for the shelves next to him. It was so slow, it was almost hypnotizing. Stevie stopped munching at himself and watched.

Thor took hold of one piece of white printer paper, delicately, in a two-finger pinch. Then he tugged on it, sliding it out from under the heavy glass paperweight.

It was the only thing happening in the room. Natty leaned forward to see, hands wrapping his knees in a hug. Stevie watched, too, his gun hand lowering slightly, until it was pointing mostly at the floor.

Thor set the paper flat on the floor between his jeans-clad legs. He started folding it. He had big hands, both long and wide, with square-tipped fingers that looked too large to be as deft as they were. They folded the paper precisely, one short nail running down a crease he'd made. He tore a strip off at the crease, and then he had a perfect paper square.

He folded and refolded, crimping and shifting, making the paper square bloom into three dimensions. I could already see it was too complicated for an airplane.

Natty watched with big, interested eyes, and I saw Stevie was watching with that same expression on his face. Mouth slack, all else forgotten. I realized then that he was younger than me. Seventeen or maybe eighteen, tops.

The paper folded up even smaller and became more complicated in Thor's deft hands. When he stopped, he was holding a paper bird. He set it in his palm. He showed Natty, turning it this way and that, and Stevie looked, too.

Natty reached for it, but Thor lifted one finger in a wait-and-see gesture. He turned the bird in his fingers and gently grasped the tail. He pulled it, and the bird's head dipped down, like it was bending to eat a seed.

Natty smiled outright, and reached again. Thor surrendered the bird to him. People don't really notice eye color, but we were so close, I noticed his as he looked at my son. A pale, plain blue, like chambray denim. Stevie was watching Natty, too, with envy, as my child pulled the bird's tail and the head dipped up and down.

I opened my mouth to thank Thor for the bird, for the slight calmness that had come into the room with it, but what came out was a piece of a Dickinson poem, one that Walcott had said for us in the car earlier.

I said, "The thing with feathers."

Thor's gaze flew back to my face, and what happened then was only between us. I can't explain it. It didn't happen to Stevie, still bird-watching, or anyone else, even Natty. It happened in the air over Natty's head.

His pupils went wide, spiraling open into dense black holes, pulling me inexorably to him. He stared at me like he was seeing me for the first time. His breath came out. A current sparked and caught and flowed between us, opening us up to each other, and I felt like he saw all the way down into the bottom of me, saw how scared I was, how helpless, saw me at the top of that seesaw. He saw how perfectly unable I was to save me and Natty, but how some secret piece of me wished he could. How I wanted him to be magic and save us all. He nodded, faintly. Like he was saying I could have my way. He would save us. And then a great peaceful calm washed out of him and into me. I swear.

"I'm William Ashe." But he wasn't saying his name so much as making me a promise.

"Shandi," I said, and my voice was steady.

Because I knew then. William Ashe was going to save us. William Ashe was the brave one, the bold one. He *was* the great god Thor. I wanted to lean across my son's head and press my mouth to his and taste him and let him suck all this certainty out of my mouth. I wanted to be his, or maybe just be him.

I heard Stevie say, "Can you make anything else? That moves like that bird?"

While he was speaking, under his question, I said three words to William Ashe, barely audible. Three perfect, beautiful words that left a taste in me like honey.

"Gun. File cabinet," I said.

He nodded, like he was saying yes to Stevie, but I knew it was for me. He was telling me, message received. He knew where the other gun was. I felt myself easing. It was like he'd put his big hands on the seesaw. He couldn't let it down slow until my feet touched ground. Not yet. But he had me held steady for now, and it was enough.

"I can make a jumping frog," he said to Stevie. "I can make a top."

When he turned, it broke our stare, and that was probably all that saved me from leaning in closer and actually kissing him, Stevie be damned. The electric connection was over, but my certainty remained. William Ashe was going to make this right or die trying.

There was a concentrated pause. Stevie's eyebrows knitted together, like his biggest decision now was which paper toy to choose for himself.

The air conditioner went off. I hadn't noticed it while it was running, but the sudden quiet startled me. I think I held my breath, and Stevie's head went up like a dog who smells something bad coming on the wind.

The phone rang again.

Chapter 4

*T*he thing with feathers," Bridget says. She changed Shit Park into a beautiful place full of birdhouses. People followed her lead, wanting a piece of that completeness that had let her do it. By summer the park had butterfly flowers and bird feeders and wind chimes strung in all the trees. Bridget had willed it into a re-claimed space.

William's heart catches, stops, and then bangs his paused blood forward again. The restart is so rapid that William feels it as a rev-ving in his chest. He stares at the girl in the poppy-covered dress. She has opened her mouth and pulled his wife's voice out of his head and into the room.

Of course, it isn't Bridget speaking. It only sounds like her. Exactly.

"I'm William Ashe," he tells her. He wants her to say more words.

She says her name, "Shandi," banging down on the first syl-lable and almost swallowing the *i*, just as Bridget would.

William has his own idea of destiny, separate from fate, or signs and wonders. So for a moment he has no explanation for the way she's lighting up the room with Bridget's presence. Bridget's high, clear voice is so very different from this girl's scared, husky whisper. It isn't the words themselves, either, though the first thing she said was one of Bridget's go-to quotes.

Then it clicks for him; it is the accent.

It's not a common way of speaking. William, born and raised in Morningside, is a true Atlanta native. He talks like everyone on television.

Bridget spent her first sixteen years in a small town across the Georgia border, in North Carolina. Years of Atlanta living shortened her stretched vowels and clipped her blurry consonants, but her voice retained a mountain flavor, a muddling in her *a e i o u*'s.

"Atlanta straight up, with a twist of hick," Bridget called her accent.

Now this girl has said, "The thang with feathers," just as Bridget would: flat, very Atlanta, but *i* gets away from her.

Stevie is asking about the origami bird, but William can't look away from the girl, trembling in her poppy dress. Her dark eyes are nothing like Bridget's wide-set, celery green gaze, but he looks anyway.

As Stevie speaks, Shandi says more words. "Gun," she says. "File cabinet."

William's head dips in an involuntary nod at the way the *i* becomes an *ah* in her mouth. *Fahle cabinet.* Perfect.

"I can make a jumping frog. I can make a top," William says, to pacify the cranky infant with the pistol. So he will shut up and let this girl talk more. If the bullet is his destiny, what can it hurt him to think of his wife's voice, a little, now?

The girl doesn't speak, though. She only leans in a little closer, as if she might stretch her neck over the head of the frightened child sheltered between them and kiss him. Her breath is warm. She smells clean, like Ivory soap and mint. He stills. He leans in, too, readying to put his lips on the mouth that makes sounds like Bridget's mouth. But that isn't what he wants.

He wants something else. Fiercely, a pulse so centered in his body it could be his own heart beating. It is the first time he has wanted anything in months, and it is ridiculous.

He wants to hear Bridget talking.

Not this girl. And not the Bridget he is angry with. He doesn't want to hear the wife who could slough off her own body, the body he loved, and fly unthinking into a white light that her oxygen-deprived brain cells told her she was seeing. She went fast, joyfully soaring with their daughter toward her God, handing Twyla, safe and giggling, into the arms of the nicest possible Jesus. A PBS Jesus, unwounded and clean. That Bridget nodded and smiled, accepted it, saying, "Yes. Let the little children go to Him." Even William's little child, who might well have grown up to be a rationalist.

He doesn't even want to hear his barely remembered wife, the one that Angel Bridget, hauling their baby cheerfully up to heaven, has superseded in his fury. His wife drinks small-batch bourbon straight up, has a flash-fire Irish temper, swarms under and around and over him in bed. Loves poetry and Stephen King novels equally. Plants a patchwork garden every spring, pansies in the carrots, crazy oregano trying to twine with shepherd's needles. He knows these things, but they are like facts he read in a *National Geographic* in a waiting room one day, explicating the genus *Bridget*. She's so distant she might as well be theoretical.

The Bridget he wants is an earlier version. Ponytail Bridget in pink Converse high-tops. Before there was a marriage or a Twyla or a Saturn wagon with no backseat.

He closes his eyes, simply to not be looking at this girl who isn't Bridget, wanting to hear Bridget's young voice in a single-minded, desperate, impossible way. An echo of his old obsession, from when he was seventeen, and she was the new girl at school. When he followed her from class to lunch to class to bus.

She read books—novels, nothing interesting—as she walked the halls, oblivious to him. She found a place at the brainiac girls' lunch table; these were not the kinds of girls that football players noticed, so his stalking went uncharted. He was so invisible to Bridget that twice she passed by close enough for him to smell her lemony shampoo, and yet she never returned his gaze.

No one had yet proved the existence of human pheromones, but William became certain of them. There was no other explanation for his reaction to her solitary joy as she destroyed the park to raise it, to the way the basic shape and smell and sound of her undid him; she was indefinably correct for him. He knew it on the cellular level.

Weeks of this, sick with crazy, silent longing, and then Paula said it was starting to be "Unabomber creepy." She made him skip class and took him up on the roof. She'd had a key, lifted off a janitor, since her freshman year, and often snuck up there to smoke.

William lay flat on his back, squinting up at the sun, still warm though the air had a decided chill. Paula stripped down to bra and panties, shivering, to bask in it. She might as well have been wearing one of her mother's voluminous caftans. His own body was attuned only to where Bridget sat, two floors below. She was a red laser dot on his mental map of the school. The sun was nothing. The real heat licked up at him from Bridget. His whole body warmed and flushed, burning at the idea of her under him, even with a building in between them.

Meanwhile, on the roof, where his brain was, Paula said, "You have to make a move before you end up torturing puppies in a basement full of Bridget-themed blow-up dolls."

"I don't have a move," William said. "Tell me a move."

But instead Paula spent ten minutes cataloging all the ways in which William was not allowed to wreck it. ". . . *and* you're forbidden to talk about how to make really stable explosives. Or poisons. That will scare the shit out of her. Don't talk about any of the six boring-ass books you are reading, or the fact that you're reading six books concurrently, and God, don't use the word *concurrently*, at all. Ever. I can't believe I used it. I can't believe I even know it. I probably caught it from you, and it's the least sexy word on the planet."

William listened with his brain, while his body, an entirely separate animal, tried to melt shingles and brick and wood and plaster so it could plummet into Bridget.

"So far, you've told me nineteen things not to do."

"Really? You counted?" Paula said, sitting up. She was making an expression at him.

When William was little, he had a book called *How Are You Peeling?* It was full of pictures of vegetables with faces. The radish is happy. The eggplant is sad. His therapist wanted him to learn to recognize the same looks on the faces of his classmates or his parents. He'd outgrown the book, but he was still supposed to do the exercise. Right now, he should ask himself, *What is she feeling, if Paula raises one eyebrow up and not the other?* But Paula generally said exactly what she meant with him. It was one of his favorite things about her. He was free to take the question at face value.

"Yes. Exactly nineteen. Do you want me to say them back to you?"

"God, no." In his peripheral vision, he saw Paula lean forward so that all her shaggy black hair dropped around her face. She said, "I have made myself a hair tent for thinking in."

They could hear the bell ring even through the roof. Bridget would be rising from her desk, moving toward her locker. He tracked her on his mental map, wishing he was on her level. He would like to look and look at Bridget's face, try to guess what she meant when she lifted just one eyebrow.

"Tell me three things to actually do," William said to the hair tent.

"You could go the secret admirer route?" Paula used both hands to part her hair and her up-tilted eyes peered out. "Perfume and anonymous love notes. Girls eat that shit up."

Not a bad start, but too circular. "That ends with us back here, because I have to eventually talk to her."

"Yeah, there's always a downside," Paula said, then put her finger up in the air, making a hook.

William grinned. Last year, after they'd had sex, he'd felt comfortable enough to ask if he could practice his assigned peer conversations with her. He'd been bad at picking up on jokes, sarcasm especially, which relied so wholly on inflection. He was much better at it now. At one point, early on, she'd suggested making the finger hook every time she was kidding. He had said it was a good idea, and she had rolled her eyes and made the finger hook, because she had been kidding.

"I got it!" Paula said. "Make *her* talk. I'll write you a list of questions. Then you listen and say all nineteen parts of her answers back to her. That way she knows you listened, and plus it makes her think that you guys have stuff in common. I read it in *Cosmo*."

"She'll ask me questions back," William said.

"So, answer them. Maybe she'll like you." William made the finger hook, and Paula grabbed it and shoved it down. "I'm serious. She could like you. I like you, Bubba."

"Yeah, but you don't want to be my girlfriend," William said.

"Please. I'm a senior." Paula flopped down onto her back, her shoulder pressed companionably against his. He barely felt her, his whole physical self yearning itself ragingly down. William sat inside his overheated skin, trying to think and failing with a torrent of hormones clotting up what was generally an excellent brain. He could feel his body starting to rock itself.

Paula curled toward him on her side and bit his shoulder. Hard, but friendly. It was Paula's version of one of his therapist's old tricks, like origami or football; give the body-animal something to do so his mind could go about its business.

When he looked at her, fully present on the roof at last, she let go with her teeth and said, "Sex ambush. You need to drop her down, but hard. Get her hooked on the bod and the crazy-hot moves before she clocks how ever-fuckin' weird you are."

This might well work on Paula. She could be caught up and swept along, laughing, into any plan that pleased her in the moment. But it depended on Bridget being like Paula in this way. The Bridget he'd observed was wholly self-contained and thinky. She made plans, and people fell into them with her. She did not lie on rooftops in her underwear biting male friends. She changed parks with subversive tulips. She sat at the smart girls' lunch table, observing more than participating, reserved. She seemed . . . not untouchable, not at all. But not something he could lay his hands on without express permission.

"That plan will end with me in prison," he said, but everything Paula had told him to do and not do was folding itself into a shape in his good brain.

"Well, a kiss ambush then." Paula was still talking. "It's not like you can win the girl by doing chemistry."

"Yes, I can," William said, a variation on her plan growing clearer and more detailed by the second. "You just said I could."

"Uh, no?" Paula said. "I didn't say that."

"Yeah, you did," William told her. She simply hadn't realized it, because like most people, Paula didn't understand that the entire world was mostly chemistry, doing itself.

He hears ringing again, so Bridget is in English class. But it is not the bell. It is a phone. William blinks and feels the room reload around him. Oh, right. He is having a robbery. He is having a robbery while all the carefully compartmentalized sections of his life jumble and collide and refuse to be contained.

"Fuck!" screams Stevie, so shrill he sounds like a child. William's paper-bird spell has been broken.

The girl in the poppy-covered dress stares up at him. She is making the face that William recognizes as the far end of anxious, and her little boy's body is trembling, pressed against William's side. Yet here is William, wanting to re-court his teenage pre-wife, still so angry with her that the only Bridget he can stand to desire is two stories and sixteen years distant from him.

He shakes his head to clear it. Bridget's priest has failed, spectacularly. *Anniversaries can open up old wounds,* he'd said. What an asshole. William is not a fan of metaphors; they are so often inaccurate. *William,* the priest should have said, *anniversaries are just like being vivisected.*

The phone rings again. William was better a week ago, watching Paula drink up all his beer inside his quiet house. He was better twenty minutes ago, even, when he was angry with laundry soap. He was best of all a few breaths previous, calmly making an origami bird in the peace of knowing that a bullet belonged to him. He should stick with that.

But the desperate mother eyes of the girl with Bridget's voice are telling him he needs to reprioritize. Young Bridget would agree. She'd say that what he wants doesn't matter here. This girl and her child love each other. The little old couple, they love each other, too. Even the clerk with her disturbing front teeth must matter to someone, somewhere. He must get them all out of here, safely, and now teenage Bridget is more than a voice in his head. She is a presence. She is a haunting with an Irish temper, telling him to get up off his ass and fix it.

Fine. William draws white lines on a blackboard in his head, mapping the play. He can't go for Stevie directly. He has to cross to the opposite wall first. That way, when Stevie shoots at William, the bullets will move perpendicular to the other hostages. It also means Stevie will have time to pull the trigger, perhaps multiple times, as William turns at the wall and goes toward him.

He is almost certain that the gun is a .32, and it is the perfect gun. Shoot a guy as big as William with a .22, and it's only going to make him angry. A .38, however, could push him backward in midstride, and a good hit from a .45 would blast a huge hole in him and drop him instantly.

But a .32? William has crashed through hosts of offensive linemen, barreled into massive blockers, bulling forward to get to the ball carrier and take him down. He has waded willfully toward pain a thousand times. He knows how to overbalance, tip his body forward and dig with his feet. The gun will tear him up, but he is stronger than it. He was practically built for running into gunfire from a .32. Unless Stevie gets lucky, hits his heart or brain, William's big body can absorb the bullets long enough for him to sprint close. There is a large glass paperweight near him on the lowest shelf of the desk. He will smash this paperweight into Stevie's head and lay him out.

If he does it right, this girl and her little boy get to walk out hand in hand, and the old couple, too. The clerk can stop weeping and go back to work, save up some cash, and fix her teeth. Stevie can wake up in prison with a bad headache. Life will go on for all of them its inexorable way.

Meanwhile, William can stop thinking. Stop remembering. He can lie down quietly and bleed. Hopefully, Stevie will shoot him enough times to be definitive. Everyone gets what they want.

The phone rings again. It is close, sitting on the desk beside him. He looks from the phone to Stevie, who is standing in the sunlight under the windows. William can see a million dust motes floating in the yellow light.

"You gonna answer that?" William asks, meeting Stevie's eyes. Man to man. A dare. The same look he learned to use on guys on the opposing team at the ten-yard line.

Stevie pants and his eyes roll around. "You think I'm stupid, big guy? You want me to come over by you? Lean across you, get that phone, huh?"

William shrugs. If Stevie comes close, William could take control of his gun hand and have Stevie pinned and helpless in seconds. He likes his first plan better, though, and Stevie doesn't move toward him anyway. Stevie is stupid, and his limited synapses are misfiring because of the stimulant he ate or smoked or snorted, but he has a roach's instinct for self-preservation.

"I could answer it," William says. He reaches for the phone.

Stevie panics, brings the gun to bear. "Hell, no!" William

hears Shandi's breath catch as the gun swings. He stills. Stevie wastes another ring puffing a short breath in and out. "No one needs to talk to the cops but me." He eyeballs the phone, then William, wanting one, rightfully wary of the other.

"I could slide it to you," William says, impatient now.

While Stevie is thinking it over, the phone stops.

William says, "I'll get it to you for next time. They will call back."

A phone call is a distraction. It could give William a tiny opening. It's all he needs.

Stevie stops looking for the trap in the offer and nods. William half rises and turns to the desk, on his knees now with his back to Stevie. His right hand reaches up for the phone, but his left hand reaches into the shelving and closes around the large glass paperweight. As he turns back, he keeps the paperweight behind him, setting it down easy with an almost silent *click*. Then he slides the phone across the floor. It comes to rest at Stevie's feet. Stevie bends at the knee, watching them all as he fumbles around with his free hand, trying to find it.

Finally, he gets it and rises. It hasn't rung in a good thirty seconds, but he clicks the button anyway. "Hello?"

William can hear the dial tone. Stevie says, "Hello?" again, louder and angrier. A red flush does a fast creep up the back of his neck and washes into his cheeks.

"It went to voice mail," the old man says. He sounds angry and aggrieved and at the same time patronizing, explaining the obvious to someone very stupid.

Stevie stares at the phone, and then at the old man. He blows his breath out of his nostrils in a fast, loud snort. The old man will not look away. William smells ozone. Hormones—or something truthfully electric—crackle the air between them. Stevie is shocked into moving. He runs at the old man in a short, vicious charge, yelling as he moves, "Shut up! Shut up! This is your fault!"

William starts to move, too, his right hand closing on the paperweight behind him, but at the same time the clerk lets out a short, sharp scream and Shandi clutches at his arm. The little boy grabs his shirt in two panicked handfuls, yelling a long, scared vowel sound.

Stevie stops short and kicks wildly at the old man's gut. The old guy falls sideways into the wall and folds, curling into a fetal shape. Stevie kicks his head, his shoulder, arms flailing.

William says, "Let me go," pushing the words between his teeth and trying to peel them off him.

Stevie's arms pinwheel in crazy circles, gun in one hand, phone in the other. The old lady screams and puts one hand on each cheek, as Stevie kicks the old man a third time.

Shandi yells, "Stop it, stop it!"

She lets go of William to put both arms around her son, pulling his face into her so he can't see. The boy lets go to push at his mother, trying to see anyway. His cap comes off and falls against William's leg.

Stevie is already dancing back to the wall with the row of high, slitted windows. The old man gasps and coughs, holding his kicked ribs. William puts his hand with the paperweight beside his thigh, on the floor, breathing hard, his body full of pent motion.

"Your fault," Stevie says to the old guy, loud. The sheer physical exertion should have calmed him, but instead he seems exhilarated. He is panting, so energized his arms twitch and his voice breaks.

The old man's wife is on her knees now, arms going around her gasping husband.

"It's not," she says to Stevie, and her eyes are so cold. She would kill Stevie right now if she could. Kill him and never lose a minute's sleep. William likes her.

"Shut up, you old bitch," Stevie says. His lips are twisting up into a feral, panting smile. "This is your fault."

William feels Shandi's arm tighten around her child at the ugly word.

The clerk's head is back down. She is crying with her hands slack by her sides. She snorts and hitches, pulling Stevie's gaze.

"I want to go home," the clerk says, tears streaming unchecked down her face.

She has a cartoon bird tattooed on one breast. Another thing with feathers, bobbing up and down, yellow and cheerful, as her chest heaves from the weeping.

"Don't you even," Stevie snaps at the clerk, furious. He looks at Shandi and her big-eyed child, who has succeeded in getting his head up. He peeks out from his mother's armpit. "It's them, not me. Stupid rich shits."

Stevie waves his free hand at the old couple, huddled together. The clerk keeps sobbing. Stevie turns to the couple, and spit flecks come out as he speaks. "How many of these you got, these gas stations. Like ten? How many you got?" It doesn't sound rhetorical. He takes a stamping step toward them again, as if he might go kick an answer out of the old man. William shifts his legs, readying, his grip firm and easy on the paperweight. It is heavy and hard, larger than a softball, built for his big hand. The orange daisy is cradled facedown in his palm.

"Six." The old lady's nostrils flare as she speaks.

"Yeah, so, six," Stevie says, almost a growl. "You make a crap ton of money, and you don't even work. You got her for that, right?" He jerks his thumb at the weeping clerk. "Her and a bunch more like her. They get, what? Minimum wage? Maybe a free slushie come Christmas? You swing by to get your big piles of scratch in your Cadillac. You sit in your fat house, charging guys like me five dollars for a pack a smokes. You got everything. Guy like me, what have I got? Huh?"

"A gun," the old woman says, not backing down. "And no heart. You worthless trash."

The words make Stevie's spine jerk straight. His arm swings up as he takes another stamping step toward them. His whole face is twisted now, his teeth bared in a display of dominance that the gun renders ridiculous.

The sound of the gun cocking is huge. It is a sound that eats all the ambient noise in the room. William feels the earth slow in its rotation, his perception of time elongating to a single heart-beat. He can see the spunky old lady's hand reach for her husband. Stevie brings the gun to bear with murder written so plainly on his face that William needs no help to read it. The old man is lying down with his head in his wife's lap, but his hand reaches for hers at the same time. He is closing his eyes. Hers stay open.

William is already moving, his big athlete's body well ahead of his brain, his mouth saying, "Get down," to Shandi as his body carries him away.

He is at the wall before Stevie understands what is happening. William turns and overbalances forward, digging with his feet, hurtling toward Stevie. His hand holding the paperweight is also in motion, eating the momentum, loading it all into the swing.

He is less than a third of the way there when he knows he has miscalculated. The paperweight, with all the force of his big body behind it, is moving too fast. But his body is committed, plunging forward. He cannot slow it or call it back.

Stevie has turned, but now he is wasting all this luxurious slow time by making his eyebrows rise. His mouth drops open into an expression so exaggerated it is like a page out of William's old vegetable book. The radish is happy. The eggplant is sad. The potato is surprised.

Stevie is the potato.

The gun is pointing at the floor now. His other hand opens and the phone hovers in midair, waiting for the next endless second to pass so it can obey gravity and clatter to the floor. The gun hand starts to move now, but it is not bringing the gun to bear. It is coming up defensively, as if Stevie's pale, fleshy forearm can stop William, halt the raging force of his charge.

William's blow connects as the phone smashes on the floor, so that only William hears the shivery bone crunch as the paper-weight meets the side of Stevie's head. Stevie pauses, still making the same expression, and then time snaps into its regular track.

Stevie thunks to the floor, faceup. Momentum from the swing spins William to the wall. He stops there. Stevie lies where he has fallen. He is still and his eyes are open, staring sightlessly up.

There is a breathless pause. The cocked gun lies ready by his slack hand.

William holds tight to the paperweight. He looks at Stevie, who has absolutely failed to shoot him. He hasn't shot William even once.

William shakes his head, back and forth. He was so sure. It was destiny, by his own definition, a thing you choose. A thing you follow relentlessly, no matter what stands between you and it. He leans against the wall, breathing hard from the adrenaline.

The clerk has stopped crying. She has gone quiet, almost as still as Stevie.

Shandi rises to her knees, staring at Stevie, but her child's dark-fringed eyes are fixed on William. His mouth is a solemn slash. William slides along the wall until the corner stops him. He is trying to understand the shape his own face is making.

The tomato is relieved. The lime is disappointed.

His brain feels stuck, remembering that as a child, it bothered him no end that many of what his therapist called "vegetable pictures" were actually fruits.

Outside the Circle K, someone has brought a megaphone. A huge voice says, "This is the police. Please pick up the landline. We just want to talk."

A muffled ringing begins. Apparently, only the phone's casing has broken. The hand piece is somewhere under Stevie.

It is the little old lady who finally moves. She lets go of her husband, who is folded in a huddle around his own ribs. She clambers quickly to her feet. William thinks she is going to dig under Stevie and get the phone and answer, tell the police they can come in now. She doesn't. Instead she runs at Stevie in a tottery five-step sprint. She goes right to his hand and she kicks at it, his gun hand.

This is what cops do on television, William realizes. When a suspect is down, they kick the gun away from him. She kicks and misses, and William is surprised to hear himself say, "Wait." The second kick connects.

The rusty silver gun goes spinning away, and she must have caught it exactly right, because as it spins there is a huge, unearthly boom.

Interesting. He feels an inner tick, a soft, internal echo of the gun's sound. He sits down suddenly and very hard.

He feels his body shaking, and it is because it is laughing. His laughter feels unnatural, rasping in his throat. He realizes it has been a long time since he has laughed.

"Oh my God," Shandi says, and she is up and running to him now, her child in her arms. She sets the boy onto his feet as she drops to her knees beside William, yelling, "Give me your cardigan," over her shoulder to the old man.

William folds at the waist and tips sideways, lying on the floor by the wall. Perhaps she wants the cardigan to cover Stevie's face. This is not funny, but William can't stop convulsing with this endless laughter.

He laughs so hard it hurts, a stitch in his side.

Shandi leans close, peering down into his face, still demanding sweaters.

Somehow William has rolled onto his back. Perhaps she rolled him?

"Destiny," he says to Shandi.

Maybe he is laughing too hard for her to understand him. But maybe not. Maybe it is only that she doesn't know it is a joke. He tried to hold his finger up, make a hook for her, but all at once he is too tired. William stops laughing and stares up at the ceiling, and it is only the plain ceiling. It has big square fluorescent pans of light set into its tiles. No holy beam of sentient gold glows down at him. No fiery chariot comes to ride him up to heaven.

His eyes would like to close now. He allows it.

Chapter 5

*F*ifteen seconds ago, William was invincible. I'd never seen a person move like that. How foolish for me to tell him about the file cabinet. As if he needed a gun. He'd been like something on Discovery Channel, surging up out of long grass. Now he had a hole in his side, and his blood came out of the hole, just like it would do on anyone. It didn't seem possible for him to be so humanly shot in his body.

He pulled in a long, raspy draught of air, shunting it fast out. My own breath wouldn't go all the way down into me. It stuck in my throat, so that I had to take little panting sips of oxygen.

Then he said one word to me. He said, "Destiny," and I felt my heartbeat and my breathing stop, everything in me pausing for a tick, because he was telling me he knew. He felt it, too, this thing between us.

The old lady was trying to hand me her husband's sweater. I stared at it blankly, then realized I had asked for it.

"Go get help," I told her. I took the cardigan, pressing it down hard onto the hole under his ribs. The startling cherry red of William's bright blood soaked into the lemon-colored cotton.

My mother used to say *Red and yellow catch a fellow,* in warning tones when I wore this silly poppy-covered dress. I thought, *Now this sweater I am holding on him is the same colors. It's like we're already one of those awful couples who dress to match.*

Outside, the cop with the megaphone was saying a lot of things, but it all sounded like garbley-goo, as if Charlie Brown's teacher heard shooting and was now blatting and blaring, asking Snoopy what the hell was going on inside that doghouse. William's slow blood, soaking through the sweater, was so very red. I didn't want Natty to look at it. But Natty was looking away. I followed the line of his gaze and saw Stevie.

Stevie was super, super upsetting to look at. He was so still. His head was dented in. His eyes were open. He wasn't breathing.

Good, I thought, savagely. I only wished I had been the one to put him down like that, down like a bad dog, instead of dangling stranded way up high on an imaginary seesaw, letting every awful thing happen.

"Natty," I said. "Natty!" Natty shook his head like he was waking up, and met my eyes and blinked at me. I made a smile shape out of my mouth. "We're good, baby," I said. "You and me, we are safe and good."

Someone needed to take Natty outside to all the real, solid things that belonged to us—his basket full of Matchbox cars, my sunshine yellow VW, our Walcott. Someone needed to call in help for William. I hoped that someone was. Me, I had to press down hard on the hole, feeling William's inhale pushing up, like an answer. His eyes were drifting closed.

"William, look at me!" I said, but he didn't. It felt important to not let him slip away into some kind of sleep or darkness. I put my face near his face and said, "Say things at me. What day is it?" It was a dumb question because I had no idea what the date was. I never did. I even sometimes got the year wrong on my checks.

But he croaked out a word. "Friday."

His eyes opened and focused on my face. He was still with me.

Outside, the cop with the megaphone had stopped talking, and the phone started ringing again, muffled under Stevie. I was so not digging that out.

"Say more things," I told him. "Where do you live?"

"Morningside," he said, talking fast in a gasp on his exhale, adding something that sounded like "Near Shit Park," but that could not be right.

"What do you do? For a job?"

"Researcher," he said.

I blinked. "Like at a library?"

"A lab. Gene therapy."

A scientist? He looked more like a lumberjack, or a forest ranger. "Where do you work?"

"Geneti-Tech," William said. I knew the name. That company was huge in Atlanta; their disturbing logo was everywhere. It had the words *Food-Medicine-Life* wrapped around a winged tomato, like a visual admission of how creepy-far they were willing to bend nature. Hard to imagine William, so tan with all that sun-streaked hair, in some sterile room swathed in a lab coat, cloning sheep.

"Are you dying?" Natty asked William. He was still holding his paper bird, and now he was looking at the bloody sweater. *Red touch yellow, kill a fellow*, I thought, but that was a different rhyme, meant to help Natty know which snakes were dangerous.

William took another of those long, raspy inhales. "I'm just a little shot," he said on the exhale.

He seemed so calm. Was it shock? Or had the bullet hit something vital? I had no idea what kinds of organs he might be keeping in his shot place. Too low for lungs. Too high for intestines. Why had I made Walcott do all our dissections in high school? Typical.

I realized I was five seconds from losing my complete shit, panic rising up in me like a gorge. Losing my shit sounded so wonderful, too, a delicious luxury. I wanted to fall into terrible screamy little chunks and weep and flop on the floor and let someone else press their hands hard into this yellow cardigan, saving William, getting their palms slick with his warm, red, living human blood. But Natty's face was pinched and white. He was looking to me. I'd already sat like a lump through a whole robbery, not saving him. I had to be better. William had said the word *destiny* to me, and he'd taken a bullet for us. I had to become a whole 'nother better person, worthy of William, able to protect my son, right this second.

The clerk, Carrie, stepped into my peripheral vision, her head moving, looking first at Stevie, then at William, then at Stevie, like there was some kind of invisible tennis ball bouncing back and forth between them.

Stevie's chest jerked. He inhaled. It was a bubbling, mucus-y noise that I thought I would hear in every bad dream I had for the rest of my life.

The paperweight lay nearby, daisy side up, wrongfully cheery. Stevie's eyes were open, but not in a looking way or even an alive way, in spite of the breath he had just taken. They were like glass eyes someone had put into his head. He'd breathed in, but it was obvious that Stevie-Our-Robber-Today would not be getting up and resuming his duties.

But maybe it was only obvious to me. When Stevie took a second thick breath, chest hitching, Carrie's mouth yawped open and the most ungodly howl came out. She galloped right to the door, scrabbling at the ridiculous flip lock Stevie had turned before his head was all stove in. She swung the door wide and sprinted away, her animal howl evolving into a human word: "Help, help, help!"

I heard her pounding footsteps receding, then the jingle bells went off as she exploded out the front door. I waited for the police to shoot her by accident, but I didn't hear anyone shoot her. Maybe she had thought to put her hands up, or they were just good, smart police.

Natty asked William, "Does it hurt you to be shotted?" It sent a ting of worry up my spine, because Natty at three often spoke like a forty-year-old accountant. I had heard him say, "Let me compose myself," and "This hill makes me exhausted." He hadn't added extra *ed*s onto his verbs for more than a year.

"It doesn't feel great," William said.

Sweat was beading on his forehead and upper lip, though I was shivering myself half to death. I had no idea which of us was right, if it was hot or cold. I could feel the pulse of his heart in the heat of the wound. It felt good and strong. It felt unstoppable. But only the tiniest piece of time ago, he had surged across the room like some huge, unfolding beast of prey. He had seemed unshootable, and look how that turned out.

I heard the jingle bells chiming like crazy, a lot footsteps pounding toward us. A whole crowd of people, coming to help.

"They're almost here. Hold on," I told William.

"No, thank you," William said.

Then they burst in the door, a huge, confusing wave of human noise and color. Policemen first, fast and cautious, then paramedics, and some other people in uniforms I did not recognize, and some in regular clothes.

Paramedics swarmed around William. I got moved back, out of the way, by a guy in a kind of boxy jacket thing that made me think he was a fireman. He was tall and very calm. He wrapped us up in a blanket, asking me if we were hurt.

"We're good," I said. "Please just help William."

"Don't worry," he said to me, and to Natty, "We're taking good care of your dad, okay, buddy?"

I blinked. The fireman thought we were together, me and Natty and William. We were three things that looked like one thing. Like a family.

I thought Natty would correct him, but instead he turned and looked up at me, a wide-eyed, questioning look.

I looked back and thought, *Destiny. Why shouldn't me and Natty get to have him?*

Could a man like this belong to me? Today I'd sat on my ass, clutching my child and waiting my turn to be shot like a good little rabbit. How could I do otherwise? I had such practice being weak. I'd been practicing for about four years now, from the second I decided to take my lovely Natty as a gift, unconnected to the awful night I got him. No, even before that, when I'd made Walcott take me home and snuck inside and kept my mouth shut.

Natty had a human father. When I tried to imagine him now, I saw a golem with a lumpy face of red Georgia clay, rising from the earth around the beanbag chair, leaving streaks of himself on my clothing. I'd let him stay faceless, stay anonymous and unaccountable. That was not okay. I should never have allowed that. I should have gone after him, found him, laid him out. But instead I had pretended that it didn't happen at all, until Natty made that particular pretend more complicated.

Even then, I did nothing. Didn't call the cops, didn't try to stop him from doing it again, if he wanted to in his clay heart. Didn't grieve. Didn't learn. Never made him pay. Hell, I never even had to tell anyone I was pregnant.

Walcott did that for me. He came over with his momses, who looked at me with concern and reassuring love while Walcott spoke. They'd treated me like a favorite niece since I was five, when Walcott and I went running back and forth between their B and B and my house nine times an afternoon. Walcott sat between me and them on our toile sofa, telling Mimmy about finding me drugged and half-naked behind a frat house on the Emory campus. He spoke all halting with his face the color of the reddest red Crayola.

I didn't even listen to him tell it. I couldn't bear the kind gazes of his mothers, or watch my own mother's face. Instead, I tried to stare right straight through Mimmy's closed drapes. I pretended a meadow on the other side, full of all kinds of fairy-tale things: talking squirrels and little fauns and tree nymphs. I imagined opening the drapes, stepping through them, going into the butterflies and sunshine while Walcott finished up my dirty work. I could lie down in the magic grass and call up some unicorns. Why not? I was ten weeks along, but I still had everything I needed to make them come to me.

Mimmy sat across from us in the matching chair, all alone. She heard him out, and I was so safe in my meadow that I barely registered it even when she started yelling.

"What poop, what poop, what utter poop!" Even in a state, Mimmy's vocabulary didn't lose its sugar. "You did this. You did this!"

Walcott's taller mom, Aimee, put her hands out, like she was surrendering, and said in her kindest voice, "Charlotte, I know how upsetting this must be, but Walcott is telling you the truth. We drove Shandi to see my gynecologist. She confirms that your daughter is pregnant, and also that her hymen is intact. Dr. Kaye believes that the boy who drugged your daughter might have ejaculated prematurely at the . . . oh dear. At the gate, as it were. Close enough so that—"

My mother was positively gawping by then, her jaw unhinging and swinging up and down about nine times before she could get it under control and form words. "You took my daughter to the doctor? *You* did?"

"Drove her, yes. She asked us to."

I stayed in the sunshine place, pretending a meadow full of fairy mushroom rings where nothing any of them said had one damn thing to do with me. The magic yellow motes of cheery pollen in the air had probably made the baby happen, but I felt a distant kind of sorry for Mimmy. She'd been blindsided in her warm and lacy living room, all pink and cream and gold. She'd served sweet tea to the whole family, unfailingly polite, only to have them tell her this? She'd given Walcott free run of her house for years and years, against her better judgment, and now he was explaining that her daughter had caught pregnant at a party, the way other girls catch colds.

Mimmy bared her teeth into a shape that was nothing like a smile. "Are you stupid? Do you know your son sneaks out of your house fifty times a week? Do you know how many times I've caught your kid in my daughter's very room, after midnight?"

That snapped me back. I activated and said, real mad, "Mom, he always had his pants on, though."

Mimmy turned on me with her gorgeous eyes gone all slitty. "Why are they even here? You could at least do your own explaining."

A fair point, but I turned my face and looked past her, back at the drapes. Now it felt like the only thing behind them was our little front lawn.

Walcott's shorter mother, Darla, said, "According to our doctor, no one is having sex with your daughter. Not our son, certainly. Walcott is not sexually active yet."

Aimee said, "I don't think we should speak to Walcott's sex life, Darla."

"Of course not. I'm just saying he doesn't have one," Darla said, smoothing her Indian-print skirt down over her legs.

Walcott turned to me and said in a low, conversational tone, "I want to die now. You?"

"Ten minutes ago," I said, but all the mothers in the room kept right on talking.

Aimee was still focused on Darla. "When the time comes, I hope he will talk to us about it. But we have to respect his privacy." She turned back to my mother. "I can tell you this, we've given him fistfuls of condoms. Absolute fistfuls."

Darla chimed in, "This happened in Atlanta, anyway. Walcott wasn't even in the same county."

That brought my mom up short. She paused, blinking, and her righteous fury dialed down a notch. It wasn't like the news delighted her, nothing like. But I saw her get a tiny tickle in the schadenfreude as she registered that this happened on Dad's watch.

"Does her father know?" she asked, and she sat up a little straighter when Aimee shook her head. "So when was this exactly?" She was talking to me, but I looked away, as if all the things happening inside me were not really my business. My mother turned back to Aimee. "Do you know? How long ago? How far is— Does she want to—"

She couldn't even say it, but she needn't have worried. If I was going to have an abortion, I never would have let Walcott tell her I was pregnant at all. Stopping the little wad who was so busy making himself into a Natty—it didn't seem fair. I didn't know this small person who had taken root in me, but his existence felt like a trick that had been played on *both* of us, together.

Aimee said, "Shandi doesn't feel that's an option."

"Although it is, Shandi," Darla said in a low tone.

She might have gone on, but my mother said, "She said no. Don't you push that child."

Darla held up her hands. "Not pushing, just making sure she knows her options."

My mother got frosty and said, "She knows her Christian options."

Aimee stepped in, peacemaking. "We're not trying to overstep our bounds here. Shandi already made a decision, and we can all agree to respect that and deal with the situation as it is." While Aimee was helping everyone tread quickly over unstable ground and back to good manners, I leaned into Walcott and whispered in his ear, desperate. "Go call my dad and tell him. Fast."

Walcott jerked and turned to me. "Are you frickin' serious?" he hissed.

I nodded. If I let my mother tell him, it would become another weapon in the endless war. She'd imply that I'd never have gotten pregnant here, where an ever-vigilant Trinity had six eyes on me; in Atlanta, Judaism's single God had blinked. She wouldn't be able to help it.

To be fair, had the situation been reversed, Dad would have found the same scant solace in pinning it on Jesus. They were both from such devout families, but when they'd met in college, those traditions hadn't felt important. All four of their parents had pushed against them, and they'd pushed back super hard, eloping at the tender age of twenty. It was them against the world, until I came. I know all kids blame themselves when their parents get divorced, but I was the one kid who was actually right. The question of what faith to raise me in put a chink in them; their families hammered at the crack I'd put in their foundation until they shattered.

I held Walcott's gaze and whispered, fierce, "I can't let her enjoy telling him. I could never look at her again. I'd have to run away to New York and be a hooker and eat a pound of heroin and dic."

Walcott swallowed, looking sick, but he got what I was saying. He always did. "Well, we can't have that."

I passed him my cell phone.

He got up, said, "Bathroom," to three pairs of questioning mother eyes, and left the room.

He took care of it. Again. I didn't even have to try not to listen, much less explain it myself. Never. Not once. Just sat there, like today, waiting for my turn to get a bullet.

I looked at my hands, still streaked with William's blood, and knew I couldn't sit quiet and helpless ever again. I couldn't be that person anymore. Natty deserved better. So did I.

"You ready?" The fireman said. "We're taking him out."

I carried Natty, following the fireman over to William, now up on a gurney. He had a paramedic on one side, holding up a bag of fluids that were running down into his arm. There was room for me on the other side. They had given me the wife slot, where William's wife would go if this were a hospital drama on TV.

He met my gaze as we started moving, and I knew he felt it, too, how of a piece we three looked. How right this was. Even in this crowd of busy strangers, the fireman and the paramedics could see how we belonged. As we walked, I put my hand on his warm, bare chest, high up on the unshot side, the way a wife would. And why not? This was destiny. He had said so, and right now, today, I had decided to deserve it. The girl who was walking out of the Circle K with William Ashe was not a person who would wake up spraddle-legged on a beanbag chair and just fucking take it.

I put the top down, and Walcott drove, mostly because a cop who looked alarmingly like Samuel L. Jackson had said I shouldn't. But I didn't feel shaky. I felt like I could have flown home.

Walcott drove fast, and once we were back on the highway, I put my arms in the air, cupping my fingers. The wind pushed at my hands, and I pushed back.

"Suck it, wind," I hollered. "I'm bigger than you."

"Tamp it down, Easter Candy," Walcott said, grinning. I gave him raised eyebrows at the nickname, and he explained, "You're like a kid on a bad sugar high." He jerked a thumb back to where Natty slumped heavy-lidded in his car seat. "That one's crashing already. Turn your volume knob down, and he'll blink out like a bug light."

"You're right," I said, softer. Natty was so done in he had pink circles around his eyes. "Do you realize you saved someone's life today?"

Walcott had grabbed one of my beach towels out of the car and pressed it to the shot cop's bleeding shoulder, which was a weird synchronicity, considering I did pretty much the same thing with William such a short time later. Me and Walcott, on this day destined to practice the first aid we'd quasi-learned together while passing endless notes in Health class.

Maybe Shot Cop had been young and sweet and beautiful; I honestly couldn't remember a single thing about her except how the blood had opened up like a red poppy on her pale blue uniform. Maybe Walcott already loved her secretly, and would ditch CeeCee and track Shot Cop down and poem her into loving him back. He and I could have a double wedding. My traitorous brain added *if William is all right*, and at that thought, my heart gave a panicked little hiccup.

Busy saving the cop, Walcott hadn't called anyone except 911. Not Mimmy, not my dad, not even his own mothers. Even after the cavalry of cops arrived, he hadn't thought to do it.

"Why didn't you?" I asked, as we zoomed down the highway toward Dad-n-Bethany's, so freaking late. The actual being-a-hostage part hadn't put us much off schedule. It was the paperwork. We'd had to wait around until that older cop who looked so very disturbingly much like Samuel L. Jackson was ready to take my statement.

"I was busy," Walcott said in a quiet voice. I could barely hear him.

"Doing what?" I asked.

"Praying," he said, which shut me up.

I never thought of Walcott, son of yoga-obsessed, quasi-Buddhist lesbians, as a prayer. I thought of him as more of a meditator, really, and then I got the giggles, imagining him cross-legged with hands at heart center in that parking lot, trying to om my sorry ass to safety.

Natty fell asleep—deep, fast, floppy asleep—three minutes later. We drove on, quiet for his sake, but my head was full of plans. William would be fine. I was making him be fine with all my faith in it, because he had to be. If he was going to die now, then why would destiny put us together in that Circle K? William would recover, and I would go to him and he would help me. I wasn't sure what a gene therapist did, but genes were the only link I had to finding Natty's father. William would finish falling in love with me over his electron microscope, helping me seek justice.

Natty didn't even wake when we got to Dad's house and I peeled him out of his car seat. He lay slumped on my shoulder, in that drooling, boneless state that only cats and little children know.

Bethany answered her pretentious wind-chimes doorbell and stood blocking the door, staring me down, a gin-and-diet-tonic clutched in her perfectly manicured claws.

"Well, look who finally decided to put in an appearance," she said.

Here it was, past dinner, the little boys already upstairs, and Bethany still had perfect makeup and a perfect blowout and was wearing perfectly understated, wildly pricey jewelry. She was exactly like her house, expensive and elegant, but not at all comfortable. She wasn't actually beautiful, but no one noticed because she was always so smashingly put together, plus she had that kind of raily, curveless body made for hanging clothes. I always felt bigassed and bobble-boobed and like I probably had food on my shirt around her.

But not today. Today she looked like a sun-bleached bone with a hank of black hair on the knob end, and I was chock-full of living juices.

I said, "I'm sorry, we—"

But she was already turning away, talking over her shoulder, heels clicking against her immaculate terrazzo floor as she walked away to grant us access.

"I don't want you to be sorry, Shandi. I want you to be courteous and thoughtful. I want you to realize that other people, inconvenient as it may be, have lives and plans that do not revolve around you. This would be so much more useful than being simply sorry." Her tone was frosty and instructional, but I wasn't fooled. This was how Bethany did righteous fury. "I, for example, had a Pilates class this afternoon. It's my one time all to myself, to take care of me and de-stress, and instead I waited here for you, endlessly."

Dad must have heard us. He came into the foyer, looking comfy in jeans and a soft cotton shirt.

He dropped a kiss on the top of Natty's sleeping head, tugged my hair, and said, mildly, "We were getting worried, kiddo." He wasn't on call; I could smell scotch and the ghost of a good cigar on him, and I could hear the news on TV in the living room ahead of us: warm brown daddy smells and sounds. "Want me to go lay the little man on the sofa? He looks like he's down for the count."

"Yes, please," I said. "He weighs five hundred pounds. Maybe even tuck him in bed? I don't think we can finish the move tonight, Dad. Natty's done in."

"Sure. It's not a problem if they stay over, is it, B?" Daddy said, his easy smile including Walcott. He took Natty, who stirred and stuffed his index finger in his mouth, the way he had when he was just a baby. Dad headed for the basement.

"We'll see," Bethany said, her already thin lips disappearing entirely into a pressed-together slash.

If I didn't have the ace of almost being shot nestled sweetly in my pocket, I knew we'd be back on the road in half an hour, as soon as her lecture was done. Then tomorrow Dad would FedEx me a pony by way of apology.

Bethany said, "Your father didn't give you that expensive iPhone strictly for playing that game with the upset birds and texting your little friend here. He gave it to you so you could call, should you for some unimaginable reason need to be almost four hours late."

This was a true Bethany-style reaming, and the longer she went on, the happier I got, basking in the stream of icy invective.

Walcott beetled his eyebrows at me. He knew I could stop this lecture any second. I had the best excuse in the universe for not calling—"Sorry, B, there was this gunman, and he wouldn't let me use my phone!"—but I didn't.

She owed me, for all the times she had given me oblique crap about getting knocked up—"Being ready to become sexually active, Shandi, includes understanding all your options in regards to birth control, and also having the maturity to openly discuss these options with your chosen partner . . ."—and me unable to defend myself and say, "Do you think I never practiced putting a condom onto a banana in Health? Do you think that I, a doctor's daughter, believed that I would not get pregnant if I jumped up and down twenty times after intercourse?" But I never did defend myself, because Bethany didn't know how I got Natty.

That information stayed in a tightly closed circle: Walcott. Mimmy. Dad, who was smart enough about his second wife to leave her outside any loop involving me. Aimee and Darla, who'd loved me since I was little, and who decided to love Natty, too, on principle. I hadn't even let *myself* think about it, until now. I was simply another knocked-up high school girl, certainly not the first one seen in Lumpkin County or Atlanta.

Now I stood in Bethany's vaulted ice-blue foyer, getting deeper into a giddy form of PTSD every second, deserving reassurance and a belt of medicinal whiskey, or maybe a Valium. Bethany had an endless supply of those. But instead I was getting martyred.

It was too delicious to pass up. I sent a psychic look at Walcott that said, *Beloved friend, go beetle your brows elsewhere because I have more than earned the coming moment.*

He grinned, rueful, conceding my point with his complicit silence, and Bethany harped on, digging herself in ever deeper, until finally, finally, she asked me the million-dollar question: "Why didn't you call?"

I'd been waiting for that one, the way a baseball savant waits for the soft, fat pitch he knows is coming, right over the plate.

"I was held up," I said, deadpan.

Walcott snorted and then bent a little at the waist, felled by a sudden coughing fit.

"That's it? That's your whole explanation. You were held up?"

When she repeated the phrase, Walcott lost it. He couldn't hold it to a cough. He outright howled, and I was so punchy and crazed by then I lost it, too. We folded, helplessly gaffawing and shaking like Jell-O, leaning on each other to keep from sinking down to the floor. Bethany's salon-shaped eyebrows arched up high and higher and ever-angry highest. Actual color rose in her cheeks, as she stood furiously on the outside of my awful joke.

"You were *held up*," she said, not yelling yet, but close, closer than I had ever heard her come to a harsh, raised voice, and Walcott laughed so hard tears spurted out of his eyes.

"Yes," my dad said. He had come back into the foyer. He looked pale and sick. Our laughter clicked off. I stood up straight, still hanging on to Walcott, though. "She was held up. It's on TV. Shandi is on the television."

"She whatted? She what?" said Bethany, her voice getting shriller and higher with every little barked question. "She was what?"

I pushed past her, dragging Walcott. We all followed my dad back into the living room. Sure enough, there I was. It was so weird to see myself on Dad's big flat-screen. I hadn't noticed anyone filming, but the camera had caught the scene from pretty far away. They must have been in the Hardee's parking lot when we came out. I hadn't clocked the news van, what with the host of cops swarming all over. Even SWAT had been there, standing around their black van, smoking.

But it was recognizably me with Natty perched on my hip, bending over William Ashe on the gurney. I could see my palm resting on his chest, near his shoulder on the unshot side. They'd cut his shirt off, and his chest had been sprinkled with khaki colored hair, sun-bleached a shade lighter than his warm, tanned skin. My hand balled into a fist, closing over the remembered feel of him. It had been like touching the top of my dresser; there was no give to him at all.

The reporter was talking over the footage, saying, ". . . ended after twenty minutes when one of the hostages rushed the gunman . . ."

So strange, watching myself touch William, hearing a newscaster tell a distant version of a thing I'd actually lived. I knew the real soundtrack, though.

Good job, I was telling William. Like nine hundred times. As if William Ashe was a professional robber-thwarter instead of some kind of scientist.

Walcott blew a raspberry. "You look like you're about to kiss his dying lips and then set him on fire in the parking-lot version of a Viking funeral."

I hadn't realized how every muscle in all my whole body

had bunched up, watching this, until Walcott made me smile. I knuckle-punched his arm and glanced up, saying, "Shut up, you," but he didn't have on his joking face.

On the screen, Natty leaned down to touch William, too, pat-pat-patting his arm. I knew what he was saying. He was telling William, *You did what Batman would have do'ed.*

Then the talking head of the news anchor replaced the shaky footage of us by the ambulance, but I knew what had happened after that. They'd loaded him in and closed the doors and drove him away from us, because I didn't really belong in the wife slot. Not yet, anyway.

"Shandi?" Walcott said. He sounded weird. He said my name in a strained tone I'd never heard before.

The talking head was replaced with a picture, an informal thing, snapped at a park. It was William. But he wasn't alone. He was holding a baby. He was sitting by a woman.

All at once I was intensely interested in what the talking head might say, so of course this was the moment that Bethany decided to finally take up yelling, after years of snow-soft, well-modulated, disparaging comments.

"Are you goddam kidding me?" It was almost a shriek. "You mean you were literally held up, in a holdup, you were held up, and you stood there, you stood there in the foyer and you *let* me go on and on! You made a joke of it, you—"

"Shut up!" I hollered back. On TV a bubble-haired blond lady was saying vital things about William, and I couldn't hear her over Bethany. Then my dad joined in.

"Bethany! Stop! Shandi is in shock. Go get her some water! Go get her some wine!"

"Hush, hush," I said, even more desperately. "Walcott, turn up the TV."

"Okay, okay!" He turned and began digging around in all the Bethany-inflicted silken throw pillows that were infesting the couch.

"No, I will not hush!" Bethany was talking over Dad and me and the TV, too. "Do you think I am some kind of monster? I never would have said those things to you if I had known! But you, you *let* me!"

In the picture, William Ashe was sitting on the grass. He had a good, sharp-looking haircut and a serious, reserved smile. A baby girl, maybe eighteen months old, was flopped barefoot and happy-sleepy in his lap. Her hair was gathered into a ridiculous sprig of strawberry-blond floss on top of her head. Beside him, leaning into his broad shoulder with her legs curled under her, was a smiling redheaded woman. The anchorman was talking now; I heard him say "William Ashe" and "hero of the hour," and "tragic accident." Did he mean the shooting? Was William all right? But I couldn't follow because Bethany was yelling now. Really yelling.

"Why didn't you tell me you were in a robbery? You hid it! Deliberately! To make me look bad. What kind of a conniving person does that?" She was right. It had been low, and I was getting a hard and instant karma-slap for it.

The red-haired woman was Mrs. Ashe. No doubt about that. I could see it in the way she leaned her head toward him and tucked her shoulder close against his. I hated her, a little, for existing.

"Walcott!" I hollered over Bethany. "Remote?"

"—stuck in this house all day waiting and then she comes here *knowing*—"

"Shandi, honey, you need to sit down," my dad said. "Shut *up*, Bethany."

"Everyone, shut up!" I screeched.

I stepped close to the TV, staring at the wife for the few seconds they left the picture up. She had freckles and a long, bony Irish face, but a really good smile. Her thick, wavy hair was flat gorgeous, but she was no Mimmy. She was like me; pretty enough for real life, but not television pretty. She looked happy, though. They all three looked happy. Still, I didn't think William Ashe was married to her now. In the Circle K, he had showed all the signs of being a recently, but not too recently, divorced male.

The picture was replaced with the blond anchorwoman, with an I'm-making-a-sad-face-but-not-the-kind-that-leaves-a-wrinkle expression.

"If you think I am going to apologize!" Bethany raged on, with Dad talking over her, saying, "Well, Shandi is not going to apologize. No one needs to apologize," and me saying, "Just stop yelling for one second," and Walcott digging in the pillows.

"Got it," Walcott said, and the volume bar appeared and shot from left to right, filling all the way in.

As the sound came up, the anchorman blared, ". . . killed in a tragic auto accident, exactly one year ago today."

It was so violently loud, everyone did finally shut up, and I rocked back from the TV, blinking, as if the words had literally slapped me.

In my peripheral vision, I saw Walcott come up beside me, but he wasn't looking at the TV, he was looking at my face.

"Walcott, please," said my father, very loud over the TV, and Walcott turned the volume down.

The camera backed up, showing the blonde beside the man anchor. She was making complementary what-a-damn-shame eye-brows.

"It's so ironic," the woman anchor said. "To become a hero, to save other people, on such a sad anniversary."

In that moment, I understood his wife was dead. As under-standing dawned, I realized that I'd read the shaggy hair and the pale band of flesh on William's ring finger wrong. He was not divorced, and I was standing here curling my lip and checking a dead woman's looks against mine. I was selfishly wishing her out of the picture, only to find out she was. Really, really out of the picture. I felt exactly like the piece of crap I was. I glanced at Walcott, my eyes swimming with tears, and saw him swallow, his Adam's apple hopping up and down once in his long, narrow throat. His eyes on me were, for maybe the first time in our lives, unreadable.

Bethany was staring me down with fury written in every line of her face, but she kept her yap shut, and my dad just looked shaken.

The anchor kept talking, reporting about Stevie now, showing what looked like Stevie's old mug shot. The man anchor said he had a long criminal record, no shock there.

Yes, I was a lowly worm, but I hadn't *willed* his wife into being dead. They said the accident happened a year before I ever laid eyes on him. His heart must be broken, and I would never have wanted that. I'd only wanted, desperately, for him to be a thing that I could have.

Which he was. Feeling like an awful person for being glad of it couldn't stop me wanting him for me and Natty. Couldn't stop me wondering about him. Maybe he was a single dad, like me. Maybe he was lonely, like me. An inadvertent tingle buzzed in my belly. Maybe he was really good at sex. Unlike me. But sweet damn, I was so willing to learn.

That weird predestined feeling that I had run smack into the love of my life intensified. He was sad and tragic, and helping a girl like me hunt justice might be exactly what he needed.

Then it occurred to me that the baby, the daughter, could have been in the accident as well. I had that mom-reaction I think every parent gets. A fast *Please, never, not my kid*, aimed at heaven, combined with the red-hot slicing empathy that cuts you when you understand a nearby soul has already fallen into your worst fear, and for them it is real and forever.

I felt a clenching of the mother node inside me. That little girl with the silly, flossy sprout on her head? She was gone, too, with her mother. That was why William had moved so immediately, putting himself between the gun and Natty. He'd leaned in to make a human tent with me over Natty, too, without even thinking about it. He had lost his child; he knew how fast things could spin out of control. He knew a person could lose anything in half a heartbeat. William understood. The tears spilled all the way out of my eyes, and I brushed them fast away.

"Baby," Dad said, and he came over and took me in his arms. "What a day you've had. Of course you are staying here. Bethany, go get some sheets for the couch downstairs, for Walcott."

I felt Bethany's cool gaze on me growing even cooler, but she turned away and went to get the sheets. The sports guy came on then, and a whole new terrible thought occurred to me.

"I have to call Mimmy. I didn't think it would be on the news. We were only in there, what, half an hour?"

"It was a long half hour, though," Walcott said darkly.

"I can imagine," my dad said, snuggling me closer.

I said, "Oh God, Mimmy can't see it on TV before I've talked to her. She'll lose her mind."

Bethany came back with her arms full of bedding, passing through on her way to the basement stairs, but she paused when I said "Mimmy."

"You didn't call her from the car?" asked my father. I shook my head. He rubbed my back, and he couldn't help but smile faintly. "Don't worry. Your cell phone would be ringing right now, if she had seen this."

I knew then that he would never hold it against me, the fact that I stood in the foyer and let Bethany yell at me, because I hadn't called Mimmy. He had been the first to know. In fact, *Mimmy* might hold a grudge, because I had come here to him instead of having Walcott drive me two hours back to her place.

Bethany said, "You should definitely call." She looked like she had a whole alive mouse trying to scrabble its way up her throat and out. She was trying to choke that mouse back down. Now that she had banked her temper, she knew I was a solid ten points up in the endless game of Who's the Asshole? that we'd started playing the instant she married my father. He was the show's host and the judge, as well as our lone target demographic. "You should go call her right now."

But Dad didn't let me go.

Well, I'd had a crap day. I'd been held at gunpoint, been so scared for my kid, fallen in love with a shotten-up stranger with a tragic past, and had decided to risk everything, even Natty's peacefully fatherless childhood, to stop being a coward. Sometimes, on a day like that, you need a victory. Even a little one. Even if it is thorny and vicious and small-minded.

So. For just a few seconds more, I made The Mimmy wait, and I stayed right damn where I was, smiling beatifically at Bethany from inside the circle of my father's arms.

Sometimes karma takes years to pay a person back, but that day, it had a fast backhand return; I snuggled in, and that's when Natty started screaming.

Natty was up and down all night, chased out of his sleep by a spider, by a ninja, by a silver gun with human legs and feet.

I'd moved him into my bed, so I didn't have to leap across the room to wake him all the way out of the scary dream and pet his sweaty hair back from his face. When he was a tiny baby, he'd work himself into such deep and earnest sleeps that he would sweat hard like this. The side of his head that had been pressed against the mattress would smell a little bit like a foot. Baby Foot Head, Walcott called him back then, and remembering this, my heart lurched around and got wobblety against my ribs. I could have lost him today. I nestled him in close, crooning, "Hush, baby, hush."

His eyes gleamed huge in the dark. Walcott appeared again in the doorway. The last three times, he'd been in boxers and his T-shirt, but I clocked that he was fully dressed now. Shoes even, though the clock by my bed said three A.M.

"I had a bad dream," Natty said in an aggrieved voice, like he was accusing someone of something. "That gun camed back. It chased me on its legs."

"That's terrible," I said. "What a terrible gun. I hate that bad gun. But now it is just you here safe with me and Walcott."

"Want me to pet your feet some more?" Walcott said.

"Yes, please," said Natty.

Walcott sat down on the edge of my bed, his long fingers petting and petting the bottoms of Natty's feet. Natty was the least ticklish child on the planet.

"I think a bad thing," Natty said.

"What bad thing?" I asked.

"I think Stevie shotted William into being dead now," Natty said, barely a whisper, and it worried me that those effed-up baby verbs had stuck.

"It's not true," I said. "William is very strong, like a big, smart lion."

"Seriously?" Walcott muttered, his hands going still. I made questioning eyebrows at him, but he wouldn't look at me at all.

"Natty, do you want to go and visit William at the hospital? So you know he is okay?"

"Yes," Natty said, and then, "Walcott, you didn't pet my feet now."

Walcott resumed.

"You want to take him some balloons?"

"Yes, please," Natty said.

Walcott petted, and I whispered a long list of get-well gifts that we could take William Ashe: flowers and a puppy, a new car and chocolate cookies, a giraffe in a nurse cap to fluff his pillow, a water pot of singing flowers or a mermaid in a bucket, either would do for lullabies, and on and on, replacing the awful footed gun that had chased him around inside his head with prettier friends, until Natty's eyes closed and his body became a limp bit of boy-string in the bed.

When Natty was good and out, Walcott stood silently and tipped his head at the door. I got up and followed him out into the rec room. The bedding was folded neatly on the end of the sofa. I sat down, but he stayed standing, both of us facing the big flat-screen that dominated the room. There was also a Wii, a hundred thousand Legos in buckets, and a shelf full of board games. The basement smelled like popcorn and a full herd of little boys, though it was supposedly for me.

Once I'd had a room upstairs, but every time Bethany had a baby, I got moved into a crappier bedroom. When my third half brother was born, I got stuffed down here in what used to be the basement office, with Bethany saying, "Teenagers need their space!"

"The basement den and bathroom will be your own domain, too. Teenager heaven, right, Shandi?" Dad had asked.

The truth was, I would have liked to stay near Davie and Simon and giggly, round-bellied Oscar, who was barely a year older than Natty. I liked little kids, always had, and these three had my same dark, round eyes, and exact replicas of my dad's long-boned, elegant feet. Not to mention there was still a huge, posh guest room, with trey ceilings and a California king. It had its own bathroom with a garden tub. It sat empty by the boys' rooms, a showpiece reserved for Bethany's parents or her sister.

But Dad had to live with her, so I'd said yeah, that sounded cool. He felt bad about it, though. He made Bethany grant me free rein in the bedroom—my first deco job—and set a budget generous enough for me to do the walls in a faux suede finish, have the curtains custom-made, and get a wrought-iron bed from Anthropologie. But "my" downstairs den had quickly degenerated into a playroom, and now my toilet seat was always sprinkled with little-boy pee.

Walcott had never rated the guest room, either. The few times he'd stayed here, he'd slept on this couch, not really a guest. Or at least not Bethany's guest.

"Where are you going?" I asked. It was obvious he was skipping out, though it was the darkest wee hours of the morning.

"Over to CeeCee's," he said. "Can I borrow your car?"

It took me a second, but then I got it. CeeCee could offer him all kinds of comfort that he wasn't getting here.

"I'd need you to come back and take us to the hospital to see William in the morning."

He said, "Seriously?" then rolled his eyes. "Whatever, I'll be back by ten."

Something was off about him. Way off. "What is it?" I asked.

He didn't deny there was an it, just said, "Can we talk about it later? I need to go if I am going, before us yacking raises Bethany from her crypt."

That sounded more like him. I grinned and got up to hug him, but he stepped back from me. Like, literally, took a step back and away.

"Walcott!" I said, really worried now.

He shook his head, his eyes hooded and unreadable, and then shoved his hands through his hair so it stood up in mad Beethoven tufts.

"I'll call you," he said, and went fast and quiet up the stairs.

It wasn't right. He wasn't right. Maybe he was having some kind of post-robbery meltdown, but why shut me out? It was my robbery, too. I started to go after him, to track him to the driveway and make him talk to me, but just then, Natty went off like an air-raid siren again.

I ran back to my bed and picked him up, said his name until he was all the way awake. The ninja had made another appearance. He had red eyes like a jawa and he was chasing Mimmy, chasing me. He had already ninja-starred Batman into pieces.

I back-burnered Walcott and climbed into bed to cuddle Natty. I heard my little VW start up, carrying Walcott away from us, to CeeCee's.

Maybe he hadn't wanted me to touch him because he was purely desperate for some sex. Earthquake syndrome. I'd read about it, how a herd of babies are always born in a little run nine months after a natural disaster. Death brushing past makes people hungry to connect to other people, to make even more people in a big push toward life, a celebration of surviving.

It made sense to me today in a way it hadn't on the pages of a magazine at my dentist's. Deep down in my body, I had a niggling push rising, too, a desire to go and get a cab, to go to William Ashe. I'd kept my hymen, but I'd lost more than my sandals and my panties the night that Natty happened. Was this what it felt like, to actually want sex? Did it start low in the belly, a buzzing kind of hunger?

Pushed deep into lemon-fresh bedding, pinned beneath the great god Thor, I thought, and there was a trill in my below half, like I was sitting on a speaker and it was blaring out my favorite song at volume nine, but I couldn't hear it. I could only feel the pulse in the base of my hips.

Had this feeling sent Walcott all the way across the city in a borrowed car full of everything I owned? Did he have this crazy rhythm beating low through all his bones, calling him to his girl? I couldn't imagine how Walcott's long, bony body would work, would fit itself to CeeCee's. She was built rounded and bouncy all over, like a blond me.

I said sweet things to Natty, telling him the story of Pigling Bland, a favorite of his. He was drifting off again, but in my head the pictures I saw were nothing like Beatrix Potter's pastel talking animals. More like me and William Ashe, with his huge, fast hands and his chest like carved wood, starring in *Caligula*. Glorious Technicolor. Dolby surround sound.

Bring it.

Chapter 6

At the end of his workday, William's skull feels hot, and his eyes are grainy. His brain is waxy and tight from subverting the agenda of a being that is not truly alive. Viruses might not meet the definition of life, but William knows these faceless strings of DNA and RNA contain immense will. They invade, change their host, replicate, survive. The trick is placing them correctly so they attack faulty DNA strands with sequences loaded to fix them. Because they invade, because they change their hosts, and because their will is so absolute, they are a perfect tool to correct poorly written human genetic code.

It is interesting work, but after hours of peering at computer screens and down into the microscopy, up to his eyes in the clean, white science of it, his body is a restless animal, shuddering and tense from being still. He runs five miles in loops through his neighborhood, then hits the weight room in the basement before making dinner. He likes the simple chemistry of cooking. He follows recipes exactly, and his food always comes out looking like the picture.

But in the before, Bridget liked cooking, too. She never cracked a cookbook. She dug around in the crisper and the pantry, setting unrelated things out on the counter. Goat cheese, an aging Roma tomato, leftover grilled chicken, some fresh herbs from her garden, maybe an egg. In the end, it would all agree and be a dinner. Her food shouldn't have been better than his, but oftentimes it was.

On nights she cooked, he would keep Twyla. It was an easy, pleasant job, even though Twyla was a very busy person. He would lie down flat on the rug in front of the fireplace, and she would pad back and forth, toting things from her play kitchen to pile around him, or she'd run in circles, making a buzz sound, or clack Duplos together like huge castanets. She would pause frequently to show him one of her fat plastic animals, or climb him, or simply sit on him, backing up and then lowering her butt in the careful way of little bipeds who are not yet certain of their center of gravity. She'd perch on his side, as at ease as when she sat on her tiny, solid play chair, taking his presence underneath her for granted.

His eyes are closed, but he does not need to see to know that she is perched on his side now. He feels her there, uncharacteristically silent. She weighs one thousand pounds.

He tries to keep so still. She is welcome to crush him, if only she will stay. He wants to reach for her, run his fingers over the familiar planes of her face, feel the sprout of hair Bridget would have gathered up onto the very top of her head, but his arms are so heavy and unwieldy. He manages to lift one toward her, anyway.

"Look who's awake," a woman says. Not a voice he knows. "How're you feeling, Mr. Ashe?"

A nurse leans over him. A few beds away he can hear a woman moaning. Someone is murmuring to her. He orients; he is in a hospital recovery room, with institutional green walls and a row of beds. The light is harsh and yellow, making him squint. It feels as if his eyes have been closed for a long, long time. He remembers being wheeled into surgery, and here he is, apparently out, technically closer to being a living system than a virus is.

"Fine," he says. His voice is so creaky and weak he doesn't recognize it.

He still feels that painful pressure on the side of his abdomen. It isn't Twyla sitting on his side. It never was. It is only the feel of a hole in him.

He drifts until they move him to a room. It is painted the same flat, pale green and has a square, boxy television set hanging on a metal arm in the corner. There is another bed in the room, by the window, but it is empty. A new nurse explains how to work his morphine pump. All he has to do is press the button, and the pump will give him a premeasured dose. He can press it again anytime he needs it after the timer reaches zero. It is set at zero now.

He isn't interested. Narcotics will make the fuzzy room around him look even fuzzier. They make him grind his teeth.

Then a doctor with a broad, soft-looking mustache over a wet mouth comes in to tell him how lucky he is. The bullet hasn't hit anything vital. He should, the doctor says, still consider himself to be a person who has had major surgery, though. He will be in the hospital at least another day or two, for observation. Then he needs to take it easy. He will be off work for up to six weeks.

"You can catch up on your soaps," the doctor says, jovial. He is very satisfied with himself, with the surgery's good outcome. A pleasing picture appears briefly in William's head: his own arm snaking out and punching his fist into the doctor's slick, wet lip.

He holds his arm back as the doctor lists all the things William should not do, which include running and lifting anything over ten pounds. There is more—wound care and medications—but William has stopped listening. He is pressing the morphine button.

The pressure in his side eases as the doctor finishes and goes away. The lights are dimmed. William floats up and off sideways. He drifts along, half sleeping. The morphine is a trick; it can't fix pain. It only moves pain over a few steps, setting it down at a distance where he can see it as something separate and not all that compelling. His thumb works the button, over and over. He floats on the drug as the endless night winds on and on. His jaw gets so tight from the narcotic that it feels welded shut.

The window takes on a faint gray glow that tells him dawn is finally near. That's when he smells her coming. Orange blossoms and fresh-cut rosemary, creeping in under the tang of antiseptic. He should have known this would happen when he woke up in the recovery room. There, he'd felt his daughter's weight pressing him down, so heavy that it should have sunk him through the bed and the floor, through grass and tree roots, until he'd been pushed a good six feet under the red dirt. Of course Bridget is coming.

Her scent is in the ducts, blowing out the vents, moving toward him. The air is full of her. The only strength in his whole body has been wired into his jaw. Even his bones are soft. Tulip colors move and bloom on the ceiling. He closes his eyes, but this will not stop her. He can still see her colors, washing over one another in waves on the backs of his eyelids.

"She's coming," Paula hisses at him from somewhere overhead. Paula has climbed a ladder so high she is at the very gates of heaven. She can see everything. She calls down, "Bridget's almost here."

He tries to sit up, pushing, straining up so hard he finds himself standing. He is seventeen years old, and Paula is right. Bridget is on the way. He can't stop her, and why would he want to? He has worked so hard to get her here.

He's in Ben Caster's backyard. Ben, the team's best wide receiver, has gone with his family to a wedding down in Florida. The Casters' house is right across from the place that used to be Shit Park. Paula calls it Holy Shit Park now because, holy shit, has it changed over the course of this school year. Old people come and sit on the benches now, to look at all the little things with feathers that have moved into the birdhouses. The birds eat from the feeders and preen themselves in the stone baths. Someone has put in a Japanese cherry. The bulbs Bridget planted last fall are up and blooming: yellow, deep pink, orange.

Paula lies flat on her belly on the roof, watching the impending Bridget's progress. It is finally time. His jaw is clenched so tight. His heart feels constricted; his chest is one size too small for it.

"What is it with you and roofs?" William asks Paula, as she climbs down the ladder.

"I like to be where I can see people, but they can't see me. Secretly, I was born a panther." Paula is amped up, eyes bright with the joy of all this crime they are doing. She looks at the rockets, lined up in perfect rows, their trajectories carefully mapped and set, and asks him, "How illegal are these?"

"In Georgia? Very, very illegal," William says, and Paula grins, bouncing lightly up and down on the balls of her feet.

William is not bouncing. His eyes are not bright. He ran nine brutal miles today, so he could be very calm in his whole body. Most of his body. Except his jaw. Except his heart. And he has a new, strange buzz in his hands, a tingle like they have been asleep and now the blood is moving again. His hands buzz with the possibility of touching Bridget.

He checks to be sure the lighter works. "You know what to do?" He has to say it through his clenched-shut teeth.

"Yeah. Stand down, Bubba. I got this. Put flame on fuses. How hard can it be?" She eyeballs the rockets. "Are these things going to blow both my thumbs off and burn the Casters' house down?"

"Probably not," William says, distracted. He is making sure the backup lighter works.

Paula says, "For the record, this is the coolest thing I've ever seen science do. Like, if chemistry was a person, it would prolly be a jack-off pimply kid with a mucus problem. But this here is like if that jack-off pimply kid bought a Porsche and banged a supermodel."

This makes William smile, in spite of the feel of a wired-shut mouth. Paula seldom says nice things about chemistry. It's odd, what impresses girls. Given the right equipment, William could make an acid that would eat right through the Casters' car and smoke the concrete underneath it. But no girl would like that.

This took months to set up properly, but he wanted to make all the pieces, not just the rockets. He even made the paper, using a simple suspension of cellulose fibers in water, with grass fiber for color, and tiny, dried petals off some yard weeds suspended in the paste to make it beautiful.

He already had thirty different invisible inks and catalysts in his notebooks from when he was nine and obsessed with invisible inks and catalysts.

Once it was all finally ready, he took his handmade paper, thick and soft as stiff fabric, and used his own concocted ink to write, *Go to your tulip bed in the park and stand by the post where you hung the first birdhouse. Saturday. Just past sunset. Something good will happen.* He watched the words disappear, and then he put the note in a plain white envelope from Walgreens. On the envelope he wrote in regular, visible pen, *This is not a love note. A love note would be scented. A love note would have words.*

William wanted to write more on the envelope, to warn Bridget against throwing the handmade paper away or using it for Civics notes, but Paula said that wasn't necessary. No girl worth her salt would use his torn-edged, elegant paper for a grocery list, especially when it was so clearly a mystery. William bowed to her superior wisdom, and Paula broke into Bridget's locker, planting the envelope there.

"You could have put it through the slots," William told her after.

"Nah. I would have had to bend it. Plus I wanted to have a look, see if she was on the pill. Or if she had a secret stash of porn or cookies underneath her math book." William started to ask, but Paula shot him an amused look and said, "She isn't, she didn't, she didn't, and wow, you have it so bad, Bubba."

On Friday, Paula broke in again to place the cranberry-colored glass perfume atomizer. That, he hadn't been able to make. He'd spent sixty dollars on it at an antiques store. He'd attached a tag with a piece of ribbon, and the tag read, *This is not perfume. If it were perfume, it would be sprayed onto a love note.*

It smelled like perfume, though. Like orange blossom with green, herbal undertones to cut the sweet. This took longest, as it was a considerable revision of his favorite old formula. When he was nine, he hadn't cared much if his catalyst had a hard chemical smell, or if spraying it onto a person would blind them or burn their skin off.

Now it was Saturday night, and Paula was right. Bridget did figure out that the perfume should be sprayed onto the paper; she'd read his note. And here she came, to the right park at the appointed hour, in the right frame of mind for what Paula calls "The PG Disney Princess Lips-Only Sex Ambush."

He holds another three minutes to give Bridget time to cross the park to the flower bed.

"Go time," he says.

He leaves the Casters' backyard. Holy Shit Park is no longer the worst park in Morningside, and the lamps on the tall posts lining the path are all in working order. Paula wanted to throw rocks, smash out the bulbs, but William nixed this plan, not wanting to fill up Bridget's resurrected park with broken glass. So Paula came up with alternative vandalism. They busted into the maintenance shed and William tripped the fuses. None of the lights are working. Now William picks his way carefully across the darkened green, sensing more than seeing Bridget up ahead of him, by the bed.

The sky lights up.

William's fireworks whistle as they go, then bang open into perfect round blooms of blue and green and gold. They drop in a host of tinted shooting stars. In the flashes of light, he sees Bridget's face tilt up, sees her lips part. It goes on for almost three full minutes, a barrage of sound and color. He has skipped the traditional show and gone right to the huge, booming finale. In every flash he sees how wide her eyes have gone. She puts back her head, the line of her throat so lovely. She lifts her arms, reaching and laughing as the sky lights up again and again. She dances her feet, opening to all the light and sound that William has made happen for her.

He has summoned the Bridget of the flower beds. The Bridget who believes that tulip bulbs, some black-eyed Susans, and a garage-sale birdhouse can remake a park. The girl who believes it so hard that she becomes right.

William knows that science and magic are the same thing; magic is only science that hasn't been explained yet. Tonight he has made chemistry into magic for her. He can see it in every line of her body. His heart bangs around, pushing against his ribs. His hands buzz and rumble.

The last array opens up, three small pops that open into green flowers, and then the secondary booms, huge, spraying a gaudy splash of gold across the whole of the black sky.

The final sparks wink out. There is a breathless pause in the darkness. The air itself is hot and soft. A dog is barking, very far away.

He steps toward her. Bridget turns, sensing his approach. This is the time that Paula says will be good to grab her with his shaking hands and kiss her, but he doesn't. This is not a girl who can be grabbed. He doesn't have words for all the ways she seems complete inside herself, but the reason he cannot use this moment to simply lay his hands on her is part of the thing that makes him want to so deeply.

As her eyes seek him out in the darkness, he has no idea what will happen next, and he is dizzy with it. He feels the buzz in his hands rising and spreading up his arms, all his blood tingling as he steps in close enough to smell her: Cherry ChapStick. Spearmint gum.

She peers at him, leaning toward him, and then she stops. She recoils, her whole body jerking backward.

"You did this? You?" She crosses her arms across her chest.

Her shoulders fold in toward themselves and her spine hunches. She is only a girl now, with pressed-together eyebrows and a down-turned mouth.

William thinks, *The squash is disappointed.*

She shakes her head and says, with almost no rancor, "You jerk."

She turns away and starts walking off, cutting directly through her own flower bed, pink Converse high-tops sinking into the loam.

"Wait," William says. She doesn't wait, so he follows her. Now the buzz has reached his throat, and his eyes burn in his head. He has fucked it up, somehow. He has fucked it up by the simple act of being him. She glances back over her shoulder and sees that he is following.

"Don't bother. How stupid do you think I am?" she asks. "What, you think I can't read?"

"You read all the time," William says, unable to stop stumbling along in her wake. "You walk down the halls reading."

"You're watching me go down the— Ugh." She speeds up, zooming fast through the darkness so smoothly it is as if she operates on sonar. "I've read the back stall in the second-floor girls' room, and I wondered, you know? I mean, yeah, you're good-looking. Obviously. And the football thing. But still, I wondered how you got so *much* play. But I see now. I bet this works great, huh?" Her voice is heating up. The live, electric energy she emits is coming back into her body.

"What does the bathroom say?" William asks, pacing her.

She ignores the question. She keeps talking over him, her words coming faster and faster until they tumble over one another. "I bet this stuff, so super romantic, I bet it really makes the panties drop. You think I don't see through this? I'm not some shiny piñata, double points if you bang me open. I'm a person. I'm a person. You think this hasn't been tried? Well, okay, not this, with the magic perfume and the fireworks, so, points for effort, but I'm a living, breathing person."

"I know that you're a person," William says. "Of course you are a person."

"Well, you're not. You're a jerk who only wants to nail me." Bridget finally stops surging forward, at the edge of the park now. She pauses and turns to him and now they are back where the streetlights are working. Her eyes are very shiny. "What I want to know is, who told you I was going to be a nun?"

"Whoa!" says Paula, rising up out of the darkness. Bridget startles and stares at her, openmouthed. Paula has left the Casters' backyard quickly, as instructed, in case the police come. She must be on her way to see how the sex ambush is going; so far, it is an abysmal failure. "You're going to be a nun?"

Bridget doesn't answer. She takes one stamping step back toward William, ponytail swinging, and her words are only for him. "I already went through all this 'get in the nun's pants' stuff at my last school. How did you find out?"

She is so fierce, her shoulders braced, her neck extended. This anger, so complete, it is as self-contained and lovely as her joy. William swallows and simply looks at her.

Finally, she shakes her head, and turns away. She stomps off, and William and Paula stand there, silent, watching her go.

"So, that went well," Paula says, when Bridget is out of ear-shot.

William asks, "What does it say about me on the second-floor girls' bathroom wall?"

Paula turns to him, surprised. "Man, for a new girl, she picks up on stuff quick, huh? It's this thing I wrote in Sharpie last year, after we hooked up. A silly thing."

William waits.

"It's nothing," Paula says, but he is still motionless, waiting. "Fine. It says, 'Honk if you've ridden Space Mountain.'"

It takes him a few seconds to get it, and then he asks, "I'm Space Mountain?"

His lungs feel small and his body wants to rock itself. His last nickname was back in middle school. They called him Moose-tard, and he hated it.

"Oh, stand down, Bubba, it's a compliment," Paula says. "It

means, like . . ." He won't look at her. His skin feels hot. "Space Mountain is the best ride in the park."

William sucks a piece of his inside cheek in between his teeth and bears down, hard enough to hurt. He'd spit his penny out in the Casters' yard because he thought there might be kissing. That has not worked out.

He fishes in his pocket, but the only penny he has is from 1970. No good. Pennies minted before 1982 don't taste right.

Paula blows out a short huff of breath and shuffles her feet. "Stop swelling like a mad toad. I'm going to say a nice, true thing to you now, William. So don't you ever give me shit about it, okay? I call you Space Mountain because back when you and I did it, you were nice to me. The whole time you were nice, and you didn't even love me. The next day, you acted like we were friends. In public. Guys never do that after. Before, sure. When they have you off alone and they want something. But you were my friend, after."

He can look at her now, but her whole face is crimson, and she won't look back.

"I started calling you Space Mountain. The ho brigade got interested. That's why Denise and Amy and that Michelle girl all hooked up with you. You were nice to them, too, I guess, and damn, but you can use that body. So your legend grew. Then one day at school—I may not have been wholly sober—I wrote the honk thing. It caught on. Girls started writing 'Honk!' and the date they'd been with you under. There's like thirty honks there now."

William's eyebrows rise.

"Are we okay?" Paula says, with her shoulders hunched up around her ears.

William shakes his head, but not to say no. He shakes it because the math is wrong. "There should only be eight honks."

Paula smiles and the tension in her body eases. "Girls lie about sex, just like boys do. So, Bridget saw all the honks, and now she thinks you're this enormous man-whore, out to nail a future nun."

Paula has breezed right past whatever complicated girl-feeling she just had, and now she is back on topic. It is his favorite thing about her, this ability to stay on point. Her brain is really quite fine. "Do you think she was serious? About the nun thing?"

"Yes," William says. It explains a lot, actually.

"Well, I'm sorry I told everyone you were this amazing lay," Paula says. When he doesn't respond, she makes a finger hook and waves it in front of his eyes. He stares up the street after Bridget, and she puffs out an exasperated sigh. "I really am sorry, Bubba. I can fix it, though. I'll talk to her."

"No," William says. "I will." He starts down the road.

"Now?" Paula says, starting after him.

In answer, he breaks into an easy run, loping fast up the street after Bridget, who is a tiny figure under a streetlight four blocks up, turning right and disappearing. Paula sprints and keeps up with him, barely.

"Oh yeah, this is going to go well," Paula says, and even though she is huffing, she exaggerates her inflection to leave him with no doubt that this is sarcasm. He speeds up.

When he rounds the corner, he sees Bridget has stopped about a block ahead of him. She is sitting on one of a pair of brick posts that stand on either side of someone's driveway. She is scrubbing at her eyes. She looks up as they get close; Paula is huffing very loudly now. She's fallen a few feet behind.

"You followed me? Really?" Bridget says. Her nose is swollen and very pink.

He shrugs and then sits on top of the other post. Paula stops and bends at the waist, trying to get her breath back.

He says to Bridget, "It wasn't because you want to be a nun. I didn't know."

She pushes at her last tears, shoving them off her cheeks with mad, flat hands. "Well, now you do."

"I wasn't *only* trying to nail you," he says, and she lets out a startled bark of laughter. "I wanted to make something nice for you."

"Why would you do all that?" Bridget asks. She is really talking to him now. Not angry talk, and the crying has stopped. This is a conversation, and he is having it with Bridget. His veins fill up with fast, red blood, and he is glad to have Paula standing by, like a referee or a coach, ready to step in when he begins to fuck it up.

"I saw you tearing out the phlox, in the park," he says. He spreads his hands helplessly.

It is a bad answer, incomplete, but she doesn't say that. Instead, she says, "Last year, at my old school, this one group of guys had a bet on who could, you know, talk me out of it. The nun thing. Except not talk. You know what I mean?" William doesn't, and it must show on his face, because she adds, "They bet on who could fuck me out of it."

Paula has her breath back. She straightens and stands with one hip cocked, appraising Bridget. "Boom, William! You just got f-bombed."

"I'm just quoting what those boys said." Bridget's cheeks have pinked.

"Pretty bold quote, for a nun," Paula answers.

"I'm just a person," Bridget says, clearly exasperated. "Every nun is always just a person. But no one seems to get that. So I didn't tell anyone here, and now instead of not having friends because I'm Weirdo Nun Girl, I don't have friends because I can't talk about anything that matters."

"William will be your friend," Paula says promptly. She grins and adds, "You probably don't even have to nail him."

Bridget blinks, looks back and forth between them. "I still don't get it. Why you did all this, the fireworks and the perfume, the note thing. Why do it, if . . ." She trails off.

He stays still with his hands still spread, still helpless. He doesn't have words for it, how it was to see her in the park. She is a thing he wants to be near in his whole body, to understand with all his mind.

"No one said you could tear out those flowers. I saw you doing it, and I liked you," he says.

"That's a little weird," she says, but not mean at all. Like she is interested in figuring it out.

"A little?" Paula says. She cackles. "Sis, wake up! Weird is his go-to setting. He's a total Aspy freak. Computer brain. Ask him to do math in his head. You'll die. And if you're friends with him, you get free A's in Calculus because he doesn't have the world's best moral compass. Though maybe future nuns don't cheat, I dunno. They sure do seem to cuss and lose their tempers . . ." She is saying sassy Paula things, but her voice sounds like it is being kind to Bridget. This is Paula, being his wingman. "I'll tell you one more thing. He's the best friend I've had in my whole life. Only guy who's never shot me full of bull, and he can keep a secret. Maybe because he almost never talks. Be mad he made you fireworks if you want, Sister Potty-Quotes, but don't be stupid. You think Space Mountain here has to work this hard to get laid? Please. Look at him. They come to him. He likes you, dumbass. He just likes you." She grabs William's hand and tugs him up to his feet, off the post. "You're done here, William," she says, and starts pulling him away.

He lets her, because most of what she has said is right. Only most, because of course he does want to have sex with Bridget. Avidly. But he doesn't think this is a thing he should explain right now. Paula has the gist of it; it wasn't *only* to fuck her. He wants to fuck her and love her and marry her, in any order she will take these things.

That Monday, at lunch, William and Paula are sitting at their small four-top right beside the long table full of the football players and their girls. Paula calls it the Annex. They don't sit with the team because Paula has had sex with a lot of them. But they sit near, because the team is not allowed to ignore her or talk shit. They have to say hello to her and wave back if she waves. These are William's rules.

Paula has a new rule, too, this year: William's teammates cannot hit her up for sex. She only goes with college boys now.

Paula's telling him some long, involved story about a party at Emory when he sees Bridget, walking toward them. The air heats and vibrates around him. Bridget is carrying her tray. Her walk is not hesitant. With purpose, she approaches. She has made a decision. She passes the smart girls' lunch table, beelining toward them.

Watching the bright tail of hair swinging in tandem with her curvy hips, he is not sure how to be friends with a Bridget who is going to be a nun. He cannot lie down by Bridget and have her bite his shoulder the way Paula can. His body would unstoppably roll toward Bridget, and his mouth would bite her back. Paula's nearly naked body is null to him, no longer viable, as if she is, in spite of their disparate ethnicities, his sister. He could not be remotely peaceful if Bridget were prone on a roof near him in her underpants. When Bridget says that she will be a nun, she means that she will not belong to him, and he cannot belong to her.

She says, "Hi," and drops onto the seat beside Paula, across from him.

He can smell her. Orange blossoms, undercut with green herbs. She is wearing his catalyst.

Paula says, "Yo, Mother Superior," and after that, they are three, William and Paula and Bridget, always together, untouching, each in their separate skins.

But he is waiting. He can wait, because she can say with her mouth that she is going to be a nun, and never love a man, never be in love with him, but chemistry is truer than anything a person says. She has sprayed the thing he made onto her skin. She has marked herself with his scent.

He never stopped making it for her, and she never stopped wearing it. His waiting body stayed blank, done with being the best ride in the park. He was waiting for the contact that he knew was coming. Orange blossoms, and green herbs; that was the smell of Bridget, always, then and now. Exactly now.

He is not seventeen, and Paula is not here. He is in the hospital, floating slowly down from the morphine; pain is closer, more relevant, but only by a little. Pain and Bridget's scent, both faint, have come into the room together. The smell makes the air heavier than when Twyla was a thousand pounds pressed into his side.

He opens his eyes. Dawn has come. So has his wife. She floats and wavers. Sunlight pushes in the window behind her, turning her hair into a halo of molten copper-blond around her face. She is wearing a long pale dress, and the sunlight comes through that, too, lighting up the outline of her body.

It is Bridget, and she still believes in miracles. She believes that if he puts his hand out, his arm could span time, reach backward, past the whole bleak silence of the last year, into the before, before they put her in the ambulance, before she did the unforgivable. If only he believed it, too, he could pull her to him now, put his mouth on hers, and have her, bullet holes and trucks and gravity and God and space and time be damned. The look on her face—he knows this look, though it is tempered now by sorrow. It is permission.

He breathes in the air and the air is full of her smell. Her scent chokes him.

"Are you here to pray for me?" William asks. "Don't pray for me." His throat is parched, and his voice comes out of it in a raspy, burned-up whisper. His words are slurred. His blood is thick with drugs. He will not reach. Her body bends and ripples in the rising sun, and her hair is made of light. "I'm going to close my eyes now," he says. "When they open, you won't be here anymore."

He blinks, a long, black blink that could be twenty seconds or an hour. Morphine has stolen all his sense of time. In the dark of it, her scent begins to fade. He rolls onto his unshot side to face the wall, dragging the box with the button with him, pressing and pressing. He keeps flooding his blood with the drug, so everything stays distant. He's willing to accept the spine shudders, the woozy unreality of the room, and the clenched jaw, if these things come with unconsciousness. Better darkness than seeing Bridget, at any age. He has worked so hard, for months now, to blank out any memory that might have her in it. To push it away, unexamined. He cannot keep remembering his wife tearing up a garden at sixteen, must stop watching her take on his scent at seventeen. He can't have the grown-up version wafting into his hospital room, looking so holy, so forgiving. He has not, will not, cannot forgive *her*.

He wakes up facing the flat green wall, still rolled onto his unshot side. He sucks in a great, heaving breath through his nose. The air is still and quiet and smells only like cheap cleaning fluid.

"Are you awake, Bubba?" Paula's voice, speaking quietly in case he's not.

He rolls cautiously onto his back.

The room is full of silent people, looking at him. His jaw aches. He feels woozy and nauseous and all the people in the room are undulating inside their skins. The only one he recognizes is Paula, who is sitting on the other bed in a black skirt and a white blouse, her expensive jacket in a crumple beside her.

She smiles when she sees his eyes and says, "What did I tell you about getting shot? What did I tell you?"

"Nothing," William says. "Though in retrospect, you meant to tell me not to?" His voice comes out hoarse and overloud.

"I see the bullet missed your smart-ass gland," Paula says. Her head wavers back and forth on her wobbling neck, and he weaves his own head back and forth, trying to match the movement to hers. "Bubba? Did you get shot in the brain? Or do they have you on the good drugs?" He holds up the box with the button, and she smiles. "Yummy. Okay, but don't be shot again. Ever."

"Check," William says.

The tall, skinny boy standing to her left shuffles impatiently. William doesn't know him. He's college-aged, wearing long shorts and flip-flops. His face looks like he is eating something sour.

Closer to his bed, in the room's only visitor's chair, sits a familiar dark-haired girl with a little boy in her lap. The boy is holding a tattered, grimy origami bird.

"Hello, Natty," William says. He picks up the bed remote and presses the button that raises him to sit.

"Hello, William," the little boy says. "Mommy said you wasn't killed."

"How are you feeling?" the girl says, shyly, and the name comes back as he hears that familiar accent. Shandi.

"Yes, William, how *are* you feeling?" says Paula, raising her eyebrows at him. She waggles them significantly. "I see you've made new friends. Pretty ones. With . . ." Behind Shandi's back, Paula hovers her hands over her own small breasts, honking large imaginary ones.

Shandi says, "Natty's been really worried."

"Psssh," says William, looking at Natty now. He waves one hand expansively, which causes a long, shuddering pain to radiate from his side, but the morphine makes this only mildly interesting. "I'm hardly even scratched."

A lie, but it is oftentimes expedient and kind to lie to children. The last two months that Twyla was alive, he nightly had to shoo away the Hommy-Hom who lived in her closet. It was an idea he resisted at first. Instead he explained the natural world to Twyla, the nonexistence of monsters in general and Hommy-Homs in the specific. Twyla listened and nodded, and at the end he said to her, "So monsters don't exist, do they?"

She answered, very serious, "No, Daddy. 'Cept dis Hommy-Hom." And pointed at the closet.

"My bird has blood on it," the little boy tells him, mournful. "I'm not allowed to keep it."

He holds it out, showing William the rusty streak on the tail.

"I'll make you another," William says.

Paula, sounding very much like herself now, says, "By the way, I'm glad you're not dead."

"Me, too," William says. It is expedient and kind to lie to adults sometimes, as well. "Why aren't you in court?"

"I need to be. I had to get a continuance, and now my bitch client has decided we should renegotiate and go after that second summer home. All because you couldn't wait to get shot until tomorrow."

Shandi says to Natty, "Walcott will take you to the cafeteria to get that ice cream now, okay?"

Natty nods, and Paula is still talking. "You're very popular. Mrs. Grant—the lady who owns the Circle K—stopped by to weep and abjectly apologize. She's very, very sorry that she shot you with her foot. Her husband has a couple of cracked ribs, she said to tell you, but he should be fine. He's in a room down the hall. He wants to say thank you. That clerk came by, too—"

"Carrie," Shandi supplies. She is handing the little boy up to the much larger one, angry in his flip-flops. All the motion in the room makes William more nauseous.

Paula talks over her. "—on the same errand, one assumes. They didn't stay, though. Only this one stayed. And watched you sleep. Which isn't creepy." She says it in the way that means she does think it is creepy.

"So did you," William says.

He feels his mouth stretch out long into a smile. Too long. It feels like half his head could yawp open and hinge back entirely, until he is staring upside down at the wall behind him.

"Yeah, but I love your sorry ass," Paula says.

Shandi startles and draws in her breath, fast and sharp.

The angry boy flairs his nostrils. "We'll be in the cafeteria, when you get done with this lunacy."

He carries Natty out.

Natty waves as he goes, and William waves back. So, this is what three looks like, big-eyed and quiet and intense. William has not spent much time with children other than his own daughter, who stopped at two. She was all noise and chaos in glittery pink clothes, a ball of willfulness with short, fat legs. He can see the physiology is different. Three is longer and straighter, the back no longer bowed and the stomach losing its baby roundness.

Paula says, "He's gone. You can stop waving now, Bubba."

He didn't realize he still was. He stops, and stops smiling, too, trying to narrow his mouth back down, make it shorter. He can't do it, and he deliberately sets the morphine button aside.

Shandi says to Paula, "Could you give us a minute? Alone?"

Paula chuckles. "Absolutely not. Your friend said that you are here for lunacy, and this man is clearly helpless. What if you eat him?"

"William," Shandi says, like a plea. Her eyes are big and desperate, like they were in the Circle K, fixed on him like she expects him to bang Paula in the head now. It reminds him.

"Did I kill him? When I hit him with the paperweight?" he asks her. He doesn't want to have killed anyone. Not even Stevie.

"No," Shandi says. "He was in surgery, they said, and now he's in the ICU. They put a cop outside his door, but I don't know why. He's in a coma."

She stops talking and looks down at her hands, glancing over at Paula a couple of times. William picks up Natty's dilapidated paper bird, pulling the tail to make it peck. It's so rumpled that all it can manage is a lurching, sad movement. Shandi still keeps glancing back at Paula.

Paula says. "I'm not leaving, crazy lady."

"I'm not crazy." Shandi turns to William and says, "Or maybe I am. In the Circle K, when you, when you were shot, you looked at me and you said a word."

William shakes his head. He doesn't remember.

"You said 'destiny,'" Shandi tells him.

Behind her, Paula sits up straight, and now she is looking at William with intensity. She knows his definition. Her eyes narrow.

"William," Shandi says, and he sinks back to that moment, when their eyes met over the head of her frightened child. He thought then that she might kiss him. She leans in close again, speaks barely above a whisper. "Do you believe in miracles?"

Behind her, Paula's eyebrows disappear into her bangs.

"Define the term," he says.

"Like when the Red Sea parted, or when Lazarus got back up," she says. She swallows and looks away.

"No," he says.

She shrugs. "I was a virgin when I gave birth to Natty. For a long time now, I've told myself it was a miracle."

Miracle is another word for magic, and magic is only science, unexplained. The simplest explanation for her sentence is a need for antipsychotic medication. Paula, twirling her index finger by her forehead behind Shandi's back, is advocating for this one. William, even in the grips of morphine, doesn't think so. He was with her in the Circle K. She was steady and cool, doing her best to keep her child safe. She did all the ugly things that needed doing when he took the bullet. She doesn't strike him, even now, as unstable. Though certainly his judgment is impaired. Right now, it looks as if she has two or three overlapping faces.

"There's no such thing," he tells her.

She shakes her head, rueful. "I know. I'm not even sure if I believe in God. But I pretended it was a miracle anyway. It was easier. If there's something you can't live with, you have to get it off of you. You do whatever you need to do, to push it far away." This, of course, makes perfect sense to him. "It can come back, though. You never know what's going to call it back."

"Detergent," he says and Shandi's eyebrows knit.

"Okay, stop," Paula says, standing. "He's in no condition to talk to you about whatever your disturbance is."

Shandi ignores her and bulls onward, talking faster now, and her voice is fierce, telegraphing urgency. "There was no miracle. I killed it in the Circle K. I killed it dead, and now I only want to know the truth. You said that word, *destiny*. You said you were a scientist. I think that you could help me know."

"I mean it," Paula says, looming up over her. "Time to go."

Shandi retracts under Paula's glare, sinking herself deep into the chair. She grips the edges with her hands so hard the knuckles whiten. She will not easily be moved, but Paula is about to lay hands on her and make it happen, easy or hard. Someone could be hurt. Probably Shandi.

"Wait," William tells Paula, and she pauses to boggle at him.

His mind, even soaked in narcotics, is engaging. Something rose for this girl, too, inside the Circle K. She says she killed a miracle, and while he understands that she means this figuratively, the concept pleases him. She wants willfulness and science now, to help her. "I'm interested in doing that," he tells her.

Paula is so startled she does an actual double take. Shandi only nods. She looks relieved, but not surprised. It's almost as if she expected him to agree, and this is interesting, too. William himself would not have predicted it, right up until he heard himself say it.

"Are you fucking kidding me?" Paula says. She is examining Shandi again. She's been teasing William about having a young woman hanging around to watch him sleep, but now she's taking Shandi seriously. Her gaze rests on the girl, appraising, suspicious, and then she's glaring at him. "William, do you hear yourself? Is your brain in a cloud?"

He shoots her an impatient look. "You know I don't like metaphors before I've had my coffee."

She laughs in spite of her confusion. "Or after," she says.

"Or during," he agrees. He understands what she means, of course, but why should he have to? Why ask if his brain has been encased in a visible mass of tiny water droplets when what she really wants to know is why he's acting out of character.

"Whew, you've bounced back sassy," Paula says. "I should have shot you months ago. You've really thrown me, though. This girl just said the most ass-crazy mess I've ever heard, and you're all in? Just like that?"

William shrugs, though he can tell from a distance that his wound is not reacting well. It also wasn't the best idea to sit up, now that he's noticing. The two women undulate in the fuzzy room, each wanting different things. His loyalty is to Paula, but the night was long and black; the morning seems impossible to navigate with loyalty alone.

Shandi may well have saved his life with a borrowed sweater and quick thinking. The common perception would dictate that he is in her debt, although he isn't grateful. Being saved was not the outcome he was seeking. But now she's said a lot of things that have left him feeling curious. He's almost interested, his mind engaging with something far outside himself for the first time in a year.

And why not? It isn't every day he meets a girl who killed a miracle.

"Sure," he tells Paula, tells them both. "Just like that."

PART TWO

Chemistry

The Brain is just the weight of God—
For—Heft them—Pound for Pound—
And they will differ—if they do—
As Syllable from Sound—
EMILY DICKINSON

Chapter 7

*T*his is what I knew: William would find Natty's biological father. He would banish the red-clay golem I'd imagined rising, malformed and anonymous, from the earth around the beanbag chair. He would make it have a human face, a human body, a human vulnerability to justice. I had finally become a true believer.

"He's not Sherlock Holmes," Walcott told me on the phone. I was hurling a load of laundry into the machine at the condo, getting ready to go back over to William's. I hadn't seen Walcott since we'd visited the hospital. I'd told myself it was only because he lived in Lumpkin County in the summertime, working for his momses. But he hadn't answered my texts, and that was unprecedented. I called the B and B and had Aimee go and get him. Now we were in this stupid fight. He didn't think William could do it, and he was irked that I'd even asked him to try. "You believe it the same way Natty believes that he saves Tinker Bell by clapping, every time I read him *Peter Pan*."

"Yeah? Well last I checked, Tink was still breathing," I told him, irked back.

"Don't go back over there," he said.

But as soon as we hung up, I went.

I'd been taking care of William for more than a week, cooking healthy meals in his kitchen and making him stay flat as much as possible, so his abdomen could heal. His friend Paula took the night shift, and I do mean took. With both hands. She showed up every night but Tuesday, arriving near enough to Natty's bedtime that it was hardly more than our paths crossing. I might have let Natty stay up later, though, if it wasn't for the way she filled up the house, pushing me aside until I felt like an invading bug scuttling along the walls.

She'd bring a six-pack, pop open a couple, and pass one to William. She'd plop into the armchair and only then say, "Oh, did you want one?" She shut me outside the conversation, engaging William in an odd, truncated sparring or saying things soaked in so much history and reference it was almost shorthand.

I might have been jealous, if he wasn't so completely unromantic with her. It was like watching some alternate-universe version of me and Walcott, where Walcott was the quiet one, and I was kind of an asshole. I wondered if they weren't cousins or some other flavor of family. Paula was such an indecipherable mix of races she could theoretically be related to anyone.

That night, she showed up early.

We'd finished eating dinner but were still sitting at the table, chatting, with William at the head and Natty and me on either side of him. This was the third day he'd felt well enough to sit at the table instead of having a tray in bed. He was barefoot, wearing a T-shirt that said E. COLI HAPPENS, and a pair of ancient Levi's that looked so soft I wanted to drop to my knees and rub my cheek along his thigh.

I heard her letting herself in as Natty began agitating to go see the little brown bats before it got too dark. She sauntered into the kitchen and put a six-pack down on the counter.

I told Natty, "In a minute, baby," mostly because I didn't want to let her run me out in the middle of an hour that was still my time.

She gave me a cool nod, then said, "Hey, Bubba, how're you feeling?" to William.

"Twenty-six percent less dead," William said.

I said, too loud, "There's more salmon if you like?" She shook her head. When I added, "Can I at least get you some coffee?" she laughed outright.

"I'll get my own drink, Susie Homemaker. Take a load off."

She popped the cap off one of the beers and leaned against the counter, drinking and looking at me over the bottle.

Natty was out of his chair now, coming around the table to tug my sleeve and say, "It's bat o'clock immediately, Mommy."

But I wasn't ready to give the room, much less William, over to Paula. "I have to get the dishes done."

Paula said, "Why don't you take him, William, since you have pants on, for a change."

"Sure." William got up, his palm pressed lightly against the place where he had been shot, as if the bullet was still there and he was holding it in.

I started to follow, but Paula said, "I think they have bat-watch covered, don't you? You finish clearing. I'll rinse." Paula struck me as having the domestic instincts of a barn cat; I thought, *This is a ploy to get me alone.*

But then she gave me a wide, bland smile and started running water in the sink. Not a ploy at all. She wasn't trying to trick me. It was a clear request for a tête-à-tête, designed to run under the male radars in the room. I grabbed a couple of the dirty plates and took them over, curious enough to let her have it. We'd never been alone together, and when William was present, she'd never shown the slightest interest in talking to me.

Paula took the plates and began rinsing, but the second the front door closed, she shut the water off. She turned toward me, sharp-eyed and canny, wiping her hands dry on the dish towel to save her sleek, bitch-black suit.

"This was one thing when you were a cute little stray with a crush. But now you're trying to get a dish in the house," she said with no preamble. "William's feeling a lot better, and so I think you're done here."

All at once I felt so awkward that I didn't know where to put my hands. I found myself clutching them together in front of me like Natty caught sneaking a jelly bean. I made them drop down by my sides.

"Ooh! You're spooky," I said, "but I don't think you get to decide that."

"Are we going to let William decide?" She chuckled, but it was not a friendly sound.

"I guess," I said, because I wasn't sure where this was going.

"You think he'd pick you?" Paula asked.

For a moment I wondered what his other choice was. Then I realized that, while I'd never seen him so much as glance at her in a romantic way, she was a harder thing to read. She was pushing me, though, so I pushed back. "He still needs help. It's not like you're up for the job."

I hated how defensive I sounded, but there was enough truth in it for her to incline her head and say, "Touché."

When Natty and I first drove over to his house, a renovated Tudor in the heart of Morningside, we'd found him spaced out on pain meds, swaying and eating cold noodles directly from a carton. He was in no shape to continue the conversation I'd started at the hospital. Paula had driven him home, but then she'd left him with nothing in the fridge but milk, OJ, and a bunch of take-out Chinese food for reheating. I'd put him to bed, and Natty and I stayed. We'd come back the next day with real groceries and stayed longer.

I kept thinking someone—family, maybe, or close friends— would show up and kick me over a step, saying, *Oh thanks, Shandi, you almost perfect stranger, we'll take it from here.* But Paula didn't come until seven, most nights. A neighbor dropped off a coffee cake, and Geneti-Tech sent a huge crate of pears, individually wrapped like they were diamonds. I made fun of that until I bit into one and felt its perfect, crisp sweetness flood my mouth. Until Natty and I came, the house was a beautiful void: breezy sheers, glass bricks, and silence.

Paula's head cocked and her eyes were so cold. She stepped in closer still, and she *was* spooky as all hell. I caught a whiff of what it might feel like to be some hapless deadbeat dad, about to get creamed, stuck alone on the witness stand with Paula bearing down.

"I appreciate the casseroles, okay? But you can't have my autastic Dr. Ashe. I don't care what he's said or what it looks like. I'm telling you, he's not available."

I tucked my chin down, eyebrows rising. Paula was claiming him like territory, but my brain stuck on the other thing. "Your what?" I said, and then, processing it, I said, shocked, "William's not autistic." But I had a click in my head, like, *Oh. That slight lack of inflection. The way he looks off sideways when I talk. It isn't the Percocet.*

"On the spectrum. Whatever. He's a grown-up, Shandi. He's learned how to pass. Mostly," she said, then added in a sweet nursery-rhyme singsong, "Asperger's, autistic, a green and yellow biscuit." Her lip curled up and her voice went from kiddy-sweet to bullets. "Try to stay on topic. Stop coming here, wearing the shit out of those cast-me-as-the-wifey sundresses. This one looks like you dug up June Cleaver and ripped it off her corpse. No one dresses like that to get help with a science-fair project, or whatever crazy bullshit you were spouting at the hospital."

I was instantly ashamed of my own stupid vintage apron, which was unfair. I'd come to remind William of his promise to help me, but I had found him hurt and alone. There'd been no one else, and he'd gotten shot saving my life. Saving my kid's life. So, yeah, I'd Mimmy'ed around a little, tucking blankets under his feet, greeting him with the smell of Lemon Pledge and a big-ass slice of pie when he woke up. Now it had somehow turned into a full-on Mim-vasion. But Mimmy's life was a dress rehearsal for a show that never opened. I wasn't her, and I didn't want to be her, cooking and smiling and dead from the neck down.

It was true I wanted more than his help as a scientist, though. I wanted wine and kissing under bridges. I wanted his big hands buried in my hair, and I wanted to be with him in Paris. Hell, I wanted to be under him in Paris. It was only that I had no idea how to get to there from here. I'd never seduced anyone. I'd never even tried. I felt my cheeks heat up, and she nodded, like my blush was confirmation.

"So what. So I like him," I said, hating that she had me on the defensive. "Is that so awful?"

"Yes. It's awful," she said, like she was explaining something obvious. She moved so she could look at me, up and down, appraising me like I was bad cattle. I was getting angry now, too. Her gaze was so intimate, it felt insulting. "You're angling for Bridget's place?" she asked. I'd never heard the name, but of course I knew who Bridget was. Instantly. "Please. You're not even half a Bridget, you fetus. You're not even Bridget Lite. How dare you try to step into her shoes."

"It's not like she's using them," I snapped without thinking, and instantly felt my flush turn into beet-red shame.

"Wow," Paula said. "At least we know where we stand now."

"I guess we do," I said. I was ashamed of what I'd said in anger, yes, but I would not back down.

I'd figured Paula out now. How ironic that I'd thought of Bridget as my rival, when I saw her photograph on the news. A part of me had been relieved to find his house was not a shrine to her, as if she were the first Mrs. DeWinter. It was the opposite. No clothes, no leftover lipstick or perfume. Not even any photographs, just a bunch of square shadows on the wall where framed things had once hung.

I'd only found a hint of her yesterday when I was looking for a hand towel. I'd seen a broken rosary in the back of an otherwise empty bathroom drawer. I'd thought, *Is William Catholic?* He didn't seem Catholic. He didn't seem anything. I'd wondered idly, like a girl testing out last names in her notebook, if I'd have to convert. It would upset my parents, but at least it would upset both of them equally. Dad would feel I'd chosen a form of Christianity, and Mimmy would be equally certain that I hadn't.

When I'd pulled the rosary out and saw its pale coral beads, the delicate silver crucifix, I realized it was too feminine for William. I'd shoved it way back in the drawer again, quickly, like it had gone red-hot.

Now I wondered who exactly had cleared all Bridget's things away so thoroughly. Had Paula done it, to make room for herself? I was willing to bet she had. She knew where William kept the garden key, and she let herself in every night like she already belonged here. I'd thought she was William's Walcott, but she wasn't worth even one of Walcott's toes.

The front door reopened, and she turned her attention away from me. It felt like a hook being peeled out of my skin. As they came in, Natty was talking in his outdoor voice, loud and excited.

". . . that kind of beetle. Don't scare him! You'll make him smell like fart!" and William laughed.

Paula had started forward, but she froze at the sound. William had a big laugh, weirdly overloud, like his volume knob was busted. I hadn't heard it since the Circle K. He'd laughed like this when he got shot.

That was strange; since I'd practically been living here, I hadn't heard him laugh. For a second I didn't know if that was because he was some flavor of autistic. Maybe he didn't laugh because he didn't feel things. I had some vague idea that that was what Asperger's meant. But that picture, with Bridget, holding his little girl in his lap . . . Maybe I only hadn't heard him laughing because he was so damn sad, like anyone would be.

The sound of it changed Paula's face. She swallowed and her eyes pinked up. I stopped wondering. I didn't know much about

Asperger's, but I damn well knew William. I'd seen all the way down into him, back in the Circle K. I knew him even better now. I'd watched him be so sweet and patient with my kid, and I'd poked my nose into the crannies of this scraped-out shell of a house, even the smallest bedroom, the empty one, with walls the color of orange sherbet. Happy fat bluebirds flew in a hand-painted line up near the ceiling. A child's room, now with no toys, no window treatments, just a sad dust bunny drifting across the bare floor with no bed or dresser to hide under.

He wasn't incapable of feeling. He was heartbroken. Even Paula the hard case was halfway to crying because his big laugh was a good sound, a familiar sound. One that had been missing.

Natty paused in the doorway, pointing up at the porch light, so excited. "William! That's a Cope's Gray! It's not typical for him to go down out of trees."

William leaned down and swung Natty up, favoring his shot side. He held Natty high to see the frog who'd come to eat the porch light bugs. He was saying something about its thigh coloration, feeding facts to Natty's information-hungry brain, both of them squinting into the light.

Watching him hold Natty, their heads bent together, the whites of Paula's eyes had gone even redder.

William set Natty down, and Paula turned her back and started rinsing the same two plates she'd already rinsed. Natty invaded the kitchen, begging for a Tupperware to catch the slimy friend they'd found out there. William followed at a slower pace.

"No, honey, we have to leave him out. It's mating season. He's come down to find a girlfriend." I still sounded shaky. Paula's spine got even more rigid as she stood, rewashing the only clean dishes.

William came over, too, walking into air so thick with cat-fight tension that to me it tasted just like estrogen. He didn't seem to notice, saying, "He says he misses the 'yell-y frogs' at night."

Up on Mimmy's mountain, the treetops were full of about a

million of those bloaty-looking fellows. They hollered all summer long, clamoring for love.

"Maybe we can get a CD," I said, trying to sound normal.

Natty scrubbed at his eyes with his fists, saying, "Real frogs is better." It was full dark now, and these days, the closer he came to the badlands of sleep, the more baby-talk invaded his sentences.

William said to him, "We could make a terrarium. You could have frogs chirping in your room."

"No, you cannot," I said.

"You don't like frogs?" William said, surprised, as if frogs were universally beloved, like chocolate or songs.

"I like frogs fine. Outside. Not in the house where Natty could leave the lid open, and they could come and touch my sleeping face with their sticky little creep feet."

It was the longest conversation we'd ever had in Paula's presence. Usually, she took over, shutting me out. Now she finally had herself together. She turned around and reached for her abandoned beer.

William saw her reddened eyes. "What did I miss?"

Paula waved one hand dismissively, "Shandi and I were discussing history. She thinks Columbus is a superhero, landing on an 'undiscovered' continent. It upset me. There was a whole nation of people who belonged here already, with a far more valid claim."

He looked to me, his eyebrows raised.

I said, "It's sad, but it's history. We were all born in the country that came next. I'm a big fan of the fresh start."

The silence after that was strained. William looked back and forth between us like he'd heard a few bars of a song he knew but could not place.

Natty said, "We could have catched him for a minute, though," claiming William's attention.

"Another night. I see Green Tree Frogs here quite frequently."

Paula pitched her voice low, talking under them, so only I could hear. "Oh, kitten heels, it's on. I'm gonna sink your battle-

ship." Then she walked past me, took William's arm, and walked
him away from me manually. "So, Kai still won't call me back. I
heard from Tank that she joined some sort of a farm co-op. I'm
guessing cult?"

William snorted. "Your mother selling airport flowers. Yeah.
I can see that."

Natty was yawning. He came over to lean on my leg, saying,
"But I do want that frog termarmium, Mommy."

Natty could say *anaphylactic* and *ludicrous* and the Latin names
of fifty kinds of bugs without a hitch, so I knew he was done for
the day.

I ceded William to Paula, but only for the moment. Tomorrow was another day.

I took my kid back to the condo. I tucked him into bed with his
light saber and his big Darth Vader mask and helmet. In my son's
post-Stevie world, a decapitated Dark Lord was better comfort
than poor old Yellow Friend. His room at the condo also had a
star-shaped night-light from Dad, plus Praying Hands Jesus and
Mimmy in her red bikini watching over him from the wall. A
growing flock of William's origami birds stood sentinel on the
bedside table, but none of these things could stop big black bombs
and guns with feet from hunting my kid. By midnight he'd
crawled into bed with me.

I didn't need the shrink Dad was paying for to tell me these
bad things were all substitute Stevies. She specialized in PTSD in
children, but so far it looked to me like Dad was shelling out two
hundred bucks a pop for a kindly old lady to watch Natty make
little plastic good guys beat the crap out of little plastic bad guys.
I did that with him every day for free.

It surely wasn't helping him sleep. He spent the rest of the
night fisting his hands in my hair, throwing out his arms and
punching me in the throat, and flipping around like a slinky and
then shoving his little toes up into my nostrils.

I lay there, drifting in and out. I loved him way past crazy, but he was not the man I wanted in my bed. That man was in Morningside, sleeping the hard sleep of the recently shot. Alone. I hoped.

I might not know squat about seduction, but Paula, I was willing to bet, knew it sixteen ways from Sunday. She was slinky and so exotic-looking with those pale eyes, up-tilted like a cat's. All her suit skirts were two inches higher than what I would consider to be strictly professional.

They'd said on the news that the accident had happened exactly a year before the robbery; I'd appeared on the horizon exactly one day before it became socially acceptable for her to make a move on him. No wonder she hated me.

And me, stupidly casting her as a bitchy lady Walcott, hadn't realized I had competition. I'd been too busy Mimmy-ing out, and Mimmy, post-divorce, had lived what the Baptists called a blameless life. She kept her lamp trimmed and waited for nothing, immaculate. She sold all her candy and gave her fried chicken to families that had been invaded by new babies. No man was invited in to eat off her table and admire the way her house sparkled. Mimmy looked hot, but inside, the only thing less sexual than Mimmy was a puffy baby kitten eating pudding. Vanilla pudding.

I'd been broken for so long that the first time my body woke up to a man, I'd pulled on my circa 1957 clothes and started dusting, wearing pearls. It made sense, I guess. I'd fallen hard for William on the same day I decided I could no longer pretend my son's conception was a miracle, immaculate and tidy. It helped that the bullet hole made William a supersafe man to be alone with. While I was playing nursemaid, I didn't have to move ahead with any of it. Not finding my red-clay golem man, and not sex.

Paula, who walked in heels like she was sex itself, shaking out her oil-black hair, thick and coarse as a pony's mane, was marking him like territory. I couldn't stall any longer. Not on either front.

The next day, I got up early and dressed myself so carefully. A full circle skirt with a white midi blouse. I even went for the

Peter Pan collar. Hair in a high pony. Perfect red lipstick, like a stop sign aimed at kissing. I wanted to take the sex out of today, all of it, to keep it safe for later.

Natty and I ran a bunch of errands, first thing. That afternoon, when I headed toward William's house, I had two bags in the car. One was full of everything I needed to make Mimmy's best corn chowder. The other was my old gym bag, unearthed from my closet at Dad and Bethany's while Bethany was at Pilates.

I set them down on William's kitchen counter, pushed all the way against the tile backsplash. William was in his room. I loaded the dishwasher, then went to put Natty down for his nap on the loveseat in the office. He made me pin his sheriff's badge on before he could sleep.

"I need it for being brave in," he said, which broke my heart. I stayed, petting his feet until he drifted off.

When I finally left him, I found William drinking coffee at the breakfast bar, still in sweat pants and an old white tee.

"You look like you could use a nap, too," he told me.

"Thanks! I love it when men tell me that," I said, smiling, but if I looked half as sick as I felt, I couldn't blame him.

I'd never actually told anyone. Walcott had handled all those parts for me. I was scared to even try, but my spine was set. I knew inside the Circle K that I should have told this story a long time ago. I had to tell it, now. I wanted William Ashe to be the first.

I went into the kitchen, letting the breakfast bar create some space between us. I got the first bag and began laying out the soup ingredients on the granite countertop, very tidy, like the fate of nations hinged on whether or not the onions lined up straight. Making this soup would be my last act of Mimmy-hood. I wanted it to count.

"In the hospital, I asked you for a favor, but you were kind of glassy. Do you remember?" I asked him.

In my peripheral vision I could see his head cock to the side in that odd, un-human way he had. It reminded me of the velociraptors from *Jurassic Park*.

"You said you killed a miracle. You said things about science and destiny. I told you I'd help you, and I meant it. I've thought about it since, quite a bit. But you never brought it up again, and I was coming out of anesthesia and taking opiates. I was beginning to wonder if it happened as I remembered it."

"It happened pretty much like that," I said, low. It made it easier, to have him say he really meant to help. So I began talking, taking him with me to just before I started my senior year of high school.

It was my dad's weekend, and I was supposed to be at the late movie with a bunch of kids from synagogue. I barely remembered calling Walcott a little after midnight, but I did. He heard Pink caterwauling over a heavy dance beat, heard me yelling that he should please come to the party and get me now. I laughed in a high-pitched cackle, and when he asked me where the hell I was, I said, "I think the Kappa house? Kappa Lappa Something?"

He heard a boy's voice talking, close to the phone, which meant close to my face. Then I'd disconnected.

He called me back, again and again, but he only got my voice mail. I'd sounded so weird. After the ninth call, he was alarmed enough to go downstairs and steal his one mom's Visa and his other mom's Prius. He came galloping over the hills in a white hybrid, getting forty-six miles to the gallon, to save me.

He picked Emory, because it was the closest campus to my dad's with housing for the Greeks. By the time he found Kappu Nu, it was after three A.M., but inside their big white house, a party was still raging. He loped through, doing a lap of the ground floor before taking the stairs two at a time. He opened every door he found, busting in on kids having all kinds of probably consensual sex, on a naked couple so busy yelling at each other they never knew he was there, on three frat boys passing a water pipe, and finally a bathroom full of buzzed girls smearing on fresh lipstick. He pushed his way in, but none of the girls was me. He went back downstairs and waded around the impromptu dance floor until he'd peered into the face of every shortish girl with dark hair he could find.

He left the house. He walked down the road calling my name. He was about to go back to his car, thinking he had chosen the wrong campus, when he saw a yellow VW parked on the next block. He knew that Mimmy-enraging DA DS GRL vanity plate; Dad had had the car delivered in the middle of my Lumpkin County Sweet Sixteen. So Walcott went back. He stood in the front yard, pacing back and forth, hollering my name over the muffled sound of dance-music backbeats trapped inside.

I heard him.

I said his name back, though my tongue was so thick and dry it was like a wad of cotton in my mouth.

My eyes opened, and I was staring up at the stars through the branches of some oak trees. I could hear the party, and over that, Walcott's voice sounded again, now hollering, "Marco?"

I called back, "Polo," through my cotton wool mouth.

I was lying on a half-deflated beanbag chair, weather damaged and sad. I lifted my head and saw him coming, a long, thin line of vertical Walcott, appearing through the trees in the backyard. I let my head tip back, and above me, through the leaves, the stars were spinning on strings, like a baby's mobile some crazy god had strung up just for me.

I could feel thin grass sprouting from the red clay soil under my feet. I flexed my naked toes. My silver sandals were gone, baby, gone. I lay there trying to remember what had made me skip meeting up with my Atlanta friends, heading off instead to a party with two older girls I'd just that second met at Starbucks. Oh, right. I'd been pissed about some stupid fight with Bethany.

"Marco?" Walcott called again.

I put my head up to say "Polo" and the world spun, but I saw him see me. My head tipped back. I blinked such a long blink that when I opened my eyes Walcott was there, as if he had teleported to me.

I heard him saying, "Shandi, Shandi. Oh shit, Shandi."

I felt his hands, first scrabbling at my waist, then brushing my bare thighs. He was pulling my bunched-up skirt down. It registered then, distantly, that I felt too breezy down there to be wearing any panties.

"Hi, Walcott," I said.

"Shandi, are you *drunk*?" Walcott asked.

We weren't that get-wasted-every-weekend kind. Sure, we'd snuck a bottle or two of his momses' organic Pinot, but always together. Never out in the unsafe world where I could end up on a beanbag chair with my skirt hiked up, showing Walcott and the crazy swinging stars all of my private business.

I said, "I only had Coke," but I was sick and hot, and my jaw felt permanently clenched. I felt drunk plus plus; it was not like any kind of buzzed I'd ever been.

Walcott helped me sit up, and the world swayed around me. I leaned the other way and puked a thin stream of bile onto the ground. Walcott sat back on his haunches. I ran my hands down my body. I had my T-shirt on, but my bra was down around my waist, like a weird padded belt. My scared hands went shaking farther down my trembling body. I let them go sneaking up under the skirt Walcott had just pulled down. Yes, my panties were missing, and there was a strange slick of something tacky, drying in a trail that ran down the crook of my thigh.

My perma-clenched jaw was sore and shivery, but nothing else felt sore. My hands kept wandering around between my legs. They couldn't help it. Walcott sat, not looking away, as my hands went feeling and digging, afraid. My whole body was filthy and sweaty and sticky, the back of my bare legs glued to the ancient, cracked vinyl, but I felt like regular old me down there.

"Did someone . . ." Walcott couldn't finish. Couldn't say the word.

"I don't think. Because it would hurt, right?" I asked. "I mean, how many times have we watched *SVU*?" And we sat looking at each other, thinking of hot actors pretending to be cops and saying words like *tearing* and *vaginal bruising* and *brutal*. But I kept touching myself, down between my legs, and I felt regular and fine.

"Your underpants are gone," Walcott said, so earnest that it struck me as hilarious. I started giggling, and Walcott said, "Shandi, you are so messed up."

"I don't remember drinking," I said. "I don't remember anything."

"Someone dosed you," Walcott said, sparking into a kind of savage rage I had never seen on him before. "Who the fuck? We will go in there, and you show me. I will kill him."

But I didn't know, not at all. I shrugged. Walcott deflated as fast as he had swelled, and his mouth worked like it did when he was nine and had decided boys were not allowed to cry, no matter what his momses told him. He scooted closer and picked something out of my hair. He showed me. A piece of grass.

I kept rooting around in myself, not realizing my fingers might be pushing more of that tacky slick up inside myself. I was too sick and dizzy. I couldn't understand how all control over my basic human person could be taken away from me so easily.

I said, "The ground looks like a damn kaleidoscope. You're right. Someone dosed me, but I don't think he . . ." I stopped, too, caught on that word.

I should have kept talking. If I couldn't say it to Walcott, I wasn't going to say it to anyone. And I didn't. Not then and not ever, until now.

I told William all the things I should have told the cops four years ago, or at the very least my parents. It took a long time to get all the way through. I had to pause and savagely hack up the red pepper or wait until tears stopped splashing down and salting the butter.

William made it easier.

Nia or CeeCee—my best girlfriends at GSU—would have gotten all moist and huggy until I choked and wept myself into a snotted-up silence. Some dry, judgmental detective might blame me for not policing my Coke.

Not William. He didn't even look at me. He got some of Natty's art paper from the stack on the bar, tore it into squares, and started folding. Our eyes never met. Not once. I told the garlic and the corn and the beautiful white cream while William sat on the other side of the breakfast bar, so involved in making origami animals it was like we were in separate boxes with a wall between us.

He was listening, though. I'd learned that the more he fiddled or folded or tapped out an arrhythmic pattern while staring out a window, the more of his attention was engaged.

I told him how I lost myself. I'd lost time, too, lost memory. Lost my shoes and my pink lacy panties. If I'd lost nothing else, that wasn't due to me.

The Golem had put himself in charge. He could have called in friends. He could have held my head underwater in the frat house bathtub until I was drowned and dead and gone. He had left me, helpless and exposed under the stars for any number of strangers to find, to do whatever they wanted, too. It was pure luck I'd called Walcott earlier, pure luck that Walcott had chosen the right campus, had seen my car and found me. Nothing had been up to me.

By morning, what memories I had were misty and riddled with holes, courtesy of whatever had been fed to me. At first, it was only that it was easier to think of it as a dark blue dream. After Natty happened, I thought it was necessary. I made my son be wholly mine, scared I couldn't love him unless I let my intact hymen mean he *was* some kind of miracle. Too scared to test it, until the Circle K. There, ready to put myself between Natty and bullets no matter where he came from, I'd learned that I'd been lying for no reason. There, I'd finally stopped.

By the time I finished talking, the soup was bubbling on simmer, and William had an army of paper animals lined up in front of him. I realized they were all different sizes of jumping frogs. For Natty. He'd been making the frogs Natty was missing, and that almost undid me. I put my head down and breathed through it, my whole face crumpled up like an angry fist.

He stayed seated with the breakfast bar between us, and that was smart. I think I would have stabbed anyone who tried to touch me in that moment. I had the onion knife still handy.

When I stood up straight again, he said, very low and simple, "I'm sorry."

Not like an apology. Just sympathy, but I almost dissolved again. I tamped it down and flapped my hand at the air, like I was moving us along.

I said, "That day in the Circle K, I stopped pretending. Nothing like a gun in the face to make a girl reassess her life choices. If I let my pregnancy stay a miracle, then whoever the guy is, he still owns me. It's complicated, because I wouldn't trade Natty back for anything. But that man took something from me. I got Natty, and I technically still had my virginity, but I lost other things that night. I want them back. He owes me those things back."

William said, slow and thoughtful, "You want me to help you find him."

"Yes. I don't know anyone else who *could* help. I don't remember what he looks like, sounds like, or anything about him." I said. "All I know is, Natty's carrying parts of him, inside his cells. I thought because of your job, you might know how to find him."

After a thoughtful pause, William said, "I'll tell you what's of interest to me. The gym bag, with your clothes from that night. Was it plastic?"

"No," I said. "It's cloth."

"Excellent," he said. "Do you still have it?"

"You have it." I nodded to the bag I'd pushed to the back of his kitchen counter. "I dug it out for you this morning. I didn't touch anything. I wasn't even sure it would still be there. It was buried under about fifty pairs of shoes." I took in a huge breath, pulling in good, clean air, and then pushed it all back out, trying to imagine it was taking every bad thing inside me with it.

"Okay. Here's what I can do." He starting ticking things off on his fingers. "A detailed analysis of fibers left behind. If he's left hairs with a follicle or semen"—I winced at the word—"and it hasn't decayed, I can get his DNA fingerprint. I should probably get samples from you, too, to distinguish your cells from his. And I'll need Natty's for comparison." He steepled his fingers together and pressed his hands into his forehead. "Do you understand what you lose, if I take that bag? I don't know police procedure, but I'd guess this would invalidate the bag's contents as evidence."

I nodded. I'd walked out of the Circle K thinking the Golem should be found and put in jail, but by morning, I'd realized this would never be an option.

"I can't do that to Natty," I said.

Up until now, only a select group of people knew how Natty came to be, and they all loved my kid right straight down into his bones. They would never tell him. Finding or even prosecuting his father wouldn't change how I felt about Natty. I knew now that nothing could, but it would change how he felt about himself. My child would not grow up thinking of himself as a rapist's kid, the product of an awful thing that happened to his mother. There could never be a trail of arrest and court records. He could never know a man was in prison for making him. This was nonnegotiable.

William asked, "Why do this at all? You plan to take my results to a private detective?"

"Probably," I said. "I want to know who he is."

If I asked, Dad would pay for one, no question. But I had this crazy-firm belief it wouldn't come to that; William would deliver Natty's father to me. I'd long avoided faith, because in my family, it meant an awful choosing. There was no acceptable third way. It was synagogue or church, Bible or Torah, brisket or bacon. A burger ordered with cheese or without was such a statement that by kindergarten I knew to pick the chicken nuggets Happy Meal. The mildest allegiance was proof one parent was the rightest and the most beloved, and I refused to call the winner and the loser in their war.

Natty's eyelashes were still the holiest thing I knew, but I found I could have real faith in my gas station Thor. Both kinds. The assurance of *'Aman* I'd learned in Hebrew school, and the substance of things hoped for, too.

"Say your detective finds him. Are you going to hurt him? Kill him?"

I almost smiled. Then I realized William wasn't kidding.

"No. I can't go to prison. I have to raise my kid. But he doesn't get to know me and me not know him. I can't let him . . ." This was the part I hadn't been able to put into words. Walcott had asked me this same question. If I couldn't maim him or put him in jail, why ask William to help me at all?

But William was nodding. "If you know who he is, you're one up on him. Right now he still has all the power."

"Yes!" I said, staring at him. God, but he was beautiful, and he got it. Paula could call him her Au-tastic Dr. Ashe—how I hated that oh-so-possessive pronoun—but he'd seen right into the meat of this and nailed it in two sentences. It made me mad that Walcott, a poet, supposedly able to plumb the human heart, couldn't. He thought since I couldn't prosecute the guy, I should walk away. He'd gone all Yoda on me. *Do, or do not.* He couldn't see that the in-between was all I had.

"Okay." William put his hands down flat on the counter and stood up, barely favoring his shot side now.

He came around the counter, toward me, and my breath caught. I turned toward him, waiting, something warm uncoiling in my belly. I realized that now, yes, now I was ready to be touched. Not in sympathy. Not all moist and huggy. I wanted him to come around the counter and put his hands on me and pull me to him. I wanted him to erase whatever had been done to me with the force of his own body and my absolute consent.

He came in close. So close, I could feel leftover, sleepy heat coming off his skin. He reached one long arm around me, took the bag, and stepped away.

"I'm going to grab a shower. I'll go into the lab tomorrow, see what I can learn." He headed for his room.

I literally felt myself deflating, all the air going out of me. I leaned against the counter, watching the man I wanted walk away. Damn, but he looked good doing it.

I watched William until he disappeared around the corner. He had recovered a good measure of the animal grace I'd seen in his body at the Circle K. I pulled a plush white paper towel off the roll on the counter. I scrubbed my mouth, wiping my kiss-me-not thick coat of lipstick away in a crimson smear. I took the band out of my hair and shook it out.

Walcott was right, in one way. I had been clapping to save Tinker Bell, throwing my whole heart at a pretend. I'd had a lot of practice. But the pot of velvet chowder on the stove behind me was my last. I was finished playing pattypans, and Paula better watch her effing back.

This was real. This was right-now real. I'd told the truth and handed William the bag, setting more than one thing into motion. I was done with lies and miracles, done letting my body be a dead zone under a crinoline. My body was broken in a different way from William's, but ever since the Circle K, we'd both been busy healing.

Mine was ready.

As soon as his was, too? I was going to try it out.

Chapter 8

*W*ednesday night, and William is driving home from the lab. He's gone in twice this week, but not to work. He's still on leave. He's been picking through the flotsam of Shandi's nonmiracle. It's the only thing he's found that can distract him as he waits for Detective Bialys to call him back and give him an update on Stevie's medical condition.

Very few other people on the planet are seeking this information. According to Bialys, only the Grants and the clerk from the Circle K robbery have called the hospital to ask. The only ones who care to know if Stevie is still living are people Stevie himself might have killed.

The doctors won't release that information. They tell the police, though, and Bialys passes the news along to William. He makes an exception because if Stevie dies, then William is the one who killed him. Bialys behaves as if this gives William the same rights as a relative, or perhaps a cop.

William spent the morning analyzing the fibers gleaned from Shandi's skirt and T-shirt, but today, Bialys should know if Stevie's life support will be continued or not. The simple molecular structure of ancient polyester couldn't hold William's attention. He did what was necessary, but by lunchtime, he returned to the cell samples for targeted testing, learning more than Shandi had ever asked to know.

Natty interests him enough to be distracting. They've been constructing a giant Lego spaceship. The child grasps the spatial relationships, even though the set is meant for teens and adults. As they work on it, he climbs William as if William were playground equipment and plops himself unceremoniously into William's lap. William, whose brain is also exceptional, was never a cuddlesome child. Natty reads phonetically and can intuit the meaning of unfamiliar, complicated words from context. He also looks directly into William's eyes and begins dialogues. William was nonverbal until he was almost two. At that point he began speaking in fully formed, precise sentences, but mostly for the purpose of disseminating information. He didn't engage in true back-and-forth dialogues until he was well into his preschool years.

William was only supposed to compare Natty's DNA to the other samples, establishing parenthood. But he kept testing. The human genome has been fully mapped, but not fully interpreted. Otherwise, William could have looked at the fingerprints and seen all that Natty was and is and will be. Natty has a superior intellect, but has paid no genetic penalty that William can find. His intelligence is like William's athleticism. A gift. William's speed and his excellent hand-eye coordination are atypical for a person with his genome.

Curious, he took the genetic material he had left from Shandi's Person X, amplified it, and checked for strings of code linked to the autism spectrum. William has these abnormalities stacked in every cell of himself, deletions and duplications on chromosome 16.

Shandi does not. Natty does not.

Natty's father does.

Interesting.

Early in his marriage, the idea of children made him physically aware of the absences and wrongfully duplicated base pairs that he carried. To procreate would be to risk a specific kind of failure. But Bridget, deeply Catholic, felt guilt over birth control.

It fell to him to be meticulously careful. It was William, always, who stopped, who opened the bedside drawer, who rolled on one of the condoms he kept stocked there. He did not believe in sin as such, but he posited for Bridget that he performed the bulk of theirs. Bridget didn't argue it, but she took it to confession every week.

A couple of years into the marriage, she stopped him as he reached for the drawer, boosting herself up on an elbow to kiss his shoulder, his neck. "Will, I think you've made your point."

He hovered over her, braced on his arms.

"I'm not making a point," he said. "I'm having a basic understanding of human biology."

She kissed his neck again, ran her hands down the length of him. "I'm having one, too, and I want babies."

He was taken aback by the plural. "How many?"

"Oh fifty, at least," she said, her breath in the hollow of his throat. "But we can start with one."

Poised over her, body surging toward her cell by cell, he heard his voice saying a true thing. It sounded harsh and loud, almost angry. "It could come out like me."

Bridget dropped onto her back and grinned up at him in her best way of grinning, the way where her eyes crinkled up until they were almost gone. She pulled him to her, saying in his ear, "I want *your* babies, stupid man. Specifically."

After, they lay face-to-face with their legs in a tangle, his genetic material already making its way to the only exact, specific egg that could ever have been Twyla.

He brushed her hair back from her eyes and said, very solemn, "Bridget. God was right. It's better with no condom."

She laughed, looking up, pretending to scan the ceiling for

impending lightning. "Dial the blasphemy down a notch, if you please. You know anything over seven gets me antsy." It was a sentence she said frequently, but never when she actually thought he'd been irreverent. A private joke for William and Bridget. God wasn't in on it.

Twyla had not been a genius. Her developmental progress fell within the norms delineated in the book that Bridget kept on her bedside table. Twyla achieved milestones on schedule, rolling over, sitting up, and babbling in the proper order, at the proper time.

In a room of a thousand human babies, an impartial panel of judges would not have chosen Twyla as superior. But to William, her genome was so beautiful. He could find himself in her, literally, and all that was not his belonged to Bridget. The genome told him Twyla was nothing that did not come from one of them, and yet, in a way so unquantifiable it had smacked of magic, she had been more than the sum of their parts. She had been her own empirical self. Twyla *had* been best, and William could have found her in that room of a thousand babies with his eyes closed.

He is approaching his regular turn into Morningside, but he doesn't take it. Shandi will be there, helping Natty refill the bird feeders while something bubbles on the stove. He doesn't want her as a witness when Bialys calls to tell him Stevie's fate. She was present when he introduced air and light to the previously closed environment of Stevie's skull cavity, and she has a vested interest in Stevie being dead. She'll feel relieved. Perhaps even pleased, and he's not sure what his face will do.

This road takes him into Decatur, and once he's there, he finds himself following a familiar path. It's not a good idea. He knows this, even as he comes to a stop in front of the painted brick cottage where Bridget's parents moved after their youngest started college.

There are lights on inside, and multiple cars are parked in the driveway. Bridget's parents' old Volvo is blocked in by her brother Michael's van and a couple of Toyotas that he doesn't recognize. The dented Honda Civic on the street belongs to her youngest sister, Maggie. Pieces of the Sullivan clan are gathering for dinner.

William is excellent at compartmentalization, but coming to this place is a mistake. It isn't good for him. He hadn't so much as thought the syllables of her name for months, until the Circle K. Now her memories rise thicker every day. He will not think of her. He thinks, instead, of Baxter. Baxter is inside, no doubt milling around the crowded kitchen, hoping someone will get clumsy and drop a slice of cheese or some chicken. He feels a tightening in his chest. He should put his foot down on the gas. Speed away. Go home.

He is not welcome. This is not acceptable behavior. But he pulls to the curb, letting the car idle. His breathing has accelerated, as if he sprinted all the way here. As if he is still sprinting.

William wants to get out of the car, go up the walk, and bang his fist against their silly purple door. When Bridget's father opens the door, William can say, "I want my damn dog."

William can't imagine what would happen next. Nothing pleasant. The Sullivans are mostly redheaded, and they all have quick tempers. He is not thinking of his wife, of what she called "the flash-fire angries." He will not. He thinks instead of her youngest sister, Maggie, who combines that same temper with poor impulse control. One day last year, she drove over to his house, rang the doorbell, and then hit him. She slapped her open hand hard up against the side of his head, making an angry face so like Bridget's angry face that he simply nodded in response. She looked instantly sorry, with Bridget's own instant-sorry face, and he stopped being willing to look at her at that point. When he finally opened his eyes again, his porch was empty.

He can't picture anything specific past demanding Baxter. Whatever happens, it won't be clean or kind or simple. He did not behave well after the accident.

His lips twist up then, because he is sitting in his car across the street from their house, like a stalker. He's still not behaving well.

But he leaves the car in park, trying to get air all the way down into his constricted lungs. Bialys's call is not the only reason he doesn't want to go home to Shandi.

Yesterday, dozing in his old familiar place on the rug, smelling fresh flowers and roasting meat, he heard a woman humming and the sound of small, bare feet slapping earnestly against the hardwoods. He fell into a strange peace. He forgot when he was. It was a nine-second sink into before.

He jerked awake in a belly-dropping swoop of vertigo.

The child running up and down the hall was only Natty, but Natty was no threat to Twyla's place. That's not how families are structured. In families, he realized, children are added to, not superseded. The addition of a child is not a betrayal of previous or current children.

Wives are structured differently.

His body is rocking itself forward and back from his hands, squeezing the wheel at ten and two. He can't have Shandi in his kitchen. He can't go home, risk taking pleasure in her approximation. He has come instead deliberately to this house, though he knows he shouldn't—

The headset at his ear chirps, and his whole body jumps and shudders out of rhythm. His hands are strangling the steering wheel, and he loosens them. He must not sit churning outside this house, thinking about procreation and the replaceable nature of wives.

Caller ID tells him it is Bialys.

William puts the car in drive, pulls away from the curb, pointing toward Morningside. He taps the earpiece and says, "Hello?" He has a practiced phone voice, pleasant and well modulated, but it fails him. It shakes and lacks volume.

"Dr. Ashe? That you?" It is Bialys. William focuses, thinks only of the detective. Bialys is a large, crumpled individual, soon to retire. The last time they met, Bialys had food on his tie.

"Yes," William says.

"Steven Parch is being taken off the ventilator. His uncle made the call this morning. I'm sorry. I only heard it now."

Now Bialys has his whole attention with no effort. A silence stretches out between them, very long, but Bialys doesn't seem to mind it. The uncle is Stevie's closest living relative, so Stevie breathes or stops breathing at his sole discretion. Stevie is not brain-dead, but he is in a "vegetative state." When Bialys first said this phrase, William thought, immediately, *The carrot feels nothing*. The longer it continues, the less likely it becomes that it will resolve itself favorably.

"He said he had a child," William insists. He remembers it perfectly, Stevie saying, *I'm a daddy myself. I ain't gonna shoot no little kids* . . .

"Not that we can find. Even if, Parch's kid would be a minor, and Parch wasn't married to the mother," Bialys says, as kindly as he can in his gruff, barking voice.

"When will it happen?" William asks.

"Not long. A day or two? It would be immediate, but the uncle's doing ten in Alabama. Prison complicates the paperwork. It doesn't help he's in another state."

William is turning into Morningside now. On one side of the car, the well-watered lawns of his neighbors are deep green. On his other side is Holy Shit Park. Asters bloom in the beds, and behind them, tall copper sneezeweed daisies are surrounded by butterflies. They flutter and pause, preening on the blooms. A hummingbird feeder hangs on a wrought-iron post, bright red and yellow, and north of here, a machine is breathing for Stevie. The machine is keeping him alive.

A day from now, or maybe two, William will have killed a man.

Into this second long silence, Detective Bialys says. "You understand, William, you're not in any legal trouble."

"I know," William says. He is on his street now. Paula's BMW is in front of his house. Shandi's yellow beetle isn't. So there's that. He pulls into the drive and stops. "This is the only possible outcome?"

"Just have to dot some *i*'s." There is another long pause, and then Bialys says, fast and low, "This is lucky. You have time to get right in your head. That's not how this works, most times. He had a gun, okay? A bunch of citizens lined up. It wasn't going anywhere good. You did the right thing." This is the most words William has ever heard him say in a row.

"I understand." William says. "Please call me. After."

"I will," Bialys promises. They hang up.

Perhaps there is no child.

But then why say it? It's an odd lie for a nineteen-year-old armed robber to tell. William has never been good at nuance, but when Stevie told Natty he was a daddy, it didn't sound like comfort. He didn't say to Natty, *I promise I won't shoot you.* He was boasting: *I made something. I am a father.*

With the engine off, William's car is quickly turning into an oven. He should go inside, but instead he hits the button, and the driver's-side window scrolls down. The July air outside is not much of an improvement.

So somewhere in the world, a child will grow up with no father instead of a drug-addled, criminal one. Six of one, as his own father used to say to indicate equivalence. But after Monday, there will not be a possible outcome where Stevie opens his eyes and stands up and says, *I'm better now. You didn't hit me all that hard.*

He wants this, though it is not rational. He doesn't care what happens to Stevie then. Stevie can go straight from the hospital to jail. In jail, William could forget him very quickly. Dead, he is an absence in the world that William has created.

Perhaps Stevie was lying, and there is no child. Perhaps when he dies, no one will care. Paula says that's pathetically sad, but it seems preferable to William. A dead person, wholly unconnected from other humans, is only so much meat.

Paula is standing in his open front door now, waving him in.

He gets out, and as he comes up the walk she says, "I managed to run Shandi off, for tonight, anyway. You're welcome. Did Bialys call you back?"

"They're taking him off the ventilator." He spreads his hands wide. There isn't any more to say about that.

"I figured they would," she says. "We could get truly, deeply drunk?" William shakes his head. "We could comfort-eat a vat of Mr. Feung's?"

"It's about half MSG," William says, going inside, walking with her toward the kitchen. "Might as well eat cat food."

"I like it," she says.

"Liking shit don't make it smell good," William says, and then he and Paula stop dead and look at each other.

It is a Bridget line, a colloquialism she learned from her mountain granny, Twyla Grace, up in North Carolina. She often quoted this earthy bit of wisdom when assessing Paula's latest boyfriend.

"Wow," Paula says.

"I don't know," William says, answering a question she hasn't asked.

Paula boosts herself up to sit on the kitchen counter. "You should get at least a little drunk. Grab us both a beer?"

He gets two from the fridge and tries to hand her one, but instead of taking it she grabs his wrist. She pulls him toward her until he is up against her knees on the counter. She wraps one ankle around his leg, pinning him, then stretches her spine up to put her face closer to his face than he likes. She has set all her features to be stern, pulling her eyebrows very far down, her mouth also down at the corners, to indicate that she is very, very serious.

"You better not be hoping to luck into another way to kill yourself. Even after Parch dies. I won't allow it."

William is much stronger than Paula; he could pull away. But Paula knows his definition of destiny. She knows he said that word in the Circle K, to Shandi, right after he took the bullet. Shandi told her, at the hospital. Paula is saying now, quite plainly, that she guessed the destiny he chose there. She is angry with him for it.

"You're very smart about people," William tells her. "It makes you good at your job, but I'm finding it a little inconvenient."

She refuses to be joked out of this. Her face stays stern, and she doesn't release him. "I'm a damn good lawyer, but I *planned* on being a clinically depressed, alcoholic, part-time barmaid. Just like Mom," she tells him. "You're the reason I'm not. You expected better of me. So don't be a glib little turd when I'm saving your sorry ass back."

Had Stevie been remotely competent, Paula would possess a large piece of the absence *he* left in the world. He owes her this.

"I won't do it again," he says. He holds his body still and lets her keep her face uncomfortably close to his as she continues.

"I don't believe you." Her voice is hard and low. "Why wouldn't you kill yourself? I've seen your style of grieving, and it flat sucks. For everyone. You shove comfort sideways. *No one* is allowed to be comforted. So now what? Should we all jump in front of bullets with you? Try something else, because you're rotting from the inside out. Stop rotting."

"I'm not rotting," William says.

Paula lets him go, taking one of the beers from him as he backs up.

"You're pretty much rotting, Bubba," Paula says. She twists off the cap and drinks. "Don't front like you're moving forward, either. You've got this pretty little object sublimating sex into nine thousand quarts of soup, and you stand there like you've misplaced your dick." She sounds like herself again. "Not that I think putting it to Shandi is the answer. God, please, spare us all *that* fresh-faced hell. But you have to do something with the rest of your dumb life. What are you going to do?"

"Work," William says. His work is valuable. In ten years, maybe less, his team could well end Parkinson's. Maybe he should go back full-time on Monday, six weeks off be damned. He can't sit through long days in the house after Stevie dies.

"You've been working," Paula says. "It's not enough."

"I need to start lifting. I'm going soft. I need to run."

"Brilliant. That sounds like the quickest way to tear your stitches open and drop your guts onto the pavement. Chicks dig scars, dumbass. Not gaping wounds," she says. "Do you want Shandi to dig your scars, William?"

He chuckles in spite of himself. Paula has a gift for making sentences have two meanings, and one of them is often dirty. "Quit it. Shandi isn't—" He has to stop there because the only word that ends the sentence properly is *Bridget*. Shandi isn't Bridget. Seven months ago, he told Paula she had to wipe that name from her vocabulary. They both did. He himself stopped thinking of his wife entirely. In the Circle K, she got back into his head; now she is threatening to become a sound in the room, an actual presence. Paula has only promised that she will not talk about Bridget until he does. He can't hand the name back to her.

"Shandi isn't correct," he finally says.

She chugs more beer, then smiles as she sets the bottle aside. "You like her, though. I know you like that kid she's got. Even though she isn't *correct*." Paula makes air quotes around the word as she speaks, to signal to William that she knows the name he almost said. The name that she is not allowed to say. "Or do you really think you two are *just friends*?"

She gives the last two words air quotes as well, indicating they are not meant literally, but he examines them in that light anyway. Making friends is not part of his skill set. Bridget made their couple friends, and most were affiliated with the parish or Bridget's work at the women's shelter. They don't come to this house now. He likes many of the people who work for him, but he likes them as a unit, the way he likes his football teams.

He knows things about Shandi as an individual. She has a sweet tooth and a running feud with her stepmother. She has an aversion to even the most interesting vermin and is attracted to primary colors. She prefers to eat things with her fingers, includ-

ing salad. She'll pick up a dry lettuce leaf and roll it around a
mushroom or an olive, then dip it into a dish of dressing on the
side. It's likely he has made a friend.

But what Paula is suggesting is a blank place in his head, like
trying to see a color that isn't on the spectrum. When he pictures
Shandi, she is all the way across a room. Holding a spoon.

Does he want to keep her there? He isn't sure. As a child,
William did not like being touched by people who were not his
parents. He'd fall down flailing and screaming if he was put into a
crowd of jostling children. Later, during adolescence, he came to
like the jarring slam of his body into other bodies during sports,
and puberty made sex an active interest. But outside these specific
realms, his body preferred to stay untouched inside a perimeter
that extended well beyond its skin.

He knew this was not socially appropriate. He'd discussed
herd-animal behavior with his therapist, who asked him to ob-
serve these behaviors in the people and animals around him. Once
he started looking, he realized social touch was happening almost
constantly, among his parents, his peers, even among his gerbils.

The gerbils were sisters, and they hadn't been complicated
enough to require individual names. He called them Mice Ladies,
collectively. William enjoyed their soothing, repetitive wheel
sounds, and they enjoyed one another. Mice Ladies slept in a
united ball, ate with their sides pressed against each other, and
took turns grooming one another's ears.

After a couple of years, the average gerbil life span, two of
them died. William didn't like to watch the remaining ancient
Mice Lady, huddling up against only herself in the corner. He
thought about distilling ether and fixing the problem, but she
died before it came to that.

Then he married Bridget and gained the pleasure of her con-
sistent, close proximity. The herb-and-orange-blossom smell of
her. Her legs twined in his and her hair spilled across his arm
every morning. Later, Twyla, lying on her back across his legs,

kicking and smiling in her toothless, charming way. He would sit still, experiencing the feel of his hand spanning his daughter's chest, the rapid, light tattooing of her baby heart, his other arm wrapped around Bridget, who liked to read tucked up against his side. He thought then, *We are being Mice Ladies. For all my higher functions, I am only Mice Ladies, after all.*

Now he thinks, *I should have named them,* and then he is disgusted with himself. Waiting for Stevie to die has put him off. Quoting Bridget's least-educated grandmother. Mooning over dead pets. Haunting the Sullivan house in Decatur. He *should* get drunk.

"Don't do anything you can't take back, is all I'm saying," Paula tells him now. "Not with bullets or Shandi."

William says, "I finished her lab work today."

It's an excellent segue. His new topic is both related to the current topic and of interest to Paula. It hits her politics correctly. She dislikes rapists considerably more than she dislikes Shandi.

"Oh good. Did you learn something useful? I promised her I'd check up on it, if she'd GTFO for the evening."

"I think so. There were eleven separate blue or gold polyester strands, probably from our guy. Those are Emory colors, so you could posit her attacker was affiliated with the school." This is good. A good, absorbing topic. He doesn't enjoy excessive drinking, but he doesn't want to think about Steven Parch. "Moreover, it's likely he was older. I'd look for an alum or even a professor."

Paula nods and helps herself to a second beer. "That's really helpful, because if some old fart crashed a frat party, people would remember him, you know?"

William doesn't know. When he went to Notre Dame, he stopped seeing the Atlanta therapist who made peer events mandatory. His parents wanted him to live at home and go to Emory, but William accepted a football scholarship at Bridget's first-choice school instead. His father was excited about the football, but both parents knew he could not tolerate dorm life. They worried his college experience would not be successful in spite of his intellect. In the end they let him go, but they rented a house for him and found him a new behaviorist in Indiana.

The new doc absolved him of parties, deciding it was fine for William to hang out with only Bridget and Paula after games. Dr. Bennett didn't know the three of them spent those hours driving William's SUV deep into the country to blow up thrift-store furniture in a fallow cornfield. William, cannier at nineteen, played up the fact that he had successfully formed two interpersonal relationships and kept his mouth shut about handcrafting explosives.

Paula asks, "Why couldn't it have been a student, though?"

"The jersey he was wearing was probably more than a decade old. That's why the fabric shed so much."

Paula sits up very straight then, setting down her beer. "The guy was wearing a blue and gold sports jersey? And it was weirdly old?"

William nods. "Weird for a college kid. Not an adult. I've got shirts that old."

Paula jams both hands into her hair, her voice rising in both pitch and volume. "No, shut up. This was Kappu Nu? That house?"

"Yes?" he says.

"Holy crap, William! Shandi's looking for a guy on the Emory Football Team!" Paula is spinning and heading out of the kitchen at a fast clip.

"Emory doesn't have a football team," William says, following her. He should know.

"Kappa Nu has one, though," Paula says over her shoulder. She is practically running into his office. "They've had one for years. It's a joke, like an old joke, or a ritual. Emory doesn't have a football team, and Kappa Nu doesn't have virgins. Like, virgins and a football team are mythological. Pledges have to prove that they aren't virgins before initiation." She sits down in the desk chair and starts swishing the mouse around to put his screen saver to sleep.

"Prove how?" William asks. Paula's sexual-knowledge base is vast, another reason she is such a good divorce attorney.

Paula clicks his browser and it opens into Google. "Not really prove. It's all bullshit, for hazing. They'll call a couple of the guys cherries to yank chains, and stick 'em on the Emory Football Team. They've got the original jerseys in a box in the attic, with all these superstitions built in around them. Each jersey has a history. Some have lucky numbers, some are duds." Paula is typing in search terms now while she talks. "The cherries have to wear their assigned jerseys to every social, every party, until they can, you know, get off the team. You get off by banging someone, 'scuse the pun, like, say, at a Kappa Nu party. Like, say, at the party Shandi visited, you savvy?"

The overhead light is putting a glare on the screen so William flips the office light off and leans down beside her so that he can see. She has typed in: Kappu Nu, Rush, Emory Football Team.

"They have a website?"

If Paula is correct, she and William could be solving Shandi's puzzle definitively, when William is only supposed to give her lab reports and options. He is not prepared to deliver a specific human male. There is an uncomfortable dissonance in saying, *Thank you for the soup and the post-op care you have administered. As a token of my appreciation, I have found the man who assaulted you.*

Paula is grinning, the blue light of the monitor shining off her teeth. "Oh, hell yeah, they do. They take a team picture every year. It went digi maybe ten years ago? Before that they used to put Polaroids on the house bulletin board."

"How do you know all this?" William asks.

"Please," Paula says, with a sideways glance that tells him clearly that he is being a dumbass.

He *is* being a dumbass. Paula knows because ten years ago, she no doubt peeled a few jerseys off aspiring Kappa Nus herself.

Paula, Paula, Wein-ah Hop-pah, she's your friendly Cherry Poppah, the rhyme began, back when they were in high school. There were multiple verses.

He and Paula met under such circumstances, at a party. He was a sophomore in high school, and it was the first night he started for varsity. His team won. More than won. At the end his teammates all pounded and slapped at him, called him William the Destroyer.

He was in the basement rec room, where Chuck K., Davis, and Chuck M. were shooting nine ball. They were drinking beer and listing their sex girls, like a contest. William wasn't drinking because he was not of legal age to drink, and he wasn't playing pool because he'd run the table twice already. Chuck K. had told him to sit down.

He shrugged when they asked him to list his sex girls, partly because he hadn't had any, and partly because he'd brought a really good book about frontier orbitals. Every time one of them spoke to him, he had to put his finger in to mark his place and make his eyes look at them until they stopped talking. His therapist had forbidden him to read during peer conversations.

"You never?" Davis said.

Chuck K. clutched his heart and pretended to die of surprise. He was the Chuck that everyone said was hilarious. Chuck K. let Davis and the less amusing Chuck have the game and went upstairs to where the actual party was writhing and pulsing in its intolerable way.

A few minutes later, Chuck K. came back. Paula was with him.

William knew who she was. She was famous at his school. Famous for sex. There were a few other girls who were as famous, but they were divided into two tribes, black and white. With her reddish-brown skin, shaggy hair, and pale, canted eyes, she was too racially indeterminate to fit at any lunch table. She ate alone and walked alone and had sex with half the school, if his teammates could be believed. William believed some of them.

She came across the rec room toward him in a short, swirly skirt, swaying her hips, her fingertips brushing the smooth skin of her copper-colored thighs.

She stepped in and stood between his legs. William could feel the cold of the fresh beer on her breath. He didn't mind her coming in this close. At all.

She looked right at him and said, "He's too cute to be a total charity case." The pronoun indicated she was speaking to Chuck K., but then she said, "Come on, if you're coming." That part seemed to be to William.

She started walking away, and William got up off the stool and followed her, in case she meant to lead him into sex. He'd played JV as a freshman, but he knew the varsity boys were often given sex.

As he caught up, she grabbed his hand and turned, tugging him down a hallway. Her hand was small inside his, the touch of it intensely interesting: he felt his way along her fingers to her palm. Her hand was dry and cool. She led him to a small guest room in the basement. He could hear Chuck K. and Davis and Chuck M. hooting as they went.

She sat him on the bed and swung her denim purse off her shoulder to plop onto the mattress beside him. She stood between his legs, weaving, looking down at him, her face framed by her shaggy black hair.

She pulled at his shirt and he lifted his arms obediently so she could peel it off. She ran her hands over the sculpted planes of his chest and belly.

"God, I love athletes," she said.

She leaned down, coming at him with her lips wet and already parted. He barely had time to hide his secret penny low in the back of his mouth, between his molars and his cheek.

Kissing was slippery, but he liked the foreign feel of her tongue, a strange beery muscle invading his mouth like it was looking for his penny. His body sparked to it in red, unfathomable ways. He could hear the party's music thumping above them, and from down the hall, the faint clatter of pool balls banging into one another and the raucous voices of his teammates, too far to make out words.

She took her shirt off. He couldn't hear the sounds anymore because his whole brain was using itself to see things. Her breasts were full on the bottom, but sloped on top, so that the nipples tilted up.

She put his hands on them. The brown skin here was paler than her other skin, and her nipples were the same color as wet maple sugar. He wanted to put one in his mouth, but he wasn't sure if it was allowed.

She knelt between his knees. His brain was swamped with images, trying to catalog all the naked ways she was for later: Her back, bending over him so her spine bowed and her hair fell forward. Her bared nape, paler, like her breasts. Her black hair falling across his lap, covering her hands as she worked him out of his fly.

She peeled his jeans all the way off, pulling his shoes and socks off, too. His gaze caught on the flare of her hips above her skirt's low band.

Her lips closed over him. He swallowed the penny. His spine stopped working and he fell back. He had a moment to wonder how a mouth could feel so molten hot and liquid but apply the rhythmic pressure all the same. Then his mind shut down and his body was an animal, unthinking and alive. His brain didn't think of anything at all. He drained away out of himself and disappeared into her.

He blinked up at the ceiling, surprised.

Her head and shoulders popped up over the edge of the bed. She was grinning. "Wow, really?"

He wasn't sure what she meant. She crawled up beside him, still topless. The tips of her breasts scraped against his side as she slid, and he felt the rhythm she'd set restarting in his hips. Her smell, her skin, her separateness, these things made the orgasm feel like more than an expedient path to sleep. He rolled toward her, his erection already back, pressing into her skirt. She laughed and said, "Wow, really?" again, but in an entirely different tone. This time, he understood it.

"Yes, please," he said, and even to his ears it sounded dry and formal. The way he'd been taught to accept a cracker from his elderly neighbor.

"Well, since you're so polite."

She flopped onto her back, which made her breasts sway on top of her chest in a wholly distracting manner. She didn't move to put him in her mouth again. He looked at her face, and she was making an expression that he recognized. It was a sports face, usually seen on someone on the other team, across the line. Someone who mistakenly believed he could protect his quarterback from William.

She was, as Chuck K. would say, daring him to *bring it*. The expression was familiar enough for him to recognize it, even out of context, but William had only the most clinical understanding of what this particular *it* was.

He sat up and assessed her, naked from the waist up. Her scuffed clogs had dropped off, leaving her feet bare. Her shoes looked small, lying amid all the parts of his abandoned clothing. Her toenails were painted pale blue. She was lying down. As he had been.

He gave her a brief nod, then slid down to kneel on the carpet where she had knelt, pushing her cotton skirt up into a bunch around her waist. She was wearing very small panties, also pale blue, so sheer he could see the dark thatch of her hair. He moved in close, so the width of his shoulders pushed her legs apart, and he pulled her hips toward him, so her legs had to bend or they would come off the bed. He pushed the flimsy center panel of the panties aside, examining the surprising complications of her in the lamplight. After a few seconds, she made a little laugh.

"Are you, what, looking at my cooter?" she said.

Rhetorical, he decided.

After another few seconds she said, "Yo, freakshow, *why* are you looking at my cooter?"

This did seem to require an answer. He didn't have one, so he put his mouth on her, using his tongue the way she had when she kissed him, like he was the one looking for a secret penny now. Her breath pulled in and her back arched. In the simple, physical immediacy of her body bowing up, involuntary, he understood her. He relaxed. She was only an animal, like him. She was only another little animal, after all.

"Boys don't really do this," she said. Her voice sounded compressed and strange. But this wasn't the same as saying not to, and her little thighs flexed and clenched against his ears. Her feet paddled at his back, but gently, not kicking. He stayed where he was, learning her interesting smells and textures, until she was only her body, too, the way he had been, her hands fisted in his hair, her breath ragged.

Then she started crying. He was alarmed, and crawled up to make sure he wasn't raping her; as a freshman, he'd had a seminar in gym about no meaning no, and crying meaning no, too, but when he got up to her face, it didn't seem to be a bad crying. She was smiling at him.

He was still hard, pressed against her bared hip. She felt him there and went scrabbling in the purse beside them for a condom. She pushed him onto his back and threw one leg over him, like she was climbing on a horse.

He'd had a therapy horse named Buck when he was very young, and what happened next was like that, except wholly different. Partially because this time he was the one being ridden, and mostly because the pleasures of this ride progressed exponentially into a madness. It felt unstoppable and oddly connective, a form of communication with cues he could read, free of the exhaustion of conversation.

Well, she talked some. She said things like, "I was only going to blow you, but, oh well." And, "Don't tell anyone, but I never came with a boy before." Nothing that he had to answer.

After, he felt as if they had completed a rigorous sporting event together. He felt warmly toward her, just as he did toward his football team's skilled kicker. And, much like in football, the team he'd formed with Paula had won, their first time out.

He knew several of his teammates had been with her in this way, and it bothered him to see she was not treated as a teammate when she carried her tray past their lunch table the next day. They sniggered and poked William with their elbows, but none of them greeted her. There was no justice in it.

He picked up his tray and followed her, sitting down beside

her at her habitual table. She made a surprised face, but didn't tell him to move along. They ate quietly, William reading and Paula doodling in a sketchbook.

At the end she said, "Do you think I'm your girlfriend now, Bubba?"

"No," he said. Then, with interest, "Wait, are you?"

"Please," she said. But she said "hey" to him in the hall later, that same *bring it* expression on her face, and accepted his returned greeting with puzzled eyebrows. He sat with her the next day, and the next. Within a month, neither of them could fathom how their lives had worked before, without the other.

They never had sex again. She moved on to the next in the long series of boys and men he would call Buddy when they came to Bridget's brunches. All the shits that didn't smell good, even when she liked them. Paula's Buddies were grateful. Easily dismissed. It was Bridget who eventually explained that Paula hadn't slept with him again because she'd decided that he wasn't one of them.

Paula, in her thirties now, still has Buddies who require so little to be pleased that she barely acknowledges they're breathing. Paula, in her late teens and early twenties, would have run across the Emory Football Team.

The subpage of the Kappu Nu website has loaded. Paula is correct. They have team photos organized by year on a drop-down menu. This year's team has not yet been assembled, so the page shows last year's. Four boys stand in a line wearing football jerseys. They all hold tiny American flags and look uncomfortable.

"That's a big team. The guys they do this to are the obligatory pledges. Legacies. The scrubs they have to take, you know?" He doesn't know, but nods so that she won't explain. "Natty is what, three?" she asks, doing quick math in her head. "So we want the team from four years back."

She rolls the mouse down the menu and the picture loads. There are only two, kneeling like football players in the front row of a team shot, one knee up and one knee down. The caption says, *Quarterback Marvin James and Point Guard Clayton Lilli*. Both boys wear the ancient blue and gold jerseys. The guy on the left, number 66, is a soft-looking black kid with a huge Adam's apple. Clearly not Natty's father.

But the kid in jersey 13? He is racially appropriate, long and gangly, with wide cheekbones and a delicate chin. He has straight brown hair and a thin nose that flairs wide at the end. Thick glasses hide his eyes.

"Could be," William says.

He still feels loathe to hand this off to Shandi in the form of a single unproved possibility with a face and a name. It's too personal, bound to be unsettling. When she asked him to help her, she was already overwrought. She cooked while she spoke, and he'd watched her putting in at least a quarter cup of salt. He poured the inedible soup down the sink rather than upset her further. Paula's knowledge base has complicated things.

Paula stands abruptly, walking quickly away toward the window. William takes her place in the desk chair, looking at Clayton Lilli more closely, squinting at his ears. Shandi's earlobes dangle, and Natty's are attached. If Clayton Lilli's dangle, he can be ruled out as a genetic possibility as surely as the black team member. But this is a whole body shot, not a close-up, and Lilli's limp hair hangs down, obscuring much of his ears. William needs a head shot. He opens a second browser window, and goes to Google images.

"Oh my God," Paula says in a strangled voice, peering out the window.

William is busy typing in the name "Clayton Lilli." It's unusual, but is it unusual enough? Perhaps he needs more search terms.

"William! William!" Paula calls. Her tone is urgent.

"What?" he says, looking up from the screen.

She doesn't turn around. She has shoved the curtains to one side and her palms are pressed flat against the glass. The room is dark, and outside, in his yard, he can see a faint orange light.

Paula says, "Your car is on fire."

He gets up immediately and comes to the window, pushing in beside her.

So it is.

For a moment, he is once again caught in the free fall of vertigo. His heart pounds when he sees the orange glow inside his car. The breath leaves his body, and the exhale shapes itself into her name. For the span of that half breath, the fire reads like a reverse love letter, a violent *no*, an angry bomb set in answer to his long-ago fireworks.

By the inhale, he knows this is ridiculous. And yet the feeling lingers as he sprints for the extinguisher.

Chapter 9

I knew nothing about seduction when I started. Now, at least, I knew that I was bad at it. I also knew it required more than a wardrobe change, no matter what music videos and a thousand romantic comedies had taught me. Most of all, I'd learned it was impossible to give it a serious go without a babysitter.

I didn't have one. Walcott hadn't returned my last three calls. Another couple days of this crap and I'd get in my car and drive to Lumpkin County to see if he had died and forgotten to tell me.

I couldn't invite Mimmy to Dad's condo, even though Dad had cleared out. (He'd stopped by twice, bearing gifts, but he'd used the doorbell like a guest. He said he wanted it to be our place, for real.) That left mixing Natty in with my half brothers for Bethany's nanny to keep. The boys all got along, and Bethany hated it as a bonus, but Oscar was recovering from a stomach flu. That closed that option off until at least the weekend.

William didn't seem to mind me and Natty showing up and hanging out, but he didn't try to jump me just because I put on my red Marilyn dress or the micro-est of all my seventies minis. I tried speaking in a husky voice, and he asked me, "Do you need

a lozenge?" like I was his wheezy grampa. I even tried to channel Reese Witherspoon, dropping a pen when he was behind me
and starting a slow bend to pick it up. He stepped around and
got it for me, leaving me jacked at the waist and feeling like fifty
different kinds of fool. It didn't help that I suspected Paula would
know exactly how to do this. Assuming she wasn't doing it—and
more—already.

My time was running out. He slept less and went on long
walks now. He spent hours at his lab, analyzing the cheek swabs
and the bag I'd given him. He spoke as if any day now he would
have a tidy file of facts for me to take to a P.I. and our business
would be done.

I still didn't believe that. I thought, instead, that the great
god Thor would find the actual guy—a name and a mailing address and a face. His identity would be the world's worst present,
wrapped in a bloodred bow, because then I'd have to choose.
Once the Golem had a face, I'd have to decide what to do with
him, or to him. What if I was the first link in a long chain of
drugged girls? Could I stop him and still keep Natty safe from
ever knowing? Part of me hoped he would be so distant that I
would have no choice but to let it go. Like if he was in Alaska, or
dead. Maybe even dead in Alaska.

God, I wanted to know who he was, though. More than that.
I knew that I would know. My heart believed in it, in William, in
spite of every rational thing my mind said.

Wednesday, I got to his house while he was still at the lab. I let
myself in with the hidden outside key, and then I taught Natty to
play blackjack, using jelly beans for chips. He cleaned me out of all
my reds and oranges and was swinging his feet and sneak-eating
his winnings when I heard the door opening.

I leapt to my feet, smoothing my pencil skirt. I'd paired it
with a low-cut top and a push-up bra that understood exactly how
to work that neckline.

It was Paula, though, hours early, carrying her inevitable six-pack. She lounged in the doorway, eyeballing my cleavage, and said, "Yowsa! Put those away before someone loses an eye."

Natty swung around on his bar seat to watch her cross the room, while I tugged uncomfortably at my blouse. She moved Natty's art supplies down a foot and then banged the six-pack onto the coffee table, like she had such immediate plans for it that there was no reason to take it to the fridge. She plopped onto the sofa, slipping her black heels off and putting her bare feet up beside the beer, claiming the space. "Hiyas, Natty."

"Hiyas, Paula," said Natty, and his wide, red smile told me two things: he'd eaten enough jelly beans to thoroughly spoil his dinner, and he liked Paula just fine. I bet men of all ages liked her fine. Her bare legs were cinnamon colored and eighty miles long.

"Pack up your stuff," Paula told him. "Tonight is grown-ups night. You and your mom are going home now."

Natty started pushing the remaining jelly beans into a heap, obedient.

"No, we're not. Go work on your poster," I said, lifting him down.

Natty paused, looking back and forth between us. The Word of Mom won; he went to the coffee table and began coloring his purely godawful diagram of all the pieces of a beetle.

Paula put her hands behind her head, elbows bent, and stretched herself upward, spine bowing like a cat's. I heard her back crack from across the room. For a minute the only sound in the room was the back-and-forth sawing of Natty's crayon on the poster board. Then Paula started talking, apparently to the ceiling. She sure wasn't looking at me.

"Did you know that Bridget once signed on to be a nun?" Paula told the ceiling. She had my whole attention the second she said that name, and she knew it. "The first vows are temporary. They last three years, in case you aren't down with how the sisters go. But they are real vows. Poverty. Obedience. Chastity. That's the one that gets me. If you take the next set of vows, it's chastity, your whole life long. Can you imagine?"

I could, actually. I *had* imagined it, vividly, every time I broke up with a boyfriend, feeling permanently borked. But all I said was, "What's your point, here?"

Paula chuckled and lay her head back, like she was done talking, but she had brought up Bridget for a reason. A nun. Who marries nuns? William, apparently. Perhaps her point was that he wouldn't pick a follow-up who was as far from pure as I was. Maybe the sexpot wardrobe was actually working against me, and I'd do better in a burka. But if so, Paula and her skirts and her constant ooze of pheromones was as out of luck as I was.

Paula started talking again, still addressing the ceiling, "She worked at a mission down in the projects. William was doing this intense MD/PhD program at Emory, but he never let Bridget go alone. Can't you see him, with those sledgehammer arms and very few discernible facial expressions, dragging a laptop and fifty pounds of textbooks, studying, while Bridget bent over a Dick-and-Jane book, teaching some detoxing, underage, illegal Mexican hooker to say 'The pencil is yellow' in English."

"Little pitchers," I said.

Paula glanced at Natty, wielding a blue Crayola with his head bent. He'd copied the bug parts diagram freehand from one of William's books, making it huge. To decorate his room, he'd said. I could have cheerfully lived out my whole life without ever knowing what-all chunks made a bug, but Natty was entranced.

"Him? He's not listening," Paula said.

"He's always listening," I said, and then added without changing my tone, "Are you listening?"

"Yep," Natty said.

Paula chuckled and said, "Fine. I'll do the Disney version. After that, she went to the convent for twelve months of prayer and meditation before her final vows. No contact with the outside world at all. William was still at Emory, but his research was so hot Geneti-Tech had already signed him on. He was working eighty-, ninety-hour weeks, sleeping four hours a night. Guess where William went, every Saturday? That damn convent. It was almost two hundred miles away. Bridget wouldn't come out, but there he was, up on the hillside every weekend, working on his laptop while the battery lasted, then doing push-ups, doing whatever crazy math William does for fun inside his head. He went all through fall, through the dead of winter. It rained every day in February, but William was there, running laps around the campus in the downpours." She looked down at Natty. "That's really cool, there, Natty. What is that?"

"A thorax," Natty said.

"Does this story have a moral?" I asked her, impatient.

I figured I already knew it. She was showing me Bridget's perfect dead-nun shoes, the ones I'd hatefully said that Bridget wasn't using. She was telling me I could never grow big enough goodness feet to fill them.

But she surprised me, meeting my eyes and speaking with slow deliberation. "That's what it looks like: William in love. Does it sound at all familiar?"

It was a low blow, and it landed. I'd never seen the William she described, but oh, I could imagine him. What that would feel like, to have him lay siege to the condo, pacing outside it like a massive wolf, howling for me to come down? I wanted, instantly, desperately, to see it for myself. Up close and super personal.

"Have you?" I challenged her back.

"Yes. Of course I have," she said, smiling a wide smile that showed me all her teeth. Her dog teeth were exceptionally pointy. "But, hey, stay here. Make him a cozy dinner. He is desperately lonely. If I get out of the way, you could very well become the thing he'll settle for."

She said it all fake encouraging, like she was bucking me up. She was so at ease on the sofa, like this was her home, too, already. On some level she was enjoying this, and I was not. William could be at the lab for hours, and I didn't want to stay here, sparring with her. Especially since I was losing. I stood up.

"Come on, Natty, let's pack up your . . . thorax."

Natty said, indignant, "It's a beetle. Only this one part is a thorax."

I picked up Natty's poster for him. He took his bag of crayons.

Paula walked us out, playing hostess in a fake-gracious way that made my hands feel itchy with a faint desire to slap her. When we got to the door, Natty went kangaroo-hopping away across the grass, heading toward the car.

I paused and said to Paula, quietly, but sharp, "Can you please at least tell William to call me if he gets done with the tests today?"

"I'm sure he'll call, if he has something for you." Paula's lemon-twist smile gave the words a second meaning.

"Oh, go to hell," I said. I turned to go.

I heard her blow out an exasperated sigh, and then she called after me, "I will make sure you get the labs."

"Sure you will," I said. I kept walking.

"Hey. Hey!" she said, and something in her tone made me pause and look back at her. "Do you know what I do for a living?"

I was surprised enough by the question to answer it. "You're a divorce lawyer."

"Yeah, a great one. I only work for women," Paula said. "I don't let men screw women over. Ever, when I can help it. Even if I think that the women are heartless, pushy, baby whores. Don't take that personally. It describes a large portion of my clientele. When your labs are done, I'll get the info to you. Period."

She shut the door, but I believed her. I hated that I believed her, but I did, enough to worry that she would take over and bring the reports to me, too. I wanted William to come to me, to follow me the way he'd once followed Bridget to a convent. I wanted him to bring me more than lab reports. I couldn't see any of it happening with her camped out here, so I went home.

By nine o'clock, Natty was asleep, and William hadn't called. Maybe he hadn't finished yet. He could be at the lab, finding the Golem right now. Or he could be putting a dent in that six-pack with Paula, while she dripped all kinds of anti-Shandi poison in his ear and ran her bare toe up and down his leg.

I'd decided I might as well go to sleep, too, if I could stop the anxious twine of waiting from unspooling in my belly long enough to drop off. I needed to get at least an hour or two before Natty's parade of bad dreams started.

I was heading up the stairs when the doorbell rang. I ran for the door with every organ in my middle trying to jam itself up into my throat. I half believed I'd see William there, in those low-slung faded jeans, coming after me like he'd once gone after Bridget, and bringing me my answers, too.

When I looked through the peephole, it was Walcott, standing on the stoop. I was too relieved to see him to be very disappointed. I threw the door open.

"Thank God, come in! Are we okay? You keep shunting me to voice mail, and I'm having desperate sorrows. When did you get in town?"

"Just now," he said, going past me into the condo's leather-and-chrome infested den. It was an awful room, made of angles and sharp glass edges, as if Bethany had told her decorator to make it a place where American Psycho would be totally at home. Right now, her cold-ass aesthetic was softened by the place being so filthy. With Dad using the on-call rooms at the hospital and me mostly at William's, it had degenerated into a flophouse. Dishes and Natty's cowboy things and all my laundry lay scattered across its sleek surfaces.

I followed Walcott, feeling strangely shy. We were almost never at odds. I didn't know how to manage it. To fill the silence—I never had awkward silences with Walcott!—I said, "My dad got Natty that Lego Death Star." It was a four-hundred-dollar toy, one of the unstoppable penance-gifts Dad was showering down on us, courtesy of Bethany being such a butthole right after the robbery.

"Oh, cool! Can I see it?"

Misfire. I flushed as I said, "It's at William's." I could feel Walcott bristling. "Are you thirsty? I have beer and Cokes and I don't know what all."

"Sure."

We passed through into the kitchen, which had a lot of stainless steel and slate gray granite countertops, but still was not as oppressive as the living room. If I were decorating for my dad, I'd do rich creams and deep, warm browns with a fat, welcoming sofa and a leather wingback.

"How's Natty doing?" Walcott asked. "He already in bed?"

"Yeah. He's not great," I said. I got a beer out of the fridge and pushed it into his hand. "Mimmy offered to come spend the weekend, which might do Natty a world of good, but Lord. I can't even imagine opening that negotiation with Bethany. I don't own anything worth her allowing The Mimmy to come pee in her territory. Unless maybe Bethany needs a kidney? I have a spare."

"Bethany's more Tin Man," Walcott said. He didn't open his beer, just held it, and added, strangely rueful, "Too bad you only have the one heart."

It was the kind of wryly mawkish joke he made when he'd been out overdrinking with the other poets, but he hadn't even touched his beer. I got one, too, and then boosted myself up onto the countertop. I took a swig and it was so good, cold and really bitey. It was one of Dad's small-batch local brews that cost the earth.

"I'm glad you're finally here, Walcott. I hate being out of sorts with you. It makes everything taste like crap. Can you stay over? Maybe take a shift with Natty? I would pay you four cherry Pop-Tarts. It would seriously change my quality of life if I could get three hours of uninterrupted sleep."

"Oh. Well. Hmm. I don't think I can do that." He said it slow, almost regretful.

"Poop. Are you still mad at me?" He shook his head. "Why then? Because of CeeCee?" I asked, rolling my eyes.

I'd introduced CeeCee to Walcott, and she knew we'd been

slipping out our windows and sleeping at each other's houses on the sly since we were nine. Ever since they got serious, though, she'd been making pushy little dabs at me, trying to step me out of territories she wanted only for herself, acting as if I were some kind of rival.

"Forget CeeCee. I broke up with CeeCee that night after the robbery."

I looked at him then, really looked at him, studying his face in the kitchen's bright lights. His mop of unruly brown hair was tufted up crazy like it got when he was stressed or his writing wasn't going well. He had thick eyebrows arched over large, deep-set eyes. His nose was unapologetically big, but it was a noble damn nose, no matter what he said about it, balanced by his wide, full mouth. His face was so familiar that I hadn't really looked at him, hadn't noticed how his skin was drawn tight over his angular skull. He had purple circles under his eyes that rivaled mine.

"You didn't tell me. Are you okay? I'm such an ass! Are you having PTSD, too?"

"I'm not sleeping great," Walcott said, setting his untasted beer aside. "Listen, I can't drink this. I can't sleep over, none of that, because you are about to be furious and want me out of here."

I blinked, taken aback, and then laughed. "I never want you out of anywhere."

"You will this time. I came to ask you to put the brakes on all this crap with William Ashe."

I sparked into an instant anger, just as Walcott had predicted, and that made me even madder. "That ship has sailed."

Walcott shook his head. "I don't mean the lab stuff." He looked away, desperately unhappy. "I mean stop going over to his house all the time. Don't let him build the Death Star with Natty. I should do the Death Star."

I puffed air out in a *psh* noise. "William is not going to replace you with Natty, or with me. You have a Walcott-shaped perma-spot with us."

"Stop being thick," Walcott said. "I'm trying—with what has to be the least amount of grace of any poet in the history of time—I'm trying to tell you, I'm in love with you."

He said it so mild and calm and simple that I couldn't process the words for a second or two. Then I said, "No, you aren't."

"I am, though," he said, holding one hand out toward me like he was offering an apology. "Apparently I've been in love with you for years now."

"No, you have not," I said, a fringe of anger tickling across my skin, because this declaration felt like a betrayal. "What are you saying? That you've been all secretly pining, the whole time, like a trick?" It was too dishonest, and I couldn't bear it if every disdainful thing I thought about Paula was true for Walcott, too. The idea that Walcott—my Walcott—had kept a secret of such magnitude! If he'd always had some nasty, sexed, romantical agenda, it negated everything we'd ever been. But he was shaking his head, vehement.

"I didn't know," Walcott said. "Or I did. But only in the back of my heart. Maybe I felt a kind of waiting? I never thought about it, same way I don't think about breathing. It was a quiet fact, that we would be an us, eventually. When we were old enough to not eff it up. I'm pretty sure you knew it, too, before all that shit went down at the Kappa house." I was shaking my head no, but he kept talking. "Then you were in that Circle K, and it occurred to me that you could die. There I was, waiting for us to grow up enough to make our real life happen, and all at once I was looking at a tomorrow with the world still spinning, except you wouldn't be on it. Natty wouldn't be on it. So I—"

"Walcott!" I interrupted. "This is a reaction to the stress. This isn't real."

He shook his head. "Remember when the cops brought you out? That's when I understood. I've been trying hard to tamp it back, but I can't. It happened, and it won't unhappen."

I remembered. They drove William away in the ambulance,

and the cop who looked like Samuel L. Jackson took charge of me. He was escorting us toward his car, when I spotted Walcott talking to another cop near the perimeter. I changed our course, beelining toward him. Walcott's face looked like it was made out of wallpaper paste. He had drying brownish blood all over his favorite Pixies T-shirt. I still had brown streaks of William's blood on my hands, and I thought to myself, *Oh, look, we match.*

Natty spotted Walcott then and came alive in my arms, hollering, "Walcott! Walcott!"

Walcott turned and saw us coming. His face broke into a wide, weird smile, an unreadable look spreading over his face as he watched us coming. It was familiar. I had seen him make this face before, but I couldn't place it. I sped up, almost running toward him with the cop pacing me.

Just as we reached him, before I could lay hands on him, Walcott turned and doubled up and puked into the grass. He heaved and heaved, with his outsize hands dangling down, his arms braced on his bent knees.

I thought, *Oh, man! I'm the only one who got to keep Mimmy's fantastic rage lunch.*

Between heaves, he reared up to look at me and say, "Hi. Oh, hi," with that weird look still on his face.

The cop went and got him a bottle of water, and then I had to give my statement, so I'd forgotten about trying to place his strange expression.

Standing in the overelegant kitchen, I finally realized where I had seen Walcott make that face before. It was his bad hangover face, from the few times when he had truly overdone it. It was a face he made when he felt poisoned near to death.

The taste of the beer soured in my mouth. It was true, then. He fucking loved me.

He was still talking, and with such calm finality it was absolutely terrifying. "Shandi, I think you were in love with me. Before. Maybe you still are, but you haven't noticed, because

I've politely chosen not to be in a hostage situation." I didn't say anything, but I guess not saying anything was answer enough. He shrugged and looked away from me, blinking rapidly. "Did I miss the window? Every time I text you, these days, you're at his house. Are you with him?"

"No. It's more like—" I stopped talking, finally clueing in, and feeling like an idiot. Walcott hadn't been objecting to my hunt for the Golem. Walcott had never been dim or missed the point. He was jealous of William.

He said, "Whatever. I don't care. I'm asking if there's room for us to try this out." He waved his hand forward and back, drawing an invisible connecting line in the air between us.

I was shaking my head, not like no, but more because I couldn't process. "Walcott, come on. We already did that."

"Did what?" Walcott said.

"You know," I said. He shook his head, mystified. He really didn't. "You *know*," I said, but I didn't have a word for it. What Walcott and I did together, while not exactly pleasant, was too funny and too friendly for that ugly f-word. Had sex? Cold and clinical. Did it? That sounded so giggly-fifties-poodle-skirt, and way too shy. Made love? Puke. "Two years ago? You know!" I yelled, thoroughly frustrated, and I saw understanding finally dawn.

"You're kidding me, right?" he said.

"No?" I said. "You were there. We did what we did, and neither one of us saw unicorns or rainbows."

Now he was laughing, but I could see that under that, he was getting angry. "I'm kind of insulted. You're going to count that?"

I swallowed and looked away. "It was enough to know there isn't any *there* there."

He shoved his hands through his hair, nostrils flaring. "We didn't even kiss! And have you ever had a *there* there? With Doug or whatever that other old dude's name was?"

"Richard," I said, feeling pretty sure he'd just changed my attraction-meaning *there there* to a much dirtier euphemism. "That question is cheating. You know I didn't."

My former boyfriend, Doug, was the only reason Walcott and I did what we did in the first place. Doug wasn't some punk college boy. He was an actual man, divorced, with a couple of kids. He had the kind of job that came with health insurance, and he took me to dinner in real restaurants. He didn't go skateboarding or drink dollar beer and he wasn't interested in making out in any kind of vehicle. He wanted a grown-up, actual relationship, one that included sex.

I wanted those things, too, but I was too freaked out to give Doug the green light.

My sticking point was, Doug believed I was experienced. He hadn't met Natty, but he knew Natty existed. In reality, I'd had exactly one boyfriend in high school before Natty happened. His name was Ajay. He had liquid black eyes and a gorgeous smile, but looking back, I mostly picked him because he wasn't Jewish or any kind of Christian. He was a cute boy I could date without picking a team. We'd eventually broken up because I could only see him every other weekend, but while we lasted, we'd had several epic make-out sessions. I'd let him put his hand under my shirt, over the bra, where he kneaded with delighted disbelief at my booby. It had been super exciting, not really because it felt that great to have my booby treated like a yeast roll, but because we had both been so thrilled that I had let him touch it.

Doug was an adult, dating a mother. He would not expect some fumbling innocent in bed. I panicked over the ugliest logistics. What if it hurt, and I cried? What if I bled? How the hell would I explain that?

So I went to the one person who had always had my back, every living second. I'd let myself into the Cabbagetown rent-a-house Walcott shared with three other English majors. He had a bedroom the size of a walk-in closet, but all his own.

He was sitting on his futon, feverishly tapping at his laptop when I came in and closed the door behind me.

He said, "I'm onto something. Can you give me half an hour?"

"Sure," I said, "but then I need you to make sex with me."

The typing stopped. "You need me to who the what what?"

"Sex," I said. "I need you to help me have it."

Walcott nodded, suddenly thoughtful. "Brilliant! Let's get to it. This sounds like the ideal way for us to never speak again. Can I finish my poem now?"

I said, "I keep thinking I'll go home with Doug, and then I freak out and don't."

He winced at the name. Doug, he always said, sounded like someone's gray-chest-haired old father. Which Doug was. Well, he was a father. I didn't know about the chest hair, yet. He did have a little gray in his hair, which I liked. But I couldn't get from where I was all the way to Doug. Not without Walcott. I begged him, and then I yelled at him. No dice. I whined that I was a dreadful virgin mother-monster who would never have sex or get to be in love for my whole life.

None of that fazed him. What fazed him was when I cried. When I sat there with tears rolling down my face and my hands in my lap and said simply, as sincere as I had ever been, "You always help me, Walcott. Why won't you help me now?"

He banged his laptop shut and set it aside on the dresser. "Gah, okay. Stop crying." I dried up, and he said, in his thinking voice. "We'll make the sex, as you say in your oh-so-charming native country, The Land of Super-Crazy, but there have to be some rules. So it doesn't get all weird and ruin us."

"Rule one." I said, "No kissing."

"Oh, hell yeah, no kissing on the mouth."

"Not on the anywhere!" I said. "I want to do this straight-up missionary. Fast and dirty, just long enough that I know what it's like."

"Right. Get in, get out, nobody gets hurt. So to speak," he said. "Also, I have to be really drunk."

I said, "Oh, ouch!"

He grinned. "Not because you aren't damn cute. You know you are. It's for later, when you never want to look at me again. I want plausible deniability. My story is, the whole thing is a blur, and I don't remember what your nipples look like."

"What about me?"

He turned his mouth down, like thinking, and said, "Mmm . . . I don't care if you know what my nipples look like."

"I'm serious," I said, and smacked him. "Should I get drunk?"

"No. You have to be dead sober. You remember it all, because we're not doing this twice. Then rule fifty-six . . ." He quirked an eyebrow at my puzzled look and said, "I lost count. Fifty-six is, we go right now. Boom! Done. No thinking, before or after."

I nodded, and he got up, heading for the kitchen. I put the futon down into a bed, and he came back with a bottle of tequila and a shot glass. He'd already downed one, I could tell from his watery eyes. I took the bottle and poured him another.

He said, "Gimme a minute. I don't want to puke it all back up and have to start over."

"Plus puking is not sexy."

He wiped his reddened eyes and said, in a teacherly and disapproving voice, "Shandi. This is not about being sexy. Can we all get on the same damn page?"

I laughed, and he downed the second one. He did five shots in all, in less than half an hour. Lord, but he was drunk.

Then we did it.

He claimed later he didn't remember much at all, just as he had said. And this was merciful, because me? I remembered.

I remembered him slurring, "This is weird to do without kissing," as he placed my hand over the fly of his jeans. There was a wad of something down there, oddly soft.

"Can you even do this? Why is it floppetty?" I asked, but even as I spoke, it stirred, like something waking up. I jerked my hand away.

He started laughing and said, "Don't be funny. Me laughing will not help the floppetty situation. Take off your shirt." When I hesitated, he said, "Big talk, but this isn't going to happen with our clothes on." He peeled his own shirt off over his head and then pulled his jeans all the way down his endlessly long body. He sat down naked. I was keeping my eyes carefully forward, but what I could make out in my peripheral vision didn't seem particularly ready to have sex.

I struggled out of my shirt and my bra, and after I tossed them aside, it seemed fair that I should get to look. So I did. In the few seconds my eyes had been covered by my top, Walcott had undergone some changes. Radical ones.

"It's that easy?" I said, fascinated.

"I'm a nineteen-year-old straight guy, Shandi. Those right there are boobs. Yeah. It's pretty much that easy."

I hadn't ever seen a penis up close in human person before. It was weird-as-hell-looking, like a space alien hiding in my best friend's pants. But a friendly alien, with a nice color. A nice shape. I leaned down to look at it up close, and me doing that, it got even readier, pushing itself up like a creature with its own life and movement, rising from the familiar long, skinny body I had seen a thousand times in swim trunks.

"Look, if this was for real, there would be kissing here," he said, waving his hand around like a drunken conductor. "And you know, some rolling around, some rubbing and stuff. And then!" He banged his hands together and then threw them apart, sideways, almost knocking his laptop off the dresser. "Then we would make the sex."

"Let's skip to the end," I said.

"You are like most guys' dream girlfriend. Skip to the end. Ha!" He started laughing again, and it went down a little. So weird. He looked at himself and then covered his eyes like a long, stringy baby playing naked peek-a-boo. "Watch this," he said. "Looking at boobs in three, two, one . . . Now!"

Bang, it was completely ready again.

I said, "How does that even . . ."

"It is what it is."

He opened his top dresser drawer, and handed me a bottle of lubricant. Then he took out a condom and started working it on.

"Why do you have this stuff?" I asked, reading the label like I thought the lubricant might have basic sex instructions. "You and Jenna broke up a month ago."

"I am, above all things, a hopeful man," Walcott said, lolling onto his back. I'd never seen him so drunk. "This is all you now. I'm going to close my eyes and think of England." He threw one arm over his eyes. "The cliffs! The Cliffs of Dover!"

So it was me on top, methodical and careful, as if I were learning how to use a tampon. The lubricant helped. I felt a weird stretching pressure, and then there we were. I was officially doing it, and it was nothing. I sat there for a minute, until the discomfort faded to an odd fullness. No bells. Not even any tingles. But not painful or scary.

I'd been so preoccupied with the mechanics that I'd almost forgotten Walcott was there. I noticed then that he was breathing weird.

"You okay?" I said, moving myself a little, like an experiment.

"Yeah. Can we be done?" he asked. He sounded slightly strangled.

"I don't know," I said. I tried moving again, and it changed his face.

"Let's be done," he said.

This was the part I didn't like remembering. Right then, for really less than a second, I had an awful impulse to not stop. Not because it felt good or because I remotely liked it, but because his skin flushed on his whole chest, and I could tell from how he breathed that he was heading toward something. In that half second, I came to understand that I could push us forward. His body, drunk and helpless, would go forward if I made it, and I wanted that. To be in charge of a man like that. To own him, and it was a mean and vengeful want that had zero to do with sex.

But this was Walcott. I never wanted to do a mean thing to Walcott.

I didn't want to do a mean sex thing to anyone. Ever.

I said, "Yes, let's be done."

I left him and cleaned myself up. I had bled, just a little. I had a weird reaction to seeing those vindicating drops of red on the white Kleenex, like a *See, I told you!* aimed at Mimmy and that pastoral counselor, at my dad and that psychologist. But I didn't dwell. I'd gotten good at never dwelling. I dressed in the bathroom, and when I got back, Walcott had fumbled drunkenly back into his clothes, too, all the way down to his flip-flops. I came and sat by him.

"I know we said no kissing, but thanks," I said. I leaned over like I was going to kiss his cheek, and instead I licked it, like a sloppy, disgusting dog lick.

He said, "Gah!" and we both laughed, and that was good.

I picked up the tequila bottle and I did three shots, dumping the liquor down into my empty stomach as fast as I dared, putting a tequila-soaked fence around all my new knowledges. Walcott had a bumper shot. We left the apartment and staggered down the road to the place we called Close Indian, having a rambling conversation about sci-fi movies, and we ate what must have been a thousand pounds of shawarma. I crashed at his place, like normal, and by morning, Walcott and me, we were back to being us.

The only thing he ever said about it later was, "I remember enough to be pretty sure it was ungodly bad. Don't worry, it will be better with Doug."

It wasn't, though. It was much the same, only sweatier, with some pawing at each other first. Doug was grunty and gross. He got lost in it while I floated through, untouched even while he touched me. I couldn't like him, during, not the way I liked him at dinner. It made me feel sick and small and broken and mean. Once was enough. I broke up with Doug, but it wasn't any different with Richard.

Now, in my kitchen with Walcott telling me ruinous things about loving me, I realized he was right. It was completely unfair to count that night against him. Especially since that absurd event with Walcott was, to date, the nicest sex I'd ever had.

"You can't be in love with me, Walcott," I said, almost sternly. "You just can't."

"Too late," he said.

"Walcott," I said, because it made me feel so helpless, "I don't know what to tell you. You say you are in love me, but what am I supposed to do with that?"

He spread his hands and half smiled. "Be in love with me back."

He didn't say it pleading or pathetic. He said it like I had asked what to do with a hungry baby or a burning house, and the answer was plain common sense.

But I couldn't. How could I even think of trying, when my whole body became something electric whenever William walked into a room or smiled or I remembered resting my hand on the sleek, polished oak of his chest?

I stood there, not being in love with Walcott back, with ridiculous numbers of tears falling down helpless out of my eyes.

After half a minute, he smiled, but not a happy smile. He nodded.

"So, I guess that's that," he said. "You have to give me some room, Shandi, if you want me to get over this." And then he left.

Chapter 10

*W*illiam is down in the basement, elbows braced on his weight bench and eighty pounds on the bar, sweating so hard he's in danger of losing his Bluetooth. He started at fifty pounds, and he's been doing sets all morning. He is working his triceps now. Eighty is not hard on his arms, but he can feel his heartbeat in his side, a painful second throbbing.

Waiting for Bialys to call and tell him that Stevie has completed the business of being killed, he has stretched his body to the limit of what his healing abdomen will allow. Perhaps beyond it. His side burns and pulses with the rhythm of the lifting and his heart.

Today Steven Parch is being taken off the ventilator. His respiration will cease, and that will shortly end all of his body's other functions. A sheet will be pulled over his face, and he will be taken to the morgue. If the uncle does not claim the body and its attendant expenses, the state will pay for a cremation. Parch will be reduced to gray dust, and even the dust will not be saved or set aside.

This isn't wholly William's doing. He can see multiple causes, high among them, Parch's own poor decisions. But it is not separate from him, either. William's causal relationship to this specific reduction of a complex living system into dust cannot be negated.

William's Bluetooth chirps. His arms set down the eighty pounds, while his abdomen feels as if he's set down more than double that. He walks over to the phone and looks at the screen, to be sure. It's Bialys. He taps the Bluetooth, leaning on the sideboard.

"Is it finished?" William says, instead of hello. His manners and his phone voice have abandoned him. He sounds raspy and too loud.

Bialys clears his throat. "No. I'm sorry."

The red pulse in his side becomes less interesting. "The uncle changed his mind?"

"No, they took him off at nine," Bialys says. "Parch started breathing on his own. I waited around, but he's still breathing."

William digests this, feeling the pain in his abdomen receding in small, lapping surges. "What's the prognosis?"

"Doctors say so much shit, who knows," Bialys says. "The uncle signed a do not resuscitate, but he won't end feeding or hydration. Says he wouldn't do that to a dog. For now? Parch is stable."

"Thank you," William says. "Keep me in the loop?"

"Will do," Bialys says, and closes the connection.

William likes this about him, how his conversations begin with what matters and end precisely when they end. More people should learn to skip the how-are-yous and see-you-soons. He wants to call Paula, disseminate this information with no preamble, and hang up. Perhaps he can start a trend. He likes this idea so much, he's a little giddy.

Why is he grinning? It is foolish. Stevie could still die. In fact, his death is probable. Were he to wake up, William wouldn't mind if he spontaneously combusted five minutes later. But in this moment, all that matters is that William has not killed him. He doesn't want to be the catalyst for loss, even though Stevie's child is a probable fiction, and if real, could be better parented by wolves.

He goes up the stairs, out of the weight room. On the hearth is a Lego Death Star, the figurines frozen in the middle of the last scenario he helped Natty reenact from a movie he has never seen. The secret hatch is open and three of Natty's favorites are imperiled in a trash compactor. Natty will be anxious to rescue them.

Also, Shandi's folder is lying on the coffee table. It contains William's lab reports, as well a dossier on Clayton Lilli, courtesy of Paula. Paula wanted to drive it over to her house, but William retained it. Shandi came to him for help, and he wants to see it through. Shandi hasn't come back to claim it, though. While he was waiting on Steven Parch's death, he was glad to be alone. Now, it seems odd. She hasn't come since Paula chased her out on Wednesday. Meanwhile, he sat on her information, absorbed in his own waiting.

He has been what Paula calls "a monstrous ass." He sometimes chooses to be an ass, at work. It can yield results when repetition and good manners fail. But in his personal life, it can happen without him noticing.

He should deliver this to her, now.

He takes a quick shower and changes, but it isn't until he is walking out the front door that he remembers that the driver's seat of his car is a charred twist of melted foam gnarled around the frame. Dammit. He forgot to tell Bialys about the car, too. Dammit cubed.

He goes back inside and gets the cushions off the armchair in his office. After a moment's thought, he gathers duct tape, wire, and towels. He finds an old pink can of Lysol in the laundry room.

He opens the car door and the smell hits him, harsh and chemical, almost like scorched microwave popcorn. The driver's-side seat is destroyed and the ceiling is streaked in black, but the car is sound, mechanically.

This is all the damage the pint liquor bottle with a rum-soaked rag stuffed in its top could do. William could have made a more effective bomb in his sleep. This one sailed into the car's open window and landed on its base, or more likely, the bomber walked up and simply set it down inside. Either way, the bottle did not break.

A Molotov mocktail, Paula called it, thrown by a poor man's carsonist.

It would have guttered out entirely if the flaming rag hadn't come to rest against the upholstery. William had put the fire out with the kitchen extinguisher, but Paula dialed 911 while he was running to get it.

Lights and sirens followed. William's neighbors gathered and milled in the street like spooked cattle, breaking and re-forming into small shocked pods, asking one another what happened. Herd animals often cluster up for comfort, but William wished they'd all go home. Two cops in uniform took a report, asking William in a perfunctory manner if he knew who might have done this.

William told them he had no idea.

He didn't say that when he first looked out the window and saw the burning car, his mouth silently formed the syllables of his wife's name. He also didn't tell them he'd been lurking outside her parents' house earlier, or that he is not welcome there. He kept his mouth shut because no one in that middle-class, deeply Catholic family would so violently break laws and social conventions. Not even Maggie. Also, they'd never own a bottle of such cheap rum.

Steven Parch's uncle is a more likely suspect. He's currently in prison, but probably has a pool of criminal friends at large.

The older cop said something about teenagers, and William nodded, as if accepting this. Paula gave him a sharp look. She'd thought about the uncle, too. But William couldn't stand on his curb, surrounded by his neighbors, explaining his part in Stevie's impending death. All he needed from those cops was a report for his insurance people.

Paula took her cue from him. She slipped her business card into the hand of the taller cop, touching her hair and smiling. "Kids today, right? But feel free to call me, Officer, if you want to interrogate me just a little more."

He meant to tell Bialys, since Bialys already has the context. He can't allow a person who would deploy even this ill-made bomb to roam his family neighborhood. If the gas tank had blown, shards of burning car would have peppered the baby-and-beagle-filled houses around him.

He's been so preoccupied, though, waiting for Stevie to be finished. The bomb fell out of his mind. He'll call Bialys back, but one thing at a time. Shandi first.

Binding the chair cushions and towels to the frame with a liberal use of wire and duct tape, William approximates a place to sit that will place his body in a reasonable spatial relationship with the steering wheel and pedals. He sprays the interior down with Lysol until the antiseptic Summer Breeze overpowers the burned chemical undersmell. His eyes are watering as he drapes a final cheerful beach towel on top of the whole mess. He has to drive with all the windows down, but it rained earlier, and the heat wave has broken. It's nice out, for July.

By the time he finds Shandi's condo, it's past two, which means Natty is likely down for his nap. Good. It seems best to take Clayton Lilli's information inside while his possible offspring is sleeping.

He rings the bell. He hears Natty crying before Shandi swings open the door. She's holding Natty on her hip, and she's been crying, too. When she sees him standing on her step, she smiles hugely and then breaks into a fresh gusset.

"Oh, William, yay," she says, and pulls him inside.

Natty, red-faced and runny-nosed, scrubs at his eyes. He looks younger when he cries, more like a toddler than a preschooler.

"Oh, William, yay," he parrots, and scrambles across the air between them, into William's arms. William shifts Natty to his unshot side. He holds the file on Clayton Lilli in his other hand, a strange dissonance.

Natty is gabbling at him through wails, his words falling onto each other so quickly, William can barely follow. The gist is, something awful was in his room.

Shandi keeps pulling William along into the chaos he has interrupted, while Natty weeps and snuffles. He tucks his face into the crook of William's neck, talking and talking, but now William can't understand him at all. They go into the living room.

"Don't look, it's a mess," Shandi says.

That's an understatement. The room is a shambles. Toys and books are scattered all over the dirty floor, and used dishes stand on every surface. Great piles and drifts of laundry lie in various stages of indecipherable cleanliness or filth.

His own house is pristine. While Shandi has been monitoring his life, her own has fallen into disarray. The disorder makes his skin itch, all of it, but Natty is soaking William's shoulder in tears. William sets the folder down on the coffee table so he can peel Natty's face up.

"Was it the ninja?" William asks.

"No!" Natty says, hitching, and the corners of his mouth both point straight down. "Stevie camed my room wiff gun hands, shoot and shoot me." William can barely understand him. He looks to Shandi, standing with her arms in an angry crisscross, her face crumpling.

"I just got off the phone with the effing stupid crap crap doctor, and she says this is progress. Isn't that so super? He's screaming himself out of his nap now, but hey! At least he isn't sublimating Stevie into spiders, and—" Her voice rises to a wail. "Walcott let me go to voice mail. Does that sound like anything like progress?"

It doesn't. The change in imagery sounds irrelevant, though admittedly he has little patience with psychology. Still, an increase in a nightmare's frequency and intensity is an escalation.

To Natty, he says, "It's okay. I can fix this." He makes his voice sound cheerful and authoritative. "Is Stevie still up there?"

He is prepared to go upstairs and beat imaginary Stevie dead, even as the real one struggles to not die of the same cause. It is a hideous juxtaposition, but this is what needs to be done.

Natty shakes his head. He's calmed enough for William to understand him. "He ranned in the closet and got away into a hole. Mommy couldn't find it. But he might come back in that hole, William."

"I'm going to close it," William says, very serious. "I know how to plug up holes, and I brought duct tape. You can help me."

Natty nods and puts his face back down on William's shoulder. William joggles him by rote. His body remembers how to properly jounce a tiny, distraught human into peace. More than that, his body is good at it. He has missed it. It is an absent range of movement that is present in his body, every day.

To Shandi, he says, "You've left the front door open." He can feel the air-conditioning whooshing out past him. As she goes to close it, he adds, "Take a minute. Catch your breath. I got this."

She looks at her son, quiet now in his arms and mouths, *Thank you.*

As she goes, he gets his phone out, one-handedly thumbing at the touch screen to find the number of his maid service. He turns to the wall, joggling and patting Natty while he speaks in a calm, low voice through his earpiece to a dispatcher, promising time-and-a-half and exorbitant tips if she will deploy a maid team to this address immediately. All the while he feels Natty growing heavier in the way of all small, soothed children. The relaxing muscles create the illusion of increasing mass.

He hangs up, but he stays facing the wall, swaying back and forth and patting, until Natty is so deeply under that he's drooling onto William's shoulder.

William doesn't stop, though. His body keeps on doing the job it was trained for long ago. It's fine, if he loves Natty a little bit. Children are added to, not replaced. And subtracted from, of course. He knows that, too, and perhaps this is why he keeps patting Natty, though Natty is asleep. He lets his own body have the simple, soothing movement.

When he finally turns back, Shandi is in the room. He's not sure how long she's been there, sitting on one of the angular chairs. The folder he brought is in her lap. It is closed. One of her hands presses down firmly on the top.

"I know what this is," she says to him, "But I didn't look. I don't want lab reports. I want you to tell me that he's in here. I want you to say you found him."

William takes his cue from Bialys, earlier, laying out the information she's waited for with blunt economy. "I can't be certain without DNA, but it's likely. His name is Clayton Lilli. He graduated Emory last year, economics, and took an entry-level job with an investment bank downtown."

She draws her breath in, sharp. "He's still local?"

"Yes. He lives in an apartment complex right by Piedmont Park," he says.

"So he's practically my neighbor. That's . . . fun." She puts one hand over her mouth, and her eyes over it are very round. She speaks through her fingers. "I knew you'd find him. Walcott said it wasn't possible, but I knew you would." She puts her hand down from her face and she is smiling with her mouth. "If Walcott was speaking to me I would put this so far up his nose. Is there a picture?"

"Several," William says.

"Does he look like . . ." Her gaze shifts to her sleeping son.

"I don't know," William says. "His earlobes are correct."

This time Shandi covers her eyes with her hand, and then drops it. She is still looking at Natty. "Could you excuse me? I can't open this in here, with him."

"Sure," he says. "I called a maid service, though. They'll be here soon."

"Oh. Thank you. That's so kind." She stands up. "I won't be long." She takes the folder upstairs.

William looks around. It's hard to wait in this filthy place, smelling dried-up egg. Is he allowed to clean it? It might be insulting. Paula, who grew up in an apartment so abhorrent it makes this condo look like a surgical theater, would think so. Paula keeps her loft immaculate, and if he so much as straightens a magazine she literally snaps her teeth at him in a double click.

But Shandi's been cleaning his house; that makes it quid pro quo. He flips Natty and lays him on the sofa in a move too quick and smooth to stir him, then blocks him with a cushion, so he can't roll off onto the floor.

He starts picking up the dishes, carrying them through the open doorway into the kitchen. The sink is full, too, so he stays there, rinsing and loading them into the machine. He finds that he enjoys the reversal. It's been so long since he's been even mildly useful to a person with whom he has an interpersonal relationship. Until he got shot, he lived in a fog of work, run, lift, sleep for months now. Paula picked up all the slack, even going online and paying his bills.

He tried to thank her, but she shrugged it off, saying, "I'm saving you back, Bubba. Whether you want me to or not."

She was referencing their move to Indiana, but William doesn't see the debt or the parallel. Taking Paula when he left for college was not solely for her benefit. It was necessary for him as well.

And for Bridget, he thinks, his wife's name rising in his mind yet again, unbidden. Almost easy now. Before the Circle K, those syllables were not allowed to form in breath or thought, for seven months. He believed it was necessary for survival.

But then he tried to walk into a bullet. Paula is right. It might be time to reassess the policy.

Bridget is still easier to think of in her earliest incarnations, when she was her simplest self. Not yet a woman, or a wife, or a mother. Just a girl, like Shandi. He sees Bridget with her ponytail set high, shoulders braced, invading the filthy basement apartment where Paula still lived with her mother, though she graduated the year before.

Paula was watching television when they arrived. Or maybe not. William had never been to her house when the TV wasn't on, even when no one was in the room to watch it.

Paula said, "Did we have plans?"

William waited for Bridget to begin, but she only bobbed her head at him, encouraging. He shook his head. Getting Paula to move to Indiana would require more than relentlessness and logic. Bridget could do tact. She compressed her lips and only bobbed her head again, wanting him to start.

Paula watched this exchange with her eyes narrowing to slits. "What is this, some kind of intervention?" Bridget blinked, surprised Paula had caught on so quickly, and Paula's lip curled up to show her teeth while her spine straightened, elongating upward from the waist. "Don't even think you're going to intervene on my ass. Don't even."

William recognized the posture; animals show dental weaponry and stretch to appear larger when threatened. He gave in and got blunt before she fully roused for war.

"We think you should move to Indiana with us."

Her spine relaxed and she grinned. "Oh, thank God. I was worried you wanted me to stop drinking."

She looked back at the TV, where an emaciated girl pranced in a circle wearing a wig made out of antlers.

Paula flicked one finger at the TV. "It's a rerun. This chick wins. Can you believe it?"

William tried a rephrase. "I need you to move to Indiana." Paula needed it, too, perhaps equally, but this was not the part that he should emphasize.

Paula ignored him, speaking to Bridget. "I thought the plus-size model had a shot this season."

William went to the TV and punched the power button off manually.

Paula shrieked, "Daddy! You killed him!" Daddy was what Paula called the television.

Bridget walked over to sit on the far side of Paula. As she went, William could hear the carpet crunching under her feet; Paula's mother didn't own a vacuum cleaner.

Bridget said, "I want you to come, too."

Paula looked back and forth between them. When neither of them gave, she rolled her eyes and resigned herself to the conversation.

"To do what?" she asked. "Farm corn?"

"Go to school," William said.

Paula snorted. "Please. You think Notre Dame is going to take me?"

"No," William said. Paula's nostrils flared and her eyes cut away. He realized too late that the question was rhetorical. "Your high school transcript is awful," he said, by way of apology.

"Who thinks William should shut up now?" Bridget asked, and she and Paula both raised their hands. "Come to Indiana."

"Seriously, and do what?" Paula said, like she was bored. She shoved a pile of magazines and her mother's filthy ashtray aside and put her feet up on the table.

Bridget said, "Go to Ivy Tech. I got you the brochure. You can get a two-year degree."

"With what money? Kai's useless, and William offed my only other parent." She gestured at the blank screen.

Now it was Bridget's turn to roll her eyes. "Oh, get a freaking job! They have Red Lobster in Indiana. Plus, here Kai hits you up for rent, but William's going to be rattling around in a three-bedroom house, already paid for."

Paula snorted. "Live free like a tapeworm and go to moron school. That's so appealing."

Bridget ignored that and kept laying out William's plan, but with her own persuasive briskness. "It's not a bad school. You make

A's, retake the SAT, and that degree will be like a high school transcript do-over. It could be a ticket into any school you like."

Her tone took for granted that Paula was capable, that Paula could accomplish these things. Her belief was a compelling thing. Last year, she'd believed Paula into making up two math classes so she could graduate on time. She'd believed William into learning the names of a good third of his classmates; William's senior yearbook was filled with notes and signatures that he could connect to faces, which was unprecedented. It was working on Paula again, now.

"You can't live in this pit, serving fried-shrimp-feast platters and dating . . . the kind of guy you date." It was a misstep. William knew it even before Paula did.

He watched Paula's strange expression shift to a familiar one, her mouth pushing into a proud curl. "Thanks, Bridge, but William's parents rented the house specifically so he wouldn't have to share his oxygen with riffraff."

"I need you to," William said, very flat, because it was such a bald, true thing. William loved lying back at the Fernbank planetarium and floating up into imagined space, loved sinking his whole consciousness into the bizarrely populated landscape of the microscopy, but he'd never lived anywhere but his house in Morningside. He could not imagine Indiana as a factual destination with breathable air and sandwich shops. He'd never traveled west of Birmingham or north of Sugar Mountain.

Paula said, "Grow a pair, William. I'm not your blankie."

Bridget's Irish temper flared. "Don't take it out on him. You're mad at me, because I insulted your awesome life here. But you know this would be great for all of us."

Paula lashed back, "Especially you. Right? If I come along, you won't end up on your back."

"What does that mean?" Bridget asked, her voice strident.

Paula sensed victory and leaned in. "How come I always have to sit between you and William at the movies now?"

Bridget flinched, cutting her eyes over Paula's shoulder to William. Paula and Bridget loved long, sweeping movies about war or doomed romance, where someone was always getting burned up in the desert or falling off a swing and dying of consumption. The films themselves didn't interest William, but he loved the experience. Last year, he sat in the middle, enjoying the comforting sounds of Paula sucking Gummi Bears like lozenges on one side and the feel of Bridget's arm pressed against his on the other. He kept his head canted so he could see Bridget in his peripheral vision, watching how the story changed her face.

This year, Bridget maneuvered so that Paula sat between them. Always, even though with other people, Bridget was unselfconsciously physical, not only with her family. She and Paula groomed each other incessantly. Her carefulness as she preserved her distance, even at the movies now, was an escalation. An admission, like the way she kept his catalyst touched always to her pulse points.

Bridget's flush deepened. Paula leaned even closer, her back almost fully to William, pressing the advantage.

"You want me in Indiana, Your Nunliness, so your plans don't get screwed. Sex pun intended. Do you honestly not know that you're in love with him? Or are you just some terrorized virgin, ready to robe up because it's too spooky to think that your nice friend William owns a penis?"

Bridget's whole face went scarlet, but when she spoke, her voice was steady. "Of course I know I love him. And I'm not scared of sex." Bridget met Paula's eyes, calm and strong, staring her down. "It's only that I fell in love with God first." Paula shifted and looked away, uncomfortable in the presence of Bridget's naked, shameless faith. She took her feet down off the table, got up, and walked away, across the room. Bridget looked to William, her eyes large and sad. What she said next was an apology. "First, and more. I love God more."

William's hands closed into fists. His nostrils flared. His interpersonal skills were not up to the moment. Another man would have known what to say. Something about concurrency? Yes.

William didn't believe in God, but he did believe in Bridget's love for God. It was a manifestation of her love of goodness, and William could believe in goodness. He saw it in her. He loved it in her. If required, he would willingly take on her rituals, and love goodness beside her in the manner that she chose. She was welcome to love goodness, to love it more than him, in fact, if only she was his.

Bridget, he wanted to explain, *these are not mutually exclusive states of being,* but this did not sound romantic.

Another man would have known how to say it. Paula could have told him, had they planned this in advance. In a few years, he would know without her help. But the moment came when it came, and he said nothing.

Paula stood silent by the wall that served as a kitchen. There was only a narrow piece of counter, already stacked high with filthy dishes. Her back was turned. She was giving the moment over to her friends.

Which was not very like her.

He realized then that Paula had derailed him. Bridget, too, shunting the conversation sideways. She'd set them on each other, then absconded to the filthy slice of kitchen.

William started laughing, really laughing, the kind that got away from him and became an overloud booming that drew the eyes of strangers when it escaped in public. Paula turned to him and Bridget looked up.

"You're the smartest person I know," William said to Paula, when he could finally speak. He wiped at his eyes, and when he looked back at her, Paula was making an ironic version of her sports face. *Bring it.* He recognized it from their one long-ago sex night.

Bridget recognized it, too. "We got rolled!" He nodded, and Bridget said, "You're wasted here, Paula, and you just proved it. Stop rotting."

"I'm not rotting," Paula said.

William said, "Yes, you are. Stop rotting. You want to lose this fight."

"I never want to lose," Paula said, a little sulky.

"This time, I think you do," Bridget said, and she was right. Two weeks later, they caravanned to Indiana: The Sullivans' minivan, his parents' coupe, and then William's brand-new SUV with Paula's army-surplus duffel resting in the back beside his suitcases.

Now, finishing the dishes in this filthy condominium, he remembers that's what Paula said to him, yesterday. *Stop rotting.* He did not realize until now that she was quoting Bridget, using his own wife's words against him. She didn't mean to push him toward Shandi. The opposite. But now he is thinking about the value of fresh starts.

Is this what he needs? Something entirely new? Before the Circle K, he made Bridget be a thing that never was, as if Twyla's interrupted, small existence and Bridget's never being born were *not* mutually exclusive states of being.

The doorbell goes off, very loud, and he jerks and spins with his heart rate jacking. Water sloshes onto the floor. He can hear Shandi answering it, letting the team of maids in. What the fuck is he doing here? What the fuck is he doing?

He begins listing prime numbers in his head, an old trick from the Indiana therapist. The one who absolved him of parties. He hasn't used it in years, but it seems fitting now, with the past resurrecting unstoppably around him. He can hear Shandi leading the maid-service team upstairs to get started there. By the time she comes back down, he is at 457, and the wild tattoo of his heartbeat has calmed. He doesn't stop following the prime numbers upward, though. He presses Start on the dishwasher and goes into the living room. Shandi is gathering her keys and her purse, readying to vacate. The folder is sitting on the coffee table again.

Shandi says, "Do I need to leave a check for the cleaners?"

William says, "They have my card on file. I owe you a clean house, I think."

"Thank you." William steps toward the coffee table, reaching for the folder, but Shandi says, "Leave it. I don't need that."

"The maids might throw it out—"

"I hope they do," she interrupts. "Crumple it up. Put it on the floor."

She sounds firm, as if this is what she truly wants him to do. It doesn't matter. He can print it out again if she likes. He tips the file off the table, and as it falls, the papers inside catch the air and sail out, spilling in a fan across Natty's scattered Matchbox cars. Clayton Lilli stares up at them from a close-up.

"I thought I would recognize him, but I don't. Not at all. I can't even tell if he looks like Natty. If Natty looks like him. It's not good enough, William. I have to really see him." She is rocking herself, unconsciously. She must be deeply upset; it's what his own body did outside the Sullivans' house. She glances at her child, sleeping in a little curl on the sofa. "I want you to take me. I think I'm scared to go by myself. Will you?"

"Of course," William says. There isn't a set of circumstances in which he would let this girl go see Clayton Lilli on her own.

Shandi is already turning to pick her sleeping child up, settling his limp weight against her chest with his head on her shoulder. He sighs and curls an arm over her shoulder, still deeply out. She carries Natty to the front door, and William follows, fishing his keys out of his pocket.

"But not today. Not with Natty. He can't even suspect there is a Natty. Today, I want to go sit in the sunshine and eat things." She stops and faces him directly. "I'm not good at this. I suck in fact. William, can we go to lunch? Here's my sleeping kid, but still. Can you and me go out? To lunch?" Shandi is speaking quickly, her words tumbling over one another. Spots of color rise in her cheeks. When he doesn't answer, she keeps on talking, faster and faster. "I know a place, really close. It's super relaxed and boho, but the food is five star. Dad took me last year for my birthday. Just us. Bethany wouldn't go there if every other restaurant in the world was on fire and her housekeeper was dead. I honestly believe she'd rather cook."

William suspects that, even though Natty is nominally present, what Shandi has proposed here is a date. He is being invited to participate in an event that sounds as foreign as Indiana did once. Back then, he'd packed and driven north anyway. Indiana was real when he arrived.

He puts his car keys in his pocket. "Sure. When the maids are done, I'll need to come back here, anyway. I have to help Natty tape up the hole in his closet."

Shandi grins. "Great, I'll drive. So we don't have to move Natty's booster."

That's good. He won't have to explain his burned-up driver's seat. He follows her down the steps. His car is beside hers, in the condo's second parking space. He folds all of himself into the tiny VW as she transfers Natty to his car seat and buckles him in without waking him.

When Shandi gets in on the other side, her arm brushes his, it's so close and small. If she has proposed a date, then he is now on it. She's still talking, very quickly, as she starts the car and drives, filling the car with chatter about the lamb burgers, the way none of the plates match, how there is a shady patio with a bocce ball court.

She says, "Today's so pretty, can we sit outside?"

This is a direct question. "Sure."

"Good," Shandi says. She starts patting at herself with her right hand, her hair, her face, manually setting herself in order as she drives. Her arm moves against his, and he needs to get his own car fixed. This car is too small, too close. The prime numbers keep winding upward in his head, and this is helping. She's gone into a maze of narrow, residential streets. There is very little traffic.

She says, "Let's drink a lot of wine. So much we have to taxi home, okay? We'll play bocce and eat gelato until we're sick. We can talk about anything that's nice. Or sit and watch the birds steal crumbs. Can we do that?"

She is turning into a parking lot. He is at 4,007 and Stevie is alive. Truthfully, everything that she is saying sounds pleasant. He can do this. Let the maid team finish. Eat a lot of protein. Let all that is complicated fall away. She is suggesting they compartmentalize, and William is superlative at this.

"Good," he says.

She grins. "Let's eat so much bread, William. They homemake it. We'll eat lunch out, like we're just people."

"We are just people," William says.

Shandi eases into a small parking space that faces the side of the patio she's been talking about. The restaurant itself is a narrow brick building with a long, low window. He can see the bocce ball court. No one is playing.

She's right; this time of day, it's very empty. Only four people are sitting on the patio, divided into pairs. A young couple drinks beer and chats. The girl's pretty legs are propped up across his lap. The closer couple is older, the man well into his forties and the woman a good ten or twelve years younger, about William's age. They sit side by side on a wicker love seat with a low coffee table in front of them. They are oblivious to the patio and all the little things with feathers, mostly house wrens and finches, around them. The man touches the woman's face. He leans in and kisses her, his hand snaking deep into her hair. The trees by the patio are strung with paper lanterns and feeders, and birds are everywhere. This place was made for legs across laps and public kissing.

This is what a date looks like. He watches through the glass. His body is rigid and still. His body does not open his door and walk toward it. It also does not lean away.

Shandi hasn't opened her door, either. The VW's engine is still running. She stares at the older couple, kissing. Perhaps, seeing these things, she has become uncertain, too. That would be excellent.

But then she says, "Hey, guess what? That's my dad," She points to the older man, who has now placed his hand on the woman's side, high, so his thumb grazes the underside of her breast. "That's my dad right there."

William's eyebrows rise. He flicks one finger at the woman. "You said she wouldn't come here?"

They can leave, of course. Her father hasn't seen her yet. He is not likely to see anyone. His eyes are closed, and William is uncomfortable with the amount of public tongue he is putting in his wife's mouth.

"My stepmother?" Shandi says, and snorts. "She would never. That woman? She's not Bethany. Not even a little bit."

As if he feels their eyes, the man who is Shandi's father breaks the kiss and turns to look right at them. He does a double take, so overblown it's comical. He leaps to his feet and the woman is shunted to the side. She looks at them, too, and Shandi makes a strangling noise. Her father's leg bangs the table, and their drinks topple. His unhinged jaw wags back and forth.

Shandi is already throwing the car into reverse and backing out as he leaps the table and runs toward them. The woman scrambles to her feet. Shandi peels away, her lips compressed, and zigzags off down the street. The car screeches around a corner and Natty snuffles, shifting in his booster seat. William crams his arm through the tiny space in between the seats to steady him. The car completes the turn, and he can no longer see the couple or the restaurant. He faces front.

"Get in your lane," William says, and Shandi jerks the wheel right and centers the car. She is still going too fast. She hits a speed bump, jouncing them all. Natty makes a protesting, sleepy noise, and that slows her.

"That woman he's with? She looks just like my mother. For one second I thought it actually was Mimmy. But no, she's much younger, and she isn't quite as pretty," Shandi says, almost to herself. "God, I wish I hadn't seen that. Now what?"

William isn't sure. All he knows is that it is important to keep moving.

Shandi's father doesn't understand. Wives aren't like children. They are not built for the mechanics of addition. Wives must be traded, one for one. Shandi's father, whether he is aware of it or not, is replacing his wife in a slow, tearing stretch, when it should be surgical. Cut. Start clean.

It was an ugly thing to witness. Betrayal is always ugly, even on a shaded patio full of little birds.

William, careening away from a probable date with a girl twelve years *his* junior, feels sick in the pit of himself. Not because the situations are exactly parallel. His wife is not at home, after all, happy and oblivious, planning Catholic Youth Alive's mission trip to Haiti.

But that doesn't make whatever he is doing here with Shandi right. And there is Natty to think of, too.

He can't let Shandi pull him in, or let himself be pushed away from her by Paula. He must choose what he wants and then act. He must turn, with the force of his own will behind the movement, one way or the other.

"Keep driving," William says, though the car feels too small to hold enough air for them. There is not enough for all of them to breathe.

"Where are we going?" Shandi asks, but William doesn't know yet.

Chapter 11

*P*aula, of all people, was babysitting Natty. Who else did I have? Walcott was out. He'd asked for space, and I owed him anything he asked for, forever. Mimmy or Dad would have expected me to say where I was going, and I'd have to lie. The truth would horrify and frighten them. Bethany wouldn't have cared what I was up to, but I sure as hell wasn't going to drop by to see if she'd share Nanny Jean for the day. Not with the knowledge banging around in my head that Bethany was far better at sharing than I had ever suspected.

Natty liked Paula, and I trusted that she wouldn't feed him bleach or bake him, but I still hadn't asked her. If I was on fire, I doubted she'd so much as pee on me to put it out. William said she'd do it, though, and called her up. He was right. Turned out, her sexual politics were stronger than both our rivalry and her personal aversion to me.

William and I were sitting in his SUV, screened behind the smoked-glass windows. We were in the backseat, and that had a lot of subtext for a girl my age. Especially since it was still mostly dark out. And he was William. But being parked directly across the street from Clayton Lilli's apartment complex sucked any possible romance out of it. I was a thousand kinds of jittery sick in my whole body.

But as time passed, and nothing happened, an air of unreality began to settle on the whole mission. William did nothing better than anyone I'd ever seen. His gaze was on the door, but it was blank. He was deep inside his head, and his foot twitched, faintly, like a dreaming dog's. It was as if he had a thousand toys packed up inside himself, and he didn't let my silent presence stop him from going down in there to get at them. It was weird, but kinda sexy. To be fair, though, I thought the way William turned oxygen into carbon dioxide was sexy.

I watched the door of the building and the dashboard clock. It ticked over to 6:01. We'd been sitting close to an hour already. It was Saturday. We could be sitting here past noon, if he slept in. Well, fine. I wasn't about to go knock on his door and ask if he'd like to buy some effing Girl Scout cookies. I wanted to see Clayton Lilli, but the idea of him seeing me made me feel like my skin was crawling off my body.

The smell of the melted foam cushioning, even under its swaddle of towels and tape, had an Eau de Pit-of-Hell that wasn't helping. More random violence, and I couldn't shake the feeling that I was connected. William's car bomb had been made by my kind of arsonist: fumbling, ineffective, yet doing damage that left a lingering stench. After all, I was the girl who'd cosmically called Stevie and (maybe) Clayton Lilli the world's shittiest criminals.

I said, "I keep thinking this lurching, lumpy Golem will come oozing out."

William's head jerked, like I'd called him out of sleep. "What?"

"He's just a guy, right?"

William nodded. "You saw the pictures. He's just a guy."

But that could not be true. Would "just a guy" feed a girl drugs, incapacitate her, walk her off alone . . . "Something's wrong with him. What's wrong with him?" It was rhetorical, or maybe a question I was asking the universe, but William answered.

"Nothing serious. He'll probably go bald, and if he smokes,

he'll have a hard time quitting. He has a higher risk of heart disease than most." He paused, because I had turned away from the door and I was boggling at him, shocked, but at the same time glad for a distraction.

"You can't know all that."

"Of course I can. I have his genetic material," William said.

"You learned all that with some . . ." I couldn't say the word. ". . . cells?"

"It's all in there," William said. "We're made out of our cells."

I didn't realize what all I was handing him, when I'd scraped the inside of my cheek. "Do you know stuff like that, about me?"

"No." He said it like I'd asked if he'd ever watched me shower through a peephole. "I did only what was needed with your sample, but"—he gestured at the front door—"I wasn't interested in this guy's right to privacy."

"And Natty?" I said.

He turned his palms up in what might have been a slight apology. "I did some quick and dirty sequencing. I checked for increased risks to common kinds of cancer, for example. I didn't see anything to worry about, or I would have told you. He's a good kid."

He didn't say it the way people do to mean a child is mannerly or charming. He was saying Natty had been well constructed.

His knuckles began tapping at his knee in a rhythm, as if a song were playing somewhere, and only he could hear it. A minute of that, with me still watching the door, and the tapping starting working my last nerve. It was stretched thin as it was.

"What's bugging you?" I said.

He looked past me, like he was watching the door now, but he said, "I also checked your son for some specific duplications and deletions that I saw in Clayton Lilli." My eyebrows rose, and William added quickly, "Natty doesn't have them."

"But this guy, he has, what, these things?"

"Duplications and deletions, yes," William said. He swallowed. I had the sense that he was telling me something significant or personal.

"Help me out here, William. I don't speak science."

William was rocking now, too, very faintly, but I could see it. His hand tapped harder. Whatever invisible song was playing, he didn't like it. "With these kinds of anomalies, I expect that Lilli would present with limited empathy. He probably has a hard time reading social cues."

I narrowed my eyes. "You're saying that's why he did this? Like, girls get so much easier to talk to if you drug the living shit out of 'em?"

"I'm not excusing him," William said, his voice level, but his hand tapped faster.

"You kind of are," I said, my voice heating.

William shook his head, vehement. "It doesn't excuse him," he said, but I was still talking.

"What about Stevie? Did Stevie's genes make him bust into the Circle K with a gun and start kicking old people? What about my dad? If we'd gone up on the patio and stolen his beer bottle, could you root around in his DNA and find out why he's screwing a girl who looks like a younger version of my mother?" I flapped my hand at the door to Clayton Lilli's building. "Poor him, he's got these duplications, and he couldn't help it."

"You're being ridiculous," William said, cold, tapping and tapping, so uncomfortable now inside his body, as if the backseat, already too small for him, had shrunk.

"You said it's all in there," I said. "You said we are made—"

"I know what I said!" His voice was harsh and loud, but then he caught himself, and when he spoke again his words came out very fast, but not angry. "I know what I said. And it's true. Our genes define our capacity. They set the range, and we have to act within it. But it *is* a range, which means it can't be simple. We are limited, all of us, and imperfect. We are broken in specific, quantifiable ways, but I do believe—I do believe in—" He stopped abruptly, looking down at his hand, like he had just noticed it, knocking against his knee now like it was trying to gain entry. He took in a very deep breath, through his nose. He willfully stopped his hand from moving. Meanwhile, my brain was trying to finish his sentence in a way that I could live with, a way that would let the Golem be Natty's biological father without dooming Natty to be awful. Had William meant to say *environment? Destiny? Free will?*

"You do believe in what?" I asked, when not asking had become unbearable.

When William's body was completely still, he turned to me and restarted the sentence. "I do believe in the possibility of goodness."

It was such an unexpected answer. He was saying Natty was a possible goodness, a probable one, even, a true and living current one, no matter where he'd gotten half his genes. I touched William's hand with my fingers, lightly.

"Me, too," I said. "I want to believe in that, too."

I'd spent years pretending Natty into a gift, a free and lovely thing, miraculous and uncaused. The closer I came to laying eyes on Natty's biological father, the more I hoped that Clayton Lilli was at least capable of goodness, whether he had chosen it or not. That we all were.

I turned back to the door. Talking about his genes made him so real. He had cells. This wasn't like watching for fanged mermaids to pop out of a storm drain. This was a human man with a propensity for heart disease and whatever chromosome thing caused male pattern baldness. I'd pretended him into being impossible. He could not exist, but William had brought me here to see him, and my faith in William was crazy absolute. Maybe that was how faith worked?

I wouldn't know, with my upbringing.

Both Mimmy and Dad would agree that Moses had faith in God when he commanded the Red Sea to part. But when he actually saw the water rolling itself up into huge wet walls, all those surprised fish staring out at him, had he gone ahead and crapped his pants anyway?

"Genes don't make it excusable," William said. "Not for this guy. Not Stevie. Not your dad."

He sounded so hard-line. Maybe he was Catholic, after all.

"Not to defend my dad, but he *is* married to Bethany," I said. I still had Moses on my mind. "Marrying Bethany is the modern version of forty years in the wilderness. It gets cold in the desert at night, William. Even Moses got to look into the Promised Land."

"I don't recall your father looking," William said, his voice so dry I had to smile in spite of the circumstances. "What happens when she finds out?"

"Oh, she knows." I'd never bought Bethany as Lady Condo-Bountiful, so excited by Natty's IQ test results that she wanted better for him than my rural, very Baptist preschool. My dad had been meeting Mimmy Junior at the condo, and Bethany moved me into town for one reason: to cock-block my own father. It made me want to take a bath in bleach and then punch her in the face with my clean hand.

I never took my eyes off the door, even as we had a nice little chat about my dad's adultery, like any normal folks might while watching for a possible fictional monster on a superfun Saturday morning. I wanted to unsee the moment when my dad took his tongue out of that woman's mouth, and she turned to look at us, face on. For a single dizzy second, I'd been looking at my mother.

The next second, I'd realized Miss Patio was younger, blonder, and not as crazy-beautiful—few were. But she'd been beautiful enough, with Mimmy-style cheekbones, Mimmy's mouth. I wondered if my father saw it. Not that I could ask. He'd left fifty messages on my cell phone, but I wasn't ready to talk to him at all, much less ask if he was aware his go-to girl was his ex-wife's baby clone.

The door opened. My spine seized up for a second, but it was only a couple of old guys, dressed for jogging. The faint gray light was warming to gold against the building's brick front, touching all the little balconies. I reminded myself that Clayton Lilli might not even be the guy. We were just checking. We were just here to see.

"It's a really nice building, and not even half a block from the park. I guess karma favors the douche-y." I was trying to keep it light, but I could hear the strain in my voice.

A woman emerged next, still in last night's club clothes, with mascara streaks under her eyes. She took her shame walk fast, in spite of her high-heeled satin shoes, and disappeared around the corner.

William kept his face pointed at the building, but after the woman passed and I didn't say anything else, his eyes began to drift off sideways. He disappeared down inside his head again.

I watched the door, glad I'd looked at the pictures of Clayton Lilli so I would know him when he finally came out. I'd lingered over the shot of the team, Lilli in his tattletale blue and gold jersey, maybe the last image taken of him before my path crossed his. It had been easier to look at this earlier version, when I could try to think of him as innocent.

"I don't know what to do," I said.

William's shoulders shuddered as he landed back inside his body. "What?"

"When he comes out. If he does. What do I do?"

"Damn if I know," William said. "I'm not good at this part."

He said it as if this mission *had* parts, like there was a manual somewhere with all the steps for stalking one's—what to even call him? I didn't have a good way to think of Clayton Lilli. Natty's father? He did not deserve the title. My drugger? My assaulter-person? Even if I could find a noun, I couldn't stand to use that pronoun in the same way I'd say "my spoon," or "my pair of shoes." I didn't want the ownership.

A young couple walked out the front door with a small dog on a leash. The girl was in front. She was a plain girl, college-aged, wearing white sneakers and a fifties-diner waitress dress, her hair scraped into a ponytail. I thought, *Someone got the breakfast shift,* and then she moved down the stairs, and I could see the man half of the couple. It was him.

I looked from the door to William. William nodded in confirmation. My breath stopped, and I turned back. It was him. The earth stopped, too, stopped spinning, but I kept on without it, whirling up and out of orbit, careening toward the sun.

It was truly him, dressed in baggy cargo shorts with his flossy hair hanging in his eyes. He popped into existence at 6:22 on a Saturday morning. The pictures had been useless. I saw how he held the leash. I saw how his head tilted to listen to the mousy girl. I saw the angle of his throat as he drank water from a sports bottle. Before he had existed in my world ten seconds, I knew he was the Golem.

I knew, because I saw my son.

When Natty was born, I had stared endlessly down into his brand-new potato face, so pretty, mostly unsquashed thanks to the C-section. I had immediately recognized my own rounded cheeks and chin. He had Mimmy's small, flat ears lying close against his head, and the long, elegant feet my dad had given all his own boys, too. The other pieces were simply Natty.

But this man? He had preowned Natty's stompy walk, leading from the boxy shoulders, as he followed his girlfriend to a sporty little Fiat parked on the street. He shared the long-waisted shape of my son's body. His brown hair had Natty's cowlick standing up in back. How dare he? How dare he be real and own these pieces of my son?

"Shandi?" William said.

I couldn't speak. I couldn't process, even though I'd known the great god Thor would find him. I was reeling, mute and gobsmacked, staring at this skinny boy-man who cocked his head to a Natty-style angle as he leaned to peck his plain brown paper bag of a girlfriend good-bye.

Clayton Lilli stepped back from the curb with his dog. It was one of those silky, fox-faced objects with the plumy tails. He was completely unaware that I had penetrated his veil of pharmaceuticals and found him. He watched the girl drive off, and then he turned and headed toward the park. I saw that he had dog bags in his pocket.

My body got out of William's Explorer and started after him. I think I left the car door hanging open. My body went, itching and burning the whole length of myself, unstoppable. Lilli was already crossing into the park when I realized William had caught up with me. My hand reached for his and caught it and held it so tight I could feel his bones grinding together. He exhaled out his nose, long and smooth, and let me keep it.

We followed Clayton Lilli across the street. It was still so early, hardly anyone was out on the green. He paused by a trash can to let the dog do his business, and we paused, too, behind him at the park's edge. I stood frozen as he cleaned up after the dog, wondering if he would come right toward me now, going home. But instead, he let his dog off the leash. It wasn't legal, but what was a leash law to a guy like him? He set his water bottle on the grass, then pulled a small collapsible Frisbee out of his pocket. The dog went nuts with joy. I sank down to sit on the damp lawn, pulling William with me. We watched Clayton Lilli indulge in an early-morning romp with his stupid, glossy dog.

To Clayton, we were no different from the older couple come to see the sunrise on a blanket, or the tired-looking mother with the hyperactive toddler, or the pair of teenage girls who had probably been up all night. The two girls walked aimlessly, orbiting each other in a little circle, each deep in conversation with her own smartphone.

Clayton Lilli didn't know that among this knot of humans, on this wide expanse of green, I was the one who wanted to kill him. It was a startling, distant thing to feel. *Here I am on the grass of earth. Here is William, and here is a golden dog. There is Clayton Lilli, drinking water from his sports bottle with all his blood tucked away inside him. Here I am, wanting to let every drop of it come out.*

I leaned in closer to William, my body pressing toward him like in the Circle K but this time, thank God, there was no Natty between us. I tried to figure out how to look at Clayton Lilli without running at him across the green and stabbing his eyes out with my keys, and without my heart breaking into tiny shattered bits because now that we were closer, I could see so many, so many expressions that belonged to my beautiful son crossing his perfect shit of a face.

"I want that water bottle," William said, and then, to my raised eyebrows, said, "Saliva."

I shook my head, no. "You don't need it. It's him."

"I like to be certain," William said.

"I'm certain," I said with such finality he nodded. My eyes burned and itched as they rested on Clayton Lilli. I looked to the dog, to rest them. "He doesn't deserve a dog that cute."

"No," William agreed. "He deserves an awful dog that poops in his clothes."

I nodded. "A magic flaming dog that rolls on his lap until he catches fire and burns up into a puddle."

"That dog already got my car."

William was helping. Being funny, that was good. Being twice as big as Clayton. That was even better.

Clayton Lilli was close to six feet, but he was even skinnier than Walcott, if such a thing was humanly possible. His legs in the floppy shorts looked like lengths of string with knots in them for knees. If he so much as looked my way, William could pick up a rock and smash his head in. I'd seen William smash a head in before, so I could imagine exactly what that would look like. I liked imagining what that would look like.

What I really wanted was to pull that dog aside, because it loved him such an ungodly amount. I wanted to tell it what an asshole it had drawn in dog lotto. I wanted to lay my case out, and have the dog nod sagely, then turn on him and bite him.

It was the way it brought the Frisbee back that broke me. It was laughing up into his face with that silly pouf of tail going like mad. It was the way he knelt and spoke to it, in his sugared voice, saying, "Who is good? Who is a good dog? Who?"

I popped up off the grass, heading right for him. I sensed more than saw William rising, moving with me.

I walked right up to Clayton Lilli, and when he saw me coming, he straightened up and turned, smiling, eyebrows raised politely, like he expected me to ask if he had the time or a spare breath mint.

"Hi!" I said. I sounded so chipper. So bright.

"Hi?" he said.

"Remember me?" I said.

His straight-line, Natty eyebrows came together, and as he searched my face, I saw that he didn't. He didn't remember me.

My fist came shooting out forward toward him, hard as it could, and it landed in the middle of his stupid face. Right on the nose. I felt it give in a fleshy, bouncing way, and then pain bloomed in my hand. Clayton Lilli staggered back a step, his hands going up to his face. His little dog started barking its fool head off. Crazy mad barking, right at me.

"What the—" he said, and took a step toward me.

I felt a wild kind of terror rise in me, but then I felt William step in closer, rising up behind me.

"I wouldn't," William said, and his voice was deep and cool. Clayton Lilli's gaze went from me to him. Watching Clayton Lilli become afraid of William made all my fear be gone.

The other people in the park were staring now. The mother picked up her toddler. He watched us, too, with one finger in his mouth. The older couple stood up, shoes dirtying their blanket. The teenage girls were closest. They stared at us, impassive, like they were looking at a TV. One of them started to lift her phone to film us.

William met her eyes and said, "No."

She lowered it.

William said to me, "I hope you're certain." His jaw was tense. He didn't like this.

"I'm certain," I said.

He nodded. "Don't make the fist around your thumb. You could break it."

I took my thumb out and it was better. A better fist, I could tell already.

I turned back to Clayton Lilli, and I hit him again. Same place. I hit as hard as I could, even though my hand felt like it was already crying. Clayton Lilli was so surprised he sat down in the grass, and the dog ran back and forth in half circles around his back, peeking out from behind one side and then the other, barking. Then it made its legs go stiff, kicking up grass behind it with its feet.

"What the hell?" Clayton Lilli said. A slow trickle of cherry red came from his left nostril and snaked down over his lips.

"Get up, buddy," William said conversationally. "I'm not sure she's done yet."

Clayton Lilli was already getting up, and as he rose, I asked him, "Remember me now? Because I can keep asking."

His dog jumped side to side, still stiff-legged and growling.

His hands rose to protect his face as he said, "What's going on?"

"Put your hands down," William said.

"She'll hit me if I put my hands down," Clayton Lilli said, outrage coloring his voice.

"I'll hit you if you don't," William said. He spread his arms apologetically.

Clayton Lilli put his hands down.

I wanted better. I wanted something more John Irving, more *Hotel New Hampshire*. Why hadn't I brought a bear? But this was what I had.

I stepped forward to hit him again, and the little dog put itself between us, growling a high-pitched warning. It broke a corner off my heart, to see its tiny, awful, misplaced act of valor.

The man half of the older couple was coming toward us now, saying, "Stop it! Stop it!"

His voice came out very loud and nasal. I could hear he was

scared under all the blustery authority. I didn't even look at him.

"Honey!" his wife called from the blanket, worried to see her husband getting close to William.

"How do you not know me?" I asked Lilli. My hands were both still balled up.

He stopped nursing his nose and really looked at me, looked in my face. It started as a searching look that went to puzzled, and then I saw faint surprise ping. His cheeks flushed a bright berry color, as if all the blood that wasn't busy coming out his nose had rushed to them.

"Mandy?" he said. "Mandy Pierce?"

William said, "There it is."

I thought I would hit him again, for getting my name wrong, but seeing the recognition in his face, the shame staining his cheeks, the desire to put my skin on his in any way went out of me. He was pathetic with his stick bug legs and his girly purse dog trying to protect him. I couldn't stand to put even my fist on him. But finally, I had a name for him. I knew what he was to me.

"This is the guy that raped me," I said to the blustery older man from the blanket. Then louder, calling it out to his wife behind him, to the mother with the toddler clutched close, to the impassive teenage girls. He hadn't met the legal standard, but I wasn't in the mood to split hairs. He'd done his level best, and I knew what he was now. I pointed at him and said, "This guy raped me."

Everyone in our square of park paused, digesting that. The teenage girls believed me. I could see it in their bodies, upper lips curling in tandem as they stepped in closer to each other. The mother looked at him, intense, trying to decide, holding her baby closer, in case. The older couple seemed unconvinced.

"I did what?" Clayton Lilli asked me. "I did not." Then louder to all of them, "I didn't."

I talked over him, firm and clear. "He drugged me at a party, and then he took me out behind his frat house, to a beanbag chair."

"That's not true," he said, speaking to the older man, not to me. I felt my jaw set.

"And raped me," I said. So loud, so clear. My voice not trembling.

What a long way I had come in that Circle K, the girl who'd never said the word was yelling it across a park, telling the truth to the only jury Clayton Lilli would ever have to face.

Lilli gulped and I felt my hands fisting up again. The little dog sensed violence rebuilding, because it started that silly, endless danger growl again, down in its throat.

"Stop this!" said the blanket man, and I smiled.

William stood behind me, more relaxed now that he had confirmation, letting it play out. He had my back. It was good, but in that moment, I wanted Walcott there. I wanted him here with me so fierce that it felt like a sickness. I knew that if I'd called him, space or no space, then he would have come. That wasn't even a question in my head. He was the one who had found me, calling, *Marco! Marco!* He'd spoken for me when I couldn't speak. He'd decided to love Natty, though it had changed his life, made it different and more serious than what most boys got in college. He so deserved to pop this asshole in the face a few times, too.

"Sir," said the skeptical blanket man to Clayton Lilli, "do you want me to call the cops?" He'd appointed himself foreman.

"No," Clayton Lilli said. He was staring at me now with a horrified expression. "Don't do that."

That made the last two skeptics on the jury sway my way. I felt their belief click into place, watched their gazes on him change. I'd made him bleed in a public park. I had a huge bodyguard threatening him. An innocent man would want the cops. I saw them all, even the interfering blanket man, realize what Clayton Lilli was. I think he felt it, too. He looked around at them. "I didn't do that. What she said. We were both drunk."

"All I had was a Coke and some Rohypnol," I said, super perky, and I swear to God he blanched.

"That's not right," he said, and now he sounded whiny, like a horrid baby.

He looked around. The young mother had gathered her little

boy so close to her bosom I was shocked the kid could breathe. He pushed at her, trying to squirm down. The young girls looked at Clayton Lilli like he was a worm.

He turned a pleading gaze to me. "I swear to you—"

He couldn't find a drop of mercy on my face, because there wasn't one, and then I saw how I could truly pay him back. Uncertainty. I could hand him the uncertainty I'd lived with for years.

I said, very low and intense, looking him right in his eye. "Do you know the statute of limitations for rape in this state?" I didn't, either, actually, but I knew it was a long one. Ten or fifteen years. "I can go to the cops anytime."

I could see fear rising in his eyes, but he said, "At least they'd listen to my side."

That almost paused me. The cops could only ever be a bluff, because of Natty. I pressed forward. "It won't be my word against yours, you know. I have a witness. My friend Walcott came and found me, after. He saw how you left me, passed out in the yard. He saw how I was drugged." Lilli shook his head, and I started free-form lying then, mixing in enough truth to be convicting. "My friend took me to get a rape kit. I have your DNA. I have blood tests, showing I was drugged." I watched him swallow, his Adam's apple working. His gaze darted around. The little jury in the park heard everything, and he could see how they were all on my side now.

He reached down and scooped his frantic little dog up. He held it close. When he straightened up, I saw that his eyes were red and wet.

"I didn't," he stammered out, his words tumbling all over one another. "We were drunk. But I remember, you said—"

"I *don't* remember. That's how date rape drugs work," I said, like I was explaining basic math to the world's stupidest child. "I could have said I loved you, and it wouldn't have been true, or right, or anything like permission."

"You did say that." His bleeding face crumpled, and he was weeping openly there in the park.

I felt an awful shift toward sweetness in the mothery pit of me. I had an unspeakable urge to pat him, and it was unfair and purely biological. It was only because his trembling lip—so like Natty's—was streaked in blood and snot. It was so wrong that he could pull mercy out of me, simply because his tears went tracking down Natty-angled cheekbones.

"I'm sorry," he said. "Oh God, I am so sorry. But I swear I didn't rape you, Mandy."

That killed it. "It's Shandi, you perfect turd," I said. "Go home now and look up that statute of limitations. See how many years I have left to decide."

He looked from person to person, his eyes pleading, but the park jury was solidly behind me. Finally, he turned, carrying his fraught little dog with him, and began walking away. After a few steps, he broke into a run. It was a shambling, sad lope, spine hunched, crossing the park toward home, with us all staring after him, condemning him.

"Miss?" Blanket Man said, solicitous now. "Do *you* want me to call the police?"

I felt a surge of vindicated exultation at the kindness in his tone.

"Thank you, no," William said, politely. "I'm taking her home."

I was panting, and I had a hard time keeping my feet from dancing. In Clayton Lilli's mind, I could go to the police at any given minute. Let him live with the wondering. Let him eat the worry of knowing I could step in and change his life forever, and he would have no say in it.

William took my hand and pulled me along through the park, in a different direction than the one Clayton Lilli had taken. He walked away from all the eyes, and also away from his car.

I clung to his hand and followed. We went so fast, the breeze felt like a mighty wind on me, like we were flying.

We came out on a road lined with little shops and two restaurants that weren't open yet. William looked from one to another, exasperated.

"Doesn't anyplace serve breakfast? You need a shot of bourbon," he said, like bourbon would be there by the eggs and toast on any decent breakfast menu.

"It's Midtown, William. They only have brunch here," I said. "I don't need bourbon."

"You do. Your pulse is way too high." I realized that we weren't actually holding hands. He'd taken mine to press two fingers on my wrist.

"Stop taking my pulse, Dr. Ashe. I'm fine. I'm just jacked up," I said. "Did you see what I did back there? I annihilated him."

He pulled me back into the park, angling for a wooden bench now. I followed, obedient, and I kept his hand. He worked my fingers as he walked, like now that was he was done being medical, he was unaware he held it.

"I didn't think Clayton Lilli would be so pathetic," I said. My earth-made monster had been shambling and lumpy, faceless and terrifying, dripping clods of red clay off his huge, filthy hands as he loomed over me. "I've been trying to imagine him, ever since the Circle K, and he was never like that."

William sat me down and took my wrist again. "Since the Circle K? Not before? Take three deep breaths, please." He was looking at his watch.

I shook my head, trying to get a lot of air down into me. Now that we were sitting still, I could feel my heart pounding all through my whole body, but it wasn't bad. It felt like victory drums. I'd be a constant sour worry at the very back of Clayton Lilli's throat, for years to come. Let him live with the same thing he'd taught me, that all his choices could be taken away in a single snap of time, at *my* whim.

"Before the Circle K, I pretended he didn't exist. My virgin birth, remember?"

"That's interesting," William said. "It's interesting that people do that."

"Do what?" I said. I pulled in one deep breath after another, calming.

He said, "Put people and events away inside their minds, and pretend they never existed. Why should something so random and banal as a bullet change it?"

"All I know is, after the Circle K, I started thinking about him. Not the real him, not like he actually is. He's so much floppier and weaker than I pictured."

"That's interesting, too. Can you say more about that?" He let go of my wrist, and turned to face forward, staring back across the park, listening intently.

I wasn't sure what he wanted, but I kept talking. "When I got past the idea of a literal monster . . . I don't know. I thought he'd be some smug, fratty, rich kid, all entitled. That's who drugs girls in the movies. Or a truly scary sociopath with dead eyes and bad teeth. This real one, I could see all the veins in him because he was so milky. I could see his veins all blue and sad under his skin." I shrugged, even though William's gaze on the horizon was so intense, he wasn't even seeing me. "This real one is . . . He is . . ." I stopped. I didn't know how to say what he was.

"He's a person," William said.

I snorted. I wouldn't grant him that. "He's an animal."

"Yes," William said, excited. "He's just an animal, like you and me."

"Not like us," I said, instantly. "Call a cab? You'll have to come and get your car back, later."

I wanted out. I would never come back to Midtown again. Or Buckhead, where Clayton Lilli worked. Natty and I had to stay east, in Morningside, in Poncey-Highlands and Decatur. In a city of four million, surely our paths would not cross. But Midtown felt like enemy territory now, and my power to hurt him lived in his uncertainty. I never wanted to lay eyes on him again.

William wasn't listening. He'd gone away, down inside his head, sitting on the bench, oblivious to the city waking up around him. The morning sky was turning blue and all the light had gone golden. Today's heat was rising, and some cars were going by on the closest road.

"William!" I said.

He jerked and then his eyes met mine, and I knew he hadn't heard me ask about the cab.

He smiled, and it was like he caught all the morning sunlight and pulled it into himself. He was golden and so lovely.

He leaned toward me, and I thought, *Really? Here? Right now?*

But I was ready for it. More than. The last time I'd come this close to kissing him we'd been held at gunpoint, so this was hardly less appropriate. I felt my spine lengthening and my body swayed his way, my eyelids drifting closed.

But his eyes were open, all the way, and his gaze passed right through me to some imagined landscape.

He said, his face too close to mine, "I know how to fix Natty."

"What?" I said, my half-mast lids flying back open at my son's name. William stood up, his movements abrupt and excitement in every line of his body.

He said, "Stevie is just a person."

"Stevie?" I said, confused, and then I realized who he meant. "Stevie who *shot* you?"

"Technically speaking, Mrs. Grant's foot shot me. But yes. That Stevie. Steven Parch." William smiled that same beautiful, light-filled smile, but it wasn't for me. He smiled it for his idea, and then he said the craziest damn thing I'd ever heard.

"We have to take Natty to the hospital. You need to let him really look at Stevie. Stevie has no fangs, no giant guns for hands. He needs to see Stevie being just a person. A quiet, sleeping person."

I heard what he was saying and it was crazy. So crazy, yes, but also? I thought maybe it could work.

Chapter 12

Natty is perched on the slate gray granite kitchen island at the condo, banging one foot into a cabinet door. He is fixing himself a mixed juice in a sippy cup. William is supervising. He keeps one hand steady on the backs of the containers as Natty pours, first orange juice, then pineapple.

"Will he see me?" Natty asks.

"No. He can't see you," William says. Steven Parch can't see anyone. But Natty's foot keeps banging the cabinet, and his serious, straight eyebrows are folded into a crinkle. "Even if you stood right by him, he couldn't see you. But you'll be on a different floor, with your mom. Can I put the carton away?"

As Natty nods, the doorbell rings. Shandi's heels clack and bang against the oak floor as she goes to answer it. With the clutter gone, he can see the whole place is composed of sharp corners. Sounds bounce off the merciless surfaces, amplified to harshness.

William says, "You've already been, remember? It's the same hospital where you came to visit me. You won't be any closer to him than when you came to my room."

Natty doesn't answer. He picks up the full cup, sucking his

lower lip into his mouth as he struggles to get the cap screwed on. William lets him, leaning back as droplets of juice spatter onto Natty's shorts. William admires the independence that comes with being three, or perhaps it comes with being Natty. He knows too small a sample to state definitively what three is like.

Natty at three wants to help. He wants to help with everything. *I can do it myself* is his favorite sentence, whether he can reasonably do it himself or not. The kid would try to drive if Shandi would give him the keys to the VW. Maybe she should. The car is sized about right for him.

Shandi has let someone in. In the living room, William can hear a man's voice, talking.

"It is not always possible to fall in love in blackberry season," the man says.

William can hear each of these odd words clearly. The acoustics in this high-ceilinged, sharp-cornered place are excellent, and the man is speaking slowly. His tones are formal, as if he is giving a speech. "You might enter the many dark chambers without this—"

"Walcott!" Natty says, his whole face lighting.

"—clustering. You might start by washing your lover's mouth in snow, or tease apart the spring tendril root of him."

Natty tries to hurl himself down off the island and shatter his bones on the cold tile floor.

William catches him and swings him up, saying, "Wait."

Walcott says, "Or scrape the old leaves out of his autumn hair, on your way to making his acquaintance in loam."

The words are intense and personal. William isn't meant to hear them.

"Put me down," Natty demands. "It's Walcott come!"

Natty wriggles and flails downward, helped by gravity. William, unprepared, must lower him or drop him. The second his sneakers touch the floor, Natty runs for the living room. William follows, feeling strongly that their entry at this point is not ideal.

Shandi has her back to them, but her arms are full of flowers.

A huge, chaotic mass of wildflowers, purple and gold, spilling out of a paper cone. Walcott, the boy who was so angry at the hospital, stands in front of her in his flip-flops, reading from a piece of creased printer paper.

"But if it is chosen in the kingdom of blackberries, that you shall be one of the ones—"

As Walcott sees Natty, he smiles around the words. Then, as he sees William, his smile and voice cut out abruptly. At the face change, Shandi turns. Her eyes are wide and bright. When she sees William, she flushes and her lips part.

"Oh, hi," Shandi says to William. "We were just . . ." She trails off and sets the flowers aside very quickly. They lie in a careless spill across the coffee table.

Walcott closes the paper at the fold, shutting it.

"I didn't realize you had company," Walcott says, and then he swings Natty up in his arms. "Hey, Natty Bumppo."

"Walcott! I mixed my own juice, perfect," Natty says.

"Cool," Walcott says, and then, to William, "Can you give us a sec, buddy?"

William doesn't like this, not at all. It is his own name for Paula's man scraps who tag along to brunch.

"William," he says, and doesn't move.

"I know who you are," the kid says, as if William has offered an introduction instead of a correction.

Then they stand there, eyeballing each other. It isn't comfortable.

William finds his weight shifting forward, to the balls of his feet. Walcott is leaning toward him, too, shoulders braced. Between them is Shandi, and is he prepping to butt antlers with this boy?

William and Shandi have had a single, ambivalent almost-date that ended in a series of sickening revelations. William has barely begun to entertain the idea of replacement, of choosing a different life. So why this animal posturing? It's ludicrous, but his body is undeniably doing it.

Is it Natty? He cares for Natty, but in a mild, relaxing way:

no ownership, no true responsibility, no desperation. Discovering three through Natty has a faint, sick sweetness to it. He still can't imagine Twyla at six. Twyla at nine. He has no frame of reference. But Natty is a window into three.

Three is oblivious to testosterone and subtext. Into the silence, Natty says, "Walcott, we're going to visit Stevie. You should come."

"Stevie? Stevie who?" Walcott asks. And then his eyes widen and he says to Shandi, "Stevie the robber?" in incredulous tones.

Shandi says, "He thinks Stevie comes into his room at night."

"We can't get the Stevie-hole taped properly," Natty explains over her.

Walcott smiles at Natty's precise diction. "Not properly, huh? Okay. I'll fix it."

As if Walcott has superior imaginary hole-taping skills. This is ridiculous enough, without William's nostrils flaring, but they do.

"Natty's therapist thinks it could help to see the real Stevie, from a safe distance." Shandi steps to William and puts her hand lightly on his arm. "It was William's idea."

As her body changes places in the room, moving to him, the tension drops. For him, anyway. Not Walcott. Walcott takes a couple of steps in closer, trying to re-create the geometry of three adult bodies, equidistant. But William has already won whatever this is, and he doesn't even know if he wants it.

Walcott says, "Shandi, can I talk to you a sec? Alone?"

"I'll be upstairs," William says, and manually removes himself from the remnants of the competition. He crosses the room and starts up the stairs, glad he is wearing his soft-soled running shoes so he does not bang and clatter. As soon as he turns the first corner, Shandi starts talking.

"I'm so glad you came! I tried to give you space, but Walcott, space sucks."

The acoustics have not yet afforded them any privacy. William might as well still be in the room.

"Yeah, that whole noble retreat from the field—I'm not that

guy. I can't toss my hat and heart and pants all in the ring and then sag off like some kind of moopy loser at your first frown." William climbs faster, and as he rounds the second corner, the voices are fainter. "Not to mention, you're my best friend, having a crap month. What kind of a tool would disappear right now?"

Natty says, "Don't disappear, Walcott."

"Never. I'm sorry I—"

William rounds the second corner, and now he can't make out the words. Good. Let the kid take his shot. At the same time, if he really wanted to facilitate Walcott's courtship, he could have taken Natty with him.

He goes all the way up to the third-floor landing, a clear space with a computer desk and the bedrooms on either side. When he came up to tape the closet hole, Shandi's door was closed. It's open now.

She has a double bed with a sharp metal frame and the kind of generic bedding that is common in hotels. It's unmade, the white sheets in a stir. He only knows it's Shandi's room because the chair is draped with a bright yellow sundress and there are red flowered sandals on the floor.

Now he can't hear Shandi's or Natty's voices at all. Every now and again he hears the wordless rumble of Walcott, saying impassioned things and failing to regulate his volume.

William shakes his head, glad to be a full two floors above it. The boy in the flip-flops is on the losing side of an either/or equation. William has been on the losing side of an even more weighted equation, much like this, before, when he was driving week after week to the convent where Bridget had tucked herself away. He paced around her walls for nine months, relentless, without so much as a glimpse of her hair.

Walcott, with his poetry and flowers, is making a tactical error. He should absent himself. William stopped prowling there three months before Bridget was to take her vows, though this wasn't a tactic. He stopped because he'd lost. He'd learned that in the either/or of God or William, God won. Every time.

The weeks after he came to terms with that fact were not good weeks.

He didn't understand the mechanics, then. It didn't occur to him that when he stopped coming after her, he removed himself from the equation. She no longer had the power to choose, and that was when she came to him.

She appeared on his doorstep in the middle of a cold, gray Saturday in March. A spring thunderstorm lingered overhead all morning, alternately drizzling and dumping water down in cold sheets. There had been no sunshine for hours. She banged at his front door with her fist, loud enough for him to hear it over the murmur of rain against his roof. He opened his door to find her standing on the small, square porch, wringing her hands.

The wind blew rain in sideways to spatter against her. Her hair was red, slick strings, clinging to her face and neck. Her shoulders were braced.

He said her name, like a question, his whole body vibrating.

She shrugged, helpless, and said, "I can't hear God."

This seemed healthy, actually, but here was Bridget, in extremis. He opened the door wider and said, "Come in. It's pouring."

"I don't think I should?" she said. Definitely a question, and he began to understand why she had come. "Do you know who I've been talking to all month? Not God. I've been talking to you. It's an awful blasphemy. At night, I lie down alone and talk to you. When we pray the hours, I'm writing you long letters in my head, and God is gone from me. He's gone. What am I supposed to do about that?"

"I don't know. I'm not religious," William said, very dry, and Bridget snorted, a flash of her own real laughter, at his understatement. Then she shook her head.

"William, I've heard the call since I was six years old, and now, when I'm this close to answering, He stops? I should hear Him ringing through the storm like bells." She took the heels of her hands and dashed tears or rain away, and then she pressed her lips into a line and met his eyes. "Maybe this is good? Maybe this is right? Maybe it's a message, calling me here, instead? If you still want me."

Of course he wanted her. He'd always wanted her. How silly, how sweet, for her to put it as an if.

His body saw Bridget, red-cheeked, soaking wet, twisting her hands. Her breath came in pants, and her pupils had expanded to wide black rings. These things were, at last, permission. She was issuing a readable, animal call, and his body rose in answer.

He wanted to bring her inside, close the door. He knew better than to take her to the bedroom. The long walk down that hall contained so much intent. No, better to lay her down on the thick rug in front of the fireplace. This knowledge made him feel a grateful wash of love for Paula and the women who came after her. Because of them, he knew exactly how to peel wet clothes away. There would be no fumbling at catches and straps. He knew a thousand different things to try on her pale novitiate's body. He could do the things, all of them he knew, until she forgot to be shy, until her head lolled back and her body became stretchy and pliable and she opened to him.

She wanted him to. It was why she came.

But William was not the boy he was when Bridget last declared her love for him, in Paula's filthy old apartment. He'd grown into his body, with all its red washes of inexplicable feeling. It no longer owned him. He owned it.

Bridget was not coming to him whole, intact inside that completeness he first saw when she destroyed Shit Park's flower bed in order to rebuild it. A nun was God's bride. She was only having wedding-day jitters. *Perhaps not God*, she said. *Perhaps you, instead.* But if he let her form the question as an either/or, he lost.

And yet, how could he help it, when she was so beautiful? He stepped out, barefoot, into the bite of rain blowing across his porch, and then his arms were around her, at last. His arms dragged her to him. It was not a thing he could have stopped. Not with Bridget asking to be his, right now. He understood that it was only for a moment.

He lifted her, pulling her up against the length of him, her own shoes falling off her feet as he put his mouth on hers. She relaxed herself into him, winding her arms around his neck so tight.

He could not put walls between them and the world. If he brought her in the house, there could not be tea and talking. He would assist her in her panicked sin. It would happen. He would become a learning experience, the mistake that clarified her place. He'd become her fond memory, or perhaps just her regret.

If he wanted to retain her, their sex could only happen as a sacrament.

He left the door open, left it behind them and carried her down the steps. He walked her out into the rain, into the cold spring storm. It beat at the outside of their bodies, the ice of it the only thing that kept him from lying down with her and having her in the grass. It soaked them, closed their eyes, bound them tighter. It could not touch the heat between them.

He kissed her mouth, her throat, her wet closed eyelids.

"You can't be a nun," he said, his voice so hoarse it didn't sound like his. "You love me. But you can be my wife and still belong to God. Still be Catholic. These are not mutually exclusive states of being." Those were the words he said, over and over. "These are not mutually exclusive states of being." He said them into her skin, the cold rain getting in his mouth. He said them as if they were romantic, after all.

Bridget clung to him, and he said the words into her hair, against her cheeks, against her jaw. She tilted her face back and let the rain fall down onto it. He said them with his mouth against the pulse point in her throat, the orange-blossom-and-green-herb smell of his own catalyst mixing with the essential smell of Bridget.

She put her hands on his face and made him meet her eyes. Her face was full of an expression that he didn't know.

She said, "I've missed you both so much. Yet here you both are, in this yard. You're both out here in the rain and the dirt of the world."

She said these things and she was laughing. She was his. He

had not won the either/or. He never won it, but she was his then anyway.

That was his final act of courtship. He walked her back to her parents' place in the rain and went inside with her to disappoint them. He converted. He married her. They came together on their wedding night as if they were immortal.

"William?" Shandi is calling.

His body shudders and turns at the welcome interruption. He can't stand here looking at one woman's bed and longing for another. The dissonance is a physical discomfort.

The drama in the den has played itself out, but here is William, remembering rain on his face and nonsensically rooting for Walcott. They are so young. Walcott doesn't understand what he is risking.

"William, we need to go," Shandi calls, and he doesn't have to do this right now. Not today. Today, all he has to do is go and look at the man he hasn't quite killed.

The Stevie who haunts Natty's room is huge and toothy, with guns for hands. The original was a dumpy little fellow. Real Stevie had mucus on his lip and a crappy, ancient gun. He wielded its authority with no grace. This is what William wants Natty to see.

Natty's psychologist convinced Shandi that direct interaction might be too stressful. She modified William's plan. While William set up his MacBook in the hospital cafeteria, Shandi walked Natty through a quiet wing of the hospital. She showed him beds full of people resting, explaining that hurt people have to lie down, and that doctors and nurses are there checking on them, every minute. The psychologist told her how to explain a coma to a three-year-old, and she did that, too. That part went well; now they are in stage two.

Shandi and Natty sit by the MacBook, running FaceTime. William and his iPad are on their way upstairs to Stevie's room. With the iPad's camera, William can show Natty reassuring things from a safe distance: the cop outside the door, the peaceful room, Stevie lying motionless and quiet. William can send select still images or a live-feed video, depending on how upsetting Stevie's tubes are.

William passes the nurses' station. It's technically illegal for William, the victim in a crime, to visit Stevie, but Stevie was transferred out of ICU after they took him off the ventilator. They needed the bed, so he has become the floor nurse's problem until he can be moved to a long-term care facility. William waves at the young nurse manning it, and she waves back, smiling. The only true barrier is the cop outside the door, and Detective Bialys has cleared it with him.

William turns right, following the room numbers as they rise toward Stevie's. He's only a few rooms away when he passes a short, stump-ended branch of hallway that only goes left. It's little more than a nook containing a few chairs, a magazine rack, and a Coke machine.

There is a girl sitting in one of the chairs. She's so familiar that he pauses. He cannot place her, but he knows this profile, knows this chopped, flat fall of burgundy-brown hair. He takes two steps toward her. She senses it and turns her face to him. She gasps and leaps to her feet. She knows him too, this very curvy girl wedged into a tight skirt, her large breasts tumbling out of a low-cut V-neck T-shirt.

A black and yellow bird is tattooed on one breast. He knows this bird, this thing with feathers, and he recognizes her even before her mouth opens into a surprised O, showing him the front teeth, broken off to stumps.

It's the weeping clerk from the Circle K, out of context in this waiting area off the hallway to Stevie's room.

She tries to dash past him, angling left, but William matches her movement and blocks her in.

"Are we going to have a chase?" he asks, incredulous.

She gulps and her eyes roll around as she backs toward the

Coke machine. He follows her into the alcove, and at his advance, she panics. She runs at him again, faking left before trying to dart right, telegraphing every move. William back-steps and matches her, blocking her path but avoiding actual contact.

William has put it together by then. She belongs to Stevie.

She is the reason Stevie knew when the Grants would be emptying their cash safe and making their weekly bank run. He can't help but admire how cool she was—how cool she and Stevie both were—working to seem unconnected. Stevie made her lie down on the floor with the rest of them. Even after the robbery went sour, he kept her up against the hostage wall, protecting her. The whole time she was his mate, her real fear making it easier to crouch and hide among them.

She pauses, and her eyes twitch back and forth in their sockets, seeking a way around him. He flexes his hands, spreading his arms out wide so she can take in the size of him.

He says, "It's no good. I'll catch you."

The stumps of her teeth bite down on her lower lip, and William has to stop himself from flinching. His tongue runs over the surface of his own teeth, checking them, and the motion causes a wave of déjà vu.

The clerk backs up to the closest chair. She plops down into it and slumps there in a heap.

Another piece clicks into place, and William says, "Did you set my car on fire?"

She hunches down, curling even farther around her own middle.

"No?" she says. It lilts up, asking if he will accept the lie.

But the timing fits. Earlier that day, the uncle agreed to remove Stevie from the ventilator.

"You set my car on fire," he says, not a question now. "Get up."

The cop outside Stevie's door can cuff her to something and call Bialys to come get her. She rises to her feet, still hunched, her elbows bent so that her hands cup at her belly. He looks at her hands, pressing into herself. The clerk, in the Circle K, was built like a taller, fuller version of Shandi. Shandi is a figure eight, her center impossibly narrow, but this girl's middle has thickened. Her hands press into her abdomen, shielding it.

She's pregnant. Not hugely so. Not yet. But enough for him to see it, now that he is looking.

I'm a daddy, too, Steven Parch said. William heard it as a boast, but perhaps it was a message to the mother of his child, sitting with her back against the hostage wall.

Steven Parch's child exists.

His earpiece chirps. He checks the phone. Shandi, wondering why he hasn't made the FaceTime connection yet.

He taps his Bluetooth and says, "I ran into some red tape. Give me a minute? I still have to check in with the cop."

"Okay," she says.

He clicks off, as phone efficient as Bialys, though her breath was on the intake, prepping for more words. He hopes that they were only pleasantries. All his focus is here.

Tears are spilling down the clerk's cheeks, making black mascara tracks. Now she looks more like the girl that he remembers.

"What's your name?" he asks her. He has forgotten it.

"Carrie," she says. "Carrie Miller. What are you going to do?"

What should he do with a pregnant girl, one stupid enough to come creeping around the edges of her own botched crime? She has probably been here most days, trying to overhear news of Stevie's condition. Blowing people's cars up, albeit poorly, when she's gotten that news.

"I don't know," he says.

"If you make me leave, I think he'll die. I've been sitting here praying him to be alive. Don't make me go." Her voice is thick with snot, and William's neck and back are stiff with tension.

Why is this day so full of awful, hopeless love? That young man spouting poetry, and now this damp, burbling girl. William is no better, racking himself into remembering the day he won his wife while staring at another woman's bed. All this overblown, untenable human feeling, and to what end, when nobody gets out alive?

Carrie crouches protectively over her pregnancy. She's been hiding out in the hospital, though her presence is tantamount to a confession. A glimpse of her, and William put the whole thing together in a matter of seconds. Bialys wouldn't have needed half that time.

She should be arrested for her shitty car bomb, and her part in the robbery, too. She stands weeping and trembling with her hands wrapped around her gestating midline. What a worthless set of parents this poor spatter of hopefully multiplying cells has drawn.

"Oh, fucking fuck," William says. He can have her arrested later. "Come on. I'll get you in to see him."

Now she stares at him with such wild hope that he can't stand to look at her. He turns and grasps her elbow, and together they go out of the alcove and down to Stevie's room.

The cop outside is an old guy, reading some kind of novel. He stands as they approach.

"I'm William," he says, and they shake hands. He doesn't explain Carrie, and the cop doesn't ask.

"You can go on in," the cop says. He opens the door for them like a butler, and he closes it behind them.

Carrie gasps when she sees Stevie. He is curled on his side, facing out into the room. His eyes are closed, and that's good, for Natty. The more it looks like he is sleeping, the better. His hair is growing in, brown fuzz over the place where William hit him.

Carrie starts toward him, but William still has her elbow. He clamps down on her.

"Sit," he says, and points to a chair by the window.

"I need to—"

"No. There are more people downstairs, and this delay could make them come up here. You sit. I need to send them video, now. You stay out of the shots and don't make sounds. You can get close to him later." He doesn't say *while I decide what to do with you.*

Carrie subsides into the chair, but she never looks away from Stevie. She swallows and wrings her hands, leaning toward him in the chair. William can't connect her rapt expression to the reality of the scrawny boy who is curled on his side. The Stevie she sees is probably no more realistic than Natty's huge fanged version.

William connects to the laptop with FaceTime. He is careful to hold his iPad at an angle that shows only his face and the wall behind him. Not Stevie yet, and certainly not Carrie. On the screen, he can see Shandi, with Natty on her lap. Natty has one finger in his mouth, sucking it. Shandi, peeking from behind him, looks tense.

William makes a relaxed smile and says, "Hello, Natty."

"Is he there?" Natty says. His voice is very low.

"Yes. I'm in his room, and you see that I'm fine. It is very quiet here, because of the coma. Stevie is here, sleeping, and that's all he does. All day and night. All the time." These are lines from the doctor's script. Shandi went over it with him. He is to describe the coma as a special kind of permanent sleeping. "Do you want to see him?" William asks. There's no reason to use still shots. Stevie is inert and his tubes are minimal, only some IV equipment and a clear line running up into his nose.

"I'm scared of see him," Natty says. He and Shandi have the same face, their eyebrows pushing inward, lips down. *The turnips are worried.*

"I'm not," William says.

"But you aren't scared of any things," Natty says, and oh, but William wishes that was true.

In the corner Carrie is trying to cry silently. William hopes they can't hear her moist snuffling over the hum and beep of the machines in the room.

"Could I see him only little bits?" Natty asks.

William turns the camera, careful to keep Carrie out of it. He takes Natty on a small, fast tour of Stevie.

"You see his eyes are closed?" he says.

"Why do he beeps?" Natty says.

"William?" Shandi says, and William flips the camera back to his own face.

"The beeps are from his heart monitor," he says. "They keep that on because Stevie is so quiet, all the time, they need it to know he's all right. That tube is to feed him. He's so sleepy, he can't wake up to eat."

He shows the heart monitor, but angles the iPad camera so Natty can see part of Stevie, too.

Natty says, "I don't think that sleepy man is Stevie." His voice sounds better. Less afraid.

"It's him," William says. He goes closer to the bed, aiming the camera down to Stevie's face. In Natty's head, Stevie is seven feet tall with gun-hands, so of course this version is unfamiliar. "You see?" The face has not changed. It is still short-nosed, puffy.

After a pause Natty sucks his breath in, and he says, "That's really Stevie."

"Yes," William says. "He can't come to your room anymore. He can't go anywhere. Not ever. He's very sick. He won't get out of this bed anymore."

Natty says, "William? Why are you sad?"

"I don't mean to sound sad," William says. It is expedient and often kind to lie to children, but William can't do it. Not right now. He turns the camera to himself. Now all Natty can see is William's face and the wall behind him. He looks and looks at Natty. Not Shandi, hovering worriedly behind him. And not beyond the iPad to the weeping girl, rocking the baby inside herself back and forth with her arms wrapped tight around it. "I'm sad because I'm the one who hurt him. It was the right thing to do. He had a gun, and he was doing a crime. I couldn't let him hurt you or your mother, or the Grants." He leaves Carrie out. She was never in danger. But he says these things both to Natty and to the girl who loves this sorry excuse for a man so much that she set William's SUV on fire. "I'm sorry it turned out this way. I wish he would wake up. I only meant to stop him from hurting anyone."

Natty's small face pushes forward so he fills the iPad screen. He peers through the technology at William's face. "You want him to wake up?"

"Yes," William says. "Very much. He would go to jail, so you wouldn't have to worry. But yes, I wish he would wake up and go there."

Natty thinks about it, then he says, "Me, too, then. I want him to wake up and go to jail. I could call him to wake up."

"It's not likely he could hear you, Natty," William says.

William looks at Stevie's face, and through the iPad he hears Natty say again, very loud, "Stevie!" Natty can't see Stevie, only William, but he yells to Stevie anyway. "Stevie! You can wake up now!"

Steven Parch's eyes open.

William feels his body flush into heat, though he knows intellectually that Parch's open eyes mean nothing. Coma patients often open their eyes, even move their limbs, following an unconscious daily schedule. It is only the timing that makes it disconcerting.

"He won't wake up, Natty," William says. William keeps his own face carefully neutral. Stevie's open eyes stare into nothing. "I'll be down in a few minutes, okay?"

"Okay," Natty says.

William kills the connection and closes the iPad cover. He sets it aside on the rolling table by the hospital bed. The second the lid is closed, Carrie is across the room, leaning over Stevie.

"Baby?" she says. She kisses his cheek, burrowing under the nose tube to kiss at his slack mouth.

"It doesn't mean anything," William tells her.

Carrie hovers over him anyway, and it sure as hell seems like Stevie is looking back.

"Baby?" Carrie says, and Stevie blinks. His mouth works.

"Wha happ'n?" Parch says, and his voice sounds rusty and unused.

William rocks backward like he has been punched. Stevie's eyes track the motion, and he looks past Carrie, blinking more at William, confused. "Did you . . . *hit* me?" Parch asks, and then Carrie leans in closer, blocking their view of each other.

"Baby, baby, oh!" she cries.

William keeps backing up, his heartbeat roaring and banging in his ears.

William can hear Stevie's rusty voice, saying, "Hey, honey."

"Oh, baby, oh, honey, oh," Carrie says. She puts a lot of little kisses on his face.

William wants to pull her back, away, but he can't bring himself to touch her. This is not medically probable.

His heart pounds in him and his rational mind begins lecturing, explaining very calmly that there was always a small chance that Stevie could wake up. Perhaps it is Carrie's voice that called him back. There is plenty of scientific research suggesting that the voice of a loved one can be heard in a coma. This is coincidence. Or it is Carrie's presence. There is no causal relationship between Natty's order and Stevie's awakening.

"We need to get a doctor," he hears himself say to Carrie, from very far away. "We need to get out of here."

"I won't leave him!" she says.

"Then you'll go to prison," William says.

That pauses her. Her hand flies to her belly. He takes her arm at last, pulls her back. He wants out of here, too. This is so medically improbable it approaches infinity. William doesn't want to be in the room with it.

In this very hospital, when he was a patient one floor down, Shandi asked him, *Do you believe in miracles?* The Red Sea. A virgin birth. In one of the Gospels, William remembers, the product of a virgin birth stands well outside a tomb and calls, *Lazarus, come forth.*

Stevie blinks and stares around, confused.

William's hand is clamped so hard on Carrie's arm now he can feel the grind of her bone. He pulls her toward the door with him.

"Don't talk," he says. He can't be in this room.

He opens the door and says to the cop, "He's awake. He's up. You need to get a nurse." Even as he speaks he is moving. Pulling Carrie out and down the hall.

"What?" the old cop says. "What?"

William keeps walking, calling over his shoulder, "You know that we can't be found here. I don't want to cause you trouble. Get the nurse."

"You're hurting me," Carrie whines as he tows her around the corner. He tries to ease his grip. It was her voice in the room, no doubt. William is positive Stevie's consciousness returned when she said *Baby*. That is how it must have been. There is research. He will not think about the fact that Natty, however technically, was born of a virgin.

But wouldn't Bridget love this? She would love this. If she were here she would be crowing at him, saying, *In your face, Will! In your face!*

He thinks he might fall down. His head is light. His lungs are constricted. He pulls Carrie back into the alcove.

"I need to be with Steeeevie," Carrie says, but she wails it in a whisper.

He releases her. "Run back there if you like, and go to prison."

She stays where she is, staring at him wild-eyed. Panting. Her hands again press protectively against her thickened middle.

"You're gonna send me anyway," she says, but her facial expression is a mix of crafty and hopeful.

He puts his head down, blowing. There is nothing he can do for this stupid, pregnant girl and her stupider lover. They have made terrible choices involving reproduction and robberies. Her life is lurching toward a bad end, whether she goes back to the room or not, whether he turns her in or not. Even if he keeps his mouth shut, Bialys might still figure it out, or Stevie could sell her out for a reduced sentence.

"What are you going to do?" Carrie Miller says again.

He knows the two of them are canny enough to lie under pressure. Perhaps Steven Parch will plead guilty and eat the jail time, to protect her and his child. He certainly protected her that way in the Circle K, which showed a certain amount of foresight. A certain amount of love.

William cannot be involved in this, but he takes his phone out anyway, and begins scrolling through his contact list. Now that he has not killed Stevie, it is his moment to walk away clean. But he can't quite. Her tear-stained face. The thickness of her middle, where she is making something helpless. However improbable, there is love here. Whether she goes to prison or not, this baby that has worried him and kept him from comfort about Stevie's fate is not going to have a good life. It will be unhappy. It will engage in crime. Probably.

But then, there are anomalies, like Paula. Carrie is no worse than Kai, all things considered. Who knows what secret combinations, what recessive magic, could be at play inside those multiplying cells?

He finds the number he wants, then gets his pen and an old *Reader's Digest* from the magazine rack. He copies it down.

He does it because Stevie's eyes opened before her voice was in the room. He knows this. He witnessed it. Stevie's eyes opened when Natty told them to.

He hands her the magazine.

"That's my dentist," he says. "If you call him next week, he'll fix your teeth. It will be paid for."

Carrie stares at him, blinking, not comprehending, as if he has now handed *her* a miracle. Perhaps he has. The air is thick with impossible things. What she does now, what happens to the baby she is floundering to protect, the world will choose. He is absolved of it.

In this breath of absolution, he has decided. He knows the risks. He knows the constant, the only human outcome. But if he is going to live on this earth—and he is—he cannot go on as he has been. He will not.

"Thank you," she says.

He isn't sure why she thanks him. Maybe only for the dentist. But maybe she understands the larger gift, which he gives her now.

He walks away.

PART THREE

Rise

A heaven in a gaze,
A heaven of heavens, the privilege
Of one another's eyes.
EMILY DICKINSON

Chapter 13

I opened the front door to find Clayton Lilli standing on my steps. I was barefoot and he was tall; when the door swung wide, I was looking at his collarbone. I had to travel all the way up his skinny stretch of neck to find his face.

A huge, surprised scream rose up inside my body, whirling round and round like a trapped tornado, winding all my guts together. My throat stayed closed, though. I would not let it out. Around the corner, in the godawful glass and chrome living room, Natty and Walcott were playing with the Matchbox cars. If the scream got out, they would come running.

Clayton Lilli was existing on my very steps, and Natty was a single wall away, secret and perfect and only mine. I bulled my way forward, out the door, and I shut it between them.

Clayton Lilli backed down the stairs as I came out, all the way to the sidewalk. It made him shorter than me. He stood on the curb, and I saw his mousy girlfriend had come, too. He looked blank, but Mouse Brown had brought a whole big bunch of feelings with her. They all showed on her face. She stood behind him, desperate and determined and a thousand other mixed-up things. It was easier to look at her, quite frankly.

"Leave, before I call the cops."

I hissed the words, forceful but not loud. I didn't want Walcott and Natty, please not Natty, coming to see if I'd gotten hung up with a Jehovah's Witness or a Girl Scout. Behind them, my two parking spaces held my car and Walcott's Subaru. They must have parked on the street, outside the high brick wall. I had to make them go there. Out the gate and out of sight. I only had a couple of minutes, four or five at most, to move them before Walcott and my son came to see what was keeping me. I wanted to yell inside to Walcott, to tell him to stay put, but that would likely bring them to us faster.

"I apologize for surprising you this way," Clayton Lilli said. "But I can't live with this. You have to hear my side."

He fumbled in his pocket. He pulled out a piece of paper, and his tall, skinny build made his movements an awful mimicry. He looked like Walcott taking his crumpled poem out to court me. Oh, but my power move in the park was backfiring. Clayton Lilli had brought me a pocketful of earnest words, too. His were for Mouse Brown's benefit, not mine. Why the hell had he told his girlfriend?

"You don't get a side. You get to leave or be arrested."

Why hadn't I let things be? I hadn't been able to live with uncertainty, so what made me think that he could? He had come to find me so much faster, though.

"Call the cops," Mouse Brown said, so close to him their shoulders pressed. Her thin lips were all atremble. "He'll read it to them, too."

"Please. It will only take a minute," Clayton Lilli said. His voice was flat. He seemed so calm, but I could see how his hands were clamped down on the paper, one on either side, waiting for permission. His knuckles were white. "It's important that you know the truth."

"I don't have a minute," I said. "And you don't have the truth."

I started down the steps toward them, and it pushed them back. They moved away from me, both of them, and this was good. Back toward the gate was good.

"You don't know this man," Mouse Brown said. "What you think happened is not possible. It's not who he is."

Clayton Lilli began reading. "'On the night of our encounter, my judgment was impaired. I had participated in a rush activity that required me to drink a large quantity of beer in a relatively short period of time.'"

I hated how he spoke, the formal grammar so like Natty. Could even that be genetic? William said everything was. It was unendurable, to listen to him talk this way, and time was sliding past, precious seconds squandered. I broke in before he could start the next sentence, saying the first thing I could think of to try to wrest away control of the conversation.

"I have a gun."

Clayton Lilli looked up from the page, and he and Mouse Brown blinked in tandem at my empty, gunless hands. My sundress didn't even have a pocket.

"It's in the house," I said, as if this would make it better.

The only gun inside, really, was a plastic Star Wars blaster that made *pew pew* noises and had lights along the side. I needed Natty's dream gun with its awful feet, so if I called it could come running out to shoot them.

In the Circle K, the gun gave Stevie all the power in the room, though he'd been so small and way outnumbered. I wanted to wave one at them, watch their little white tails bounding away over the hills. Then I could drive to Sandy Springs and shoot Bethany in her foot, for putting in the second phone line for me. I would shoot my own foot, too, for correcting Clayton Lilli when he called me Mandy at the park. He could even now be Googling an endless stream of Amandas and A and M Pierces without ever, ever finding me.

"My friend is inside, too. William. The big guy. All I have to do is yell, and he will come out here and break you into pieces."

That was better. He sure remembered William. I saw it in his sideways glance, the backward shuffle of his feet.

Mouse Brown said, "He's not here to threaten you or scare

you. He's trying to explain why he . . . went outside the frat house with you." She was a better advocate than he was, with his stiff paper and his even stiffer face, his inability to meet my eyes. I thought of William saying, *Duplications and deletions,* and of Paula telling me that her Au-tastic Dr. Ashe was a grown-up who knew how to pass.

Clayton Lilli didn't have it down yet, but Miss Mouse sure loved him anyway. She was a damp-nosed country song, standing by her man, even though her man was a total, raping asshole. What on earth was wrong with women? Now she held her hands up to me like she'd taken a job as his personal supplicant.

"If he'd been sober, he might have realized you were in trouble. He didn't know. He wasn't the one who drugged you."

She'd pulled me into it in spite of time and all my instincts. Oh, it was a smart story. The best lies contain a lot of truth, and he wasn't trying to blame me. He'd invented a defense that dovetailed with the memories I did have, and with everything I'd said to him at Piedmont Park. In his clever version, he was a random fellow, drunk at a party, who'd been enticed outside with a girl he'd thought was loose and as drunk as he was. The awful part was, it could be true. I didn't think it likely, but it could be. I had no way of knowing. All my ways of knowing had been taken from me.

I said, "You must have a good idea about who did drug me, then."

I said it to him, not her. If a different guy really had drugged me, either for himself or to help Clayton off the Emory Football Team, he would have been on the scene.

Clayton looked past my shoulder, his mouth turning down. "I'm not sure."

"That's convenient. For you and for your frat brothers," I snapped.

He faltered, looking to his feet, and Mousy grabbed the flag again.

"They are *not* his brothers. He dropped out in the middle of pledging exactly because of crap like that night."

Crap like that night, indeed. She sounded prim and disapproving, as if my assault had been a naughty frat shenanigan, equal to
pantsing some stodgy professor.

"Please may I read my paper?" Clayton Lilli asked with
dogged good manners. "It's all here in my paper."

I could feel the clock moving. He would not stop, ever, until
I agreed to hear him out. "Fine. But not now. Not here. It has
to be someplace public. I'll listen, but not at my house. If you're
really a nice guy, then you won't come invade my own house and
blindside me and try to make me." I turned to Mouse Brown,
so desperate to get them away from Natty that I would promise
anything, threaten anything. "Is he the kind of guy who's going
to make me?"

She stepped up, bobbing her head at me and practically gushing.
"No, no, that's fine. We'll meet you anyplace you want. Anytime."

She reached for his elbow, but Clayton Lilli was scrabbling in
his breast pocket for a pen. His hair was brushed and he'd put a
product in it to try to tamp the cowlick down. It wasn't working.
I bet the girlfriend had picked the outfit, a button-down shirt and
khakis, pressed to have a crease. Classic Nice Guy, with a touch of
Harmless Nerd. He shoved his thick glasses up with one hand and
fumbled for his pen with the other.

"Let me give you my e-mail."

"Just go. I'll find you. This is exactly the reason God invented
Google, so you could get the hell away from me. Right this
second."

My voice rose toward hysteria, and Mouse Brown tugged his arm.

"He's on Facebook," she said. "Clayton Dean Lilli."

I boggled at her. Did she expect me to friend him? Maybe he
could post his note to my wall, and then we'd all three go play
Farm Town.

At least they were turning away from my door. They were
walking across the lot. The Mouse set a mercifully quick pace.
I began remembering how to breathe. They reached the open
gate. There was a strip of grass and a flower bed by the entrance,

and they turned to go around it. They were so careful not to stamp through the zinnias, exactly like good, thoughtful, non-rapey people. Saving the stupid flowers cost five seconds, and in that span, I heard my front door opening behind me. I felt the push of air-conditioned cold rolling out against my back. At the same instant, Mouse Brown paused. She turned her face over her shoulder, toward me. Maybe she heard the door, or maybe she wanted to say one more thing. I don't know.

Behind me I heard Walcott saying, "Shandi?"

Mouse Brown was looking back, and I watched her whole body seize. All motion stopped. Her face went salt-white, and that's when I knew for certain Natty had come, too. She saw Natty, who was even now reaching for my hand, moving up to stand beside me.

I'd known Clayton Lilli was his father almost instantly, though I'd been farther away than his girlfriend was standing now. It was in the body, in the movements, in the cowlicks that stood up on the backs of both their heads.

She'd gone so rigid-still that Clayton Lilli stopped, too, and turned and looked. They stood in the gate, his face expressionless, and hers sizing up my son, doing math. Her eyes got wider and wider. Her mouth unhinged.

"Take Natty in the house," I hissed at Walcott, but he'd seen Clayton Lilli now, and he stepped up to stand on my other side.

"Is that the guy?" he asked. "Is that the guy? Is that the guy?"

It got fiercer and meaner every time he said it. He was seeing it, too, the pieces that Natty and this man shared, written in their every cell. I could feel the long sinews in his arm hardening and knotting, his whole body becoming something like a coil.

I had an image of them fighting. Two stretched-tall, skinny fellows tearing at each other with their spider arms. Poet versus accountant. Walcott would destroy him.

"What guy?" Natty asked, and the sound of him broke Walcott's gaze.

"Please take him inside. Please," I said in a tiny voice that had no breath behind it.

Walcott sucked air in between his teeth. He took Natty's hand and pulled him back behind me.

I said, "We all have to go inside." As if this would help.

Natty said, "That lady is throwing up on all our zinnias."

I herded them in, following, slamming the door shut, my fingers fumbling for the bolt. As if the door that had been opened up between us could be closed.

"Now what?" Walcott said.

I leaned on the door, panting. I didn't know. I looked to Walcott, desperate, but he didn't know, either. Natty stood by him with his eyebrows knit together. Natty had no understanding of what had happened, but he clearly knew that something had.

"Mommy, are you sick, too?" he said.

"No, I'm super," I said by rote. I was the mom, and the mom had to be super and have the answers. Even if she was the one who had called the monster to the doorway. Especially then, actually. I didn't have any answers, so I had to be extra super and come up with at least one.

Then I did have an answer. Just one, but it was a place to start. I could, right this second, put about a hundred miles of Georgia between my son and Clayton Lilli. This idea felt so much better than standing here and panicking.

"Natty, do you want for us to move back home? To Mimmy and the yell-y frogs?"

"Really?" Natty asked. "When?"

"Really. Now," I said. As a long-term plan, it wasn't great, but getting Natty to an address that Clayton Lilli didn't know was step one in my not going crazy.

"Let's get packing!" Walcott said, in a hearty, big voice, instantly on board. He'd become extra super, too.

Natty acted like I'd handed him a hundred puppies on the first day of summer. He stomped in a circle, yelling, "Hurray!

Oh, hurray! It is the moment of our great return!" with his odd, precise diction.

The formal way he talked had always made me smile, and it was a joy to know it still did, even now. I'd hated hearing Clayton Lilli speak that way, but he couldn't taint this. In my world, Natty had owned this way of talking first.

I took Natty up to the master bedroom and told him he could watch as much Nick Jr. as he liked. Once he'd been sucked into *Bubble Guppies*, I holed up in my bedroom with the walk-around phone. Walcott came with me and started covering small batches of my hanging clothes in garbage bags and tying off the ends while I called Mimmy.

She picked up on her cell phone; she was en route to her candy shop. I got her up to speed in a ragged whisper. It was strange, to be referencing truths we both knew but that had never been discussed between us. Walcott and his momses had done my talking for me, and then I'd pretended it away. Now, considering the hell I'd led to my doorstep, saying these words to Mimmy was so easy it was nothing.

As I spoke, telling Mimmy a truncated version of the hunt for Clayton Lilli, finding him, and how he found me back, Walcott stopped packing and sat down on the bed, listening. I told her everything, even the awful, discordant defense that he had mounted, with enough truth in it to be remotely credible. I told her that now he knew there was a Natty.

"Can we please come home?" I asked her.

"Baby, of course," she said. "I'm coming now to help you pack."

"Walcott's here," I said. "You don't have to."

I wished she would, though. I felt so small and scared right now. I didn't want to be the mommy by myself. I wanted her to come and help me be it.

"Don't be silly," she said. "I've been pointed toward you driving for the last twenty minutes."

That meant we had less than two hours until she came. Walcott and I started stuffing everything I owned back into the laundry baskets and my duffel and a slew of black plastic trash bags. We did it fast and sloppy; it would never all fit back in the Bug in such a tumble. It didn't matter. We had Walcott's car, too, and if that ran out of room, we could cram the rest in Mimmy's tugboat of a Buick.

We loaded Walcott's Subaru up first, and I saw no sign of Mouse or Clayton Lilli in the parking lot or on the road outside. They'd retreated to regroup, rethink, or maybe just break up. Natty's existence must be playing hell with her faith in his carefully typed story. I had no idea what their next move would be. All I knew was, Natty could not be here when or if they made it.

At least Mimmy had gone back to her maiden name after the divorce. She was Charlotte Madison, and if Clayton came looking, he'd be hunting Pierces. He'd find Dad easily enough, and that meant I had to return one of Dad's thousand calls. I'd been avoiding him, but he'd just become my canary in the mine shaft. I had to tell him everything and get him on the lookout. I could decide how to feel about his dalliance with The Mimmy Clone later. Right now, I wasn't interested in that; I needed Dad to have my back, the way he always had. I had to know Clayton Lilli's next move the second that he made it.

I could hear Natty happily calling out Spanish words with Dora, one floor down, as Walcott and I did a final sweep of the two upstairs bedrooms, looking for anything we'd missed. I checked the closet while Walcott dug around in Natty's bedding. He unearthed the old blue patchwork rabbit.

"Oh man, we almost left Yellow Friend."

"That would not be an acceptable loss," I said.

That was one good thing, seeing Yellow Friend there instead of Vader's disembodied head. William's plan was working. Last night, Natty had only woken twice, and I'd gotten him back to sleep in his own bed. I was willing to bet even his milder bad dreams would fade once we were home.

When we left, I felt like we should salt the earth behind us. This was a godawful place. Bethany's decorating made it so cold and unwelcoming, and, strike two, it had likely served as my dad's illicit love pad. Last and most, there was still a crisscross patch of duct tape in the closet, covering the Stevie-hole. I wouldn't come back here for a pair of sandals or some underpants.

Walcott sat down on Natty's twin bed, holding Yellow Friend. We'd already taken the pictures of Bikini Mimmy and Praying Hands Jesus and wrapped them up and loaded them inside my Beetle. All Natty's clothes and books and most of his toys were in Walcott's car. Bethany hadn't bothered much with the third floor, so what was left was a plain room with generic twin beds and a boring dresser with a herd of origami animals on top of it. They were the only sign Natty had lived here at all, except a laundry basket holding the last of Natty's toys. I began stacking the paper cranes and frogs into the basket.

I was so careful, not knowing when they'd be replaced. I hadn't heard from William since our trip to the hospital. Stevie had looked small and so pathetic, lying in a curl on the bed with a tube up his nose. William had pointed the camera at him for a minute, maybe two, before moving the camera back to his own face. I'd watched Natty shift from terrified to actually feeling sorry for poor Stevie. He'd even wished, along with William, for Stevie to wake up. I thought that was taking empathy a bit too far, and maybe William had, too. He'd cut off the feed abruptly and come down a short time later. He'd been silent and preoccupied as he drove us back here. He'd left us without coming in for coffee.

I hadn't been back to his house in two days, either. Paula had gotten to me with her description of William in love. I didn't recognize it. If he did have feelings for me, they were so well hidden that even he hadn't found them yet.

Now I was moving miles and miles away from him, and he didn't even know. That sucked, but it didn't change the plan. Natty out of the line of fire first, and the tattered rag of my potential love life later. Natty first, and everything else later. This was nonnegotiable.

"I think that's all of it," Walcott said, as I placed the last animal.

I nodded. Mimmy would be here any minute. We could load the toys and the stack of trash bags in the foyer into her big trunk. It was amazing how a tightly packed VW Beetle's worth of personal belongings expanded when you shoved them willy-nilly into bags and baskets. I took a deep breath and sat down by Walcott on the bed, but not too close. I kept a careful foot of air between us.

I said, "You know what scares me? I don't know what Clayton Lilli will do next. Not at all. I don't know what kind of person he is. I can't guess what he might be thinking, so how do I prepare? I guess I need to prep for the worst. But the worst is so bad, Walcott." Walcott knew what I meant. What if Clayton Lilli wanted into Natty's life? He could even sue for visitation and parental rights. "I should get Dad to put that awful Paula on retainer. Just in case."

I might not like her, but she was so freaking terrifying. She only worked for women, she had told me, and she knew all about custody. Just thinking the word *custody* in connection with my son and Clayton Lilli made my spine feel like a brittle string of ice. It could never come to that. I couldn't let it come to that. Why had I put him on trial in Piedmont Park?

"Don't take this the wrong way," Walcott said, and I felt myself bristling up, already taking it wrong, because I knew what he was going to say. "What if he's telling the truth? When you called me from the party, *I* thought you were drunk, and I know you really well. You were talking loud and slurry, but you *were* talking. You even made sense. I don't know what happened, but you weren't unconscious. Not then, anyway."

I felt myself hunching into a little coil as he spoke. He was right, but it didn't matter.

"There's no way I can ever know, so I can't let him be any-where near Natty. Not if I have any doubt at all. I can't."

"No, you can't," Walcott agreed.

All the air on my skin felt so chilly.

"It's dangerous, because I want it to be true," I said. "I don't want Natty's dad to be a rapist."

Just saying these things out loud, I was shivering so hard my teeth banged together.

"You can sit by me, you know," Walcott said, his eyes on me so nice. "We really are okay."

I curled deeper into my miserable huddle, not sure why I couldn't quite slide over. He'd fixed most of the damage his declaration of love had done when he came back with the flowers and the poem.

That day, after William went upstairs, Walcott told me, "That whole noble retreat from the field—I'm not that guy. I can't toss my hat and heart and pants all in the ring and then sag off like some kind of moopy loser at your first frown. Not to mention, you're my best friend, having a crap month. What kind of a tool would disappear right now?"

Natty had patted at his cheek and said, "Don't disappear, Walcott."

"Never," he said. Natty was satisfied with that simple answer. He wanted down, so Walcott kissed the top of his head and set him on his feet. "I'm sorry I bailed. I needed some time to get my head clear."

Natty went to the coffee table and started zooming one of his cars around. I knew that he was listening, though.

I asked Walcott, "So, what next? You're going to come sing under my window every night?"

He shook his head. He was looking down now, at his feet, but he had a familiar, rueful, Walcott kind of smile growing.

"You wish. This was it. The whole thing just happened." He looked up at me slyly with his head still bent, and handed me the crumpled paper. "That's right, you just got professionally courted by a poet. Boom! I'm not going to read this to you now. Not with Bruce Wayne right upstairs. I hope you'll read it later. I wrote it for you. Me. Not Auden or that hack John Donne."

"You did?" That made me smile back. I'd seen him use both those guys on Math Department girls, and Dickinson and Barrett Browning, too. I'd seen him whispering Shakespeare's dirtiest couplets into CeeCee's ear, but never his own. "You don't write love poems."

"Not usually," he said. "You were my first. But I'm done, okay? The poem, the flowers. There was candy, too, but I ate it on the drive."

"We go back to normal?" I hoped it wasn't too insulting that I said it so damn hopeful. I wanted to be with William, but my life didn't work well without Walcott in it.

"I guess. I'm not ready to throw fifteen years of friendship away because you're too effed up to know that you're in love with me. It is what it is. I promise not to gaze at you all heartlorn and be irritating like some courtly moron in Chaucer. We'll be us, but with one small difference. You have to know, I'm going to kiss you."

I glanced at Natty, but he did not stop vrooming his car. It went in an endless, breakless circuit of the coffee table.

"Kiss me?" I said, "Like a real kiss, on the mouth?"

"Oh, yeah. Tongue and everything. You owe me one, at least, for all that prime lovin' I threw your way that time."

He was right. I owed him whatever he needed, forever. Even with William right upstairs. Even with Natty three feet away, creeping around the coffee table on his knees and making engine noises. I nodded and turned toward him, bracing myself.

"All right," I said. "Let's do this thing."

He laughed outright and said, "Not now, you weirdo. Maybe not even soon. But before one of us is dead, I'm going to kiss you. It happens whenever I pick, and you have to promise that you'll kiss me back. That's the deal, if you want us to go back to normal. It may not be for years. Maybe even after whatever senior citizen you marry first drops dead. But you agree now that it's mine, whenever I decide I want it."

Natty's car found another, and they banged together. He made explosion noises with his mouth.

I had no idea how much of the conversation his big brain and his baby emotions understood, but I was glad he was there as a witness. It made it a true, sweet promise in between us, instead of some weird pressure.

So one day, maybe years from now, Walcott would kiss me. Who knows, in ten years, maybe twenty, we would be super different. I might blink and yawn like a middle-aged Sleeping Beauty, waking up to know I'd loved him all along.

"It's yours then," I said. "I promise I'll kiss you back."

He grinned and said, all mock cocky, "You don't know what you've agreed to. I wouldn't say it myself, but my friends all say I kiss like I invented it."

"Oh, you do?" I said, picking up his lighter tone, and grateful for it.

"Yeah. I've been told it's practically like kissing France."

I laughed, and after that he said good-bye to Natty and left. He wouldn't come with us to see Stevie, but I didn't mind. He had given me the world back, exactly how I liked it.

Now, the foot of space on the bed was the last awkward thing left between us. It was only air. I scooted over to him. He threw one arm around me and we sat, feeling the last barrier to us being us banished by the absolute not-weirdness of it. This was me and Walcott, his body and his smell familiar to me as my own. I leaned into him, and we stayed that way until the doorbell rang.

"I'm sure it's just your mom," he said, feeling my shoulders tighten. He got up and checked out the window. "Yeah. I see her car."

We went downstairs to get the door, and Natty joined us on the second-floor landing. He'd heard the doorbell. He bounced down ahead of us yelling, "Mimmy! Mimmy! Mimmy!" until we let her in.

She scooped him up, dropping fifty kisses on his head, then hugged me and said hello to Walcott.

As she came in, her eyes were darting all around, taking in the small foyer with its white marble floor, the ice-white walls. I realized this was the first time Mimmy had ever set foot in Dad's place. She'd never seen his house in Sandy Springs, either. The exchange of my child-self every other weekend had happened exclusively at public meeting places in between Lumpkin County and Atlanta. My mother and father would stand awkwardly in a Dairy Queen or a McDonald's, passing me and my bags back and forth. Taking the three-foot walk from one to the other was like crossing a whole tundra. It felt like the loneliest walk in the world. It had been a huge relief to drive it myself when I turned sixteen and Dad gave me the Beetle.

"Mimmy," Natty said. "Can I go with you in the big car?"

"I'd love that!" Mimmy said, at the same time I told him, "Of course you can." Walcott was already taking Mimmy's keys to load the last bags in her trunk. I handed him mine, too. "Can you move his car seat?"

"Sure," he said. "Give me a hand, Mr. Bumppo?"

Natty went with him, and Mimmy took me into another big hug, asking, "Are you okay?"

"I will be," I said.

Mimmy stepped back to search my face for truthfulness, and nodded at what she saw there. I was already better. Moving Natty actively away from here, I was able to think oh so much more clearly. I wanted to get right on the road, but Mimmy turned to the doorway to the living room, one little foot lifting, poised on the edge of the next room.

She wanted to see.

I glanced out the front door. Walcott was still moving the seat, so we had a couple minutes.

"Go on," I said.

She took a few tentative steps forward, like a deer who wants to eat your pansies but is scared of getting caught. She stopped inside the doorway. Her face was impassive as she took in the ultramodern furniture, everything cubed off in cold shades of black and gray.

"That should have had bumpers before you moved in," she

said. She gestured at the sharp glass coffee table. "Those corners could have pierced Natty's little skull like a harpoon."

"Bethany," I said, a one-word explanation.

Mimmy brushed at her own body lightly, as if the act of standing in this room had coated her in some distasteful dust. "Yes. Bethany. It's certainly not your father's taste. I'd do earth tones, chocolate brown and cream and cinnamon."

"That's what I thought, too," I said. "It would be masculine, but so much warmer. So much more like Dad."

She looked pleased, and she might have said more, but Walcott probably had the car seat moved by now. I was eager to get Natty gone.

"We should go," I said.

Out the corner of my eye, I saw her smile. It was a secret smile, only for herself. She added, so quietly I barely caught it, "Bethany doesn't really know him at all."

As she turned to leave, the smile spread, and there was triumph in her upturned lips, flashing like a victory banner. Triumph, yes, but tinged with other things. The hollowness of it stopped me in my tracks. It was such a bitter, covert smile, too much clandestine feeling for what was a very small win. I recognized it, even as she walked away.

My mother was in love with him. All these years later, she was still so very much in love with Dad.

I followed her, dazed, and saw my half-assed plan was going forward. Walcott was strapping Natty into Mimmy's car. There was no sign of Clayton Lilli. Our getaway would be complete and clean. Mimmy was already halfway down the steps. I paused to lock the door, still reeling.

I'd always thought Mimmy's vigilance was a waste: the constant diet, the exercise videos, the moisturizers. The cozy warmth of her house. The gorgeous meals she cooked and served but never ate. I thought she kept her body toned and her face so lovely and her home so welcoming for no one.

I'd been wrong. It wasn't empty. It was all for him. Whether she knew it or not.

Before I could feel sorry for her, I realized that he was equally pitiful. He'd married Bethany. My dad was charming and generous, funny and successful. Bethany hadn't been the only single Jewish lady in Atlanta when he went looking for a bride to please his family. He could have had his pick of a hundred warmer-hearted girls who would have loved him so much better. Maybe he knew that he could never love them back? Or maybe Bethany had been an angry impulse. His way of giving his family the skin of what they asked for, wrapped around a hundred and twenty pounds of bitch.

With her, he was as lonely as my mother. Now he was screwing Mim's facsimile, and I couldn't help but wonder if Patio Girl had been the first faux Mimmy to pass through his bed.

How stupid. My mom and dad had lost each other, and for what? So they could fit better at their parents' tables at Christmas and Passover? So their brothers and sisters could be comfortable? The families who had worked so hard to tear them apart had gone smugly back to their own lives after it was over. I didn't see any of my grandparents more than once a year. I got colorful birthday cards with twenty-dollar bills in them from my aunts and uncles on my birthday.

Meanwhile, my parents spent their lives so lonely. Dad wandered, seeking home in a mistress's Mimmy-canted face. Mimmy waited, her lamp trimmed, for a day that never came.

Meanwhile, all they'd ever wanted was alive inside the other.

As I came down the stairs, I knew it wasn't fixable. He'd missed me so much, seeing me only every other weekend. He wouldn't repeat that pattern with his sons, no matter what the cost, and Mimmy wouldn't ask him to. But God, I saw it perfectly, and it was such a mighty, overwhelming waste.

"See you back in Lumpkin," Walcott said. He climbed in his Subaru and started backing out. Mimmy was checking the car seat straps and then she closed the back door. She got in and started her car, and I went to mine. I watched as first Walcott's car and then Mimmy's found a break in the stream and slipped into it. Atlanta traffic pulled them away, toward the highway.

Mimmy and Walcott were taking Natty out of here. That was nonnegotiable, but it was also done. I sat in my car, and I knew I wasn't leaving yet.

I could not leave Atlanta until I'd seen William. I could send Mimmy and Walcott a text later, once enough time had passed to get them safely home. I'd say I'd had to run an errand, and I would be home soon. But I couldn't leave until I'd gone to William like an adult, and simply told him what I wanted.

A whole and grown-up person didn't play games with their own heart and their happiness. I'd let Paula and my own fear push me out. I didn't want to end up seeking substitutions or waiting for the world to change its course and swing my way. A whole and grown-up person would go and simply tell him. *I'm in love with you.* A whole and grown-up person would ask him. *Can you please love me back?*

I started my car and slid myself into the traffic, but heading the other way. I drove myself to Morningside.

I pulled over by the little square of park near his house and sent my texts. Then I drove on. As I crested the hill in my Beetle, I saw William in his yard. I hit the brakes, surprised. He was walking down his driveway, opening the driver's-side door to his SUV. He was carrying an ax. A real one, long and thick, like something for a fireman. It paused me. Not only the ax, but his body language. He moved like he was in a fury, with such fast, contained grace. I could see a world of tension in his shoulders as he loaded the ax into his car and climbed in after it. He backed out of the driveway and sped away.

I followed him. Not trying to be creepy. Not at first. A sunshine yellow VW is about the least stealthy car on the planet. I kept thinking he'd have to notice me and pull over. I would drive up beside him, and we would both roll down our windows.

I wasn't sure what I would say. Maybe leap right to *I love you.* Or maybe I'd get stage fright and only squeak, *Hello.* Maybe I would say, *Hey, William, have you got time to make hot love to me in the road here, or are you off to someplace vital with that ax?*

He didn't notice me, though. He drove more than five miles, all the way into Decatur, squeaking through yellow lights so that I shamelessly ran red ones, barely pausing at the stop signs. Now I was officially creepy stalkering, because he was obviously blind to the ball of yellow car in his rearview.

He turned off into a web of tiny, residential streets, not slowing for the wide speed bumps. His big car had better shocks than mine, and he got a couple of blocks ahead of me.

I rounded a corner and thought I'd lost him. I randomly picked to go right at the next turn, then came to a T intersection. I saw his SUV stopped half a block up on my left, in front of a painted brick bungalow with a cheery purple door.

He was already out of the car, striding across the lawn with such purpose that I was glad he didn't have the ax. As he walked, he pulled a square of white out of his pocket. A folded piece of paper, I thought. He walked to door and pressed the note against it, and it stuck. He must have had a tack or tape. I wasn't close enough to see.

He turned around, but still he didn't see me, though his face pointed briefly at me as he spun. He walked back to his SUV, got in, and drove away, the SUV bouncing high over the first speed bump. He was heading in the wrong direction to be going home, and I knew I wouldn't be able to keep up. I stayed where I was, looking at that house.

No one came out to get the note. I hadn't seen him knock or ring the bell. I pulled forward and stopped in front of the buttercream house. It was low and sweet-looking, with a lot of flower beds and a postage stamp of rich green lawn. On one side, a wrought-iron arch stood, covered in wisteria vine, with a pretty garden bench in front of it. I couldn't imagine who might live there. It wasn't Paula. She had a loft downtown. Who else could it be? I couldn't think of anyone who would matter enough to rate notes and all this purposeful stomping, much less the ax.

I turned the engine off and got out, walking up across the lawn toward that purple door. It wasn't gaudy. It was a rich, plummy color, and the paper—I saw now it was an envelope—looked very white taped to it.

There was a single word printed on it in William's economical handwriting. I went closer still, to read the word: *Bridget*.

William had left a note for a dead woman, taped to a purple door.

The hand on the end of my arm reached out and pressed the bell.

I waited, looking at that impossible word, hearing footsteps. The purple door swung open.

She was a few pounds heavier than she had been in the picture on the news. She wasn't grinning all happy, either, as she had then, sitting with her husband and her child on a cheery picnic blanket. She had only a polite smile for me, her eyebrows raised in inquiry.

The envelope, so white against the door's deep color, caught her eye. She turned to it, already reaching, and then she paused. William's dead wife paused, looking at her own name in his writing, looking at it with her dead-wife eyes.

"You're Bridget," I said to her.

"Yes," she said. She took the envelope down, running her fingers across the way he wrote her name. "Did you bring this? Did William send you?"

"You're Bridget," I told her. "You died."

She tilted her head to one side. "Oh! I see. I'm sorry. Yes, I did. Did you come to ask me about that? About where I went when I was dead?" She glanced at the envelope again, then put it away in her jeans pocket. When she looked back up, her eyes on me were so warm and so kind. "Usually Father Lewis talks to me before he sends someone, but I haven't checked my messages since yesterday." I stepped away, blindly moving backward, and she followed me out, putting out a hand to me like I was a skittish, homeless kitten. "No, no, it's fine. I have some time."

From the house behind her, I heard a man's voice call, "Honey?"

She called back, "It's someone from the church to talk to me, Dad. I'll be in in a minute." She closed the front door behind her. She took my arm in her warm, alive hand, drawing me across the lawn. I went with her like a thing with no weight, a balloon tugged on a string. "Did you lose someone recently?"

I nodded, because I had. Very recently. I'd just lost William.

"How long were you dead?" I asked her.

"Not quite three minutes," she said. She'd led me to the garden bench and sat down, pulling me to sit beside her. The bench was small, so that our knees touched. "It's subjective, though. To me it seemed much longer. Who did you lose?"

I couldn't think of a good answer. It was hard to look at her, my living rival, strange and estranged, and still think.

"I'm not here about that. I came because—" I had no way to finish that sentence. "I followed William."

"Oh," she said. Her hand went to her pocket, resting over the note for a second, digesting that. She was trying to change gears again. "How do you know William?"

"I was in the robbery. We were in a robbery."

"Ohhh," she said, and this time it was a dawning sound. "You're Shandi."

I blinked, but before I could ask, I had the answer. Paula. No wonder Paula was so set against me. I saw myself as she must see me, a pushy little girl in a Marilyn dress, moving in on a lonely man who was separated from his wife. A wife he'd once loved so much he'd stormed a convent for her. In Paula's eyes, I'd tried to slip myself between a broken couple who had lost their child. My face burned as I remembered myself saying awful, callous things about shoes and Columbus and fresh starts. Paula could have saved everyone so much trouble if she'd just said, *Hey, dummy, Bridget is alive.* I suppose it hadn't occurred to her that I thought Bridget was dead.

After the robbery, I'd heard the talking heads tutting about a tragedy, and I'd looked at that picture of his wife and child up on the screen. I'd picked the tragedy that suited me, and I'd ignored all other possibilities. I was good at that, ignoring truer possibilities, once I found a narrative that pleased me.

This, like many, many things, was partly due to Bethany. God, but that woman had an endless tab of shit she owed me! Bethany'd screamed at me all through that newscast. But it was my fault, too. I'd willfully chosen the tragedy that meant he could be mine. I'd safely buried her, mentally moving her out of my way. But William was married.

"How is he?" Bridget asked. "I came to the hospital, after he was shot. He didn't want to see me then."

She touched her pocket with the envelope again, and in that moment we were both together thinking the same thing. I knew it. We were wondering if he wanted to see her now.

"He acts like you stayed dead," I told her. "Anyone would think it, if they saw his house. I've never even heard him say your name."

It hurt her, when I said these things. I was glad and horrified to hurt her. She looked at her alive bare feet in the grass. I looked at them, too, and they were calloused, serviceable feet, wide and bony, without a pedicure.

"Are you in love with him?" she asked, and then she changed it, asking the thing she really wanted to know. "Are you in love?" She meant both of us. She was asking if William and I were in love with each other.

"What does Paula say?" I asked.

"Oh, well, Paula. She says he isn't, but she's my oldest friend. What else would Paula say?" Bridget told me, and it hurt even though she qualified it. Her eyes on me were still so unreasonably kind.

"Well, she's right."

I was happy that she'd hurt me back, though of course it didn't make us even. We would never be even, and that was something else Paula had right. I wasn't Bridget. I wasn't even half a Bridget, yet. She leaned toward me, being gracious and so gentle, while I sat, a raging, red-faced child, viciously thinking that my feet were prettier than hers.

"Do you want to come inside?" Bridget asked me, touching my leg with one hand. A gardener's hand, also calloused, with short, neat nails.

I realized I was crying.

"You're so stupid. You're so stupid," I said, though it was hard to push words through my cloggy throat, and my nose was snotting up. I'd been stupid, too, with all my different kinds of patty-pans. Pretend wife, pretend hot mistress. Running first after him and then away, like I was being Pepé Le Pew and then the stupid cat with its accidental stripe in turn. Even this, following him like some romantically imprinted duckling to declare my love. It was all little-girl tricks. Little-girl games. I should have known better. I lost my little-girl card when I got Natty.

This was another pretend, and here in a yard on a bench was his real wife, with sad, kind, tired eyes. The lesson of Mimmy and my dad was not for me. It was for her. It was for them. I was so sick with understanding that I was practically yelling at her.

"Why didn't you just stay dead, if you are going to be so stupid? Why did you even live? So you could sit in your yard and talk about some dumb afterlife experience with messed-up, mourning strangers? You love him. You think I don't know what that looks like? I don't care if he sent you away at the hospital. He was shot. He couldn't *make* you leave. Now, for all you know, I'll go right straight to him to beg him to love me and forget you. And still you sit here, being stupid."

The compassion on her face as I raged on made me simply want to kill her. I wrenched myself up and away and stomped back to my car. She called my name, but I ignored her and got in, slamming my door. I drove myself in circles, crying and crying.

Screw her, if she didn't want him. I headed for William's house to wait for him, turning toward Morningside even as I was saying every bad word that I knew. I wasn't halfway there before I turned the car around. I drove away from him, and even got onto 85 to head up north to Mimmy's, because what was I in love with, really? William?

He was beautiful and closed so shut that I could dress him up in any kind of superhero suit I wanted. Captain Animal, rising and smiting Stevie down. Dr. Genius, finding all my answers inside the microscopic mystery of cells.

He *had* actually done these things, though. He was actually brave and good. I got off after a single exit, driving back toward Morningside, but I was wondering. In the Circle K, did I really fall in love with him? Or was it just the idea of him, something big and strong and smart enough to get in between me and every bad thing in the world? A silent, strong protector. He'd let me hit at evil with my tiny fist in the safety of knowing it was not allowed to hit me back. He'd been a white knight wise enough to kill even my son's nightmares, taping up all the holes where the bad, bad things came in.

What frightened child wouldn't want that? Maybe my body felt free with him only because I felt safe with him. Maybe loving him was nothing more than wanting to be safe. If so, then it was crap. No one could make the world safe. No one on this blue ball was ever safe for even a second. I knew that. I knew that better than most girls my age.

He was so beautiful. He wasn't mine. I should run to the mountains now, and hide. I should run right into his arms and demand that he close them around me. I should run home to my mother and cry into her lap.

I stopped dead on Ponce de Leon Avenue, not turning toward Morningside and facing the wrong way to get back on the highway. Behind me four or five enraged people began squashing on their horns. I hit my flashers and sat there with other cars streaming around me, honking for me to go, go, go, but I couldn't go until I knew which way to turn.

I didn't want to choose. Both options sucked, and I was tired of every kind of running that there was. So in the end, I didn't go to either place.

In the end, I drove myself to Piedmont Park.

Chapter 14

*H*e drove directly to Paula's office after he left the Sullivans' house in Decatur, unable to stomach the idea of returning to his house alone. Paula took him to shoot pool, and for hours he thought of very little beyond the angles and the English. They went back to her loft around midnight, where he slept on her sofa for a couple of hours.

Now, dawn is close, and Paula is still hacking at the last wooden bench with her hatchet. They have Holy Shit Park to themselves in this dead hour before early morning. He's dragged the benches to the center of the green space, hoping the sound of breaking them down to kindling won't call anyone. It's the last thing.

The sidewalk is littered with shards of glass. Paula, who long ago wanted to put rocks through all the streetlights, has had her chance now. They've ripped the late summer flowers out in handfuls and strewn them across the grass with their roots torn and exposed. After that, William used the ax to smash most of the birdhouses, scattering this season's used-up nests, dry and empty here in late July. He hacked down all of the four Japanese maples he himself put in years ago, as a wedding present.

"You have to do this bench, Bubba. It's defeating me," Paula says. She is panting, but her eyes are bright and she is grinning. He isn't sure if it is because he took the note to Bridget, or if she is simply happy to be breaking things. Probably both. "Hatchets are stupid. Why do you get the ax?"

She backs out of the way, and William swings, bringing the ax down in a long, fast arc that feels good, a good stretching release of force from the muscles of his back and shoulders, though his abdomen protests. The splintered bench snaps, all the slats caving down at once, and the blade bites deep into the dirt.

"Oh. That's why," Paula says as he wrestles the ax back out.

They stand with their heads tilted to equal angles, listening for the sounds of feet or yelling or sirens, in case the smashing of the bench has notified a neighborly insomniac that crime is happening.

Nothing.

Paula cocks the hatchet to a jaunty angle on her shoulder and heads toward the final birdhouse. It is covered in hand-painted flowers that look like they've been done by a child or an adult with little aptitude for art. It is hung too low on a trunk to be a good birdhouse. Any cat who happens by could easily get to it. Anyone over six feet tall can peer inside it.

William says, "Not that one," and she leaves it be.

The rest of the small park is a jagged wreck of torn-up, dying plants, shards of glass, and wooden benches hacked into kindling. They sit down on the ground, side by side, as they have destroyed all the other places to sit. Paula's shoulder presses companionably into his.

"This is actually what I'm good at. Isn't that sad?" She doesn't sound sad. "I'm completely great at tearing shit right the hell up. Taking things apart is all I do. It's even my job."

"You do other things," William says.

"Yeah, but I don't build. I think you and Bridget, as a couple, are the only thing I've worked to build in my whole life."

William nods. This sounds accurate. "Do you think she'll come?"

The note he left taped to the Sullivans' house in Decatur said, *Meet me at your old tulip bed tomorrow, just before sunrise*. This note didn't promise something good would happen, as the first one had. He isn't sure Bridget will think this is good, what he's doing.

It's one thing to decide what you want. It's quite another to know how to get it. William doesn't know how, but he is trying.

"I hope so, Bubba, because you've certainly put some effort in." She waves her hand at the chaos around them.

Paula could have come up with a better plan, more romantic, perhaps, and put it together for him very quickly. She tried while they were playing pool, and he told her to get her head in the game before he ran the table. He didn't want Paula's ideas. He decided this all on his own before he went to get her. No chemistry or tricks. No catalyst, no puzzle. He wrote the note in plain blue ink. Then he worried that Bridget wouldn't understand, so at the bottom, he wrote, *This is a love note*. He wanted to be clear. He wanted full disclosure, so she could decide to come, or not.

If she comes, he has things to show her. The park, restored to its original shit, is only one.

At home, on the mantel, is the second thing. He took down three pictures of Twyla that were still in the attic. There could never be enough pictures to capture all the ways that Twyla was, so he chose them by year. Twyla the newborn. Twyla at one. Twyla at two.

Bridget wanted pictures out because, for her, some celestial Twyla still existed. For William, Twyla stopped when the backseat stopped. It made physical objects that were closely associated with her very hard to look at. He put them all up in the attic, quite soon after the accident, one Saturday while Bridget worked at the shelter. He thought it would be easier, but Bridget hadn't responded well.

Now, William wants them back out, too. They are a testament that Twyla *was*, and that her short existence mattered. It was wrong to put all trace of her away. There was no justice in it.

His reasons are different from Bridget's, but the result is the same. This was always true, in the before, inside their marriage. They would often follow separate chains of reasoning, and yet come to the same conclusion. Bridget acknowledged this herself, though she spoke of it in terms of paths and destinations.

The last thing is a note in his calendar. He has set up a meeting with Father Lewis. Father Lewis will probably need to talk for a long time, but William believes he can find a way to navigate the conversation peaceably. Before the Circle K, he could not allow Father Lewis, or anyone, even his wife, to say his child was in "a better place" without speaking back in the cruelest terms.

"It's such shit, and you know it," he said to Father Lewis, then, while Bridget sat silent on their sofa. She stared out the window, watching birds light and peck and flutter on the feeders. She didn't appear to be listening as William told him, "If you had faith, you'd walk into the sea and get to heaven sooner."

"Suicide is a sin, William. Are you thinking of harming yourself?" the priest asked, concerned.

William didn't answer the direct question, which in retrospect is telling. All he said was, "You're worshipping a God who sticks you to the planet on a technicality."

These conversations were not productive.

Now he has decided to return to a sustainable peace with Bridget's church. If he doesn't, he is choosing to remain on his side of the unwinnable either/or. When it is God or William, God has her, all to himself.

God has had her from the moment the paramedics lifted Bridget out of her wrecked wagon, and she saw the place where the backseat had been. She experienced a cardiac arrest, the stop that is the start of death. Bridget, inside the process of her body shutting down, dreamed she saw their child rising, whole and beautiful, and she went after her. She talked about her own brief death this way, as if it had been a choice, saying she shrugged off her body like a heavy coat and flew up to catch Twyla.

What happened after that—the beckoning light, the flight through the tunnel holding Twyla, the flooding sense of peace, the bells, the careful placing of their laughing child into huge, strong arms that held her kindly, the feeling of being welcome, of a warm acceptance—was a direct result of cerebral anoxia and the flood of endorphins that the panicked brain releases as it dies. William could likely have approximated the experience for himself, with a careful use of ketamine and suggestion.

In retrospect, however, this was not a thing he should have said to Bridget.

To be fair, there was little he could say to Bridget on the subject of Twyla's afterlife, so Bridget listened, more and more, to God.

She began going to mass every morning. When not at mass, she spent hours praying, talking to the God she imagined holding their child. At night, Bridget even started sleeping on her back, facing up, yearning toward a better comfort than any William had to offer. Perhaps because it was a comfort that William's words directly undermined.

He stopped talking when he understood how deeply it hurt her, but by then even his silence was a contradiction of her hope. William's very presence corroded it. His unbelief, his unremitting sorrow, the absoluteness of his loss—it was an assault upon her only peace. She moved farther and farther from him. She avoided him in daylight, busying herself with mass and prayer and more work for the church. The slice of sheet widened in the bed between them every night. It was Bridget and God, and there was no room for William.

As the months ticked on, her words and eyes for God and God alone, William became so angry. His longtime rival was no longer satisfied with first place. God had taken all the places. William became angry with all parts of Bridget, one by one, until he was even angry at the details of her dying hallucination.

If William's heart stopped beating, he thought, were he to dream an afterlife as his brain's electrical activity ticked down to cooling nothing, were he to find himself in Bridget's heaven, he would not hand Twyla over. He would fight and rage. He would rend the puffy cloud walls and kick holes in the golden streets. He would go to his oblivion in the peace of knowing he had demanded Twyla's life back with the last pulse of his brain. Irrational, this anger, but it came. The more she prayed, the more it grew.

The last night, with most of the bed between them, the moon was very high and bright. He'd forgotten to shut the blinds. In this abundant moonlight, she'd looked at him. It was strange to see the celery green of her eyes so close, so full of longing.

With her looking, he could say, "I miss you." Simple words, but they were true. He missed her. It was the only thing he felt now, except grief, and the rage at his inability to help her when God could. "I miss you," he said again.

"I know. Will, I miss you, too. So much. I don't want us to live like this. I want us to be better."

She moved first. It started as a slight bend toward him that he mirrored, a tentative shift together in the moonlight. Then he rolled on his side, she on hers. They both moved closer, her mouth finding his, his hands fitting themselves to her familiar, long-beloved contours.

It might have been the start of a way back, to a place of compromise. She'd always said their marriage's best trick was to hold her faith between them without him breaking it or her letting it part them. But William, aware of the simple mathematical risk, understanding all that could be lost, turned briefly away from her. He reached to open the bedside drawer. He took one of the condoms in the box he'd always kept there. When he turned back, she was already scrambling backward away from him, on all fours like an animal. She was naked, cheeks burning, and her eyes were furious slits.

She reared up on her knees and slapped him, once, hard across his face. He dropped the packet on the bed, on his knees now, too.

"No!" she said.

"I can't," he answered. His cheek burned.

They faced each other in the darkness, panting, both of them shocked, and both of them so angry. Bridget got up out of bed and walked away, snatching her thick bathrobe as she passed her closet. She did not come back to their room that night. She was asleep on the sofa in the den the next day when he went to work. While he was at the lab, the Sullivans came, acting as a tribe. When he got home, all her things were gone. All evidence of Bridget had been removed, as thoroughly as he'd removed the evidence of Twyla.

William wasn't great at nuance, but he understood this was a statement.

It was a relief, he found, not to lie beside her anymore, failing her, more angry every day. It was a relief to mourn his child in the peace of being allowed to feel his loss as absolute. It was easier, in fact, to accept the house's evidence: there never was a Bridget. Nine days after she left, he found her old charm bracelet under the sofa, and he stuffed that in the attic. There, he found she'd taken many of Twyla's things with her, and that was also a relief.

He banned her name, her image, and all thought of her, though the ban caused the only fight he'd ever had with Paula. Paula still went to see Bridget every Tuesday, but she stopped telling him, as he insisted. She let her Tuesday absences speak for her and didn't say the banished name, as promised.

He thought at the time it was necessary for survival, but then, the anniversary came. He was waylaid by detergent in the Circle K. Trying to escape his wife, he walked into a bullet. The ban was not sustainable.

So, here he is now, with the pictures on the mantel and their park in ruins. He is ready even to talk to Father Lewis. Of all the things William lost in the accident, it's strange that the one he

must work hardest to reform is the one that holds the least interest: the art of coexistence with theology.

"She's coming," Paula says.

Paula stands and melts back into the night, disappearing. Yes,
Bridget is making her way to him. He sees her flashlight bobbing
along, helping her pick a path through the wreckage. She crosses
the ruined park she once miracled into a lovely place. Her light
traces all the damage he has done, all that he has torn apart with
his bare hands. Well, and an ax. And Paula.

She comes right to him in the darkness, her sonar as accurate
as ever. She points the flashlight up, so they can see each other in
the ambient light. Her face is so sad.

"I wasn't sure you'd come," he says.

"I don't know that I would have come, for this, Will." She
gestures at the wreckage in the park, but she's using her private
name for him. This is a good sign, in spite of her sad face. She
must not understand what he has done here.

He swallows. "I want you to fix it," he says, by way of explanation. But that's not right. He wrecked the park to give Bridget
and God both something to do. Something that includes him. "I
want you to help me fix it."

Her head tilts sideways, puzzled, and then her lips part and her
eyes go wide.

"Is it— Did you make me a metaphor?" Her tone is so disbe-
lieving that he smiles, mostly with relief. He nods once in a short
yes. He has made her a metaphor. The park is his attempt to speak
to her in a language that was never his. She looks at the park with
new eyes, and her gaze on it has softened. "What does it mean,
the one whole birdhouse?"

She points to the flowered one, so ill-placed, that he saved
from Paula's hatchet.

"Nothing," he says with an exasperated shrug. "It's full of
birds."

"What?" she says.

She's right to be surprised. He is, too, because it's very late for nesting. It must be a species that breeds later in the spring. She goes to the tree, though, and while she is too short to see inside, she listens. He listens, too. They are rustling around in there, sensing the coming dawn.

"You think a cat got their first nest?" Bridget asks, perhaps a better explanation.

"Maybe," William says. If this is their second-choice bird-house, they didn't learn much from the first experience. It isn't safe. "I couldn't kill a bunch of little birds for a metaphor."

She smiles then, her old real Bridget smile, and says, "Of course you couldn't." She looks at him as if she sees him. "Will, I'm so sorry. I left you months before I packed, and it was wrong and awful. Then you got shot, and it was like waking up. I realized I could lose you all over again. You were still so angry in the hospital, though. I ran, and I shouldn't have. I should have stayed and talked to you. Yesterday, your friend came over, Shandi, and she told me how stupid I've been. She's right. I was. I am."

Shandi? It's surprising, but this is not the time to ask her to elaborate. She has to stop apologizing. They have both done many things poorly, things that hurt each other. She shouldn't be apologizing; he is close to certain that he hurt her first.

"It doesn't matter. I'm stupid, too. If I start listing all the ways I failed you, we'll still be standing here when the sun is up. We'll get arrested."

Off to their left, there is a footstep sound. The snapping of a twig. Paula? Maybe, but it could be anyone, and he would much prefer not to be caught. Even though he should be. This is a public park he has destroyed, after all. But he has good-faith plans to fix it, whether Bridget helps or not.

"Crap!" says Bridget, "William, this is crazy. Come on."

She takes his hand. The feel of her fingers in his, the pressure of her hand, is so familiar. She tugs on him, and he follows.

They are leaving his parked SUV behind, but he entrusts it

to his wingman. Paula will gather the ax and the other tools and drive away from the scene of the crime. She'll probably think to hotwire Bridget's car and move that away as well; Paula, in her youth, learned a broad and useful array of basic criminal skills.

Bridget says, "We have to fix this tomorrow. This is so wrong. It was very wrong you did this."

Her voice isn't angry, though, and he is calm and breathing easy as she pulls him toward the house. She said, *We have to fix this*. We. First-person plural. She is still Bridget, after all, complete inside herself. Last time, the whole neighborhood rallied, all because she was bold enough to rip out all the ugly, dying phlox. She can fix it. They can fix it.

Her flashlight picks a path for them through the darkness, to the house, together. When they reach the yard, she stops, but he doesn't. He lets his body intersect with hers. He turns her in his hands and kisses her. For a moment she is surprised into stiffness, rigid in his arms. Then she pushes up on tiptoe. Her mouth opens to him. Her palms cup his face.

They do not kiss the way they did once before in this yard, when the cold rain came down to save them for a better day. They are not so young or desperate for each other now. It begins as something close to comfort. It is familiar. It is sad and good to kiss her this way, to wrap his arms around her waist and lift her up, pressed vertically, full-length against him. He carries her inside this time, not out.

He can't take her to their bedroom. The history and presence of the condoms in the dresser could cause thinking. There might be more talking, more endless apology. To the rug in front of the fireplace, then. He lays her down on the thick pile. There is nothing here that he can put between them.

She knows his body. He knows hers. They are so careful to be kind to each another. He does everything that she likes best. She is the same with him, her hand touching him precisely here, her mouth moving in this favorite way. Her lips find his new scar and linger there, learning it. They come together, skin on skin. They move slow and open-eyed. They each accept their different risks.

"I'm sorry," she says. "I'm so, so sorry."

"I'm sorry, too," he says, and kisses her until all the apologizing stops.

He is almost only his body. His mind plans things from far away. Tomorrow, which is close now, very close, they will begin to fix the park. As they work, he will tell her about Stevie, rising. He will tell her about a virgin's child, calling through an iPad. *Stevie, come forth.* For William, it is always, it can only be, science and coincidence.

Bridget will make it more. Bridget will make it into hope, that thing she says has feathers, and he will let her. He will give it to her, all of it, and let her. This is where he finds grace, in giving in to hers. She is letting him back into hers, and those are all the thoughts that he can have before he is only his body and hers both, the two of them a single thing, connected, risking everything. Risking even creation.

After, they lie loosely in each other's arms, watching the sun come up through the window. The horizon is washed in pink and gold, rimmed with blue.

She traces his mouth with her finger.

"The eggplant is sad," she says, quoting his old vegetable book. He smiles, wondering what she sees in his face that she would think so.

They lie together in the growing light. Bridget tucks her face into his shoulder. He knows this posture, recognizes the slight change in her breathing. Her body is beginning to ease itself into sleep.

William is not tired. He watches the sunrise happening through the fence, a black chain-link convenience for Baxter. A bird lands, one of the many cardinals who come back every year to nest. This one is male and very red. Now, Bridget lies in his arms. His genetic material is doing its busy job inside her. There is a red bird on his fence.

"The radish is happy," he tells his sleepy wife. Her face is pressed into him, but he can feel her smile, her teeth against his bare shoulder.

"Will," she says into his skin. "These are not mutually exclusive states of being."

Chapter 15

I sat under a tree in Piedmont Park for hours, watching Clayton Lilli's apartment building. I stayed sheltered near the trunk. I only left my spot of dryish grass twice, once to walk to a park-side deli for a sandwich that I didn't feel like eating, and once to visit the same deli's restroom. From my shady spot, I had a good view of the entrance.

At about four, I texted Mims, to make sure she and Natty got home safe. She was pretty ill with me, and worried. Yes, they were home, and Walcott was unloading, she texted. She was going to make him lunch as a thank-you. Then she started texting me question after question—where was I, when was I coming home, was I okay—none of which I knew how to answer yet. All that mattered to me was that Natty was back at her house, out of the way of whatever dumb thing I was doing.

I ignored the questions and texted, *Love you, thank you, sorry. I'm fine. Home soon. Then you can ask me anything and kill me after.*

My phone immediately began playing Mimmy's calypso ring-tone, so I shut it off.

A little after five thirty, Clayton Lilli got home. I watched him park his Honda on the street and go inside. I didn't move, though. I stayed right where I was. I couldn't quite make myself go after him. I wasn't sure what I thought he would do, but I was too jacked up in my body to walk into his apartment without William at my back, ready to kill him with a paperweight. Fifteen minutes later, his field mouse of a girlfriend showed up. Today she wore jeans and carried what looked like a couple of textbooks.

She was too far for me to read her face, but her body language was grim. She shuffled with her shoulders in a little hunch. She had a key. I wondered if she lived there.

Now I had no excuse not to go. What could he do? Re-drug me and try to re-rape me in the presence of the one girl he'd managed to convince of his inner sugar-bunny nature? She was convinced enough to come back over, anyway.

But I couldn't make myself get up. It was like I was waiting for something, for a sign, or for permission. To stop being afraid. To stop wanting things I couldn't have and try to find out what was possible. I sat there for at least a miserable ten minutes, trying to make myself begin.

That was when I saw the nun.

She was cutting across my corner of the park in sensible shoes, carrying a big fake leather tote bag. She was in street clothes, a knee-length navy skirt and a white blouse with a rounded collar, but I knew she was a nun because she had on a simple version of the hat, with the white band at her forehead. A drape of black cloth came down from it and fell around her shoulders.

This nun was in her sixties, at least. She didn't look a thing like pretty Bridget Ashe, but I had this odd swoop of angry vertigo, because the second I saw her, I was positive Bridget had sent her. Why? To warn me off? Or to give me some kind of permission?

But how would Bridget even know that I was here?

The nun wasn't looking at me, anyway. She didn't even seem to be looking for me. She came abreast of me, walking briskly with her head down to pick her way across the uneven ground.

She didn't even notice my staring. Perhaps a lot of people stared. She was a nun who still wore the hat.

So she didn't have a message for me. Maybe she was the message. I blinked hard and squinted, half thinking I had invented her, but the nun was still there, still going by. Maybe she didn't have a damn thing to do with Bridget Ashe. The world held a crap ton of nuns. There were probably thousands in Atlanta alone, hunting for lepers to care for, or eating ice cream. Doing whatever the hell nuns did. I'd never noticed them before because I'd never exactly been on the lookout for them. Why would I be?

But no matter how hard I told myself that this was a coincidence, I did not believe it. It felt like that word William had said to me in the Circle K, after he took the bullet. It felt like destiny, or the answer to a prayer I hadn't even yet been saying.

Was this what a real miracle looked like? I wouldn't know. I was the girl whose life had been upended by an ugly, purely human virgin birth. Today, I'd gotten an equally shitty version of the resurrection when Bridget opened the purple door and came to sit with me in her own garden.

If this was a different kind of miracle, I was letting it walk past me. At that thought, I found myself rising. I hurried, angling to catch up to her. The closer I got, the more the movement toward her felt inadvertent, like she was made purely out of magnet. As I came up beside her I saw she had a sprinkle of flossy lady whiskers on her upper lip, and the rest of her skin looked like parchment paper, folded and refolded until it was creasy and soft. I stepped around and blocked her way, but then I didn't know what to say to her.

She stopped walking and said, "Yes?"

I didn't know how to address her. In the movies, when people talk to nuns, they say "sister," but it felt way too disco to say "sister."

"Ma'am," I said, instead. "I'm sorry. This might be too personal, or even rude to ask a nun, but my friend is . . ." I stopped. Bridget Ashe was not my friend, and I had no idea how to explain

William. I didn't even know what I was supposed to say to her. I opened my mouth, and an unplanned question came out of me. "Could you have been anything else, besides a nun? Could you have married a person or just not been one?"

She tilted her head to a quizzical angle, but she answered me. "I was called to this life, but it was my choice to answer." I stood there like an idiot, nodding at her for fifteen, maybe twenty seconds. She finally added, like she was encouraging me, "I'm sorry. I'm late already, unless . . . Did you need something else?"

I didn't know, but I shook my head *no*, anyway.

"Do you need to talk to someone?" She was beaming the kind eyes at me, still. Was this a nun thing? An endless supply of exhausting, kind gazes?

I shook my head again. "Thank you."

She started walking past me, but she glanced over her shoulder at me as she headed away toward whatever she was late for. Bridget had taught English to illegal aliens, to prostitutes, back when she was a pre-nun. Maybe this nun had a job like that to get to; she'd picked up her brisk pace again. From the back, I could see her shoulders were beginning to round down into the kind of soft hump you sometimes see on grammas.

I called to her back, "What did it feel like? Getting called to be a nun?"

She stopped, and she turned all the way around. She looked me right in the eye across the twenty feet of green park that separated us now. Once again I had the clear feeling I had overstepped some boundary, but once again, she answered anyway.

She said, "It felt like a love story."

I gave her a short nod, like a head jerk. I flat hated that answer.

I was so effing sick of other people's love stories, today in particular. Why would some higher power send me a nun, only to have her tell me this? She was what Bridget could have been, but Bridget had chosen William. Bridget was William's love story, and he was hers. In William's story, I might rate a footnote. He wasn't much for narrative, so maybe Paula would tell his, and I would be a bad digression that she edited away. This, right here, this was my story, and love had no place in it.

Looking at the nun, I thought, *Unless you count Natty.*

I realized that I did. I was on my own, but yes, I did count Natty. He was all that counted, really. No matter how ugly the night when I got him, I wouldn't go back now and change history even if I could. Any change could alter or erase him. William had told me that. All that Natty was came from his cells, and I was so in love with every piece of DNA that made him be him. I was in love with everything: his eyelashes, his serious, small voice, his overinterest in the biology of beetles. He was perfectly formed to be himself, and he was mine. I was his.

The nun called to me again. Her voice was old, old like she was, papery and fine, but what she said, she said with such assurance.

"It still feels like a love story."

I didn't answer, but I felt my shoulders squaring up and rising. Sure, I was scared to go up there and face Clayton Lilli and whatever lies or truths he had to tell. Of course I was, but I waved good-bye to the nun and then I started walking toward Clayton Lilli's building anyway.

Perhaps she had been sent—it felt that way still—so I would know there were so many kinds of love stories. This one belonged to me and Natty. I was going to make damn sure it ended right.

I went right to the door and I mashed the button that was labeled *C. Lilli.* Mouse Brown might have a key, but she didn't get billing on the intercom. Still, it was her voice that answered through the speaker. "Yes?"

"It's Shandi Pierce. Buzz me in. I need to talk to him."

There was a long pause. I suppose they must have been conferring. After a long thirty seconds, the buzzer sounded, and I pushed the door open.

The intercom labels put him in 312, so I took the elevator to the third floor. I found them down the hall on the left. His door was already open, and they stood framed in it together, watching for me. As I approached, they stepped back to let me walk in past them. It felt weird and wrong to let him shut the door behind me.

We stood in an odd triangle, all pointy with me at the apex, the two of them framing the closed door.

"Hi," said Clayton Lilli.

"Hello," I said.

"Hi," Mouse Brown said, breathy and high. A long silence stretched out, thinning all the air between us.

"Can I get you a drink or something?" Clayton Lilli asked.

That made me and Mouse Brown both look at him, me withering and her wondering. Even with that, it was several seconds before he realized how inappropriate a thing it was, to offer the girl who says you roofied her a drink. He flushed a faint pink in his cheeks.

"Let's sit down," his girl said. "I'm Beth, by the way."

Ugh. Her bland, brown name was bland, brown Beth. It didn't bode well, to have her be called the plainest iteration of my step-fridge.

I sat down alone in the center of Clayton Lilli's sofa. He had two armchairs across a coffee table, and he sat in one and Beth sat in the other. We'd exactly re-created the same awkward triangle we'd made when we were standing.

"Should I get my letter?" Clayton Lilli asked me. "I could read it to you."

I liked it that he didn't bring up Natty. It was as if that moment when Natty joined me on the steps outside the condo didn't happen. He'd rewound back to before that, when the stakes were lower, back to wanting to read his "What I Did After Summer Vacation" essay.

I shook my head. "We both have ways that we could really hurt each other. So let's try to talk this out. No paper. No rehearsed whatever. You say what you need to say to me."

"I'll try. I'm not that good at telling stories, but I can try to tell you how it was that night," he said. "I want to say what really happened, as best as I remember. I have to go back, to before I saw you, so it makes sense, okay?"

I nodded.

He glanced at Beth, but she was looking at her hands. I noticed for the first time she had a little diamond winking on the proper finger. The stakes were high for everyone here, then. I knew she'd heard this story before, and she'd believed it enough to show up on my steps and passionately defend him. She was quieter today, sitting in a separate chair with all that space between them. She didn't seem as sure of him, ring or no ring. Natty was a world-rocker, for everyone in this room.

Clayton said, "My dad died when I was a baby, and my stepdad adopted me when I was two. He and my mom never had kids. He couldn't. He loved me. Loves me, but I'm not much like him. He's a salesman, really great with people. He was a Kappu Nu. He thought a fraternity would help me be a more social person. The Greek system was designed to create automatic, useful friendships."

As he spoke, Beth tilted her hand back and forth, the ring winking at her in the shifting light. Clayton Lilli stared at a spot on the wall past my head. It made him seem dishonest, to have him not even look at me. But I remembered William saying, *duplications and deletions*, and William wasn't all that big on eye contact, either.

"At the party, they had a simple machine made of a hose and funnel, and they put a certain amount of beer through it, into me. It was a lot of beer, and I ingested it very quickly. It didn't feel like drinking. It all poured in, and I couldn't stop it."

Now Beth spoke. "They filled him up like he was a pitcher, or a beer balloon."

"Were you there?" I asked, my voice sharp.

"No," she said. She looked back at her hands.

"I was seventeen," Clayton Lilli said. "I'd never drunk alcohol before rush. Well, no. My mom let me have champagne on New Year's. I'd tried tastes of her wine. But not serious drinking."

He said it with such earnesty. The Great Pumpkin would come to this guy's pumpkin patch, he was so damn sincere. Of course, it was entirely possible this sincere and awkward boy would then drug the Great Pumpkin and try to put it to him. I had no way of knowing.

But I listened with my mind as open as I could make it be as he continued.

"I wasn't drunk, because all the beer went in so quickly. After a few minutes, I was very drunk, though, instantly. It was terrible and frightening. I had trouble walking. I had no balance."

"The floor pitched under his feet, like the whole house had turned into a ship in a storm," Beth put in, unable to help herself. It was odd, how he would say something blunt and plain, in his formal tone, and then she'd translate it into simile.

"I'm not the kind of son my stepdad would have had. I tried to be, by rushing Kappu Nu," Clayton Lilli said. "I was bad at it. They didn't like me, and I didn't like them. I thought, when I was suddenly so drunk, that I should go lie down. I made my way to the stairs, but it was hard, because there were so many people, and because the floor pitched, as she said. That's when I saw you. You were by the stairs, leaning on the wall. You were talking to three guys. At least three. Three that I noticed."

I digested that. I imagined myself there, drugged and helpless, with three guys around me. I saw us already by the stairs that led up to the bedrooms. I could feel my body curling inward protectively, thinking of being taken upstairs by three guys instead of outside to a beanbag by one who didn't even get it all the way in. Three guys was scary as all hell. Jesus, what girl would not prefer his version? If he was making this up, it was a very good story. Very crafty.

"Who were they?" I asked. It was a test.

"Rog Bently, Daren Case, and Michael Warren," he said. "I wrote them down for you. In my letter."

I'd wanted to see if he would give their names up, but then I wasn't sure if it made him more credible, or less, that he would so promptly tell me. He might have been finger-pointing at guys he didn't like to save his own ass. But it could be that he was actually trying to do the right thing.

I said, "At my house, you said you didn't know who drugged me."

"I said I couldn't be sure," he told me. He was being very literal, but I thought he might be right. In my memory, that was exactly how he said it. "I don't know which of them drugged you, or if they were all in on it, or if it was someone else I didn't notice there."

"He'll help you find out, though. He'll do whatever you want," Beth said. "He'll go to the cops with you, talk to other pledges from his year, or those three guys. He'll wear a wire."

It was staunchly said, if overdramatic. Maybe she was saying it for her as much as me. She so wanted his version to be true, but Natty must have shaken her faith in him. At the condo they stayed so physically close. Now, each sat slumped in their own chair.

"Go on," I said to Clayton Lilli.

"I was going up to pass out or vomit. I hadn't decided. Probably both. But as I came up by you, you grabbed me and pulled me over into the group."

As he spoke, I tried so hard to let it spark something inside me, some unaccessed memory, some piece of my brain that had gotten buried under whatever the drug was. I waited for an inner *Bing!* of truth to sound, but as he described me paused by the stairs with three boys, described lurching over to us, I could only imagine it in the third person. I saw it like a story I was inventing, not a memory at all.

"You pushed Rog to the side and you grabbed me. And you— Then you— It was you." He blushed a deep, uncomfortable red.

I felt my cheeks heating, too. "I kissed you?"

Beth dropped her face down into her hands. She didn't like to hear this part.

"Yes," he told me. "You did. You kissed me, and you said things to me. It was dark, and loud with music, and I was very drunk, so I don't remember it all exactly. You hollered a lot of things into my ear. You were happy to see me. You kept saying, 'Yay.' It was your idea to go outside. I was drunk, but you were— I'm sorry—you were pretty, and you seemed drunk, too. I didn't do so well with girls in high school. Pretty girls never grabbed me and kissed me and said nice things to me like that. You were so drunk you had to lean on the wall, and I couldn't stand up, either. I was leaning on you, so you got pinned. I think the wall was the only thing that kept us standing. You told me that I had caught you against the wall, so you were mine now."

His whole head, even his neck were flushed deep crimson now. Beth picked her face up out of her hands to translate Clayton into simile. "He felt like it was a game, like you were already playing a game where a girl had to be caught, and he'd walked into the middle of it and somehow won."

Clayton Lilli said, "When you kissed me, and you said all the nice things, the guys around me were whooping, cheering us on. I felt like I was finally doing something right. Like what my stepdad would do. You seemed like the kind of girl he would have known in college, pretty and wild, getting drunk. Cool. Used to hooking up. Not like me. That's what I thought you were like. Those guys were cheering, saying, 'Whoop, Clayton's getting off the team.' There's this thing the Kappas—"

I cut him off. "I know about the Emory Football Team."

He swallowed, looking unhappy, "They were all slapping my back and I was still leaning on you, and you said the thing again, like I had caught you or pinned you against the wall and now I got to have you. I wanted to get away from the other three. I thought you did, too. I was scared if we went upstairs they would come, too. To watch. For proof about the football team. That made me feel so scared and sick. So I said I was taking you to dance, and we went away from them. We had to help each other walk, we were so messed up."

"But we didn't go to dance," I said.

"No. You wanted to go outside. We were in the kitchen, I remember. It was dark in there, but not crowded like the front room. You . . ." Now he was redder than anyone I'd ever seen. A silly color, tomato almost. Cartoonish and impossible. "You took— You had a skirt on, and you took your panties off. You dropped them off right there around your ankles and when they got stuck in your shoes, you kicked your shoes off, too. We kissed and you had your skirt on, but I knew you'd taken them off and it made a lot of difference. I couldn't not think about that. That they were gone. That was when you said you loved me."

"That doesn't sound like me," I said.

"You were really messed up," he said. "Somehow we made it to the beanbag, behind the grill, in the backyard. We were there and fooling around some but I kept thinking about the thing you did in the kitchen. I thought about that and it made me be done. I thought we didn't, you know. Not quite. That's what I thought?"

It was hard to believe this boy who couldn't even say it was a rapist. But maybe that was the exact kind of person who would drug a girl? He wasn't a forceful guy. He was red and ruined from talking about it. Maybe uptight and diffident was the exact type to go the roofie route?

"You didn't get it all the way in." I said it for him, and he glanced at his girlfriend.

"That's what he told me," Beth said. Her color was high, too. "He told me this story a long time ago, when we started dating, and we talked about our pasts. He told me about that night the way he's telling it now, if that helps. He said the two of you didn't get all the way to . . ."

She trailed off. She meant Natty, but none of us were ready

to have him in the conversation yet. Thank God. But I wanted to act in good faith here. I wanted to tell the truth, in case he was.

I said, "We didn't. Not all the way. I mean, he finished, but we didn't." I'd gotten equally wound up in embarrassment and euphemism, but plain, brown Beth seemed relieved to have this part of his story verified. She also looked puzzled. "It's possible," I said. "Not likely, but it can happen."

We all knew *it* meant pregnancy. We all knew *it* was Natty.

Clayton picked his story back up. "Right after, I was embarrassed, but then I was also really nauseous from being so drunk. I got up and tried to walk away to be sick, but I couldn't even walk. I crawled. I crawled on the grass with my pants down. I crawled until I started throwing up. It's likely I had alcohol poisoning. I weighed maybe a hundred and fifty pounds?" He didn't look to me like he weighed any more than that now, but I kept my mouth shut and let him finish. "It was a lot of beer. I threw up, and then I crawled away from that place, too. I crawled until I passed out. I woke up half under the bushes in the side yard with my pants still down. It was early morning. I went around back to the grill, but you were gone."

The three of us looked at one another. I remembered none of it, but I hoped this part was true. I hoped he did wake up with his bare ass pointing skyward, as vulnerable as he'd left me.

"I wish I could believe you," I told him. "I want it to be true, for a lot of reasons. But none of it sounds like me. I can't see myself doing any of that. Ever. I've never in my life told a guy I loved him. I wouldn't say that to some stranger, no matter how effed up I was. It was still an asshole move, going off to the backyard with a superdrunk girl you just met. It's gross. I mean, who acts like that? But it's not illegal, and I could sort of empathize. I want it very badly to be true, but it . . . it's not a thing that I can gamble on." And once again, we all knew the *it* in question was my son. "I have to know, for sure. Can't you tell me something, show me something, that would prove the smallest piece of it?"

I knew even as I said it, it was hopeless. I was asking for a miracle.

"I'm sorry. All I can tell you is what I remember." He went back through it, ticking the points off on his fingers in a way so like William it made me uncomfortable. "You kissed me first, and in the kitchen you were saying that you loved me. You said I caught you on the wall, so I got to have you." He pauses, forehead creasing as he concentrates. "I remember, it was weird, how you said that part. You said you loved me because I had you pinned. *Because* I caught you on the wall."

"That doesn't even make sense," I said. "You came up to me, you said. I wasn't running."

"No," he said unhappily. "It didn't make sense. I had you pinned, though, because we were both leaning. You said it in a weird way. Maybe wall-pinned? Like the frats pin girls? But no, that wasn't it. It was a weird word, though. I remember that."

"Wall-caught?" I guessed, and then I heard what it sounded like, out loud.

"Yes! That's it," Clayton said. "Wall-caught. One word almost, very archaic sounding. I remember wondering if being wall-caught was a cultural thing I didn't know about. Like handfasting."

"Walcott? I said it like one word? I said 'Walcott,' and then I said I loved you?"

He nodded, and then his eyebrows knitted up all puzzled as wild color rose in my face and I clapped both hands over my mouth. I stood up, my body unable to contain itself even with a whole sofa to itself.

I'd called Walcott earlier that night, when the drugs first hit. I must have been looking for him. Of course I would be so happy to see Walcott, if I had three boys angling me up some stairs while I was feeling sick and off, or drunk and wrong, or even just loose and crazy. In the loud, dark party, drugged and reeling, if I saw someone so long and tall, someone with those spider arms, I might well hope it into being Walcott.

"I told you that I loved you," I said into my hands. They

couldn't understand me, probably, but I didn't care because I was speaking to myself. Was Walcott right? Had it always been between us, like a present we were waiting to unwrap when we were older? I couldn't remember it that way. But I had been so terribly derailed.

Now Beth looked as puzzled as her boyfriend.

I took my hands off my mouth and said to them, "I might know a way to find out. I might know a way that would let me believe you." None of us knew what to do with that. "I have to go home."

I started for the door.

"But then what?" said Beth. She meant Natty. She meant we couldn't stop this conversation until we found a way to talk about him. I wasn't there yet, not by half. It was possible, it was even likely, that Clayton Lilli hadn't set out to hurt me, four years ago in the Kappa Nu house, but oh, I could see a hundred ways that he could hurt me now. And I had to be sure.

I stopped at the door and said, "Let's pause, okay? For now? Let's all agree right now to not do anything fast. I don't know you, and I don't trust you. You don't know me, either, but I can promise if you push me now, it's going to get so ugly. You don't know what all I'm capable of doing. This is . . ." And then I put it all right out in the open. "This is my kid we're talking about. You need to let me think."

This could go bad, so fast. I knew it, and they had to as well. Between us, the threat of jail for him, the loss of sole custody for me. I could go back to my story, insist he was a rapist. I'd have Walcott's testimony and Clayton's DNA to back me up. His story was good, though. He could win, and end up with half of Natty's life in his untrusted hands. Also, his financial future, he must have been thinking of that. I could sue him for child support.

But I looked at their faces, and his was earnest. Hers was frightened, but also relieved. They both looked just as young and scared as me.

Clayton nodded. "Going slow is right. It's good."

I said, "Slow, or even nowhere. I start school next week, so I will be in town a lot. You can decide if you even want to talk more. That's the first thing. We could all walk away from this. It's an option, and I believe you enough to be open to it. We all cut our losses and walk away. It may be best, even. But it's possible I could be open to other things, if you let me go home and think. If we are very slow. Slow and very careful. Because for me, the only person who matters in all of this is Natty."

That made Clayton sit up straight. "That's his name?"

Beth got up and crossed to Clayton's chair. She put her hand on his shoulder.

"Yes," I said. "His name is Natty. Nathan."

"Slow," he said. He looked up at his girl. Her restored faith in him had pinked her cheeks. She looked less dour and beige, at least. I wondered if his story was really true, and if I was in love with Walcott. I wondered if I could ever come to trust Clayton. I wondered if I could stomach a person named Beth.

"We can do that," Beth said for him. She looked to him when she said it, though, and he nodded.

I dug in my bag and wrote down my cell phone number for them.

"Call me next week, if you decide you want to talk," I told them both, and then I left.

Maybe they would walk away. That would be easiest. But maybe they would want to be involved in Natty's life, in one of a hundred possible capacities. If I came to believe him, we might step toward that, eventually. Maybe I would even go after those three boys and find out which of them put chemicals into my Coke, taking away my memories and my choices. That person should be made to pay. But I didn't have to decide anything right now.

I didn't know how it would unfold. I didn't even know how I wanted it to. All I could do was go home and see what happened. My heart was divided. It mostly hoped Clayton would never call, but the small slice left hoped in a frailer way that he might come to be a good thing in my son's life.

The only thing I could hope with my whole heart was that we would all be slow and very careful with one another. So I hoped it, and I went home, to Mimmy and my baby.

I didn't call Walcott. Too much had happened. My brain couldn't think and decide if I had, when drugged and helpless, looked for him so hard that I had seen him in the first long, tall shape that had come toward me. That I had told him I loved him. That I had said his name into a stranger's mouth. I was too blank and scared and tired and hopeful all at once to know if I had loved him my whole life or not. It was all I could do not to pass out from exhaustion and run off the road into a ditch.

Once I got back home, up on the mountain, I pacified Mimmy as much as was possible. I didn't bother with my room. I went to Natty's and wedged myself into my sleeping son's twin bed. I fell to deep-down sleeping almost instantly, breathing in the smell of his apple-clean shampoo.

*W*hen I wake up, it's past nine.

I don't call Walcott until after I have showered and dressed and eaten Mimmy's fluffy, buttered pancakes with Natty while Mimmy ate some fruit. I wait until Natty has gone with Mimmy to the candy shop, to see the pretty girls in their sash dresses making fudge and dipping Oreos in chocolate like I used to do.

He answers his cell by saying my name, and his voice is very worried. "Shandi? Where have you been?"

"I'm home at Mimmy's. It's a long story," I tell him. "Can you meet me at the halfway place?"

He knows right where I mean.

"Now?" he says.

"Yes," I tell him. "Now."

My hair is down, still damp around my shoulders. I haven't bothered to put makeup on. My face is just my face.

I start walking through the woods to this grassy place we know, too big to be a clearing, but not quite a meadow, either.

It lies between our house and his momses' B and B. The path is sloped, but not too steep, winding me in *S* shapes up the mountain toward him. Blackberry brambles line this path, but most of the fruit is gone here at the end of summer. There are a few left, dull black and fat and almost, almost overripe. I pick and eat them as I walk, though I have no way to wash them. I let them stain my mouth with dirty sweetness.

When I break out of the woods, I see Walcott coming toward me.

I walk toward him across the gold late-summer grass, and my body is alive underneath me. Alive and wholly mine, with the heat of all the sun caught in my skin. I am as fat and ripe as one of those late-summer berries. I am juicy and bursting under all my skin. I go toward him slow; no need to hurry through this heat. No need to hurry toward knowing when my body feels as if it may have already decided. He is smiling, and as I come close he sees my face and his smile changes and his eyes change. He slows down, too. His spine straightens and he is Walcott, long and tall, coming toward me in a grassy place too small to be a meadow.

He knows me so well. I don't have to say it. Not any of it. Not yet. There will be time for it later. For now, it is enough. It is enough and it is easy. Easy to walk the last few steps between us. Easy and so beautiful to step into his arms.

He kisses me. He kisses me.

I kiss him back.